Books by Jo Goodman

Published by Zebra Books

SWEET SEDUCTION

Looking around, Mary spied the slim bar of soap she had used on her hair. She picked it up, ignoring the cloth that lay nearby. She raised a bit of lather between her hands, then applied the soap and suds to Ryder's body.

"I don't think—" he began.

"You think too much," she interrupted him gently. Her hands worked deftly, sliding the soap over Ryder's shoulders, massaging his chest and upper arms with slippery lather. Her fingers glided to his neck before she circled around him and rubbed down his back. His flesh rippled under her touch and defined the hardness lying beneath his taut skin.

Mary slipped her arms around him from behind, resting her forehead against his back. Her soapy fingers rubbed lather across his abdomen. Her hands went lower to the arrow of hair below his navel.

That was when she dropped the soap.

And the pretense.

Made buoyant by the water, Mary slipped around Ryder again, her entire body rubbing smoothly against his as her hand went below the surface of the water and grasped him . . .

JO GOODMAN

ONLY IN MY ARMS

ZEBRA BOOKS
KENSINGTON PUBLISHING CORP.
http://www.kensingtonbooks.com

ZEBRA BOOKS are published by

Kensington Publishing Corp.
850 Third Avenue
New York, NY 10022

All Kensington titles, imprints and distributed lines are available at special quantity discounts for bulk purchases for sales promotion, premiums, fund-raising, educational or institutional use.

Special book excerpts or customized printings can also be created to fit specific needs. For details, write or phone the office of the Kensington Special Sales Manager: Kensington Publishing Corp., 850 Third Avenue, New York, NY 10022. Attn. Special Sales Department. Phone: 1-800-221-2647.

Zebra and the Z logo Reg. U.S. Pat. & TM Off.

First Printing: September 1996
10   9   8   7   6   5

Printed in the United States of America

For John Scognamiglio
—from the start he said I had to write this one,
and told me about his sixth grade teacher to prove it.

One

July 1884, The Hudson Valley

Stillness surrounded him. He welcomed it, absorbing it in much the same way a leaf absorbs light, turning into it as if it were necessary to his very existence. He was aware of his slowing heartbeat and of the near-silent passage of each breath. He didn't concentrate on these things, but let them be. They happened of their own accord as he embraced the quiet and calm of *being* in this moment.

He had positioned himself on the lip of a large rock a few feet above the clearing's water hole. He hunkered more than sat, his lean, agile frame folded so that he could rise without hesitation. For now, he did not move. Waiting was its own pleasure.

Had he been asked for what or whom he waited, he would have had no reply. It wasn't important to him, and it wasn't why he sat perched on the edge of the inclined rock. Waiting did not foster impatience or anxiety. Instead, it carried with it a certain heady anticipation that was like the scent of wildflowers lifted on the back of the wind, fleeting and elusive, but something to embrace and enjoy. Waiting gave rise to possibilities and expectations. Anything could happen in the passing of a moment. Anything. It was what he knew to be true and what he felt now.

Ribbons of morning mist rose from the water hole. The perimeter of the clearing was marked off by red cedar, river birch, and white pine, but even their sweeping branches could not crowd out the sun's sure ascent. Heat lifted the shroud of water vapor, and light glanced off its surface. He watched the shifting patterns of light glint and sparkle like so many stars and could almost believe this was a place where the heavens were captured.

That thought brought about the first movement he made, a slight lifting of one corner of his mouth. An observer would have wondered at the smile, for it was at once derisive and amused, a little mocking, a little secretive. He was not embarrassed by the thought that had crossed his mind, but he knew of others who would be embarrassed for him. Poets and philosophers could entertain notions of the heavens being captured in a well of water but United States Army scouts were better off keeping their own counsel.

The hint of a smile faded and his features returned to their resting state of impenetrable impassivity. It was not a cold, stoic expression. The shape of his mouth was not tight or thinly set, and the cleanly carved line of his jaw was not clenched in stony hardness. The source of the implacability that defined his expression was calm.

Through the sleeve of his black oilcloth duster he could feel fingers of heat on his shoulder. As the sun rose higher a band of warmth touched the side of his neck just above the collar of his shirt. A moment later it skimmed across his cheek and then the glossy black thickness of his hair. He made no move to shed the heavy coat or lift his hair where it brushed his collar at the nape. The heat was as welcome as the stillness and the waiting. He raised his face, shutting his eyes momentarily, and breathed sunshine.

She was there when he opened his eyes. She stood on the opposite side of the water hole, flanked by twin birch sentinels. Her path to the water was marked by the natural placement of large rocks rising from the bank like a stone stairway. She made no move toward the water or even to put her bare feet on the flat, sun-warmed rocks. Instead she remained very still and maintained her hold around the clothing she carried in her folded arms. The bundle of fabric draped in front of her was the only clothing she wore.

At first he thought she didn't move because she had seen him. But as he continued to watch her he realized she did not have the frozen, startled posture of a frightened doe. She was not clutching her clothing in front of her protectively to preserve modesty or dignity, she merely held it. He was struck by the reverence of her posture, the respect she had for this quiet clearing he had only just discovered. Her stillness had nothing to do with him at all, he realized. She was unaware of his observation, and he wished that it might remain so. With no small measure of regret he knew he would have to make his presence known to her. But not yet, he thought selfishly. Not just yet.

Her contemplative state ended abruptly as she tossed her clothing carelessly on the rocks. It lay like a darkly raised bruise against the pale, sun-drenched stones. She didn't appear to give it another thought, not pausing even briefly to straighten or arrange it so it wouldn't wrinkle. In a way he was disappointed that she didn't care more for her garments. He had only an impression of healthy pink skin, elegantly slender curves, and rose-tipped breasts as she ignored the stone stairway and launched herself into the water from where she stood, entering it cleanly and shallowly in an arching, graceful dive that sprayed diamond droplets in her wake.

She didn't come up immediately, and he followed her path as she moved swiftly just below the water. She was as fluid as the element she moved in, her body undulating sleekly in a current of her own creation. The tapered length of her legs moved in unison, propelling her forward in a seductive, almost lazy rhythm. Once he thought she would surface for air in the middle of the water hole, but she dove abruptly and only the curve of her bottom broke the waterline before she went deeper. A smile flickered on his face.

When she finally came up for air it was directly below his perch. He was no longer smiling when she looked up and saw him for the first time. He was still hunkered on the lip of the rock like a bird of prey. His glossy black hair and the long black duster draping the ground around him, furthered that impression. Intense gray eyes watched her narrowly above the straight, but somehow aggressive line of his nose.

He didn't say anything, just continued to stare at her. In spite of the flush that was creeping across her skin and heating her cheeks, she didn't duck beneath the water. It wasn't in her nature to run even when common sense dictated she should. With characteristic directness she stared back at him.

Her eyes were remarkably green, he thought, as deeply green as the forest around her. It was a pure pleasure to look into them, and he was in no hurry to look away.

"I don't think you have any shame," she said. In other conditions, in another setting, she would have been able to infuse her words with enough acid to etch glass. This stranger merely smiled at her.

"It's that obvious?" he asked.

She had to draw on a contemptuous glare which she had been told could leave a bruise. It left the man above her unmoved. She was realistic enough to acknowledge that he had all the advantages. He was on the high ground, on solid footing, and more importantly he was the one wearing clothes. There was simply no dignity in treading water naked. Worse, she was getting tired of doing it.

He watched the tempo of her movements change as she sought purchase among the submerged rocks. He was prepared to lend her a hand when her feet touched on a narrow ledge that would support her. She made no attempt to raise herself out of the water, rather she remained very satisfactorily cloaked by it while she rested. Water glistened on her shoulders and at the hollow of her throat. His eyes strayed up the length of her neck, glanced off her smooth cheek, passed her ear, then fastened on the red-gold cap of hair that was like a damp helmet on her head.

If her eyes were her most remarkable feature, then her hair was her most unusual. It was not merely the color that made it so, but the length. Closely cropped to follow the shape of her head, it defied any fashion. It lay sleekly against her scalp, the ends of it already drying and curling in the early morning sunshine. Apache women cut their hair when they were in mourning. It was on the tip of his tongue to ask her if she had lost a loved one, a husband or father perhaps, when he remembered she wouldn't understand the question, that New Yorkers certainly didn't observe the same rituals as the Chiricahua, Kiowa, or Mescalero. He touched the back of his neck where his hair brushed the collar. Even at this length it was still longer than hers, yet shorter than he had worn it for most of his life. He had cut it out of respect for the passing of a friend and more regretfully as a concession to New York mores.

As the stranger continued to stare at her hair, she surprised herself by touching it with an air of self-consciousness, tugging on a damp strand near her temple to make it seem longer. That simple gesture was enough to cause him to look away. She wondered what construction he had put upon her cropped hair. Did he think she was ill? That she had lice? That she was a branded adulteress? The sense that he was pitying her forced her chin upward at a defiant, proud angle.

"You're trespassing," she said coolly. "This is private property."

He was unperturbed. "I was invited."

"By whom?"

"The owner."

"That's not possible."

He shrugged. It didn't matter if she believed him or not. "You're not his wife, are you?"

She blinked at that, startled that he thought she would be anyone's wife. Glancing over her shoulder to the opposite side of the pool, she saw her discarded clothes piled on the rock. No, she realized, there were no clues for him there. She looked up at him, her eyes narrowing suspiciously. "Whose wife would I be?"

"Walker Caine's."

She sidestepped the issue. "This isn't Walker Caine's property. The Granville mansion is a few miles farther up the main road." As she watched with some fascination, color crept just beneath the surface of his sun-bronzed complexion. He was clean shaven with no beard or mustache or side-whiskers to hide the telltale tide of embarrassment. When it receded a faint smile touched his mouth, and it was rife with self-mockery.

"I don't think this is a story I'll be sharing with Walker," he said. "Or anyone else."

Before she could ask what it was that amused him about being lost, he stood and shrugged out of his duster. He was tall and leanly muscled, limber and loose in spite of the fact that he had been crouched throughout their conversation. She had no difficulty appreciating that he was what her mother called a "fine figure of a man," but it wasn't his physical appearance that made her react with a small gasp. The gun belt resting on his hips accomplished that.

"You're not from around here, are you?" she said. She supposed she deserved the smirk he tossed off like a flippant remark. "What I mean is, men in Baileyboro don't wear guns."

"Gun," he said. "Singular. Short-barreled Colt .45." He had it unfastened by the time he finished commenting and laid it with some care on his duster. His fingers were deftly moving over his shirt buttons when he added, "Just like the gunslingers wear." He glanced down at her, a single dark brow raised, wondering if she'd rise to the bait. She didn't. The fact that he was taking off his shirt had riveted her attention.

She found her voice when he began to unbutton the fly of his jeans. "What do you think you're doing?" she demanded.

His fingers didn't pause even a beat. "I'm going swimming." He wondered if he could. He had no illusions that he would be as expert as she in the water. At best he would be awkward. At worst . . . At worst he would drown.

He had been seven years old the last time he was in water deep enough to swim. That was twenty-three years ago on the banks of the Ohio River. He had balked on that occasion until his father had held out a hand and told him once he learned he would never forget. He was about to test the truth of those words now. There was so little he remembered about his father, he hoped that memory wasn't playing him false.

"Not here you're not," she said firmly, as though she believed it was in her power to stop him.

He didn't respond to that. Instead he sat down on the rock before removing his pants and pulled off his dusty boots. He felt as if his entire body was layered with the same dust. The decision to sluice it off in this water hole seemed more inspired with each passing moment. When he stood again to strip out of his jeans and drawers he saw that he was, for all intents and purposes, alone. She had dived, pushed off the ledge, and was swimming toward the center of the water hole. His face wore its calm, impenetrable mask as he flung himself into the water.

He didn't come up for so long that she grew worried. From her position in the water it wasn't so easy to follow his progress. She ducked below the surface and looked for him. His deep dive had worked up clouds of silt and all but eliminated her underwater vision. She came up when she felt him brush her leg, either by accident or design.

He raked back his thick hair. Droplets of water and sunlight lent it a blue-black sheen. He was very close to her and instinctively she moved away before a swell of water drew them together.

"My father was right," he said.

"About what?"

"I didn't forget."

She supposed he knew what he was talking about. She certainly didn't. "I don't think you should be in here. I told you this is private property." She noticed that she expended a great deal less energy staying near the surface than he did. It would serve him right if he drowned, she thought. Or at least believed he was drowning. She had no illusions that she could let it happen.

"I know. But you also told me it's not Walker's, and I imagine it's safe to assume you're not Walker's wife." He leveled her with his gray glance. "Are you?"

She considered lying. After all, before Skye Dennehy had become Walker Caine's wife she had been known to occasionally skinny-dip in this very pool. "No," she said finally. "I'm not Walker's wife."

He considered that as his eyes grazed her face. "Good."

She wondered how he could give that single word so much meaning. His voice had not changed at all. The smooth, husky quality of it made her think of her father's best bourbon. His light gray eyes were still like frost, yet it wasn't a chill she felt but searing heat. For no reason that she could understand she was drawn to him and the sensation of being pulled in was unnerving.

She knew she was the better swimmer, but it no longer mattered. Here, in the familiarity of the placid little pool where she had spent so many enjoyable summers with her sisters, Mary Francis Dennehy acknowledged that she was out of her depth.

"I have to go," she said. She wished her voice did not sound regretful or uncertain.

"Not yet."

She didn't reply. She struck off for the bank of rocks that held her clothes. He easily caught her by the ankle as she swam past and pulled her back. Her instinctive struggle brought her within inches of his slick, wet chest. She calmed herself to keep from being brought flush to his naked body. "I want to go," she said clearly. This time there was no mistaking her resolve.

"All right." As he held up both hands to surrender to her wishes he sank a little in the water.

She watched him warily while he sputtered. When she was sure he wasn't in need of rescuing, she swam for the stone stairway. Before climbing out, she darted a look over her shoulder. The eyes that met hers were certainly predatory. "Turn around," she said, making just that motion with her index finger. "Or go under the water while I get out."

"You weren't always so shy."

"I didn't know you were here, and you knew I didn't."

"Guilty." There was no remorse in his tone. If he had it to do again he wouldn't do it differently. However, he saw she was willing to wait him out this time and now he was the one tired of treading. He ducked under the water and counted to ten before resurfacing.

She was sitting on the sun-baked slab of stone wearing a plain white cotton shift. Her knees were drawn toward her chest, and she hugged them with her arms. The shift was damp in places as it absorbed the water she hadn't had time to towel off. "You could have surfaced with your back to me," she told him. "How could you know I'd be covered?"

"I trusted you to be quick about it even if it meant diving into the brush." He realized she was feeling a little more confident now that she was clothed. He was not going to disabuse her of that notion by pointing out that the sunlight made her shift an ephemeral covering at best. If she stood up now she would be more exposed to him than she had been in the water. "Is the house I passed on the way here yours?"

"No," she said truthfully.

"You're a guest?"

In her parents' home? Hardly. "No," she said. "Not a guest."

"A servant, then."

She had a serenely quiet smile, and she graced him with it. "No. But it's a mistake that's been made before in my family." She saw him working out another question and saved him the trouble by asking one of her own. "What's your business with Walker Caine?"

"No business. Just reestablishing an old acquaintance."

She regarded him steadily, weighing his words. "Walker Caine has enemies. How do I know you're not one of them?"

"You don't."

She considered that. Her sigh was audible as she came to a decision. "Walker Caine is my brother-in-law."

One of his dark brows arched slightly. "Then Mary Schyler is—"

"My sister."

His eyes narrowed now as he studied her, and he felt his skin prickle with the sensation of wariness. "And you're . . . Mary Michael?"

The serene smile returned. She shook her head. "In Denver."

The water seemed several degrees colder than it had moments before. "Mary Renee?"

"Laying track for Northeast Rail somewhere in the Rockies." The smile had now reached her forest green eyes.

"Mary Margaret?"

It seemed that Walker had written to his friend about the whole family. She cautioned herself that she shouldn't be enjoying this stranger's comeuppance quite so much. "Recently graduated from the Philadelphia Women's College of Medicine and back home on the Double H in Colorado."

"I see."

She gave him credit for masking his discomfort so well. She smoothed her cotton shift over her knees and looked at him expectantly.

"That makes you Mary Francis," he said finally.

She couldn't help it that her smile widened. "That's right."

"The nun."

"The nun," she confirmed. He surprised her again by turning the tables. In spite of the fact that she now commanded the high ground, had solid footing, and was wearing the clothes this time, he was able to stare her down.

"I don't think you have any shame," he said. Turning in the water, he swam with strong but awkward strokes toward the opposite bank.

Mary Francis sat as still as stone. Several moments passed before she got to her feet. She was reaching for her own clothing when she heard him climb out of the water. Knowing that he wasn't looking in her direction now, she began to dress. The black habit was creased by her earlier carelessness, and she made a halfhearted attempt to smooth it. She adjusted the stiff white collar. Out of her pocket she pulled her rosary and attached it to her waist. She did not have her cornet or veil and her red-gold hair was incongruently bright against the severity of her habit. She threaded her fingers through it quickly, squeezing out the last of the water droplets.

He was fastening his gunbelt when he heard her voice coming to him quietly from across the water hole. He paused, raising his head, and looked at her. She was standing there in her plain black gown, both somber and simple, and he was thinking about a flash of rose-tipped breasts. She was standing there with the serene features of an angel, and he was thinking about kissing that mouth. She took a step closer to the water, the movement making the habit shift against her legs. Suddenly he was remembering the undulating rhythm of hips and thighs and calves as she parted the water with her body.

"Did you hear me?" she asked.

His eyes never leaving hers, he shook his head.

"You're welcome to come to breakfast at the house. If you're hungry, that is."

He was. The train from West Point had deposited him in Baileyboro long before any boarding house was serving a meal. He'd chosen to walk the five miles to the Granville mansion rather than cool his heels at the station. Now, not only was he hungry, it seemed he hadn't walked far enough. "No, thank you," he said. "I think I'll go straight to Walker's."

She could have said, "Suit yourself." God knew as well as she did that it was what she wanted to say. Mary didn't, however, believing she might as well behave with charity in her heart right now rather than confess a lack of it later. "Walker and Skye have returned to China," she said. "They left soon after Maggie's graduation. There's no one at the mansion except the groundskeeper and his wife." She took the path that led into the forest and then to the summer house, leaving it to Walker's friend to follow her or not.

He drew abreast of her more quickly than she would have thought possible. His passage was both swift and silent. She made no comment about his decision to join her. The fingers of her right hand ran absently along the length of her rosary.

"My name's McKay," he said. "Ryder McKay."

Mary acknowledged the introduction with a brief nod. "I don't recall Walker mentioning you, but then I haven't spent much time with him. It's unfortunate he's not here to greet you."

"I doubt he'll think so," Ryder said. "He wanted to return to China."

"My sister was excited as well. Skye imagines herself to be some sort of adventuress."

"Then she married the right man."

Mary glanced at him sideways. "Yes," she said quietly. "I think she did." They walked along in silence, their path shaded by the sweeping boughs of pine and oak and hickory. When it rose more steeply she raised her gown and revealed she was still barefooted. She had no difficulty crossing the uneven ground. "What led you to the pool?" she asked as they came over the rise. The summer home was a hundred yards across an open field, in front of them. Black-eyed Susans, columbine, and daylilies dotted the field. "Why didn't you come to the house if you thought Walker lived there?"

"It was too early. I looked around, but no one was up. It seemed more polite to wait."

"But what led you to the pool?"

"The scent of water."

"The scent? But—"

He shrugged, cutting off her question. It wasn't something he could explain and it wasn't something she could understand. She probably wondered why he hadn't gone directly to the river, but that had a different scent than the place she called the pool and he called a watering hole.

Mary didn't pursue her question. The summer home beckoned her, its newly painted, white wooden frame gleaming in the sunshine. The windows winked at her. At the entrance to the enclosed back porch she wiped her feet on the hemp mat, then slipped them into a pair of soft black leather slippers. She picked up a pail of raspberries she had picked earlier in the morning. Raising it in front of her, she said, "I was already up when you came by. I just wasn't home."

"I stand corrected," he said somewhat stiffly.

She hesitated a beat, fighting the urge to look away. "I'm sorry about what happened at the pool," she said quickly, before the apology stuck in her throat. "I should have told you at the beginning. I knew it would make a difference."

There was a hint of roughness in his voice and an intensity about his light gray eyes. "Why didn't you?"

Mary didn't respond. She preceded him into the kitchen, knowing it would take a lot of soul-searching to answer that question honestly.

The kitchen of the summer house was spacious. A large, solid rectangular pine table dominated the center of the room. Kettles and skillets and cooking utensils dangled from iron hooks on a wooden frame which was suspended from the ceiling. One of her sisters—she couldn't say now which one—had christened it the pan chandelier and the name had stuck.

"Will pancakes be all right?" she asked, reaching for one of the cast iron skillets.

He nodded shortly and looked around for something that he might do. Her hospitality confused him. Ryder McKay wasn't used to a welcome mat. An invitation into any home was rare, and the circumstances of this invitation were most unusual.

"Just have a seat," she said, pointing to one of the six chairs gathered around the table. "Unless you'd rather eat in the dining room? You could wait in the parlor while I cook."

He nudged one of the chairs out with the toe of his boot. "No," he said. "This is fine." More than fine, he thought, but he didn't say the words. He was conscious of his dusty boots, of his clothes that looked as if he'd slept in them, of his dark, damp hair that was just beginning to dry at the back of his neck.

"You can hang your duster on that hook by the back door," she told him when she saw him hesitate. Mary glanced at his empty hands. "You don't have a hat?"

Ryder shook his head. Most often he wore a bandana tied around his forehead and hair. He had one in the pocket of his duster, but he hadn't worn it since leaving Fort Apache two weeks ago. He touched the back of his neck again. It was when he had cut his hair. He was aware suddenly that Mary was looking at him expectantly, and Ryder realized he'd still made no move to take off his coat. He did so now, hanging up not only the coat but his gunbelt as well. Although his hostess made no comment, he could sense her relief.

The black iron stove was a monstrous contraption that generally needed more coaxing than a contentious child. On this occasion it fired up easily, and Mary set the skillet, adding a dollop of butter upon it to heat. She quickly put the pancake ingredients in a bowl and placed it in front of Ryder along with a wooden whisk. "You mix this while I clean the berries."

Welcoming something to do, Ryder didn't object. Butter was popping on the skillet by the time he had the batter smooth and without direction from Mary he left the table and began pouring the first cakes.

At the sink Mary paused and glanced over her shoulder to where Ryder was working. He was intent on his task and didn't appear to sense her interest. There was nothing tentative about his work. His movements were crisp and efficient as he measured out the batter and, later, when he flipped the saucer-sized cakes. She turned back to her own work, finished rinsing the berries, and sugared them lightly to bring out their own juice.

"Do you want coffee?" she asked, realizing she was remiss in not thinking of it earlier.

"Are you having it?"

"No. I'm drinking milk."

"Milk will be fine." Better than fine, he thought, trying to recall when he'd last had a glass of cold, sweet milk. It wasn't as long ago as the last time he'd been swimming, it only seemed that way. He expertly flipped another cake and placed it on a warming plate. "Do you want me to get it?" he asked before he poured more batter. "I saw the cooler on the back porch."

Mary accepted his offer, reasoning he wouldn't have made it if he minded. It gave her the opportunity to set the table. In a matter of minutes they were sitting at a right angle to one another, unfolding their napkins. Ryder started to pick up his fork when he saw Mary bow her head. His lean fingers released the fork and his hand slid onto his lap. He lowered his head, but didn't close his eyes, watching Mary instead as she said the blessing quietly. When she was finished she smiled encouragingly in his direction.

"Please help yourself."

For a moment he couldn't think what she meant. He was staring at her mouth, at the smile that had some extraordinary power to tilt him off center. He blinked. His world was righted as her smile slowly faded under his penetrating stare. He looked away abruptly, picked up his fork, and stabbed at the pile of pancakes.

Out of the corner of her eye Mary watched Ryder stack his cakes, spread them with butter, and add the sweetened raspberries. She appreciated his appetite and wondered when he'd last eaten, though good manners dictated she couldn't ask. "How do you know Walker?" she said, lifting two pancakes to her own plate.

"We met at West Point." He saw her startled pause. The reaction didn't surprise him. "I was two years older than Walker, but we began at the same time. He finished. I didn't." She resumed preparing her pancakes. "But then that's probably more in line with what you'd expect of me."

Mary's red-gold brows arched. "I don't believe I've formed any expectations regarding you, Mr. McKay. We've only just met."

He said nothing and applied himself to his meal.

She was silent for a few minutes, then asked, "How is it that you came to go to West Point?"

Ryder looked at her frankly. "How is it that you came to go to the convent?"

Mary's head jerked a fraction in response to his candor. He

couldn't have let her know any more clearly that she was intruding upon his privacy.

"Look, ma'am," he said. "If the price of breakfast is having
to answer your list of questions, I think I'll pass." Waiting for
her reply, Ryder leaned back in his chair and pushed away his
half-eaten plate of food.

Mary found herself apologizing for the second time that
morning. "You're right," she said softly. "I was being uncon-
scionably rude. There are no strings to breakfast." She pushed
his plate toward him again, even as she felt her own appetite
fading. "Eat your fill. I won't bother you again." She noticed
he did not require a second invitation. He tucked into his food
with relish while she mostly pushed hers around her plate.

"This is a big house for just you," he said, looking around
the kitchen again. "Are you here alone?"

"Right now I am. Jay Mac and Mama were up here for most
of June and they'll return again next month. They hire some
help in Baileyboro to maintain the house. I didn't want anyone
here, so I sent them away." Her sigh was a trifle wistful. "But
you're right, it's a big house to ramble in alone. Every room
has memories, this one perhaps more than any other. Sometimes
I can almost believe I hear the Marys laughing and bickering
and chattering." She smiled gently now, thinking about squab-
bles at the kitchen table over who would clean the berries and
who would make the pie crust, who would set the table and
who would pour the milk. "There were too many of us and not
always enough jobs."

"The Marys," he said thoughtfully, interested. "Is that what
you call yourselves?"

Her smile deepened to a grin. "No. My father called us that.
He came up with it after we started calling him Jay Mac. He
mostly used it when he was thinking of some collective punishment."

"Collective punishment?"

"You know, when one of us had done something wrong and
wouldn't admit to it. Jay Mac would line us up, oldest to young-

est, and pace the floor in front of us, speaking to our mother as if we weren't in the room at all." Mary's voice deepened, her brow furrowed, and she tucked her chin lower and looked up, as if she were looking over the rim of invisible spectacles.

Ryder watched, fascinated by this imitation of John MacKenzie Worth. The man was a leader of industry, the owner of one of the most powerful and successful rail lines in the nation, a personal friend of presidents and generals. He was not a man to be taken lightly or to be made light of. Yet his daughter showed no compunction about sharing this intimate glimpse into their family life.

" 'Moira,' he'd say, 'the Marys have perpetrated a most heinous crime. I count two of my cigars missing from the humidor on my desk. Not one Mary will admit to it, so all the Marys must bear the responsibility.' " The impression she gave of Jay Mac was quite credible, but then all her sisters agreed she'd had more years to practice it. Mary straightened and resumed her own sweetly melodious voice. "He'd go on for a few minutes, hoping to wear us down, I think, but he never did. Being one of the Marys made us stronger. Against a force like Jay Mac, it was necessary to band together." Half her mouth curved in a quick smile that also lighted her eyes. "Poor Papa, he's smart about so many things, but he's never quite learned how to divide and conquer his five Marys."

If only a third of what Walker had written him about the family was true, Ryder imagined that five young Marys were a force to be reckoned with. "Why were you all named Mary?"

"Mother's idea." She took a sip of milk. "Tradition, I suppose. She's Irish, you know. And Catholic, of course. But Jay Mac's a thorough Presbyterian, and then there's the problem of us all being bastards because Jay Mac didn't marry my mother until a few years ago." She glanced at him, wondering what Walker had revealed to him. "Did you follow that?"

He nodded, but he was paying more attention to the fact that she had a milk mustache on her upper lip. Her youthful smile, the odd cropping of her red-gold hair, and now the milk outlining the shape of her upper lip made her seem as young as a schoolgirl. As innocent as one, too. He needed to remind himself of that. He cleared his throat and touched his own lip. "Milk."

She understood immediately. "Oh," she said a bit self-consciously. She dabbed at her mouth with her linen napkin, then looked to him. "Better?"

"You got it all," he said, not quite answering her question. "So you were all Marys."

"Well, yes," she said, picking up the threads of her story. "But not really. I'm called Mary. Sometimes Mary Francis. My sisters were always Michael, Rennie, Maggie, and Skye. They only heard Mary precede their name if they were in serious trouble."

Which sounded as if it had been rather frequent, he thought. "Who stole the cigars from the humidor?"

"What? Oh, the cigars." Mary gave up any pretense of eating. She carried her plate to the sink and scraped the uneaten pancakes into a pail. "It was Michael. She actually liked the smell of cigar smoke."

"What was your father's punishment?"

Turning to face him, she leaned back against the sink. Her nose wrinkled with the power of the memory. "We smoked until our faces were the color of pea soup."

"Michael, too?"

"Michael, too. She lasted longer than the rest of us—which of course confirmed her as the perpetrator of the heinous crime in Jay Mac's eyes—but eventually she succumbed. Jay Mac was pretty certain she'd never pick up another cigar as long as she lived."

"Did she?"

Mary shook her head. "Not that I know." She gave Ryder a dead-on look and added dryly, "She gave them up for cigarettes."

One corner of his mouth lifted slightly, acknowledging the irony and humor. He resumed eating while Mary collected the skillet from the stove, the crusty mixing bowl and dirty utensils, and began washing. She didn't hear him come up behind her, didn't know he was there until he slipped his plate into the dishwater. Surprised, she jumped a little. Before she could say that he had merely startled her, he was backing away as if he had been the one who'd been burned.

"Don't worry," he said tersely. "I'm not going to touch you."

Her forest green eyes regarded him curiously. "I didn't think you were. And I wouldn't jump if you did. You caught me unaware, that's all. I didn't know you were there. I'm not frightened of you."

He was quiet, measuring the truth of her words. "Is it because you feel safe in that getup?"

Her brows rose a fraction in reaction to hearing her habit described as a "getup." Her tone was patient but cool. "It's because I don't think you intend me any harm. You're Walker's friend, aren't you? Why would you want to hurt me?"

"You weren't so confident back at the water hole."

"Back at the . . . umm . . . the *water hole* I wasn't so confident you even knew Walker Caine." She turned her back on him and continued washing. "And, yes," she added softly, with almost pained honesty, "perhaps some of it has to do with my getup."

Then it had nothing to do with him, he thought, wondering if he could believe her. Nothing to do with his sun-bronzed skin, straight inky hair, or the gunbelt he wore low on his hips. Ryder reached in the pocket of his jeans and pulled out an envelope. It was wrinkled and dog eared. There were a few smudged fingerprints on the back. He opened it carefully and took out the contents. The letter was two pages long, front and back. It had been handled with more care than the envelope. He held it out to Mary.

"You don't have to prove anything to me," she said.

"Take it."

Mary pulled her hands out of the water, shook them off, and wiped them on a towel. She took the letter Ryder held in front of her. "This isn't necessary."

"Read it."

She had only taken note of Walker's handwriting once before, at the occasion of her sister's wedding when he'd signed his name to the marriage papers. Mary quickly turned the pages, and her eyes flickered to his signature. She would recognize the scrawled and sweeping lines of his "W" anywhere. Having established the letter was really from her brother-in-law, Mary went back to the beginning and read it through carefully.

Most of the letter was about Skye, about the hasty marriage, and the circumstances that had brought Walker to the Granville mansion. There was anecdotal information about Skye's family and descriptions which brought a smile to Mary's lips. Walker certainly had them all dead to rights. The letter concluded with an invitation for Ryder to visit Walker and Skye whenever he wanted. "Walker didn't know yet about his assignment to China," she said, returning the letter to Ryder. "He's been there and back and gone again."

"He didn't know when I would take him up on it," Ryder replied. "I haven't been much good about writing back myself."

"It was a rather nonspecific invitation."

"He meant it."

"I know that. Walker didn't make the offer to be polite. That certainly isn't his way." Mary was able to see the envelope clearly as Ryder replaced Walker's letter. "Is that where you came from?" she asked somewhat incredulously. "Fort Preston in the Arizona Territory?"

"That's where I was when I got the letter. I came from Fort Apache."

"You traveled over most of the country to see Walker without ever thinking to check if he was here?"

"There's no need to be scornful," he said evenly. "Or have I given you the impression I'm a stupid man?"

No, she thought, that wasn't her impression at all. "Quite the opposite," she said.

He folded the envelope and put it away. There was a gravity to his voice that hadn't been there before. "I came East to pay my respects to a teacher who died recently. I missed the funeral the military gave him, but I spoke to his widow and made my peace. That was what was important to me."

Mary saw that it was. The cleanly defined lines of his face were still impassive, but there was a certain solemnness about his eyes. "An instructor at West Point?" she asked, beginning to piece things together in her own mind.

He nodded. "General Augustus Sampson Thorn."

It was an impressive sounding name but one with which Mary was unfamiliar. "I don't believe I know of him."

"A veteran of battles at Shiloh and Manassas and some of the early Western campaigns against the Cheyenne. It's all right," he added when she continued to shake her head slowly in nonrecognition. "He would have rather been remembered for his career as a teacher."

"What was his subject?"

"Mathematics."

Once again she was disconcerted by his ability to surprise her. "This was a subject you liked?"

"Very much so."

"I see," she said, wondering what to make of him.

He almost smiled then. "No," he said. "You don't see at all."

Mary noted that he didn't seem bothered by the fact, which meant that he didn't care for her opinion one way or the other. She supposed that was as it should be. They were virtual strangers in spite of a common acquaintance and a perfunctory exchange of names.

Mary finished up the last of the dishes while Ryder stood by. "When do you have to return to the Fort?" she asked.

"I'm not going back to Fort Apache. I have a new assignment."

"Here in the East?"

"No." Was that disappointment he glimpsed? Relief? "In the Southwest Territory."

"You're regular Army?"

In Ryder's opinion there was nothing regular about the Army. "More or less," he said. "I scout for them."

Mary Francis Dennehy's laughter was not for the fainthearted. It exploded from her like a burst of Gatling gunfire. It was loud and raucous, yet wonderfully lively and infectious. The features that could be solemn and serene under the most trying circumstances became animated and mobile. Her eyes crinkled, her nose wrinkled, her generous mouth split widely, and she flushed from the hollow of her throat to her scalp. Her family appreciated it. Little Sisters of the Poor made allowances for it. Mother Superior suffered it. And Bishop Colden prayed it would never happen during his mass.

Ryder McKay took a step backward and stared mutely.

"Oh," she said, trying to catch her breath. "Oh, I'm sorry. No, I'm not. Not really. Oh." Mary felt another burst of laughter rising in her, and she fought to stifle it. Brushing at the tears that had gathered at the corners of her luminous eyes, she held her breath as if she had hiccups. "But it's so funny, don't you think? You . . . an Army scout . . . lost on your way to . . . to . . ."

"To Walker's," he finished without any hint of humor. "It was amusing when I realized it. It's humiliating when you do."

That cut her laughter short. "Oh, I didn't mean . . ." Her voice trailed off when she saw his eyes were not so sober as they had been a moment earlier. He was teasing her, she realized. She dabbed at her eyes again. "I wouldn't mention this to anyone," she said.

"I think I said that earlier," he reminded her.

"So you did." She picked up a dishtowel but he took it out of her hands and dried things himself. She leaned against the sink and watched him and wondered why he was here now, why he had lost his way, and what it meant. "There's a sign at the fork in the road," she told him. "Walker's place is clearly marked."

"There was no sign," Ryder said.

Yes, she thought, there *was* a sign, but it was one meant for her, not for Ryder McKay.

It was after midnight when Mary left the summerhouse and retraced her steps back to the pool. The night was cloudless.

Starshine and a first quarter moon lighted her path. Mary hadn't even considered carrying a lantern. She had found her way unerringly to the pool on much darker nights. This evening presented no problem.

Wearing only her white cotton shift, she was like a wraith as she crossed the field of wildflowers. She padded silently where the grasses had been beaten down. The earth was cool on her bare feet as she wended her way over the hillside, and in the forest the bed of fallen pine needles was soft. At the edge of the clearing she paused as she had on so many occasions, as she had earlier this morning. This place was a sanctuary to her, a place of peace and worship, and she gave thanks for it now.

Stepping forward to the natural stone stairway, Mary pushed the wide straps of her shift to each side of her shoulders and let the fabric glide against her skin like a caress. She stepped out of the puddle of material and unhesitatingly launched herself into the pool.

From his perch on the far side of the water hole Ryder McKay watched the graceful, supple arc of Mary's body as it slid almost soundlessly into the inky depths. He should leave, he told himself, because she valued this place for its solitude. For the second time he was the trespasser, and for the second time he had failed to make his presence known. The thought came to him again that he should leave, but Mary surfaced then and raised her arms, stretching, and moonlight limned the slender length of them and Ryder stopped thinking about what he *should* do and considered instead what he *would* do.

Mary turned on her back and floated with little effort, kicking her feet just enough to keep her on the surface. The water was warmer than the air, and her skin prickled and her nipples hardened. She ducked backward into the water, warming herself all

Jo Goodman

over until she completed a circle and surfaced again. She could see her own breath like mist in the air . . . or cigar smoke.

She smiled. Now why had she told Ryder McKay that story? Or any of the others during the afternoon and into the evening? He had wanted to be on his way after breakfast since there was no chance of seeing Walker, but she'd pressed him into helping her with a few of the heavier chores around the house. He hadn't seemed to mind, she reflected, and he was the one who offered to finish painting the porch rails after lunch. Neither of them mentioned dinner, but it seemed natural somehow that he should stay, and then they sat on the swing at the front of the house and time slipped away. She was the one who realized he was missing his opportunity to get out of Baileyboro, yet she hadn't said anything about the train schedule. It seemed only right that she offer him one of the summer home's five bedrooms for the night.

She hadn't thought about not being able to sleep while he was in the house, while his bedroom was across the hall from hers. She was tired when she bid him good night; she hadn't expected to toss and turn and wonder if Ryder was finding his own bed comfortable. After thirty minutes she had risen and gone to the window seat. She had tried to read, but the starshine on the field outside her window was more intriguing. The path to the pool unwound through the field like a dark grosgrain ribbon. Even though she sat at the window for another half hour she knew where she'd find a measure of tranquillity.

Only it wasn't the same now, and she knew better than to blame Ryder McKay. His intrusion wasn't the problem. That rested within her. There could be no measure of peace anywhere if she didn't find it first in her heart.

It came without warning: the ineffable sadness that was so much a part of her life of late. The weight of it lay heavily on her chest, crushing it. Each breath was labored. The movement of her arms became listless and leaden. Mary was too experienced with the sensation now to fight it. She gave in and allowed herself to slip beneath the surface where her tears could mingle with the water.

Ryder raised himself up slightly, anxious now for Mary to resurface. He counted the seconds and wondered how long she could possibly hold her breath. He was on the point of diving for her when she came up and headed for the bank.

In the stillness of the night he could clearly hear her pained gasps for air, and it was only by slow degrees that he realized the rhythm was wrong, that what he was hearing were really Mary's anguished sobs. He came to his feet, intent on leaving now. Whatever was pulling at Mary's heart was between her and her God, he thought. It wasn't about him. He had no place in it.

Still, he found himself walking the perimeter of the water hole and coming to stand beside her prostrated body. He scooped up her shift and crouched beside her. "Put this on," he said softly. And when she couldn't quite manage it herself, he helped her.

After that it seemed the most natural thing in the world to take her in his arms.

Two

September 1884, New York City

Mary went home to write the letters. The convent in Queens was not the place where she could put her thoughts to paper this time. Although it had been her home since she was seventeen, for just a month more than thirteen years, Sister Mary Francis needed to go to the place of her youth.

The mansion on the corner of Fiftieth and Broadway was a palatial affair. John MacKenzie Worth had had it built when he'd recognized the populace of Manhattan was moving north. Central Park was mostly farmland when they first moved in. In the beginning their house sat alone on a street that, though it later became a thoroughfare in the heart of the city, was then a muddy tract in the hinterlands.

The gray stone home was large and solid, built to accommodate Jay Mac's mistress and his five bastard Marys. There was a lot of gossip among society's upper crust when Jay Mac's plan was first revealed and still more during the residence's construction. After all, matrons tittered, Jay Mac and his wife lived not far from the planned site. How could he do this to Nina? How would that woman hold her head up? Only Nina's death finally silenced the gossips on that subject.

On another front, one closer to his heart, Jay Mac heard from Moira that she really didn't want to leave the flat where she had been living with her daughters. True, they were cramped, and

Mary was old enough to deserve her own room, but it was hardly a squalid setting.

John MacKenzie Worth had not become one of a dozen of the most powerful and influential men in the nation by listening to what everyone else said. The construction went ahead.

Now, as Mary Dennehy came to stand in front of the spiked iron fence that bordered the property, she appreciated her father's decision as she had never done before.

She pushed at the gate and it swung open easily on well-oiled hinges. Mr. Cavanaugh's work, Mary thought. Their grounds-keeper worked hard to present the house in its best light. The shrubs were carefully manicured, the rosebushes pruned lovingly. Now that it was fall, marigolds and hardy mums followed the perimeter of the house and touched it with a deep, rich rainbow of autumn's finest colors.

Mary let the gate swing closed behind her and paused briefly before starting up the walk. She drew a calming breath to order her mind because she recognized that the serene and stoic presentation of the house was not what one necessarily encountered inside.

A maid she didn't recognize greeted her at the door and took her shawl. "Where's Mrs. Cavanaugh?" Mary asked. The groundskeeper had a perfect counterpart in his wife, who oversaw all of the inside work. Mrs. Cavanaugh had been with Moira Dennehy and her children since they'd moved from the flat to the palace.

"M'name's Peggy Bryant, Sister," she said, making a little curtsy. "Mrs. Cavanaugh's having a row with the butcher this morning. Something about being charged twice for lamb chops that weren't worth their price once."

Mary smiled. It had been disconcerting not to see a familiar, loved face immediately, but Peggy's story was pure Mrs. Cavanaugh. She loved to haggle with the green grocer, the butcher, the flower vendor, and the milk man. She watched every one of Jay Mac's household accounts as closely as she watched the stock market. In her mind the two were related. The housekeeper

supposed that whatever she could save on the front end would
be returned to her twofold through her stocks at Northeast Rail.
Jay Mac tried to explain once that it didn't work that way, but
there was no telling Mrs. Cavanaugh anything once she had her
mind made up. To Mary's way of thinking that trait went a long
way to making Mrs. Cavanaugh one of the family.

"Your mother's gone shopping," Peggy offered. "I don't think
she expected you before tea."

Mary did not let her relief show. The cornet of her habit
continued to frame delicate, serenely untroubled features. "And
Jay Mac's at his office?"

Peggy nodded, and several strands of dark hair slipped from
beneath her dainty, starched cap. She tucked them back quickly.
"Since early this morning, Sister."

"I'm just Mary here."

Peggy's hazel eyes were skeptical as they took in Mary's habit
from head to toe. "That will take some getting used to," she
said uncertainly. "I was raised by the Sisters at St. Stephen's.
They weren't likely to ask me to call them by their given
names."

Mary saw Peggy glance upward as if she were expecting
lightning to strike. She said dryly, "In my experience, Peggy,
our Lord uses more subtle means—at least before tea."

Peggy's eyes widened so the whites were completely visible
around her hazel irises. "Oh my, you're just like they said you
were."

Mary didn't ask who "they" were or what "they" said.
Clearly the newest member of the staff had had her head filled
with tales. "I'd like to use my old room," she told Peggy.

"That's fine, Sister . . . I mean . . ." Her voice trailed off as
she tried to correct herself. "I just finished cleaning it. Mrs.
Cavanaugh said you might want to have a lie-down there."

"Thank you, Peggy." When the girl started to precede her up
the stairs, Mary laid a gentle hand on her shoulder. "It's not
necessary. I think I know my way."

Peggy flushed. "Very good." She made another small bob and hurried down the hall.

Mary's room was much the way she had left it thirteen years earlier. Dolls from her childhood crowded the overstuffed chair by the fireplace. Photographs of herself and her sisters as young hoydens took most of the space on the mantel. Her collection of small glass figurines was still on one corner of her vanity. An ivory-handled mirror, a gift for her sixteenth birthday, still lay on the other corner, her initials worked carefully into the pattern of roses on the reverse side. Two brushes, both made of boar's bristles and imported from London, lay beside the mirror. The small cedar box beside them held ribbons and tortoiseshell combs.

Mary's slender fingers trailed lightly over the lid of the box. Her hair had been her one true vanity, she thought, so it was good that it had been cut. She had had to fight tears as the weight of each long curl was lifted away from her head and lopped. There was no mirror for her to watch the shearing, but a single glance at the floor, at the red-gold carpet of hair surrounding her feet, told its own story. The face of Sister Benedict told another. "She knew it was my vanity," Mary said softly to herself. Her fingers left the box and ran across the tips of the brushes. "She took a lot of pleasure in watching it go."

Even now Mary could hear the snapping of the shears. There had been no public tears for the loss of her hair, only private ones. And they fell silently in her solitary room as she prayed for forgiveness for being so proud. "Maybe Sister Benedict knew I would always struggle with pride." But Mary didn't believe it. Sister Benedict was a small-spirited, spiteful woman who liked nothing so much as making others feel they were not as worthy as she.

Mary ignored the four-poster with its eyelet lace comforter and pillow shams. She had not returned to her room for a lie-down as Peggy imagined. She was set on a different purpose this day.

Sunshine from the French doors fell across the writing desk

and polished floor in slanted rectangles of light. Mary sat at the desk and opened the middle drawer where the ecru stationery was neatly stacked. She had been composing the letters she was about to write for months in her head. Knowing what she wanted to say did not make her task any less difficult.

The first letter was to Maggie. Wise Maggie whose skill at healing often extended to those with no visible wounds. She wrote to Maggie about her decision, what it meant to her, and what she suspected it would mean to the family. Maggie would understand where there would be hurt and where there would need to be healing.

The letters that followed were copies of the first in some of the content, but each missive accounted for the uniqueness of the sister who was going to read it. To Michael, the reporter for the *Rocky Mountain News,* Mary described her decision as writing a new chapter in her life. For Michael's twin Rennie, a construction engineer for Northeast Rail, Mary wrote in terms of building bridges with her past and the foundation of her spirit. Composing Skye's letter was perhaps the easiest. To Skye, her baby sister who wanted nothing so much as adventure, Mary wrote of just that. Change was its own adventure, and the change she was planning would give her that ten times over.

Each letter was carefully folded, the envelopes neatly addressed. Three would find their destination in different parts of Colorado. One would find Skye months from now in Shanghai.

Mary relaxed in the ladder-backed chair and stretched. Her fingers uncurled stiffly. The small of her back curved until she felt the lines of tension ease. There was a tiny popping noise in her neck as she moved it from side to side. She picked up the letters and carried them downstairs. She considered giving them to Peggy to post, but decided there was no one she wanted to entrust with the mailing of these particular letters. Mary found her shawl and left the house unnoticed, accomplishing her mission by the time her mother arrived home from shopping.

Moira Dennehy Worth was a petite woman who stood only as high as her oldest daughter's chin. That didn't stop her from hugging Mary to her breast as if this grown woman were still a child in braids. "It's good to see you, darling," she said cheerfully. She took a step back, examined Mary carefully, and pronounced herself satisfied. "You're looking very well. You've a bit of color in your cheeks this afternoon."

"You just squeezed it in there."

Moira wagged a finger, but she was smiling. "Don't be insolent."

Mary kissed her mother's softly lined cheek. "All right."

That lifted Moira's dark red brows a notch. "So agreeable? Are you certain you're not sickening with something?"

"Mother."

The dry, level tone was more familiar to Moira. She smiled and rang for tea. "Come and see what I've bought for your nieces and nephew."

"Your grandchildren, you mean."

"You always were the quick one," Moira acknowledged with a sly smile. She began opening the packages from A. T. Stewart's and Donovan's which covered the cushions of all the available sitting space in the front parlor. She paused long enough in her enthusiastic recounting of choosing the perfect dress for Madison to order tea and sandwiches when Peggy arrived.

Mary dutifully admired each outfit and accessory her mother unfolded from the tissue-paper packaging. There was enough ribbon, lace, and bows to set up shop as a milliner. Every item was quite lovely and obviously chosen with an eye for color and the individuality of each of the grandchildren. "Are you going to send these out for Christmas?" she asked.

"Actually I was thinking I might get your father to visit Denver before then."

"Oh."

"That's all?" Moira asked. "Just 'Oh'? Don't you think it's a good idea?"

Mary injected the proper note of passion into her voice. "I think any time you can get Jay Mac away from the Worth building and Northeast Rail, it's a good idea. You'll have an argument, though, since everyone was just together for Maggie's graduation."

Moira sighed, surveying the bounty of purchases. "I know. But that gathering made me want to have all my babies under one roof again."

"Babies or grandbabies?"

"Both."

"Mother," Mary said, giving her a level stare. "Skye and Walker can't possibly—"

"Oh, I know that, too. It's just a dream. I'll take as many of my babies as I can get."

Tea arrived and Mary helped her mother clear the loveseats to make sitting room. The small watercress and cucumber sandwiches had a delicate taste, and Mrs. Cavanaugh had prepared Mary's favorite spiced orange tea. "Will Jay Mac be late this evening?" asked Mary.

"No more than usual, I think." Her mother frowned slightly. "Why? Is it a problem? You can still stay for dinner, can't you? We have raspberry sorbet to finish the meal."

Mary couldn't help but smile. She supposed her mother hardly realized she was tempting her with sweets as if she were a child. Perhaps it was the nature of motherhood to always see the little girl in the grown woman. "I'm staying," she said. "Even if raspberry sorbet is not on the menu."

The twelve-course meal was served in the smaller, family dining room. Moira and Jay Mac sat at either end of the walnut table, and Mary, in spite of the fact that there were five chairs she could have chosen, chose the one in which she had sat for every meal with her family. Perhaps, she reflected later, it was in the nature of childhood to always be a little girl in the presence of one's parents.

Jay Mac was full of news from the business world. Moira and Mary had no trouble following it. They were familiar with the vagaries of the market, the unpopular attempts to unionize laborers, the problems with getting government land, and the difficulties laying track in the hostile Southwest Territories. Jay Mac shared his information as if he were among board members, not family. The expectation was the same: they should understand what put food on their plates and cash in their coffers.

Somewhere between the artichoke consommé and the roast lamb, Jay Mac's recitation ended and he entertained questions and suggestions. Moira and Mary's contributions moved the meal through the light green salad and salmon and peas. Jay Mac listened thoughtfully to what they had to say. He accorded their opinions the same respect he accorded those of his business associates, which was to say he took everything under advisement. His broad face could be impassive, the dark green eyes distant, but when they lighted on his wife or his daughter there was no mistaking the warmth at their depths.

John MacKenzie Worth wore his authority and power as other men wore an old dressing gown. He was comfortable with the mantle of influence, enjoyed the responsibility and the challenges. Over the years it had been proven to him that nowhere was he more challenged than in his own home. He still had a thick head of dark blond hair, but every graying strand at the temples he counted as ground lost in a skirmish with one of his daughters.

They were all settled now, each with a family and a profession. Even his darling Mary had a family of sorts, Jay Mac thought. He hadn't approved of her joining the sisterhood—he considered it his first major defeat at the hands of the Marys—but he had come to accept it. He even made anonymous contributions to Little Sisters of the Poor to help them run their hospital. He suspected Mary knew where the large donations to the charity originated, but she kept her own counsel.

Moira made overtures about a November trip to Denver while the potato croquettes were being served, but Jay Mac did not bite on the dangled bait. She tried again, regaling him with a humorous account of her shopping expedition, while they ate from a selection of cheeses. He chuckled in all the proper places but showed no interest in pursuing the topic of a trip West.

Moira's unsuccessful maneuvering took them just to the end of the meal, and so it was that Mary's own announcement was finally made over the raspberry sorbet.

"I'm leaving the Little Sisters," she said. Her tone was clear, and she didn't mumble or glide over the words. Still, she had to repeat herself because neither Jay Mac nor Moira could believe they'd heard correctly. Though her resolve had not changed, it was more difficult to say the second time.

Jay Mac didn't watch Mary as she repeated the words. This time he watched his wife. Moira's complexion faded to the paleness of salt, and she looked as if she'd just swallowed arsenic. "You're serious about this?" Jay Mac asked.

"You can't be serious!" Moira said almost simultaneously.

Mary pushed away the dish of sorbet. "I've quite decided," she said calmly.

"You mean you're joining another order," Moira said, her voice at once coaxing and hopeful.

The question challenged Mary's composure, but she managed to meet her mother's eyes and answer with credible firmness. "No, Mama, I mean that I am leaving the sisterhood altogether. I'm renouncing my vows."

"Oh, my God." Moira's face crumpled and tears welled in her eyes. She was so frozen by the revelation that she couldn't raise the napkin from her lap to her eyes. "Oh, my God," she whispered softly, tragically.

Mary had had a suspicion all her life that the clashes with her father were preparing her for something more formidable. She knew now that it was true and called on an inner reserve of strength, if not Divine guidance, to see her through this battle with her mother. It was accepted, even encouraged in a subtle sort of way, to match wills with Jay Mac. It fostered purpose and initiative and clear thinking. For as long as Mary could remember, no one had ever stood up to her mother.

It had never been necessary. Until now.

Jay Mac cut through the tension at the table by posing a question and drawing attention to himself. "Perhaps if you told us what's brought this about," he suggested.

Mary's hands were clasped in her lap, the knuckles nearly bloodless from her tight grip. Her chin lifted a notch, but her face remained composed. "It's not easy to explain," she said slowly, searching for the right words.

"Sure, and it's a crisis of faith," Moira interrupted. "That's what it is. I'm certain if you talk to Bishop Colden or Mother Superior they'd tell you it's not an uncommon experience. People of the cloth go through it just like parishioners. It doesn't mean you have to leave the church."

"Mama," Mary said with rather more sharpness than she intended. "A crisis of faith is not a cold. It's not something one catches and suffers. One doesn't simply recover and go on. And I've talked to Bishop Colden and Mother Superior, and they agree this is not a crisis of faith."

"But—"

"Moira," Jay Mac said firmly, deeply. There was a caution in his tone he did not often use with his wife. "Let Mary say her piece."

Moira was stricken. Her head snapped up, and her full mouth narrowed. The usual sparkle in her eyes was a militant glint now. "You're taking Mary Francis's side," she said, accusing in her hurt. "Sure, and you never wanted her to take her vows. You should be reminding her to honor her promises, especially when they're made to God."

"Please," Mary implored softly, her eyes darting between Jay Mac and Moira. "This isn't supposed to be an argument between the two of you."

It was as if she hadn't spoken. Jay Mac tempered his tongue by taking off his spectacles and making a show of cleaning them. "In the first place, Moira, I'm not taking anyone's side. As near as I can tell there's no side to be taken. And while it's true that I didn't think Mary should take her vows, I had to finally accept it was her decision. Now, if something's happened to make her change her mind, isn't that between her and God? Don't you think she's discussed this with Him?" He rose from his chair and replaced his spectacles on the bridge of his nose. Without asking what they wanted, he went to the sideboard and poured three cognacs. Rather than returning to his own chair at the head of the table, he pulled out the one at a right angle to Moira. He set the glasses in front of them and indicated they shouldn't be shy about drinking. "Do you think it's a crisis of faith, Mary?"

She raised the balloon-crystal glass between her hands, warming the liquor, but she didn't drink. She shook her head slowly. "No, it's not that. My struggle hasn't been with God but with what He wants for me. It's not that I don't believe in Him, I believe He has something else in mind for me."

Moira stared straight ahead, looking at neither her husband nor her daughter. Her expression was stony, and when Jay Mac laid a hand on her wrist she stiffened and tightened her lips.

Mary saw the movement, and the ache in her heart grew deeper. The sympathy in her father's eyes only made her want to cry. "I've given this a lot of thought, Mama—"

"Then you should have prayed more and thought less."

Jay Mac's sandy brows arched this time and he lowered his chin, looking hard at his wife over the gold-wire rims of his spectacles. In thirty-one years of knowing and deeply loving Moira this was a side he had never seen. It was not like her to be so closed or intractable. She was more subtle about her wishes than this exchange would lead one to believe. And she was never cruel. "Moira, to twist your phrasing, you're being thoughtless."

"Mama," Mary entreated, breaking in. "I *did* pray. This wasn't a decision quickly come to."

Moira shook her head. "I don't believe it."

"I can't be responsible for what you believe," Mary said tonelessly. "But it's the truth that I've been struggling to just this point for years."

"Years?" Jay Mac asked, surprised himself. "Mary, you've never let on, never told anyone."

The corners of Moira's eyes creased deeply and she gave Mary a narrow glance. "Not your sisters? Did you tell them and swear them to secrecy?"

"No. I didn't do that. I told them today, by individual letter. I wouldn't mock you and Jay Mac by sharing with them and not with you. If any of the Marys suspect it would be Maggie and Skye, and that's only because they've been close to home until recently. They saw me more often, and perhaps there were hints that I didn't know I was giving."

Moira was not mollified, but she didn't comment.

"Mama, what would I have said?" Mary went on. "And when would I have said it? My decision's made now, and I can hardly find the right words to explain. Most of the time the conflict is grappling with uncertainty. One hardly knows whether to reach for a light or snuff one out. When I went to our summer home in July it was to be alone with my thoughts and my prayers, and find answers to the questions I could hardly express." She paused and reached forward to touch her mother's arm, stopping short of Moira's satin sleeve when her mother did not lean in to her. Mary's hand hovered for a moment then was withdrawn. "Can you understand any of this, Mama?" When Moira didn't answer Mary looked helplessly to her father.

"It's a lot for her to accept," he said quietly. "There's been no warning. It's a shock, I confess, even to me."

Mary nodded. It had gone as badly as she had feared, and her world seemed shifted for it. The only thing that hadn't been changed was her mind. "Perhaps it would be better if I didn't spend the night here."

"Don't be absurd," Jay Mac said brusquely. "Of course you'll stay here. This is still your home. God knows your room hasn't been changed in thirteen years and it's certainly ready for you now." He looked sideways at Moira. "Almost as if someone's been expecting you."

"I wouldn't put that construction on it," Mary said, coming

to her feet. In spite of her best intentions her tone was caustic. "It's more likely that Mama wanted to remind herself of the sacrifice she made."

"Sacrifice?" asked Jay Mac.

Moira stared at her oldest daughter. "What sacrifice?"

Before Mary could help herself she said, "Me, Mama. I'm the sacrifice. You offered me up to the Church to atone for *your* sins."

Jay Mac stayed Moira's hand, keeping her from striking Mary. "I think you'd better go to your room, Mary. Enough's been said here this evening."

For once Mary Francis Dennehy had no argument with her father.

Fort Union, Arizona Territory

The ball was in full swing. The officers' wives wore a brilliant array of colors, taking this occasion to show off their finest gowns from back East, or at least something they'd been able to order from San Francisco. The fabrics were satin and silk and taffeta, and their hues covered the spectrum. The wives looked especially bright against the solid blue dress uniforms of their husbands. Gold braid, white gloves, and polished black boots, all of it so distinguished on the parade ground, was now a mere background complement to a dizzying display of crimson and sapphire, emerald and jade.

Not every officer had a wife, and not every woman at the ball was married. Several of the women were mere girls, still fresh-faced from the schoolroom. Others were in their early twenties and of a single mind to leave the arid drabness of Fort Union. They were the daughters of commissioned and noncommissioned officers alike, and their dance cards were eagerly sought by the eligible bachelors. It would have been unthinkable to allow any one of them to go unaccompanied through a single dance, especially when their fathers were taking notice. Even eighty-year-old Florence Gardner did not want for partners. The interest shown her was in part because she was shockingly free with her opinions and always engaged in lively conversation, and in part because she was the widowed mother of Fort Union's commander.

Although all the women were sought as partners, one particular woman enjoyed a surfeit of attention and accepted it as her due. Her presence was suffered by the officers' wives and despised by the officers' daughters. Florence Gardner was the only one who found amusement from her presence at the fort, though she kept it to herself.

Anna Leigh Hamilton bore the stamp of Eastern sophistication that none of the other women in the room could rival, except perhaps the general's mother who didn't care to. It was not that the wives and daughters hadn't once enjoyed the same well-mannered polish Miss Hamilton wore as regally as elbow-length gloves, it was simply that the heat and hardships of the Arizona Territory, the daily threats of raids and uprisings, had worn away the pretenses and conventions. Practicalities were more important considerations in this harsh environment than polish.

Anna Leigh Hamilton didn't expect to stay at the desert fort long enough to lose the radiance and refinement that drew so many covert glances in her direction. She looked forward to returning to San Francisco, then to Washington, with her widowed father. She would play hostess for him again, attend the theater and the opera, and choose from among the most advantageous of the invitations for dinner parties and carriage rides. She would entertain congressmen and judges and generals, sometimes in the parlor or dining room of their grand Washington home, sometimes in the even more intimate surroundings of her grand bed.

Ryder McKay casually flicked a cigarette into the dirt when he heard someone approaching. Turning, he leaned negligently against the wagon wheel he had been inspecting moments ear-

lier. The woman's silhouette was outlined by the bright candle-
light coming from the officers' hall behind her. Ryder recognized her immediately and his wary, guarded features faded.
The posture that had looked relaxed now actually became so.

"Don't you have enough partners in there?" he asked. His
raised chin indicated the hall. "You're not going to insist on
making me do a two-step with you?"

Florence Gardner laughed gleefully. "And get my toes tram-
pled in three different places? I don't think I'll risk that." She
leaned a little heavily on her ebony cane as she came closer to
the wagon, and didn't offer any resistance when Ryder picked
her up by the waist and set her on the back of the wagon bed.
It was very like him to notice her discomfort and act to relieve
it. Looking at him carefully, his strong features handsomely
carved by starshine and firelight, Florence was moved to sigh.
She tapped him on the chest with the curved handle of her cane.
"If I were forty years younger . . ."

Ryder smiled at that. "You'd still be old enough to be my big
sister."

"Ill-mannered lout," she said pleasantly. She made it sound
like a term of endearment. "Why aren't you inside filling dance
cards?"

He didn't answer, turning to his inspection of the wagon
again. It was a bone of contention between them, and Florence
Gardner knew precisely how he felt. He wasn't an officer. That
covered his end of the argument as far as he was concerned.
Given the opportunity, the general's mother would have pointed
out that neither was Ryder regular Army. He had never been an
enlisted man. Though he preferred to think of himself as a scout,
he was much more of a special agent, contracted by the Army
for very particular assignments. He had as much right to be in
that room as the senator from Massachusetts, the prospectors
from the Holland Mines, or the surveyors from the Office of
Land Management.

"Humph," Florence snorted when she couldn't get a rise out
of him. She smoothed the edges of her thick white hair where

it had come loose from its combs. Her pale blue eyes sparkled a bit mischievously as she said nonchalantly, "I thought you might be encouraged to take one turn on the floor with the hussy."

Ryder's lean fingers paused on the axle. "I don't think I heard you correctly."

Florence rapped the cane on the wagon bed several times. The harsh tattoo made the wood vibrate. "You know you heard very well. There's nothing wrong with your ears. I'm the one who's older than dirt here."

Ryder stood again and rested one elbow against the side of the wagon. He looked at her consideringly. She was a diminutive woman with pale skin and even whiter hair. Her mouth was too full and wide to ever be severe, but she made an effort to clamp it down hard when she wanted to appear disapproving. In confidence she had once told Ryder that she had seen too much in her lifetime to take anything too seriously. As a result, even at her most critical, most intolerant moments, Ryder saw through the grimly set mouth to the youthful laughter in her heart and in her eyes. Sometimes, when no one else was looking, she even dared a wink in his direction. It was their shared secret.

"Well?" she demanded with some asperity. "Why aren't you—" Florence broke off as the double doors to the hall opened and closed again. Over Ryder's shoulder she saw the subject of her question come into view. "Don't look now, Ryder, but—"

He nodded. "I know. I can smell her."

Florence knew Ryder was referring to Anna Leigh's expensive Paris fragrance, but the fact that he gave it no more due than smelling cattle droppings tickled her fancy. She laughed so hard tears gathered at the corners of her eyes.

Ryder reached in his back pocket and extended his bandana. The older woman took it gratefully and dabbed at her eyes. She stuffed it back in his hand just as Anna Leigh came upon them.

"Help me down, Ryder," Florence said. "I'll go back to the ball. Even in this desert, three's a crowd." She smiled serenely at Anna Leigh as she was gently set down. Her parting smile for Ryder was a shade more coquettish. "Behave yourself."

Not certain for whom the admonishment was meant, both Ryder and Anna Leigh watched her go. When Anna Leigh turned to Ryder he was already engaged in his inspection of the wagon. "Doesn't the Army have people who do that sort of thing?" she asked.

"Yes," he said shortly. "Me."

Anna Leigh laughed lightly. It was a trilling sound, sweetly melodious. She couldn't know that it served to remind Ryder McKay of a heartier, healthier laugh. "I thought I would see you this evening," she said.

He didn't look at her, giving his full attention to his work. "You are."

She was more intrigued by his rudeness than offended by it. She followed him as he walked around the wagon. "My father thought you'd attend the ball. It's in his honor, you know."

"I know."

"You were invited, weren't you?"

"I was."

"Then why—"

"Personal." As far as Ryder was concerned the subject was closed. He had no need to explain his reasons to Anna Leigh Hamilton or her father for that matter.

Anna Leigh's bow mouth was pulled in an attractive pout. It was a practiced expression, one that she had mastered in front of her vanity mirror. One hundred strokes to her silky, butter yellow hair, gave her ample time to rehearse the nuances of expression that ran the entire emotional gamut from melancholia to madness. She had a slender face with high cheekbones, a wide brow, and clear blue eyes that could be both winsome and worldly. Her complexion was creamy. The few freckles on the bridge of her slim nose were due to nightly applications of lemon juice and morning applications of rice powder. Among her other attributes she numbered an hourglass figure, slender well-turned ankles, dainty feet, and delicate bones.

The attention that Anna Leigh Hamilton accepted as her right was due in no small measure to the fact that she was a beautiful young woman. Most of the time she was skillful enough to conceal the fact that she knew it.

"Don't you think it's a bit insulting?" she asked. "Not to come inside?"

"You're not inside," he pointed out.

She smiled now and wished he would turn in her direction to see it. When he didn't she made certain the smile could be heard in her voice. "Touché," she said. Anna Leigh ran her hand across the rough wooden edge of the wagon, following the path of Ryder's own fingers as he rounded another corner. "What exactly is it that you're doing?" she asked, curiosity quelling her impatience. "It's a wagon, isn't it? Four wheels? A solid bottom?"

More or less a solid bottom, he thought. "It's a wagon," he said.

"One of the ones you're escorting to the train station in the morning?"

At first he was surprised that she knew about it, then he reasoned she could have heard it anywhere. The trip was hardly a secret among the men. Still, he didn't deny or confirm her suspicions or ask her what she knew about it.

"I'm going along," she told him.

Ryder stopped his inspection and turned on her. The night air was dry and crisp. The harsh lay of the land was no harsher than the taut features of Ryder's face. "No, you're not."

Anna Leigh warmed to the look, thrilled by his concern. At the same time, she wasn't used to being told no. "Papa said I could."

"And I say you can't."

Her light brows rose a fraction. "I don't think this is your decision."

"We'll see." He wasn't going to barge into the ball now. His argument with the senator could wait until they could talk privately. "Shouldn't you go back to the dancing?" he asked.

She shrugged. The movement raised the half moons of her

breasts a little higher. Anna Leigh noticed the motion drew Ryder's attention but did not hold it. "Is it because you're an Indian?" she asked.

His entire body was rigid. It was an effort to be polite. "I'm not certain I follow."

"Is that why you aren't joining the party, because the other scouts aren't invited and you're an Apache just like them?"

"That's an interesting conjecture."

Anna Leigh continued to stare at him expectantly. She only came to his shoulder, but she knew the angle at which she had to look up showed her throat to its long, slender advantage.

"Who told you I was Apache?"

Anna Leigh shook her head slightly as if she were protecting her source. "It's true, isn't it?"

Ryder doubted that anyone had told her. More likely, it was her own assumption. She had seen him in comfortable conversation with the scouts, sharing a table with them in the mess hall, and had drawn her own conclusions. She was encouraged in her thinking by his physical appearance: the sun-beaten color of his skin, the thick mane of glossy black hair, his strongly carved features. She had ignored, as others had before her, that he stood six to eight inches taller than the other scouts and that his eyes were the color of early morning frost, or she had explained the anomalies away by further assuming his heritage was mixed.

Ryder's smile was cold, his eyes penetrating. Anna Leigh didn't know enough to look away. She was mesmerized. Abruptly Ryder came to a decision. Taking her by the wrist he led the senator's daughter away from the row of wagons, away from the music and lights of the officers' hall, and toward the soldiers' barracks. He didn't take her inside, but skirted the adobe building until he had her at the rear. She made no move to resist him, not when he pulled her into the shadows behind the barracks and not when he pressed her against the rough mud wall. Her breathing was light, a little unsteady, but she was excited, not fearful.

"Is this why you came out here?" he asked lowly, the line of his jaw tense. "Were you hoping to have the *savage's* hands on you this evening?" He pulled at the puffed sleeves of her satin gown so her bodice slipped lower.

Anna Leigh looked down at herself. Even in the shadows her skin was still paler than the hands that were on it. The contrast was startling, and Anna Leigh was aroused by it. "I've been watching you," she whispered huskily. From the beginning, she could have added. He was standing on the porch of the officers' quarters when the entourage from Washington had arrived. One of his shoulders had been braced against a timber that supported the overhang, and it was his indifferent, casual posture that she had noticed first. He didn't leap to attention or stiffen self-consciously as one about to come under inspection. Instead, he tugged on the brim of his hat to shade his eyes and disappeared just as the wagons were being unloaded. His insolence did not go unnoticed by other members of their party, but rather than being insulted by it, Anna Leigh was intrigued. "You're not like anyone else here," she told him.

Ryder was not particularly flattered by her observation. Not only did it have the easy comfort of a prepared speech, but there were men at Fort Union he admired. Not being like anyone else wasn't always a compliment. A hoarse sound came from the back of his throat, part growl, part purr. His hands slid across her bare shoulders to her neck. The rough pad of his thumb brushed the hollow of her throat. He saw her mouth part and felt the catch of her breath. He lowered his head. "How sure are you of that?" he asked softly. "I want the same thing from you that they do." His mouth clamped over hers as his entire body drove her flush to the wall.

Anna Leigh welcomed the pressure of his mouth. One of her legs rose against his flanks. Her body rubbed his. The bodice of her gown was pushed lower and her breasts would have been exposed to the cool air if it weren't for the protection of Ryder's coarse woolen jacket. Friction radiated through her tender skin, hardening her nipples and sending charged currents of heat from her breasts to her thighs. She felt her gown being raised and realized he was going to take her out in the open, standing up, her back pressed to a wall of dried mud. If she hadn't been clutching his neck for support, her fingers threaded deeply in his thick, inky hair, she would have lifted the gown herself.

Suddenly Ryder stopped his assault on her mouth, raised his head, and let her see the glimmer of a smile on his face. It had the warmth of a sliver of light on cold, hard steel. "I'm as white as you are, Miss Hamilton," he whispered roughly. "If you're looking for a scalp to hang in your bedroom, you'll have to look—"

Anna Leigh reared back and slapped him. "Bastard."

"Wrong again," Ryder said pleasantly. He ignored the heat in his left cheek and made a gesture near his head, tipping an invisible hat to her. It was an absurdly mannerly touch given his behavior, and she did not miss the mockery in it or in his expression.

"They said you're a half-breed," she called after him as he turned to go. Her tone was accusing, as if she'd been betrayed— not by the ones who told her but by him.

Ryder paused long enough to speak to her over his shoulder. Anna Leigh had managed to right her bodice and was smoothing what had been a carefully coifed hairstyle. "If *they* told you that," he said, conveying something of his disbelief, "then it was because *they* were warning you away from me. Around here white women don't throw themselves at Indians or half-breeds."

Anna Leigh's eyes widened. "What are you saying? Those bitches were trying to protect you? Save you for themselves?"

Ryder almost laughed. He hadn't thought of it like that, but he supposed it could be true. The mothers didn't seem to know whether to be hopeful or fearful that he would turn his attention to one of their daughters. "I figure they're hedgin' their bets until I make up my mind. Truth is, though, I'm spoken for."

"Spoken for?" she demanded crossly.

Ryder didn't miss a beat. "Florence Gardner."

The following morning Ryder reflected on the exchange between himself and Anna Leigh Hamilton as the company was preparing to depart. She hadn't been able to respond to his parting shot for almost a full minute, but made up for it later with a foul harangue that would have made the coarsest whore sit up and take notice. She was looking very demure this morning, he observed as Corporal Harding gave her a leg up on her mount. She handled the unfamiliar mare expertly, calming her quickly and demonstrating at the outset who was in charge. Ryder had never had any doubt that she could handle a horse. His objection to her joining the expedition had nothing to do with her riding ability and everything to do with the element of danger.

Anna Leigh had a sweet, saucy smile for each of the sixty men accompanying the wagons, from the lowliest driver to the troop leader, First Lieutenant Spencer Matheson. It was calculated to brighten their day, make them forget the miserable heat, and encourage them to remember how she had looked the night before in her jade satin ball gown. Ryder McKay was not a recipient of that smile. For the troop scout, Anna Leigh reserved a look that was haughty and superior, a pointed reminder that in spite of his attempt to humiliate her, she had still won an important battle. He could not have his way in all things.

Ryder dismissed the look she cast in his direction by simply ignoring it. He had more important things on his mind than Anna Leigh's petty retributions. He didn't understand or agree with her father's decision to allow her to accompany the wagons. Senator Warren Hamilton had explained it to him, of course, but to Ryder's way of thinking it didn't make sense. It didn't matter to Ryder that the senator had already made a promise to his daughter, or that he thought Ryder was exaggerating the danger; as far as Ryder was concerned, any danger at all presented too great a risk.

As soon as he realized the argument was lost, Ryder lodged a personal protest with the fort's commander. General Gardner listened, made his own attempt to dissuade the senator, and was met with the same stiff resistance. Finally the general had no choice but to order Ryder to take her along. "It's his business," he said. "And you're not the one in command."

"I haven't forgotten my place," Ryder said. "But I'm the one charged with the safety of this expedition and I don't like it. She doesn't belong."

General Gardner had held up his hand in a weary but firm gesture. The subject was closed and Ryder McKay was dismissed.

When First Lieutenant Matheson moved his company out, Ryder stopped thinking about Anna Leigh and her powerful, but ill-advised, father, and concentrated on his assignment. As an Army scout Ryder held no formal rank. His pay amounted to a little more than a captain's salary because his skills were in great demand. He carried a map of most of the great Southwest in his head. On long expeditions through rocky canyons or scrub desert, Ryder proved he could find water, forage for food in the brush, or hunt game if called upon to do so. He did not expect to be asked to fill any of those roles this time.

The troop was escorting four wagons to the rail line at Colter Pass southwest of Fort Union. They would be met by the patrol that had been stationed there for the previous month. Matheson's troop would stay, spread out along the rails; and the relieved patrol would return to the fort for a well-deserved rest. To all appearances the journey was business as usual. The wagons carried supplies for the new patrol, enough to last at least two months in the event there was a problem relieving the men. The greased axle wheels still groaned under the heavy burden of the foodstuffs. If ever there was a soldier who thought the Army's biscuits could substitute for cannon fodder in a pinch, here was proof; for the wagons scored the ground with their weight. They carried kegs of fresh water, tins of coffee, canned peaches, corn, tomatoes, and milk. Jerky and rice and dried beans filled large burlap sacks. Sweets would be provided by molasses and raisins. Flour and salt were staples, but butter in the field was made from a combination of bacon grease, flour, and water and had the consistency of gravy. A clay crock held sourdough starter for fresh biscuits that would be a touch lighter than the ones they were traveling with. The men going to take their turn at patrolling the rail line looked wistful when they had their last glimpse of the fort. Few of them were thinking of wives or sweethearts. Almost to a man they were thinking of their stomachs.

Ryder had no difficulty outdistancing the first lieutenant's men. His job could never be done beside the men in his safe-keeping. Sometimes he worked with a partner—one of the other scouts for whom there was mutual respect if not friendship—but most often he worked alone by his own choice.

The route to Colter Canyon was not unfamiliar to any but the greenest of the recruits. Ryder wasn't along to blaze a trail. He had one purpose—to find Apache.

Many of the Apache tribes that populated the Southwest Territory had been rounded up by the Army and forced to take up residence on government reservations. In spite of that there were still renegade bands that struck hard and fled fast, causing damage to themselves and the settlers alike. Ryder thought of them as resistance fighters, men who thought their way of life, their beliefs, and their families were all worth saving. It was not a popular view, and because of who Ryder McKay was, and because of how he was raised, to state his thoughts aloud would have brought suspicion on his head. He was well aware that no matter how he proved himself he was always going to be regarded with a certain lack of trust. Walker Caine was an exception to that rule. So was General Thorn at West Point. In the Southwest he counted two men who had shown themselves to be in the same vein. One was General Mitchell Halstead, recently retired from his thirty-year career with the Army, and living in Flagstaff. The other was Naiche, a Chiricahua warrior and blood brother to Geronimo, both of whom were still at large.

Ryder did not expect trouble on the journey, but he had to anticipate it. The foodstuffs they carried were especially appeal-

ing to Chiricahua raiders who would be looking to feed themselves and their families. Ryder watched the ground closely.
Displaced rocks were clues of someone passing on the land in
front of him. He knew how to determine how many were in a
raiding party, if they walked or were on horseback, how fast
they were traveling, and if there were women and children
bringing up the rear. Nothing he saw indicated the Chiricahua
were on the trail of the wagons or the company's horseflesh.

Ryder circled around and back, covering the company's left
flank and rear. He waited on the high ground among the red
rocks for Matheson's men to catch up to him. Along the length
of a nearby wash was a low-growing, spreading mesquite tree.
Saguaro cacti spotted the desert floor, bristling guards for the
unwary traveler. A tiny elf owl, no bigger than a finch, had
taken up residence in one of the thick arms of a cactus, his
home compliments of a woodpecker who had deserted the hole.

Ryder felt the skin at the back of his neck prickle. He did
not try to dismiss the feeling. It was more important to accept
it and understand what it might mean. In the distance he could
hear the approach of the company, the shuffled cadence of men
and horses, the creaking rhythm of wagons on the hard, dry
earth. Ryder could not see the column as they wended their way
through the canyon, but he followed the fine cloud of dust that
rose high in the air above them like a morning mist. By the
time they reached him he had formulated a plan.

Three

First Lieutenant Matheson listened gravely to Ryder's concerns. Matheson was a graduate of West Point and a veteran of two Western campaigns. He had been a quick study in the classroom and in the field, and it was generally agreed he was a young man with a future in the Army. One of the things he had learned was to trust his scout. This time Ryder was making that difficult to do.

Tell me again about this premonition," he said impatiently. The heat was battering them all in spite of the fact that it was not yet eight o'clock. He lifted his hat momentarily and wiped his brow. The Army issued the same navy blue wool sack coat, flannel shirt, and kersey trousers to soldiers from the Northern Plains to the Southwest. The clothing was as ill suited for the bitter cold of Montana as it was for the unrelenting heat of the Southwest Territory. There was leeway given to men in the field, especially among the privates. First Lieutenant Matheson was expected to adhere to regulation dress. Now he was baking in it. "What signs have you seen?"

Ryder was honest. "None. There's danger anyway."

Matheson swore softly. "Jesus, McKay. What the hell are we supposed to do about that?"

"How many of your men are new recruits?"

"Half, maybe a little more."

Ryder didn't like those odds. He had trusted the makeup of the company to others and now he wished he hadn't. These men weren't seasoned to fight well in an ambush. "Split the company in two," he said. "Two wagons for each group. Divide the greenhorns in half; they'll need help if it comes to a hand-to-hand fight. You lead half through the canyon. Sergeant Shipley can take half on the longer route around."

Matheson wasn't certain he liked it. Splitting a fighting force, especially one as small as a company, was always risky. To do it all because Ryder McKay had a "feeling" could cost him the lives of his men and a promotion. He looked around at his troop. "What about her?" he asked, his chin jutting in the direction of Anna Leigh Hamilton. She was sweet-talking Corporal Harding into giving her a drink from his canteen. An unconscionable flirt, he thought, since she was carrying her own canteen. Matheson sighed and returned his full attention to Ryder. "For two cents I'd send her back to——"

"I'd do it for a penny," Ryder offered. "But for right now it'd be better if she stayed with you."

Matheson shook his head. He rubbed his chin with the back of his gloved hand. "She's safer with you. You'll be out ahead of the rest of us. If there's an ambush you'll have warning before we will."

Ryder didn't repeat that there was no one out there. He saw that the first lieutenant was having a difficult time accepting the reality of impending danger. To remind him that there were no signs on the trail ahead would not support Ryder's own case. The sensation that prickled his skin earlier had not left him since. "I'll take her," he said at last, weighing his options. "I won't be able to move as fast, but I'll take her."

Matheson nodded. "I knew you would." He also knew Ryder McKay would go to his death protecting the Hamilton woman, if it came to that. The first lieutenant called Sergeant Shipley over and rapped out his orders. There was a murmur of surprise up and down the line, but it was quelled quickly.

Ryder did not wait for the sergeant to split the company and organize the departure along two different routes. He nudged his horse forward to Anna Leigh's side, took the reins from her hands, and began leading her mount away. She was almost unseated by the sudden jerk forward, and she gave Ryder a hard stare after she caught herself.

"What's going on?" she demanded. She looked around for someone to help her, but everyone was busy carrying out Matheson's orders. "Where are you taking me?"

He didn't answer her.

"I can take the horse myself," she said, trying to grasp the reins back.

Ryder didn't want her to have control until he was certain she would stay with him and not return to the company. He jerked on the reins and the cinnamon mare followed dutifully, even when Anna Leigh tried to dig her heels in and hold her mount back.

As they climbed higher on the uneven, rocky ground Anna Leigh kept looking back and below. She could see the company reconfiguring to part ways. "What are they doing down there?" she asked. "Why are they breaking up?"

Her questions were unimportant to Ryder, and they weren't answered. "Save your strength," he told her instead. "We still have a long way to go, and this route is the hardest." Even as he said it, her horse stumbled. Loose rock and gravel shot out from under the mare's hooves and clattered down the canyon walls.

"Are you trying to get me killed?" Anna Leigh snapped. "I want to go back with the lieutenant." She stared daggers at Ryder's spine when he didn't respond. It was too dangerous to fight him for control of her animal, so she concentrated on staying in the saddle until they reached the top and the land flattened out again. In the end she didn't have the opportunity to wrest back the reins because Ryder tossed them negligently in her direction.

"Don't make the mistake of trying to return by the way we just came," he warned. "Your mare can't do it, and you'll break your neck."

A single glance down told her he was right. "I'd have thought that would please you," she said tartly.

Ryder merely shrugged. "Let's go."

"Wait a minute," she protested. "I'm thirsty."

"I just saw you get a drink from Harding's canteen. You can't need another one already. C'mon."

Anna Leigh stubbornly held back. Her broad-brimmed straw hat shaded the upper part of her face from the sun, even so, her blue eyes glittered with anger at Ryder's high-handedness. She sat stiffly in her saddle, refusing to move.

Ryder glanced over his shoulder. "You can drink as you ride." He kept going, expecting her to follow. He had covered fifty yards before he realized she wasn't behind him. When he looked back she was exactly where she'd been minutes earlier. In this test of wills Ryder could see that as long as she was conscious she had the upper hand. As he reined his mount around he actually considered knocking her out and throwing her over his saddle. Only the burden that would have put on his mare made him think better of it.

When he came upon her he didn't say anything. His level gray stare bore into her. His mouth was expressionless.

"You needn't look at me like that," she said. "I told you I was thirsty."

"And I told you to drink on the way."

Anna Leigh pointed to the canteen she had strapped across her shoulder. The leather strap had left a light sweat stain on her white blouse where it slanted between her breasts. "There's something wrong with my water," she said. "It doesn't taste right."

"It probably tastes like the canteen," he said. "That happens in this heat. There's nothing wrong with it."

Anna Leigh's lower lip was thrust forward. The saucy pout usually got her what she wanted. On this occasion she got what she wanted in spite of it.

"Take mine," Ryder said, unstrapping it from his horse. He held it out to her.

Anna Leigh offered hers in exchange. She unscrewed the top

on his canteen and drank her fill. Droplets of water slid over her chin and onto her blouse, flattening it against her skin.

"Easy," he said. "You'll get a belly ache."

Lowering the canteen, Anna Leigh wiped the bottom of her chin with a gloved hand, then plucked at her damp blouse. "Concern? From you?"

"You can't ride if you're sick."

"Is that why you're not drinking?" she asked. "Or do you believe me that the water's bad?"

Obviously she required some proof before she was willing to move on. Ryder uncapped the canteen she had given him and took several deep swallows. It was no different than he'd expected; it had the tinny taste of the container. "Satisfied?"

Anna Leigh wrinkled her nose and let her distaste show. "I don't know how you drank that," she said a trifle breathlessly.

He strapped the canteen in place and gave his mount a kick. "Let's go."

This time they covered a distance just short of two miles before Anna Leigh pulled up. She watched Ryder move on ahead of her, weaving unsteadily in his saddle. His horse slowed, uncertain of where to go with no firm direction. Finally the mare halted, shifted her weight restlessly, but could not be urged forward. Anna Leigh's approach was cautious as Ryder remained slumped, but essentially upright in the saddle. He managed to lift his head as she drew up beside him. His pale gray eyes were glazed, unfocused.

This time it was Anna Leigh who took the reins. She led the horses to a squared-off section of boulders that formed a shallow cave. There would be shade, even when the sun reached its zenith. It looked like a shelter Ryder would have chosen for himself.

By the time they reached the rocks Ryder was no longer self-supporting. Anna Leigh had to ride closely abreast of him and lend her shoulder to hold him in his saddle. His dark head was unprotected by a hat, and his black hair fell forward on either side of his neck. The red bandana he wore was soaked with his own sweat. His head lolled and his chin rested heavily against his chest. When Anna Leigh withdrew her support Ryder's slide from the saddle was ignominious at best.

She looked down at his sprawled, unconscious body. There was no remorse on her face or in her voice. As far as she was concerned, he deserved it. "I told you the water was bad."

Her sentence was punctuated by the first of a volley of shots echoing in the canyon below.

There was no time to take cover. Matheson's first indication that something was wrong was the return of the split-off company. No wagons accompanied them and less than half the men who had gone formed the new column. Sergeant Shipley was no longer in the lead. They looked like troops who had just engaged in combat yet Matheson hadn't heard a single shot.

Matheson motioned to his second lieutenant. The man was a recent arrival at Fort Union, trained at West Point but a virgin in the field. "Go back to that column and find out what the hell's going on," he ordered. "I want to know what's happened to Shipley and the wagons." Matheson looked up into the canyon rocks. Ryder and Anna Leigh hadn't been visible for the last half hour. He added impatiently, a trace of alarm in his gruff voice, "And see if Ryder circled 'round to their side and saw something."

Second Lieutenant Davis Rivers lifted his hand as if to make a smart salute. Spencer Matheson went to his death with that vision in his mind.

Ryder's vision was fuzzy when he woke. His hearing was distorted. He could hear shouting and shots and an Apache war cry that instantly took him back twenty-three years. He tried to come to his feet. He couldn't even lift his head.

Anna Leigh's voice was soft and soothing. "Here," she said encouragingly. "Drink this." She held a canteen to his lips.

Ryder used what remained of his strength to clamp his lips shut until Anna Leigh laid her gloved hand over his nose. When he sucked in his next breath she trickled water down his throat. He stared at her for a long time. Her eyes were not cruel, merely frank. Looking into their light blue gaze he felt as if his will were being leached, his energy sapped. He tried to speak, but in spite of the water she had given him, his mouth was dry. He felt her hand slide into his. With her free hand she was undoing the buttons of her blouse.

He shut his eyes and slept.

Davis Rivers was in command now, and he rallied his men. They fought hard and took the advantage. The battle was a bitter one. Many men died without clearly seeing the enemy. Some scaled the rocks, but there was no quarter given. They were hunted down, and none of them made it to the top of the canyon rim.

The battle was over by noon. Five of the surviving men set grimly about the task of collecting the dead. Others removed foodstuffs from one of the wagons to make room for the bodies. Second Lieutenant Rivers called in another group and gave them specific instructions. One soldier was sent back to the fort for reinforcements. Rivers assigned himself and a private to go in search of Ryder McKay and the senator's daughter.

"That half-breed son of a bitch is going to have a lot to answer for," he told his men. They kept on working—time was short—but they exchanged knowing glances.

Private Patrick Carr was the first to spot Anna Leigh. She was hatless and walking away from a grouping of boulders that would have afforded her some protection from the sun. Carr and Rivers pushed their mounts hard to get to her. They knew she had seen them when she dropped to her knees in an attitude of prayer and exhaustion.

Carr dismounted swiftly and knelt beside her. His eyes grazed her face, her hair, and her clothing. The assessment only lasted a few moments, but it was enough for the private to draw his conclusions.

From his saddle Rivers regarded Anna Leigh. Her hair was disheveled, matted to the crown of her head by a rivulet of blood. Dust streaked her face. The bridge of her nose and her cheeks were sunburned. Two buttons were missing from her blouse, and there was a rent in the seam of the sleeve. Even though her leather skirt was tan and meant for traveling, it was covered by a film of dust.

Private Carr raised Anna Leigh's hands and examined them. The manicured nails were broken and bloody. Carr glanced at Rivers. "Looks like the son of a bitch has more to answer for than we thought."

Davis Rivers said nothing. "Did he leave you here?" he asked Anna Leigh.

Her sob was wretched, but she managed to shake her head. She let Private Carr help her to her feet and leaned heavily against him. "He's over there." Anna Leigh pointed in the distance behind her. "In those boulders. He said they would shelter us." Her pale eyes darted pitifully between her rescuers.

"How did you get away from him?" Rivers handed her his canteen.

"The shots . . . they distracted him. I hit him with a rock." She shuddered delicately, causing Carr to hold her more tightly. "I was afraid after that . . . My horse bolted and Ryder's mare wouldn't let me mount. I didn't know what to do. I stayed there with him until it got quiet again, then I came looking for someone."

"Good girl," Carr said. He asked Rivers, "You want to stay with her while I check out McKay?"

Rivers shook his head. "I'll go. Wait here. We're going to need him to show us another way down. We'll never get these horses down by the route we took."

Anna Leigh nodded. "He told me that. He knows another route."

Second Lieutenant Rivers kicked his mount in the flanks. His mare was high-strung from combat, but she was still game. She covered the ground quickly in the direction of the shallow cave.

Ryder was lying on his side, knees drawn toward his chest. There was blood at the back of his head and there were scratches on his face and neck. His jacket was lying on the floor of the cave, but he still wore his shirt. It was open at the throat, and where the second lieutenant could see Ryder's skin, he saw evidence of claw marks.

"Looks like she got some of her own back," Rivers said with certain satisfaction. He saw Ryder move slightly. Rivers grimaced, took him by the wrist, and jerked him hard to his feet. Ryder came up, staggered, and dropped to his knees like a felled tree. Rivers yanked him up again, this time by a handful of Ryder's thick hair. Half-dragging, half-lifting, the second lieutenant got Ryder McKay to his own mount.

Ryder's vision was clearing at the edges, but his arms and legs still felt too heavy to move. He was aware of Davis Rivers, of the second lieutenant's intention to put him on his horse, but he couldn't cooperate. More importantly, he wasn't certain he should. "Where's Miss Hamilton?" he asked.

The words were slurred, but Rivers was able to make them out. "Carr's got her. She's going to be fine, no thanks to you."

Ryder tried to think what that meant, but he needed his concentration to help Rivers get him in the saddle. There was no time to explain about Anna Leigh and the canteens. Ryder wanted to see Lieutenant Matheson and warn him about the real danger.

He allowed himself to be pushed unceremoniously into the saddle and registered some surprise when the second lieutenant tied his wrists to the leather horn. "What—"

"You can ride like that," Rivers said tersely. "I've seen you sit a pony without any reins at all."

Ryder's struggle was to keep his head up. He didn't know

how he was going to find the strength to guide his mare. And now Rivers was asking him a question about the route down to the canyon floor. He tried to think. It was important for him to get there . . . he had to tell Matheson . . . he had to—

"Which route, McKay?" Rivers demanded again.

Out of the corner of his eye Ryder saw Rivers raise one arm and make a gesture to someone in the distance. Ryder turned his head slowly, careful not to lose his balance, and saw Anna Leigh sharing a mount with one of the company privates. He said something unintelligible, but uncomplimentary, under his breath and nodded to Rivers. "This way," he rasped.

As he led them all by a longer, less dangerous route to the canyon floor, Ryder began to consider what he'd say to Matheson. His foggy mind still couldn't make sense of the ropes around his wrists when the one who deserved stringing up was Anna Leigh Hamilton. He planned to use words to that effect when he came face-to-face with the first lieutenant.

By the time Ryder's mind cleared enough for him to understand his predicament, he was already chained and under guard and on his way back to Fort Union.

New York City

At the knock at her door, Mary looked up from her reading. "Come in," she said quietly. Twenty-four hours had passed since she'd shared her news at dinner. Her mother hadn't spoken to her in all that time. In fact, Moira hadn't come out of her room. Mary knew who to expect.

Jay Mac walked in carrying a tray. "Disappointed?" he asked.

"Disappointed?"

"In it being me here and not your mother."

Mary shook her head. She was wearing a nightshift and her robe. Her legs were curled under her on the chair. She put down the book and made room on the small end table for her father to set the tray down. "I don't anticipate Mama will have a change of heart any time soon," she said. "I'm quite happy to have you here."

Jay Mac took a seat in the large Boston rocker while Mary poured tea for both of them. "I've tried talking to her," he said.

"I know. I don't think she's ready to hear."

"I've been thinking the same thing."

Mary handed him a cup of tea. "You didn't go to work today."

"No. I thought I should be here in case she needed me."

"You mean you stayed in case Mama and I argued again."

Jay Mac didn't even try not to look guilty. He sipped his tea and enjoyed the peacefulness of Mary's company. Even in the midst of her own troubles she had a calming presence he had always appreciated. "I had a telegram from Rennie and Jarret today. A messenger brought it over from the office."

"Business or family?"

"Business this time," Jay Mac acknowledged. "I'm sure she has her hands full with the twins, but you'd never know it from her work for Northeast. She says Jarret's midway through the negotiations for a tract of land in Arizona."

"Arizona? That's interesting. Northeast Rail in the Southwest," she mused. "You might want to think of changing the name of the railroad, Jay Mac. It hardly fits anymore."

"I'm aware of that," he said. "But I'll keep the name just to remind myself what a small thinker I can be at times."

Mary laughed. Northeast Rail was all over the country now, but in the beginning she knew her father hadn't had a plan so grand as all that. Northeast's expansion had been prompted in part by the war. The Union industrialists laid track at a rate they had never dreamed possible. After the war some predicted there would be a lull, even a decline. If it had happened to Northeast, Mary wasn't aware of it. Jay Mac's railroad continued to supply low-cost transportation for goods and people as the country's Western move enjoyed a resurgence.

Northeast had made a specialty of providing for small mining communities cheap methods of moving their ore. Rennie had been responsible for several sidelines in Colorado, and had linked Denver with silver mines in Madison, Queen's Point, and most recently, Cannon Mills. Jay Mac had worked hard to keep Rennie out of the business, but in the past few years he had grown quite fond of the taste of crow. Her expertise at knowing where and how to lay a track, coupled with her husband's ability to supervise the labor gangs and negotiate the deals, had pushed Northeast's profit margins beyond even Jay Mac's expectations.

"Are she and Jarret in Arizona now?" asked Mary. "I just sent her a letter yesterday, to Denver."

"Michael will send it on, but yes, that's where the telegram originated. I didn't know she was thinking about it. There's been so much trouble on and off with the Indians."

"Are the twins with her?" Mary asked immediately. "Are she and Jarret safe?"

"Yes and yes." He chuckled. "The Office of Land Management is conducting a survey for them now. Somewhere southeast of Phoenix. Fort Union, I think she called it. She and Jarret are waiting for news in Phoenix and planning another trip to the Holland Mines." He saw that Mary was still frowning. A small vertical crease ran between her feathered brows. "What's wrong? What are you thinking?"

"I don't know," she said. "Nothing really." But she was vaguely unsettled, and she felt her father looking straight through her. "There must be other places Rennie can go. What sort of ore is mined there anyway?"

"Gold." He refreshed his tea and added a little to Mary's cup. "Drink," he insisted. "It's good for whatever ails you."

She smiled because she was meant to, not because of any easing of her disquiet. "Is it an old mine?" she asked. Perhaps there was a chance it would play itself out before the negotiations were complete.

Jay Mac shook his head. "Your sister wouldn't be interested in it if that were the case, not without an extensive geo survey. Rennie's telegram indicates this one's about six months old. She must believe it will produce long enough to turn a profit for the railroad."

Mary's hands tightened slightly on her teacup before she set it aside. She forced a lightness into her voice that she didn't feel in her heart. "You know, Jay Mac, this is all very interesting."

"How so?"

"Well, I was thinking of leaving New York myself soon."

"Mary!"

She ignored him. "And I've considered Arizona."

Jay Mac had to use more than a little self-control to stay in the rocker. What he wanted to do was leap out of the chair, tower over his daughter, and shake a finger in her face. "What the hell do you think you're going to do in Arizona?" he demanded, red-faced.

Mary blinked once in reaction to Jay Mac's blustering then drew calmness around her like a cloak. "I thought I might teach."

"Teach?" he said dismissively. "You're not a teacher."

She went on as if he hadn't objected. "There are missions in the southern part of the territory that are always looking for help."

"You have no credentials."

"No one at the mission will care about that."

"But—"

"Jay Mac," she said firmly, meeting her father's probing eyes with a steady, level stare of her own. "I think I know enough to teach children how to read and write."

She knows that and a lot more, Jay Mac thought. Each of his daughters was uniquely accomplished, but it was tacitly accepted by the family that Mary's star shone brightest. This was one of the reasons Jay Mac had been so adamantly opposed to her taking vows as a nun. To his way of thinking she was burying her special gifts. "I don't like it," he said. "If you want to teach, then I'll send you to school as I did your sisters. You can get a position in one of the local colleges when you're through. You would be a good professor."

Mary didn't say anything for a moment. Her features never

lost their trademark serenity, but inside she was seething. The effort not to scream showed in her hands, twisted tightly together in her lap. "I did not allow you to run my life when I was seventeen," she said evenly. "Why in the world would you think I'd give you permission now?"

Jay Mac put his cup and saucer aside. "Because," he said heavily, "you've finally realized I was right all those years ago. You should never have become a nun. I told you from the first it was a mistake." If she was going to teach children, he thought, then they damn well should be her own.

The vision of her father blurred as tears welled in Mary's eyes. "You still don't understand," she said quietly, sadly. "I thought perhaps that by now you'd—"

"What?" he interrupted tersely. He thoroughly disliked the impression that he was somehow being narrow minded or obtuse. He hated it even worse that his daughter was crying. "What is it you think I don't understand?"

Mary used the cuff of her nightgown to swipe at her tears. The strain of remaining calm now took its toll on her voice, which shook slightly as she spoke. "It was never a mistake, Papa. I don't regret what I've done with my life. The years I've been in God's service haven't been barren and joyless. I became His servant gladly. That's what I don't think you'll ever understand." Mary's eyes were still awash with tears, and her tone became more earnest, more convincing. "But if I didn't leave now, *that* would be a mistake. I don't know if Mama will ever understand this."

Jay Mac thought about that. For once, he thought about it quietly. Mary's distress was very real to him, and he felt her pain as an ache in his own heart. He valued his daughter's courage in the face of his censure. She had brought his disapproval down on her head when she had joined the sisterhood, now she had to cope with Moira's rejection as she was going to leave it. Jay Mac firmly believed that he only wanted what was best for his daughter—for any of his daughters. How was it, he reflected, that there could be so much disagreement surrounding what was best?

He expelled a long sigh and saw a glimmer of a smile touch Mary's lips. She knew he was done keeping his thoughts to himself. "I don't suppose there's a husband in your future," he said.

She shook her head slowly.

"Are you answering my question?" he asked, trying to read the bemused response. "Or telling me you can't believe I asked it."

Mary's smile became more fulsome, and she dried the last of her tears. "A little of both, I suppose. I'm not out of my habit yet and you're thinking husbands."

"It's a reasonable question."

She leaned forward and tapped her father on the knee. "Only you would think so, Jay Mac." Mary picked up her cup again. The tea was cool now but she didn't mind. It soothed the back of her throat where the uncomfortable, aching lump had been. "Don't bother presenting me with a list of prospective husbands, and don't consider for a moment that I'd let you do any sort of matchmaking."

"Humph," he grunted softly, trying to look offended. "I don't make matches. I make deals."

Mary nearly choked on her mouthful of tea. "Oh, God," she said feelingly. "Truer words have never been spoken." She pointed a finger at him meaningfully. "And don't try to negotiate a husband for me. *If* someone is of a mind to ask me, I'll work out the terms with him."

"Then it's not out of the question?" he asked hopefully.

Mary realized she might as well have saved her breath. "Everything's a possibility, Jay Mac. I just don't imagine I'll be meeting many prospects in a Southwest mission."

That reminder sobered Jay Mac. "You're not still serious about going to Arizona, are you?"

She simply stared back at her father, letting him read what was in her eyes.

"Your mother's not going to like this."

That made Mary catch her breath. Sometimes Jay Mac didn't play fair. "She doesn't like the decision I've made anyway," she said after a moment. "I may as well be hanged for a sheep as for a lamb."

"I don't like it either," he said.

"Rennie's there."

"She's with her husband so she has someone to protect her. Don't forget, a little while ago you were the one wondering about the danger. Now you're talking about throwing yourself into the midst of it."

"I'm talking about going to teach at a mission," she said patiently. "Not about laying rails down in the middle of Indian land."

Jay Mac's dark green eyes narrowed. "Was that a criticism?" he demanded.

Now Mary was genuinely bewildered. "What do you mean?"

"If we lay down tracks it will be because Northeast owns the property. It's not Apache land."

"Oh, Papa," Mary sighed. "Do you really want to argue about whose land it is?"

"No," he said after a moment. He repeated it again, more heavily this time, and came to his feet. "We're done arguing. My mind's made up. You're not going to Arizona—at least not alone."

Before Mary could recover her wits to ask what he meant by that, her father was gone.

Fort Union, Arizona Territory

Like most forts built after 1876, Fort Union was not enclosed by a fence along its perimeter. It was the prevailing thinking of the times that a fort was better guarded by alert soldiers than by a barrier that gave a false sense of security and encouraged sloth instead of vigilance. Fort Union consisted of nine separate adobe buildings all a stone's throw from one another. There were quarters for the officers and their wives, quarters for the bachelor officers, three garrisons for the soldiers, a mess hall, offices for the staff, an infirmary, and a stockade for prisoners.

Ryder McKay sat on the dirt floor of his cell, his back against the wall, his knees bent, and idly manipulated a silver dollar between his fingers, passing it back and forth across his hand with such easy dexterity that it seemed to have the quickness of a bead of mercury.

Second Lieutenant Davis Rivers had had Ryder placed in the stockade immediately upon returning to the fort. Except for his brief interrogation by General Gardner in the general's office, Ryder hadn't been outside the eight-by-eight room in thirty-six hours. Except for his brief responses to the general's questions, Ryder hadn't spoken in all that time.

In the beginning he believed his confinement would end after the general heard him out. It wasn't until he listened to the tone and tenor of the questions put to him, that Ryder realized he wasn't going to get an objective hearing. The evidence against him was already overwhelming.

Outside the stockade the moon was rising. Ryder raised his eyes to catch the light and saw the moon's face was bisected by the black iron bars that divided his window. A moment's fantasy had him believing the moon was the prisoner behind the bars and he was the one who was free. It lasted only until the moon continued its upward path and slipped out of his line of vision. Ryder went back to studying the silver dollar in his hand, threading the coin from one finger to the next as if his life depended upon doing just this task.

The commotion in the office area of the stockade made no impression on Ryder. He didn't hear the argument or the outcome or have any idea it was all about him. When the door to the cell area opened he wasn't anticipating company.

"Get me a chair," Florence Gardner snapped at the hapless guard. "If you won't let me in his cell, then the least you can do is provide a chair here in the corridor."

In spite of Florence's tone the guard still hesitated. "Are you certain the general said it was all right?" he asked. "I have or—"

Florence drew herself up to her full height of exactly five feet and brought the tip of her cane down hard on the guard's instep to emphasize her point. "Don't talk to me about your orders," she warned him. "The general is *my* son, and he and I are quite clear about orders."

The guard swallowed hard. "Very well, ma'am." He felt the cane being removed from his boot and offered a relieved smile. Turning quickly before she could get him again with it, he went to retrieve a chair.

Florence now applied her cane to the bars of Ryder's cell, running it back and forth to get his attention. "You could say you're happy to see me," she said with some asperity.

Ryder came to his feet in a fluid motion, pocketing the dollar that had provided him with his sole amusement until now. "Here comes your chair, Flo." He pointed to the guard who was trying to bring it in quietly.

Florence turned on the fellow again. "There's no need to sneak up on me, young man. Give me an attack of angina and my son will see you on kitchen duty for the rest of your Army career."

"She means it, Harry," Ryder told the guard.

"Don't I know it," Harry muttered before he shuffled off.

Florence and Ryder exchanged glances as Harry made a point of closing the door between the cell area and the guard room.

"Does the general know you're here?" Ryder asked.

"What do you think?"

"That he believes you retired early."

She gave Ryder a prim smile. "Know-it-all." She arranged the chair so it was close to the bars and sat down. "There's no need for you to stand," she told him. When he didn't respond immediately she added brusquely, "Go on with you, you'll give me a crick in my neck."

Ryder slowly sat down on the edge of the cot, stunned by the fact that she was fighting tears. "What are you doing here, Florence?"

"I had to see you for myself," she said, "though it pains me terribly that you are here. Are you being treated well?"

"Well enough."

She studied his face. The single lantern in the corridor shed enough light on him that she could see shades of bruising on his cheek and temple. One of his eyelids was slightly swollen. If these were the marks she *could* see, Florence wondered about the ones she couldn't. "My son didn't give orders for you to be beaten," she said. "Joshua isn't like that."

"I know." He shrugged. "It doesn't matter."

"Of course it matters. I'm going to tell—" She stopped, realizing that she wasn't going to tell her son anything. It would only go worse for Ryder if the men guarding him were reprimanded, and then she would be forbidden from entering the stockade again. "Can I bring you anything next time? Witch hazel? Bandages?"

"You shouldn't come again."

She dismissed that with an unladylike snort. "You're in no position to tell me what I should and shouldn't do."

"Point taken." He paused and absently rubbed the back of his head. "Witch hazel, then."

"What happened to you there?" Florence asked.

Ryder's hand dropped away. "It's not important. I've got a gash and a lump, nothing I haven't had before."

Florence's mouth thinned. She hated the thought of Ryder being mistreated under her very nose.

"No," he said. "It's not what you think. It didn't happen here. When I came around en route back to the fort I already had it."

"It happened in the fighting?"

Ryder didn't say anything for a time, wondering what he could or should say. "You must have heard that I wasn't part of the fighting," he said.

Florence Gardner's shoulders sagged a bit, and in spite of the fact that she was sitting down, her hand rested more heavily on her cane. "So it's true," she said with a certain unhappy finality. "You were with her when the attack came."

"I was."

"Why?"

The only indication of Ryder's surprise was the fractional narrowing of his pale gray eyes. He didn't answer her question directly. "Haven't you heard the answer to that as well?"

The subtle accusation in his tone got Florence's attention. She pounded her cane once against the floor where it made only a dull thud in the packed earth. "Don't lump me with the rest of the idiots around here—my son included. I'll draw my own conclusions, thank you. Now tell me why you were with that baggage."

"Lieutenant Matheson and I agreed she needed to be away from the company." He added carelessly, "I lost the toss."

"Why did she need to be separated?"

"Her safety. I suspected there was some danger."

"You knew the attack was coming?"

He shook his head. It was no easier to explain now than it had been then. "No," he said. "I knew there was danger but not the form it would take. There were no signs of Chiricahua anywhere in the area."

"Yet they attacked."

"So I've heard," he said without inflection.

"You didn't see any of the attack?"

"None." Or the scene afterward. Ryder only knew what he had been told. The company had literally been cut in half, men slaughtered where they stood. According to Rivers's account to the general, the enemy seemed to come out of the stones themselves.

Florence tried to make sense of it. "How can that be?" she asked. "You were only a few miles past the canyon rim. I know you, Ryder. You would have gone back at the first sound of gunfire."

Ryder only had a fleeting recollection of the sound of a single shot. He remembered wanting to move, trying to move, and not being able to lift his head. "Miss Hamilton was complaining about her canteen water," he told Florence. "I drank a few mouthfuls to show her there was nothing wrong with it." His brief smile was humorless and self-mocking. "That's just about the last thing I remember."

"The water was bad?"

"I know my horse and I didn't cover much ground before I keeled over in the saddle. Miss Hamilton managed to get me to a shallow cave of rocks and let me fall. The next thing I recall is being yanked awake by Rivers and ordered to lead the way back to the canyon floor. I was in and out of consciousness most of the way back to the fort."

Florence was interrupted by the guard poking his head into the corridor. "You can only have a few more minutes," Harry said. "I have to take the lantern for lights out." He withdrew before he encountered Florence's verbal expression of wrath or her cane tip.

"I've a good mind to change the duty roster myself," she said under her breath. "That boy should mind his manners."

"Don't be too hard on Harry, Flo. He's all right. Just doing his job."

Florence's mouth pursed to one side sourly. "You're not taking this seriously, Ryder. You're in a lot of trouble. The only reason you haven't been summarily hanged is because you know a few people in high places who think your scalp may be worth something more than it would as a trophy." No one had ever accused Florence Gardner of not speaking her mind. "Now suppose you tell me why Anna Leigh Hamilton wants everyone to know you tried to rape her if it isn't so?"

"Revenge?"

"Is that a question or your answer?" she asked with little patience.

"I don't pretend to know what Miss Hamilton hopes to gain by telling her tale," Ryder said. "But I assure you, it's a tale."

Florence nodded her head once, an emphatic gesture that indicated her satisfaction. "I *knew* it," she said. "Why didn't you tell Joshua that she's lying?"

"I did tell the general."

"I see," she said slowly, unhappily. "He didn't believe you."

"It's not difficult to understand why," Ryder said. "Miss Hamilton looked pathetically ill used, and she had Rivers and Private Carr to corroborate her story—at least as far as to how they had found her wandering on the flats." He rubbed the lump on his head again. "She says she hit me with a rock to get away."

Florence snorted, the expression in her eyes patently disbelieving. "Seems to me the last thing she wanted the night before was to get away from you."

"That was before I showed her I wasn't interested in what she was offering."

It began to make sense to Florence. "Aaah," she said softly. "So that's what you meant by revenge. She saw an opportunity to turn the tables on you and didn't hesitate to use it."

He shrugged. "It appears that way."

"Did she know the company was under attack in the canyon?"

"I don't know," said Ryder. "Probably."

"But doesn't she see how it looks?" Florence demanded. "Her tale is wagging the dog." The attempted rape of the senator's daughter was not the sole charge against Ryder. He was being accused of dereliction of duty for leaving the company with Anna Leigh. What he said he had done for reasons of safety now appeared more suspiciously motivated. His advice to First Lieutenant Matheson, overheard by Rivers and a sergeant, to split the company, was viewed as the strategy that led to the company's almost total demise. Then there was the matter of the gold.

The four wagons the company guarded were not only loaded with foodstuffs for the future patrol. Each wagon bed had a false bottom which concealed gold ore ready for refining. The Army had an agreement with Holland Mines to provide armed escort to the Waterhouse Station on the Southern Pacific rail line. The plan had been worked out in some detail over the past few months, and Ryder McKay had been essential to its development and its follow-through. There were very few people who knew about the contents of the wagons; even the secondary officers of the escorting company didn't know what they were carrying. The loading had been done in secret, under Ryder's strict supervision, and only a few men—all murdered in the attack—were privy to the knowledge that they were escorting the mother lode.

Now, with gold ore valued at over $100,000 in the hands of the Chiricahua Apache, Ryder McKay stood charged with treason.

New York City

"I've made a decision," Jay Mac announced at breakfast. He had purposely delayed going to work so that he could speak to Moira and Mary Francis at once. Although neither of them looked up from their food, Jay Mac knew he had their full attention. "I've had quite enough of this silence." Not only weren't his wife and his daughter speaking to each other, neither was speaking to him. "Nothing good can come of it, so I want it to cease."

"Very well," Mary said obediently. "Mama, will you please pass the salt?"

Moira's reply was stiff but perfectly audible. "Of course, dear. Would you care for anything else?"

Jay Mac was not amused, but he managed to keep his expression just this side of thunderous. He cleared his throat to signal his disapproval. "Suit yourselves, but it will be a long journey across the country if that's the best you can manage."

"Journey?" Moira asked, her head coming up.

"Across the country?" Mary asked simultaneously.

Now that he had their attention, John MacKenzie Worth allowed himself to bask in it. It was very nearly impossible not to gloat. It would not be so difficult to get Moira and Mary to come to some understanding of their differences, he thought. His strategy was simple. He would give them both what they wanted, but together, and they would be forced to sort it out from there. The smile he turned in their direction was more than a little self-congratulatory. "I'm sending both of you to see Rennie," he said.

"Sending us?" asked Moira. "What exactly does that mean?"

Jo Goodman

"He's packing us off," Mary answered flatly. "Like baggage."

Jay Mac ignored that. "I'm inviting both of you to take my private cars across the country. You can visit Michael in Denver, Maggie at the Double H, and then Rennie in whatever part of Arizona she's in at that point." He didn't add that he'd ship them both to China to see Skye if they hadn't come to terms by then.

"You're not coming with us?" Moira asked.

"I'll join you later, probably in Arizona. I'd like to see the land and the mine Rennie's talking about."

Mary studied her father with more suspicion than affection. "And you'd like to see the mission."

"Mission?" Moira interrupted before Jay Mac could answer. "This is the first I've heard of a mission." Her hopes were just being raised when Mary dashed them again.

"It doesn't mean I'm not firm in my decision, Mama. I thought I might like to teach, and there are missions in the Southwest that could use teachers." She watched her mother's eyes widen, then look to Jay Mac for help. "It's no good, Mama," she said with gentle resolve. "Jay Mac already knows and he hasn't been able to talk me out of it."

Moira's confusion showed clearly in her eyes. She placed her fork down as her appetite deserted her. If her daughter wanted to teach, then she could do it closer to home. If she wanted to do it at a mission, she didn't have to leave the church. "One or the other," Moira said, half pleading, half demanding. "You have to choose one or the other. Dear God, Mary, you can't have it both ways. You can't do it."

Mary's aching expression was framed by the headdress of her habit. "What can't I do?"

"You can't abandon us *and* abandon God."

Four

December 1884, Arizona Territory

There were still moments when Mary did not recognize her own reflection. It happened the first time as she was packing her trunks in preparation to leave New York. Passing the tall, narrow swivel mirror in her room, she had been taken aback by the presence of a stranger. She stopped in mid stride and stared blankly at the person returning her gaze. It was an odd, disconcerting feeling to realize she was looking at herself.

Mary's red-gold hair was still unfashionably short, but the new maid had proven herself adept at making something out of nothing. The cut had been reshaped and smoothed to flatter Mary's face, and where her headdress had once framed her features in severe black and white, they were now offset by vibrant color.

Her manner of dress had given her pause as well. Her traveling costume featured a tight-fitting bodice with a narrow-banded collar and a pleated overskirt which fully draped her hips. The soft apricot color tinted her complexion until the embarrassment of staring at herself flushed her cheeks red. It was at that point that Mary had jammed her straw bonnet on her head hard enough to dislodge the apricot ribbon trimmings.

In Denver it happened again, only this time Mary was passing a dress shop with her sister beside her and her niece in tow. Out of the corner of her eye she caught sight of Michael and young Madison reflected in the glass, but she didn't immediately recognize the woman who accompanied them. As Michael paused to point out a gown she had had her eye on, Mary came face to face with her faint image in the store window.

With complete childish candor Madison had remarked, "What's wrong, Aunt Mary? You look like a ghost."

Michael had corrected her daughter offhandedly—"She looks as if she's *seen* a ghost, Madison"—before she realized the little girl's observation was more accurate.

Mary dismissed her sister's concern and never explained satisfactorily that it had been the unfamiliarity of her image that had caused her momentary distress.

It wasn't only seeing herself that gave her pause; it was seeing herself through the eyes of another. In the course of their travel across the country Mary had yet to feel her mother's glance in her direction without it registering a small start of surprise. Michael, even though she was prepared to see Mary out of her habit, had remarked on the fact a half-dozen times in the first hour. At the Double H where Maggie and her husband Connor lived, Mary became aware that the attention she drew from the ranch hands was not inspired by her habit. They were still respectful, still polite, but they didn't hold themselves at the same distance they might have had she been Sister Mary and not simply Maggie's sister Mary.

Now, as the train slowed on pulling into the station in Tucson, Mary wondered at the reception she could expect from Rennie. Michael and Maggie, while accepting Mary's decision with more grace and encouragement than their mother had shown, demonstrated their confusion in small ways. They would have sworn they had never treated Mary any differently because she was a nun; they would have told anyone who cared to listen that Mary had been *their* sister first. Yet there was no mistaking the subtle change in their manner toward her now that she was out of the habit.

Mary had good reason to wonder how much she had been shielded by her black gown and veil and how often she had been deferred to, not because of whom she was, but because of what she was.

* * *

At the first sign that the train was ready for boarding, Rennie Sullivan thrust the daughter she was holding into her husband's free arm and began running toward the private Northeast rail cars. Jarret looked down at the twin girls he held, both of them wriggling for all they were worth, shook his head, chuckling, and followed his wife at a less frantic pace. He set both girls on the platform just as Moira stepped onto the balcony of her car.

She saw Jarret first, his dark hair and easy smile drawing her eyes immediately. He was a handsome rogue, Moira thought, just as she had the first time she had seen him. And every bit the right match for her fiery daughter Rennie. Her smile was brilliant for him, and if anything, it became even brighter as her eyes dropped to her twin grandchildren. Moira's hand went to her heart in a dramatic loving gesture that was meant to signify breathlessness, surprise, and joy. "My grandbabies!" she cried happily.

Mary Caitlin and Mary Lillian gamely tried to climb aboard the train to get to their beloved grandmother. Their sturdy three-year-old bodies had enough strength but not enough height. Jarret scooped each of them up and set them down behind him. They stayed there long enough to allow him to help Moira down to the platform.

"It's good to see you," he said sincerely, kissing her cheek. "Rennie's been looking forward to this since we got your first telegram in October. Once she finally got your arrival date last week, she's been impossible to contain."

Moira smiled at that. Her gently lined face was creased becomingly by her happiness. "And how would that be any different than it usually is?"

Jarret laughed. "You're right. It's not any different." He looked over Moira's feathered bonnet as his children tugged on their grandmother's dust cloak. They were anxious for kisses and treats, knowing perfectly well that Moira would have plenty of both. Jarret's eyes scanned the windows of Jay Mac's private car, but the sun's reflection on the glass did not permit him to see inside. "Rennie's in there with Mary Francis?" he asked.

Moira nodded. "Sure, and she practically knocked me over to get to her sister."

Jarret refrained from responding. Moira's tone was not especially approving of Rennie's show of sisterly affection. Jarret had been warned through correspondence with Jay Mac that there was still considerable tension between Moira and Mary. Until just this moment, when he experienced the coolness in Moira's lilting brogue, he had had a hard time imagining it. Now he was a believer.

Jarret lifted each of his little Marys in turn. Cait had a hard hug for her grandmother and a loud, wet kiss. Lilly was more delicate in her affections, laying her bright red head on Moira's shoulder and fluttering her lashes coyly. He marveled at how distinct the personalities of his identical twins were, and how they blended so many aspects of himself and Rennie to become unique unto themselves.

His musings were interrupted by his wife's appearance on the balcony. She still had the power to take his breath away, he thought as his heart slammed hard once in his chest then resumed its normal beat. Her dark auburn hair, widely spaced green eyes, and full, expressive mouth drew his attention as easily as they had in the first moments of seeing her. His eyes dropped to that mouth now as its seriously set shape was transformed by a puckish, dimpled grin.

Rennie pulled Mary forward to join her on the balcony. "Isn't she surpassingly lovely?" she asked Jarret.

Jarret wondered how he was supposed to answer that. It was an undeniable truth that Mary Francis Dennehy was beautiful, even when she was looking mortified by her sister's outrageous question. Jarret was aware that it was an expression he'd never glimpsed on her face before. A moment later he realized the faint blush tinting her cheeks was also new. He continued his scrutiny, his eyes grazing over Mary's short curling crop of hair,

the perfect oval of her face, the long slender neck, and then . . .
His eyes flew back to meet hers, and this time he found himself
on familiar ground. She was boring holes into him with those
fierce, forest green eyes, just daring him to make a misstep so
she could take him out at the knees.

Self-preservation prompted Jarret to bound up the iron stairs
of the rail car's balcony and greet Mary Francis with a warm
hug and dry humor. "I almost didn't recognize you until I felt
body parts being threatened."

Mary's head tilted to one side as she looked at her brother-
in-law consideringly—and with no lessening of the mock threat.
She had once, in all seriousness, threatened to break his knees
if he ever hurt her sister. "Well, you shouldn't be looking at me
as if I've grown another head," she said tartly.

"I know that look he gave you," Rennie said mischievously,
"and it had nothing to do with growing another head." She gave
her husband a knowing glance. "He usually reserves that gleam
for me."

"You asked a very particular question," Jarret reminded her
innocently. "I was arriving at an opinion."

"And that is?" asked Rennie.

"I don't want to hear this," said Mary.

Jarret laughed. "My opinion is that my wife, as usual, is
right. She always said you were the real beauty of the family,
and I'm not going to argue with her."

The perfect symmetry of Mary's features was broken as she
screwed her mouth to one side and rolled her eyes.

Rennie raised on tiptoe and kissed her husband's cheek. "I
thought you were wonderfully diplomatic, dear. It was a very
nice compliment to both of us."

"She *would* think that," Mary said dryly to Jarret. "She'd
rather be right than beautiful any day."

Over the top of Rennie's head, Jarret's response was a wink
and a smug smile.

* * *

They were all settled in the open carriage when Rennie announced there had been a change of plans. "We're being escorted by an Army patrol to Fort Union. We've been staying there for a week now, and the general gave approval for both of you to be our guests."

Moira paused in the game of pat-a-cake she was playing with Lilly. "That's fine, Rennie, but why?"

"We moved from Phoenix to Tucson after the surveys were all complete. Jarret and I thought it would be close enough to Holland Mines to oversee the track construction, but it really isn't. And the trip, well, it can be"—she hesitated, looked at her daughters, then spelled—"d-a-n-g-e—"

"I think we get your point," Mary said, ruffling Caitlin's hair. The little girl held a parasol aloft to protect both of them from the brutal midday sun. Even in the middle of December the temperature at noon was approaching ninety-five degrees. "Here comes our escort."

Five men on horseback wearing blue Army uniforms drew abreast of the carriage as it left the station area. The corporal took the lead while Lieutenant Rivers introduced himself to Moira and Mary as he rode along beside them. Three privates took up points at the rear.

Moira glanced around at their escort. "Is this really necessary, Rennie?"

Jarret answered, turning around from his perch on the driver's board. "It is, Moira."

Rennie reinforced her husband's comment. "We stayed at Holland Mines for a while, living at the camp in a tent with the miners and the rail laborers. We decided to move to Fort Union after the Chiricahua attacked a mining camp a little farther east of here. We still stay there when work warrants it, but without the girls."

Mary was aware that Caitlin was watching her mother intently, listening hard to every word. Mary caught her sister's eye and gave a quick shake of her head.

Rennie sighed, nodding in understanding. "What one of them

doesn't hear, the other one does," she said. "It's hard. You know I was never good at guarding my tongue."

Jarret caught that comment and laughed. "Well, it would take more than these five Army regulars to do it."

Reaching behind her, Rennie gave her husband a firm slap on the back. "Mind your own business," she said, but there was no real sting in her words.

Mary and Moira exchanged their first spontaneous smiles in over two months and two thousand miles.

Rennie saw their shared laughter and was satisfied that the situation was not quite as grim as Jay Mac would have had her believe. "I think you'll both appreciate the accommodations at Fort Union. A number of the officers' wives have gone out of their way to make us feel at home. You'll be amazed at the collection of furniture and carpets that's been hauled across country. General Gardner's wife has a baby grand piano in her parlor, and Captain Avril and his wife practically have a library in their quarters."

Moira pointed to Lieutenant Rivers who had pulled ahead to converse with Jarret. "Does he have a wife?" she asked, not bothering to lower her voice.

Rennie watched Mary's mouth tighten at their mother's less than subtle interest. She felt a tug of sympathy for her older sister's position. She remembered too well what it was like when Jay Mac had tried to find her a husband. Rennie didn't doubt that Moira could be just as tenacious. "No, Mama," she said, winking at Mary. "Lieutenant Rivers isn't married."

Lieutenant Rivers heard the comment as he was meant to do. He acknowledged it by glancing over his shoulder, smiling, and tipping his hat politely in Mary's direction.

"Oh, for God's sake," Mary said irritably, "I'm not looking for a husband. My mother is."

Rivers looked confused and turned away, while Rennie laughed out loud. Moira clucked her tongue disapprovingly and cautioned both her daughters to mind their manners.

With some effort, Rennie managed to become sober. Mary,

she noticed, was still looking wonderfully militant. It struck her that perhaps this was just the right mien for an officer's wife. She couldn't resist extolling the lieutenant's virtues. "He's recently received a promotion," she told them. "From second lieutenant to first. That's because of his demonstration of considerable courage during the Colter Canyon incident in September."

"Is that right, Lieutenant?" Moira asked curiously.

"Mama," Rennie said flatly, "he's not going to blow his own trumpet."

That may be true Mary thought, but she noticed Lieutenant Rivers had slowed his horse so he could listen to Rennie sing his praises. That didn't endear him in any way to Mary. She thought he was handsome enough in a soft, boyish sort of way. He had the kind of features that would dissolve into nondescript puffiness as he grew older, and would only hint at his youthful zeal as a government warrior. It was easy to envision him as a beefy general with slack jowls and a double chin or a high-ranking politician with great side-whiskers and a bald pate.

Lost in her thoughts, it took Mary a few moments to realize she was smiling vaguely in the lieutenant's direction and he had mistaken her expression for interest. His blue eyes were wandering over her raised face, the tenor of his thoughts quite clear. Mary turned her attention back to Rennie. "I'm sorry," she said politely. "You were saying?"

Rennie snorted. "I was saying that Lieutenant Rivers managed to hold off the Chiricahua, though he and his men were beaten back into one of the canyon's dead-end passages. While they were corralled, the gold ore they'd had to abandon in the wagons was stolen."

"And you got a promotion for this?" Mary asked dryly.

The lieutenant's youthful complexion became ruddy with color, but he did not respond.

Rennie made a face at Mary. "He got the promotion because he captured the scout who betrayed the entire company and nearly caused their complete annihilation."

"Well then," Moira said, satisfied. "That deserves recognition."

Rennie nodded. "The story's been in all the local papers. I've talked to people who've been to San Francisco and Saint Louis who know about it. The Eastern papers are probably going to carry the story again now that the traitor's due for sentencing today."

Today?" Moira asked. "Do you mean it's happening at the fort now?"

Glancing at the watch pinned to her blouse, Rennie nodded. "It's already happened," she said. "At noon."

"Oh, dear," Moira said weakly. "I suppose they mean to hang him."

Rennie nodded.

"Well, I don't think we want to see that."

Lieutenant Rivers was solicitous of Moira's feelings. "It's not required, ma'am. You can stay in your quarters."

Mary's feathered brows rose slightly. "That's a relief," she said caustically. "I suppose you'll be at the forefront of the activity."

Rivers didn't mince his words. "I'd fasten the rope and pull the lever myself, Miss Dennehy. He deserves exactly what he's going to get."

Mary was taken aback by the cold virulence in the lieutenant's tone. She reminded herself it was not her place to pass judgment. Had she lived through the same ordeal as Davis Rivers she might be struggling now to find forgiveness for the traitor, or she might be welcoming his death with the same bitter hostility the lieutenant had demonstrated.

"The sentencing won't be carried out for a few days," Rennie said. "At least that's what I've been given to understand by some of the wives. It seems the entire proceeding has taken a number of unusual twists and turns." She frowned, darting a glance from her mother to her sister. "Are you certain you didn't read about any of this?"

Moira shook her head. "I'm sure I didn't."

"Mama and I have been quite content to let world events proceed without us," Mary said. "I don't think I've picked up any paper except the one Michael works for since we left New York."

"I suppose that explains it," said Rennie. "The story was especially noteworthy because the traitor of Colter Canyon is the nephew of Wilson Stillwell."

Moira's dark red brows drew together as she tried to place the name. "I know I've heard of him," she said, shaking her head as she struggled for recognition.

"The senior senator from Ohio," Mary said. "Jay Mac knows him. He's the chairman of one of the prestigious finance committees—or at least he was."

"He and Jay Mac are cordial at best," Rennie said. "I've had more success in dealing with Senator Stillwell than Jay Mac ever had."

Jarret twisted around long enough to add his two cents. "That's because the senator appreciates beautiful women," he said.

"A trait his nephew apparently inherited," Lieutenant Rivers said tersely.

Rennie shook her head. "I wouldn't know about that, since the senator has always conducted himself honorably."

Moira's interest was piqued, but Mary felt hers wandering. She didn't care about the senator, his nephew, or their appreciation of women. Taking the cream-colored parasol from her niece's chubby hand, Mary shaded them both in a way that would help to exclude them from the conversation. She bent her head and blew softly in Cait's ear, causing the little girl to giggle with delight.

Mary pointed out the giant saguaro cactus, rising thirty feet tall, its fluted columns so stately it might have been placed there solely as a desert guardian. She looked at the brown and barren ground around it and wondered if she could live for any length of time in this land. Hot, dry air seared one's lungs and scorched everything that was unprotected. The plants did not appear to bear fruit, and ribbons of radiant heat absorbed even the suggestion of water.

Yet Mary was intrigued. What kind of people called this place home, and how did the land sustain them? There was a kind of terrible beauty in the harshness that made the terrain difficult to look upon and just as difficult to ignore. The sky was almost cloudless. It stretched out to the mountains and beyond, an infinite ceiling of subtle, shimmering shades of blue. If there were animals, Mary acknowledged that she was not skilled enough to observe them. But then, she considered, perhaps some survival instinct kept them from traveling over the parched mesa at midday.

There was more vegetation as they climbed into the foothills. Scrub oaks and the occasional juniper tree marked the pale faces of the rocks with splashes of gray and green.

They stopped once to rest the horses and take a quick lunch. The soldiers ate from their canvas bags of field rations, while Mary and Moira shared the more appetizing meal that Rennie had thought to pack. Mary watched the Army men huddled around an outcropping of rocks. They didn't appear especially vigilant, she thought, as they tucked into their food with relish.

Jarret interrupted Mary's musings. "You look deep in thought," he said softly. "Care to share it?"

Mary saw that Cait and Lilly were out of earshot, occupied by their food and Moira's delightful retelling of some incident on the trip West. Rennie, she noticed, was equally enrapt. She shrugged lightly. "I was wondering about the soldiers, why they're not a little more watchful. I mean, if there's so much danger of Indian attacks, then why aren't they more on their guard?"

"Because we have a scout," he explained.

Mary's attention was captured now. "A scout?" she asked, pointing to the eating soldiers. "One of them?" She saw that she had amused Jarret, and her response was defensive. "Well? How am I supposed to know? I'm new to this country."

"And you fit right in," he said. "As prickly as a cactus."

She eyed him levelly. "I may not be wearing a habit any longer, but God is still on my side." Mary smiled sweetly as Jarret's dark brows rose a fraction. "It's something to think about, isn't it?"

There was a moment of stunned silence, then his bark of laughter had everyone looking his direction.

"Are you flirting with my husband?" Rennie called to her sister.

Jarret kept Mary from replying. "She's threatening me again."

"Then I don't know why you're laughing," Rennie said seriously. Unconcerned, she went back to helping her children with their meal and listening to her mother's story.

Jarret was shaking his head helplessly. "You Marys know how to close ranks on an outsider."

Mary took pity on him, linking her arm through his and offering the uneaten half of her sandwich. "You're not an outsider, Jarret. I'm mostly polite to them."

He took the sandwich, recognizing the peace offering for what it was.

"Tell me about the scout," she said. "Where is he?"

"Ahead of us, watching for signs."

"Signs?"

"Chiricahua signs. They're the ones who have been doing all the raiding." His eyes were grave now. "It's serious, Mary. They're not taking prisoners these days and death is brutal at their hands. A ranching family was slain recently. The five-year-old daughter was left to die, hanging on a meat hook in the smokehouse."

Mary's complexion paled. Her eyes went immediately to her nieces. "Oh, that can't be true," she whispered.

"It is," Jarret said flatly. His gaze had gone to his daughters as well. They were both laughing brightly, oblivious to the dangers. Jarret already knew his children would die by his own hand before he'd let them fall victim to Apache torture. He turned to Mary and realized she had divined his thoughts and wasn't horrified by them, only heartsick. "The Army's been going mad looking for Geronimo and his renegade warriors. Now that the Chiricahua have the gold ore from the Colter Canyon raid, it's expected they'll get more guns and ammunition."

"Surely no one will sell them any."

"For a hundred thousand in gold?" Jarret scoffed at Mary's naivete. "The sellers are lining up all the time. A detachment from Fort Union confiscated a wagon load of Henry rifles and ammo just three weeks ago. All of it was headed for Chiricahua country."

"What kind of men would—" She shook her head, realizing it was beyond her sensibilities. "Never mind. I wouldn't understand."

"I'm not sure I do," he admitted. And he had seen a lot more of the world than his sister-in-law.

Mary's eyes were drawn to the rocky cliffs around them again. "So our scout's out there, watching over us like a guardian angel."

Jarret smiled at the image that presented. "Something like that," he said.

"I hope he's a good one," she said. She was unaware of her smile or the fact that it was vaguely secretive. Mary didn't realize her eyes had taken on a faraway look as she thought of a certain Army scout getting lost on his way from Baileyboro to the Granville mansion. There was an edge of laughter in her voice when she added, "Not like Ryder McKay."

Enjoying the otherworldly expression that had crossed Mary's face, Jarret had felt a momentary lightness in his chest. It passed quickly when she spoke this name. He frowned, confused. "I thought I heard you tell Rennie you didn't know anything about the attack on Colter Canyon."

"I don't."

"But you said—"

Puzzled, Mary tilted her head to one side. "What?" she asked. "What did I say?"

"Mary, Ryder McKay is the traitor the Army's preparing to hang."

"You're looking very pensive," Rennie said to her sister.

"Hmmm?"

Rennie smiled to herself. Mary's thoughts were clearly elsewhere and had been for some time. Rennie had first noticed it not long after they'd resumed their journey to the fort. At first she had considered sheer weariness the cause of Mary's uncharacteristic silence. But there had also been the tiniest indication of a frown between Mary's brows, and she'd worried her lower lip in a way she only did when she was deeply concentrating.

Rennie hadn't asked any questions then, nor as she helped her mother and Mary settle into their quarters in the officers' building. Now that Moira was napping with her granddaughters and Jarret was engaged in some business with the surveyors, Rennie realized she had waited quite long enough.

She repeated her comment, more loudly this time. "You're looking very pensive."

Mary blinked, startled into awareness by Rennie's raised voice. "Was I?" she asked.

Rennie's mouth screwed comically to one side, and she shook her head, amused. "Here," she said, holding out a cup of tea. "I made this for us while you were daydreaming."

Mary accepted the cup and saucer that was thrust into her hands. She was curled comfortably in a large, overstuffed chair, her stockinged feet hidden beneath the full skirt of her hunter green gown. She watched Rennie settle opposite her on the short sofa and draw her legs up in a similar fashion. Rennie's posture was relaxed, yet there was a certain expectancy in her expression. There is no pretense between us, Mary thought. There was something distinctly soothing about this, and especially about Rennie's expression. They could have been children again, preparing to share secrets in their room long after they should have been asleep.

"So," Rennie prompted, "what have you been thinking?"

"Straight to the point as usual," said Mary. "And absolutely no respect for the privacy of one's thoughts."

Rennie's response was cheerful. "That's right." When Mary still hesitated, Rennie asked, "Is it you and Mama? Is nothing changed between you?"

Mary's head was lowered as she stared at her teacup. That was why her sister didn't catch the relief that passed quickly across her features. When Mary lifted her face it was stamped with its trademark serenity. "Everything's changed between us," she said honestly. "She won't accept my decision, and I can't accept that she won't accept it."

Rennie nodded, understanding perfectly. "Michael and Maggie couldn't help her see reason?"

"I didn't ask them to try." She speared her sister with frank, warning eyes. "And I am not asking you to do it either. It's not your place."

"I wouldn't know where to begin." Not that it would have stopped her, Rennie thought. Mary's vaguely threatening glance, however, was giving her pause. Unconsciously Rennie found one of her hands going to her hair in a protective gesture. When they were growing up together Mary thought nothing of yanking on Rennie's thick auburn braids to keep her in line. Rennie's hand fell away when she saw Mary's look of caution fade and amusement take its place. She stuck out her tongue.

"Well," Mary said dryly. "That certainly cut me to the quick."

Rennie ignored her and asked seriously, "Has there been no understanding at all on Mama's part?"

"I don't know. She won't let me broach the subject."

"Oh, Mary," Rennie said sadly.

Mary pushed words past that hard, aching lump that was forming at the back of her throat. "We talked about incidental things on the journey from New York to Denver. The weather. The scenery. The people in the forward cars. We shopped in various cities along the way for gifts for all the grandchildren. If I mentioned my desire to teach I was met with icy silence. If Mama saw me reading my Bible she began to cry."

Rennie felt tears pressing at her own eyelids. "How awful for you," she whispered.

"For both of us," Mary said. "I don't believe for a moment that Mama wants it to be this way. She just doesn't know how to change it." Mary raised her cup and sipped. The tea was flavored with honey and it soothed her throat. "I thought we were making some progress when we were at Maggie's. Mama's mood was lighter. She was tolerant of Maggie and me discussing my decision to leave the order." Mary's smile was wry. "Or at least she didn't run from the room when the subject came up."

"What happened?"

"Nothing," Mary said. "At least it was nothing that Mama did. I suppose it was my attitude that was altered then." Seeing Rennie's puzzled expression, Mary sighed. "It was while we were preparing to leave the Double H. Mama and Maggie were having a last-minute chat in the kitchen while I was finishing the packing. I found one of Mama's gowns still in the wardrobe so I opened her trunk to put it away." Mary was caught off guard by the sudden welling of tears in her eyes. Trying to compose herself, she ducked her head. The teacup and saucer rattled slightly, and she set them aside. She gave Rennie a watery smile as a handkerchief was pressed into her hands. "Thank you." She swiped at her eyes, then crushed the handkerchief in her fist.

Rennie knelt in front of the chair where Mary sat and placed her hands over her sister's. "What was in the trunk?" she asked quietly. "Mary? What did you find in Mama's trunk?"

Mary had to draw a breath before she could answer. "A habit," she said, her voice low. "I found a habit. Mama's been carrying it across the country in her trunk."

Rennie's shoulders sagged. She didn't know for whom she felt sorrier, Mary or her mother. "Did she expect that you'd change your mind somewhere along the route?" she asked.

"It's worse than that."

"Worse?"

"It isn't my habit."

Rennie's eyes widened. "Not yours?"

"Not mine. I think it was made for Mama." Mary noticed that Rennie looked as if she needed to sit down. At a loss to understand herself, Mary shrugged helplessly. "It's hard to say how her life might have been different if she hadn't come to America or met Jay Mac. I don't know what went through her mind when she packed it, but I know what went through mine when I saw it. It was a message meant for me." The tightening of her jaw was imperceptible at first; then, as memory and emotion swept through her, it became so clenched that a muscle worked in her cheek. She had been nearly blind with rage. Even now she could feel her heart accelerating with the fierceness of her anger. Afraid of what she might say, Mary wouldn't give words to it now.

Rennie understood the reason for Mary's silence. She squeezed her sister's hands gently and remained at her side for a few more minutes. When she got to her feet she said softly, "She hasn't stopped loving you, you know."

The knot in Mary's stomach was only slightly larger than the one in her throat. She looked away from Rennie's searching, knowing eyes. It only feels that way, she thought. Then again, as if to convince herself, it only *feels* that way.

Harry Bishop set a chair in the corridor just a foot from the iron bars of Ryder's cell. Florence thanked him curtly and sat down. She used her cane as an extension of her hand to shoo him away. She didn't speak until the door to the guardroom was firmly closed.

"Don't you have anything to say?" she demanded when Ryder merely sat on his cot facing the opposite wall.

He turned in her direction slowly. "What are you doing here?"

"Well, that's a fine greeting." Florence attempted to keep her voice crisp, but anxiety threaded her voice. It had been nearly nine hours since the sentencing had been handed down at noon. Ryder McKay had less than forty-eight hours to live.

"I mean it, Florence, you shouldn't be here. If General Gardner finds out—"

"Let me worry about my son."

"And there's Harry Bishop," Ryder said. "He can't rely on the general's good graces." Ryder knew Florence had resorted to paying off the guard in order to continue her visits to the stockade. The arrangement had worked satisfactorily for months, but there was always the risk of discovery. Over time his protests had become halfhearted but he made them because it was expected. Florence Gardner, he suspected, enjoyed the intrigue and secretly liked pooh-poohing the danger. "I didn't expect you'd come this evening," he said. "I didn't see you after the sentencing."

Florence had stayed in her room while sentence was being passed. She couldn't join the officers' wives who waited in the courtyard, eager for the final judgment. Her opinion that Ryder McKay was innocent of the charges was an unpopular one, especially since there was no evidence to support it. For Florence, the fact that her son was handing down the sentence made the proceedings intolerable. "I didn't want to be there," she explained. Now she came to the point of her visit. "Your uncle was present, though."

"I saw him."

"Oh? He said you didn't glance in his direction."

Ryder's features settled in a remote mask that shuttered his thoughts. He continued to look at Florence, but didn't respond.

"He wanted to see you this evening," she said. "Joshua permitted it, but the senator told me you didn't want him here."

"He came, but he left after a few minutes."

"And you never spoke to him."

"That's right."

Florence's lined face was grave, her eyes sad. "Wilson Stillwell believes in you," she said. "He came here because he wanted to help."

Ryder decided not to disabuse her of the notion. "Is that why you came tonight?" he asked. "To persuade me to see him again?"

She had enough good sense not to lie. "That was part of it."

"And the other part?"

Her throat began to close, but she continued to look at Ryder steadily. His cleanly defined features were calm, but the light gray eyes were penetrating. "To say good-bye. I won't be coming again. No one but officers and clergy will be permitted to see you. Harry warned me about the order. He won't make an exception this time. He says even Senator Stillwell won't get back here."

Ryder's slight smile was cool. "The general's anticipating an escape attempt."

Florence nodded. "He was brooding about it tonight at supper. I think he's fearful that the Chiricahua will try to rescue you."

It was interesting, Ryder thought, that the Army had so little understanding of its enemy and made so little attempt to come by any. "There's not going to be any rescue," he said. "The Chiricahua aren't going to attack the fort. They don't have the numbers to do it, and they don't have the weapons."

"You forget that almost everyone here believes the Apache were able to buy weapons after the Colter Canyon massacre."

Ryder didn't argue. Instead he said, "The Chiricahua won't mount a rescue. It's not their way. Even if I were highly regarded by them—which I'm not—they would only seek retribution."

"So the fighting will come later," she said heavily. "After you're—"

He finished the sentence she couldn't. "After I'm hanged."

Florence gripped her cane more tightly. Unable to look at him, she stared at her hand, at the knuckles that were thickened by a touch of rheumatism, at the thin parchmentlike skin that made her veins so visible. She should be contemplating her own death, she thought. Instead she was contemplating his. "I could help you escape," she said.

Ryder came lightly to his feet and approached the bars. "Listen to me, Florence." He waited until she raised her face, hardening his heart against her tears. She had made the offer before, and he had turned it down on every occasion. She didn't fully comprehend the wreck she would make of her son's military reputation and career. While Florence blamed her son for not looking beyond the evidence, Ryder did not. Presented with the testimony of the survivors of Colter Canyon, General Gardner was acting in the only way he could. "Don't think about it again, and don't act on it if you do."

"But—"

He reached through the bars and laid a hand over hers. "No."

Florence acquiesced with little grace. "Very well," she said sourly. "But I can tell you when it's my time I'm not going without a fight."

Ryder went to the far side of his cell and stood beside the small window. The evening air was cool, and he appreciated the fragrance of the desert washing over his face. "Is that what you think, Florence? That I'm going without a fight?"

"Aren't you?"

"I told them I was innocent. No one believed me." He corrected himself. "No one save you."

"That's not true. Your uncle lent his support, and General Halstead came down from Flagstaff to speak in your favor."

Ryder was silent for several moments. He looked past the bars of his cell to the garrison. Just at the periphery of his vision he could see the officers' quarters. "You should be going," he said. "Before the general realizes you're not reading in your room."

She waved aside his concern. "I told him I was visiting the Sullivans. Mrs. Sullivan's sister and mother arrived this afternoon, and I made their acquaintance at dinner. Mrs. Worth was quite pleasant, though I don't know what to make of the other one. Most times she looked a thousand miles away. Hardly said a word."

Ryder was barely listening. Even before his incarceration he hadn't been particularly curious about the people who came and went from the fort. Now his interest in them was even less. He couldn't recall who Florence had told him the Sullivans were or what business they had at Fort Union. "Is that so?"

Florence sniffed. "You're putting me in mind of her this very minute," she said sharply, tapping her cane for attention. "You could at least pretend some regard for my conversation. Miss Dennehy perked right up when your name was mentioned, so I think you could—" Florence broke off mid sentence, not because Ryder interrupted but because she realized that she finally *did* have his full attention. His entire posture was alert now, his frostlike eyes narrowed. She had the vaguely unsettling notion that he intended to pounce on her and the fleeting thought that she was actually glad for the bars that separated them. "Why ever are you looking at me that way?"

His expression didn't change. "Did you say Dennehy?"

"Well, yes," she said slowly, in some confusion. "She said I could call her Mary, but I thought in conversation it was only polite to—"

"Mary Dennehy?" he asked. "Mary *Francis* Dennehy?"

"I believe so."

"Sister Mary Francis?"

Florence wasn't certain what he was asking, but she said, "Yes. Rennie's sister."

He said the name almost under his breath. "Rennie." Then, "Why didn't you tell me Mrs. Sullivan was Rennie?"

Exasperated, Florence threw up her hands. Her cane clattered against the bars as it fell. "I told you she was here with her husband. I went on and on about her darling little girls. I said they were connected to the railroad." She wagged an accusing finger. "And you never showed the slightest recognition."

That's because he hadn't known the most important thing. It didn't matter now. He walked swiftly to the bars, reached through, and pulled Florence to her feet. She was close enough that he could have kissed her forehead. He didn't. It wasn't thankfulness he felt right now, but urgency. "I want to see her," he said.

His grip was tight, but Florence didn't wince. She was grateful for whatever had stirred him to life. "Mrs. Sullivan?"

"No. Not her. The sister. Mary Francis."

"She won't be allowed in here, even if you request it. I told you Joshua has said only officers and—"

"The clergy. She'll be allowed in." And it would be his way

out. Ryder released Florence but kept his face close to the bars. "Listen to me, Flo, if you still want to help, I have a plan."

Florence Gardner wasted no time. She called on Mary the following morning after breakfast, ostensibly for the purpose of having company on her daily walk. She extended her invitation to everyone and hoped for the best. Rennie excused herself because of her work. Moira wanted to be with her grandchildren. Florence sensed that Mary would have refused if it had not been left to her.

"It's good of you to humor an old lady," she said, as they left the shaded porch of the officers' quarters. "I know you really didn't want to come."

Mary considered making a denial, then thought better of it. She appreciated Florence's directness too much to offer one. The other woman would have seen right through it.

Florence raised her parasol and encouraged Mary to do the same. "You don't want to burn that fair skin of yours."

"The sun feels good," Mary said, raising her face to a clear blue sky. "It's hard to believe that Christmas is almost upon us."

"Spoken like a true Yankee," she said. "I'm from Georgia. Come Christmas Day what we got was mostly rain. The air was so humid at times you could feel it like a blanket against your skin. I appreciate these arid climes, I can tell you."

"You've been here long?"

"My son was assigned here five years ago. I came out with my daughter-in-law and my grandchildren about six months later. Joshua wanted to be certain the Indian problem was in hand. When most of the hostiles were placed on reservations he thought it was safe enough for us."

"And was he right?" asked Mary.

"There's been trouble recently with the Chiricahua. Geronimo led some of his warriors and their families off the San Carlos reservation. They've been raiding ranches and mines in and around Mexico."

"Colter Canyon?"

Florence had led Mary to the outside perimeter of the fort, taking her behind the buildings to where they were seen by the patrolling guards but still had considerable privacy. She nodded politely to one of the guards and then continued on, twirling her parasol with the flair of a coquette. "Colter Canyon," she mused, sparing Mary a swift glance. "That depends on who you ask. Me or everyone else."

"I'm asking you," Mary said bluntly.

"Then I don't know."

It wasn't the answer Mary was expecting. "I don't understand," she said.

"Neither do I," Florence told her. "That's my point. Everyone else here thinks they have the answer. I'm the only one who's certain there are things left unexplained." She noticed that Mary was deep in thought now, mulling over the cryptic reply. A passing guard eyed the younger woman appreciatively and she didn't even notice. Florence waited for him to move out of earshot. She halted Mary's progress by placing a hand on her forearm. "He wants to see you," she said lowly. "He's in a better position to explain than I am."

Mary's heart slammed against her chest. Her parasol began to slip through nerveless fingers before she caught it. "Mr. McKay knows I'm here?"

Florence watched her reaction with interest. There was a light flush on Mary's cheeks that hadn't been there a moment earlier. The forest green eyes, so ineffably sad the evening before, were bright now, alive with interest and intelligence. Ryder had been right about her, Florence thought, she would go to him. "He couldn't very well ask to see you if he didn't know you were here, now could he?"

Mary's mouth flattened. She deserved to be taken to task for asking stupid questions, that didn't make it any easier to bear. "Can you arrange it?" she asked. "Or should I speak to the commander myself?"

"I'll arrange it, dear. But it will have to be tonight. My son's already out in the field, and I don't expect him back until after dark." Florence could see that Mary was disappointed and that pleased her. It was better that way. Mary would be more eager then and perhaps less cautious. Florence was counting on that. "Of course you'll have to wear your habit," she said offhandedly.

Mary was taken aback. "My habit? But why?"

Florence frowned. "Is that a problem? Ryder told me you're a nun. I mentioned that you weren't wearing a habit when I met you, but he said that wasn't unusual."

The rush of heat to Mary's cheeks annoyed her. She had no patience for her own reaction to the memory of her meeting with Ryder. "Did he tell you what I was wearing when I first saw him?" she asked stiffly.

"No," said Florence. "But judging by the very pretty frock you have on, I'd venture that it was quite lovely."

Mary burst out laughing. The hearty, lively sound fairly exploded from her. When she saw Florence take a step back in astonishment, she laughed even harder. The patrolling guards paused in their steps and sought out the source. The sound was infectious, and quite without knowing what was funny, they found themselves caught up in it, smiling widely and chuckling under their breath. Florence discovered her own shoulders were shaking as she was swept up in Mary's laughter.

Across the compound Ryder McKay stood by the window of his cell, poised and patient, all of his senses alert. The very air around him seemed rent by the vibration of Mary's clear voice. He felt the tide of her laughter washing over him. His mouth parted as he sucked it in.

The sound had substance, and where it touched his tongue he tasted freedom.

Five

Harry Bishop lost his balance. The stool he was sitting on seemed to slip out from under him when Sister Mary Francis walked into the guardroom. He grabbed it awkwardly before it hit the floor and managed to come to his feet with a minimum of teetering. The apologies that were forming in his mind simply remained there because his gaping mouth was incapable of speech. Harry Bishop was a Boston native and a parochial schoolboy for grades one through eight. He considered the years spent under the tutelage of Father O'Donnell and the Sisters to have been his true introduction to Army discipline. Sister Elizabeth in particular had a way of bringing a classroom to order that would have done any sergeant proud.

"At ease," Mary said calmly. "This uniform doesn't require a salute."

Harry blinked, realized his hand was raised halfway to his head, and let it fall slowly. "Habit," he said.

"Yes," she replied dryly. "That's what I'm wearing."

Harry blinked again, this time collecting his thoughts. "No, I meant it was a habit to—"

She cut him off. "I was pulling your leg, private. I know what you meant."

Shaking his head slowly, Harry rubbed the underside of his chin. "A Sister with a sense of humor," he said almost inaudibly. "If that don't beat all." His hand dropped away and he looked her over from head to toe. "You arrived yesterday with the Sullivans."

"That's right. I'm Mrs. Sullivan's sister."

"I didn't know you were a nun."

Mary used one hand to gesture to her habit. "I think you can appreciate how ill-suited this manner of dress is to this climate," she said. "At least during the day. With evening upon us I find it quite cool."

"That's a fact, Sister."

"Mary Francis," she said.

"Sister Mary Francis," he repeated obediently. Harry had seen her taking a walk with Florence Gardner that very morning. Now he tried not to recall the lusty thoughts that had entered his mind. He couldn't imagine the penance that would be imposed for wanting to have carnal knowledge with a nun. He could always plead ignorance of the fact, he considered, but how much would that count for? Better to make personal amends while he could. Unconsciously his body came to attention again. "What can I do for you, Sister?" he asked in his best schoolboy manner.

"I've come to see the prisoner," she said. "I understand that it is permitted."

Harry had been warned to expect a minister from Tucson, but Mary's presence was a surprise. "You have this from the general himself?" he asked.

From his mouth to his mother's ear, Mary thought. It was just as good. "I do," she said. It didn't occur to Mary that Florence Gardner would lie.

It didn't occur to Harry that Sister Mary Francis would. "Very well," he said. His eyes dropped to the valise that Mary was carrying. "What do you have in there?"

Mary crossed the room and set the valise on Harry's desk. She opened it for the private's inspection. On top was a Bible that Florence insisted she take to Ryder. Beneath that was a fresh change of clothes, boot polish, and a shaving kit. Mary made certain that Harry saw everything. "No matter what the man's sins," she said, "he deserves to die with dignity."

Harry nearly smiled. How like a nun to think that a change

of clothes was essential to one's dignity. "All right," he said. "You can take this in—if McKay will even see you. If he won't, I'll make sure he gets it later."

"Thank you. That's very kind of you."

Harry Bishop felt as if he'd been blessed. "This way, Sister Mary. I'll take a chair in for you."

Mary smiled serenely and followed Harry through the door to the cells. Although there were three, only the middle one was occupied. Her heart raced as Harry went to stand in front of it.

"You have a visitor, McKay," he announced.

Ryder was lying on his cot, his hands cradling his head. His line of vision was toward the window of his cell, not the entrance. He made no move to rise or even look in the direction of Harry Bishop and the visitor.

"D'you hear me, McKay? Someone's come by to save your miserable soul." Harry positioned the chair in the corridor and placed the valise on the floor. "An angel by the name of Sister Mary Francis."

Ryder knew very well who accompanied Harry into the cell area, but he was careful not to show his hand. He rose slowly, stretched, then let his feet fall to the floor. Finally his head swiveled in the direction of the iron bars of the cell's door. He looked directly at Private Bishop, not sparing a glance for Mary. "You can let her in, Harry. She's not going to minister to my soul through these bars."

Harry hesitated, his eyes darting from Ryder to Mary.

"It's all right," Mary said encouragingly. "I didn't expect to be kept in the corridor. I'll be fine."

"Are you sure, Sister? I mean, if you were a man and all I wouldn't be asking."

Mary's tone changed, affecting complete confidence and authority now. "I'm fully capable, Private, even if I'm not a man. I appreciate your concern, but it's misplaced. Now, let me in to see this prisoner or you will have to account for your actions to the general first and God later."

Harry Bishop opened the door. He set the chair and valise

inside and ushered Mary in. "I'll check on you every few minutes," he said before he exited.

"Every fifteen or so will be quite enough," she said firmly.

Harry was tempted to salute again. He could not return to his station in the guardroom quickly enough.

Neither Ryder nor Mary spoke immediately once they were alone. She was struck by the changes in him; the sun-bronzed color had been washed out of his skin by months of imprisonment, a harshness was in the lines of his face, a deep, abiding coldness in his eyes. There was nothing in his manner that welcomed her; it was apparent that he resented her presence.

He found it difficult to look at her and impossible to look away. The lantern in the corridor bathed her face in warm light, but it did not account for her radiance. That seemed to come from within Mary. She was the sole source of the aura which surrounded her. Her beautiful features were composed, and their perfect symmetry gave her an otherworldly expression. Compassion illuminated her forest green eyes but her stance was faintly militant, her slender body rigid with the proud defiance of a peaceful warrior. She would not fight, he thought, but she would not be moved. He wished she had not come. Now that she was here, he wished there had been another way.

"Mrs. Gardner said you wanted to see me," Mary said. "It appears she misunderstood."

"There was no mistake," Ryder said roughly. He pointed to the chair Harry left. "Sit down."

Very much aware that it was an order, not an invitation, Mary's mouth flattened stubbornly.

"Suit yourself," he said, shrugging. He reached for the valise. "Did Florence pack this for you?"

Mary nodded. "She said it had everything you wanted." She watched him as he sat on the cot and opened the valise. "I was surprised you asked for a Bible."

Ryder glanced up. "Don't I impress you as a religious man?"

She didn't answer immediately. His question was tossed off with a certain sarcastic intent that wasn't meant to elicit conversation. Ryder had already returned his attention to the valise when Mary responded. "Not religious," she said. "Spiritual."

Ryder raised his head slowly. His narrowed glance wasn't penetrating now, only impenetrable. "Is that right?" he asked.

"Yes." Complete confidence was evoked in the single word. On an equal footing now, Mary Francis sat. "Why did you ask for me?"

"I thought that was obvious." He removed the Bible and the clothes from the valise. When it was empty his hand ran along the inside, found the edge of the piece that had been laid across to create a false bottom, and raised it. The Colt .45 felt wonderfully familiar in the palm of his hand. He left it there for the time being and placed the valise on the floor. "I thought you might pray for me."

Mary didn't take issue with his lie. "I've been praying since I learned you were here," she said simply. Without conscious thought she sought out the rosary attached to her waist. Her fingers moved over the beads, calming her thoughts as she looked around the cell. "I don't understand what's happened here."

"Surely someone's told you of what I'm accused."

"I've learned things from a number of people. My brother-in-law. My sister. Lieutenant Rivers. The general's mother. I still don't understand."

"You mean you don't understand why I betrayed the company?"

"No," she said. "I don't understand why people *believe* you did."

It was not difficult for Ryder to see that she was perfectly sincere. He had done nothing to justify that kind of faith, and he wanted to make certain she knew it. "You don't know me," he said. "You don't know the man I am or what I'm capable of. You only think you do. The little knowledge you have is dangerously incomplete. You've underestimated me."

Mary took his words as a warning rather than an explanation.

Initially there had been an urge to flinch. She had quelled it. "You're right," she said quietly. "I don't know you."

He was silent for almost an entire minute, watching her. She didn't turn away from his scrutiny but held his gaze squarely in spite of her discomfort. Ryder broke the contact when he started to unbutton his shirt.

"What are you doing?" she asked.

"Changing my clothes."

"That can wait until I'm gone."

He didn't explain that it couldn't. Instead, Ryder came to his feet and placed the basin of water at the foot of his bed on the cot. There was a washcloth among the things Florence had provided. He picked it up, wet it, and bathed his face. "I'm going to shave, too. Turn around if it bothers you."

"This is ridiculous," Mary said sharply, coming to her feet. "I'm calling Private Bishop." She would never be able to say how it happened—Ryder's movements were mostly a blur—but when his body stilled again Mary found herself facing his steady arm and a Colt .45.

"Please," he said politely. "Stay. I'd like the company."

Mary sat. She held her breath when Ryder approached, but all he did was pick up the chair with her in it and turn them both to face the wall.

He touched her shoulder lightly. Her tension could be felt through the heavy fabric of her habit. "You can breathe now," he said softly. "And don't call for Harry. You won't like the consequences."

"I don't care what you do to me," she said with foolish courage.

"I was thinking about Harry."

"Oh."

Knowing he had guaranteed her silence, Ryder released Mary's shoulder. "This won't take long."

Mary gritted her teeth. Behind her, she could hear him washing. She recognized the scrape of the razor across his face as he shed his shadow of a beard. She enjoyed her petty self-satisfaction when she heard him swear softly as he nicked himself.

"It's not a fatal wound," he said, divining her thoughts.

Mary's smug smile vanished. "You used me," she said.

"Yes." There was no apology. He stripped out of his clothes, replacing one item at a time, and dressed quickly. He would not feel clean again until he left the cell behind, but fresh clothes were a good beginning. Ryder slipped on the navy blue jacket over his crisp, white shirt and noticed Florence had repaired one of the loose eagle-stamped brass buttons. As he had instructed, she had also added a captain's insignia. "You can turn around," he said.

Mary didn't move. "This view is just fine."

"Bullheaded, aren't you?"

"I prefer obstinate."

With little effort, Ryder turned her again. He cupped her chin and raised her face. "When Harry comes back you'll need to follow my lead," he said. "Do you understand?"

"You've made yourself quite clear." She was no longer fingering her rosary. Her arms were crossed in front of her in a challenging posture. "You shouldn't have used me," she said. "You should have asked for my help."

Ryder let his hand drop away. He went back to the cot and began stuffing his old clothes in the valise. When he was done he thrust it in Mary's direction. "Are you saying you would have said yes?" he asked.

She took the valise and set it on her lap. "I'm saying it would have been polite to ask. Apparently Florence Gardner had a choice. You haven't given me one."

Ryder didn't respond. If he apologized for this he'd be apologizing at every turn. The truth was, he wasn't sorry. He picked up the Bible and opened it. The book of Psalms was hollowed out. Ryder removed an object and held it up to Mary. "The key to the kingdom."

Mary was past surprise. "Small wonder my Bible wasn't good enough for the general's mother."

He nodded, palming the key. "The Bible was Flo's inspiration. Not mine."

"Then she's a volunteer. You didn't have to threaten anyone to elicit her cooperation."

Ryder realized he had said too much. The less Mary understood about Florence Gardner's role, the better. He ignored her comment, placed his hand through the bars, and inserted the key into the lock. It opened easily. Ryder stepped out, pocketed the key, then pulled out the Colt which had been placed in the waistband of his trousers. He had half expected Harry to have checked on them by now. The private's inattention to his duty worked in Ryder's favor. "You can call him in now," he said, closing the door. "Be careful what you say."

While Mary fumed, Ryder took his position behind the door to the guardroom. When Harry opened it the door would offer Ryder cover. By the time Harry realized Ryder wasn't in the cell, it would be too late for him. Ryder cocked one eyebrow when Mary simply sat on her chair, her mouth set mutinously. When that didn't work, he cocked the Colt.

Mary's response was immediate. "Private Bishop," she called. "Will you come in here, please? I'm ready to leave."

Still eager to make amends for his previous wayward thoughts, Harry Bishop responded with alacrity. He was just as quickly dispatched to the floor as Ryder brought him down with the butt of his peacemaker.

Ryder shut the door so they wouldn't be surprised by anyone entering the stockade and dragged Harry to the cell, then he pushed him inside. He took the private's hat and placed it on his head, shoving some of his own, longer hair under it. "You can stop looking so stricken. I didn't shoot him."

"He's still been injured on my account," she said. Her eyes strayed from the unconscious guard back to Ryder. "Go on. What are you waiting for? You're free to leave." She hadn't expected to amuse him, but Mary was certain that was what she glimpsed in the frost gray eyes. "Not that it matters to me, but you're wasting time."

He gestured to her with his index finger, crooking it to indicate she was to come toward him.

Mary's dark red brows drew together. "I'm fine just where I am, thank you."

Ryder raised his gun again. He didn't point it at Mary; he aimed at Harry Bishop's hapless head. "It's not too late," he said. "I can still kill him."

Mary's own head was beginning to clear, and she had had time to take stock of the situation. She was feeling infinitely more confident than she had moments earlier. "If you shoot you'll bring soldiers running. I don't think you want that."

He didn't blink. "They're going to hang me," he said steadily. "I think I'll take my chances." He pulled back the hammer.

Mary stood. "Bully."

"Bring the valise. The Bible, too, if you want it."

She took it off the cot and stepped over Harry's body to precede Ryder out of the cell. He locked the door behind them and ushered her to the guardroom. It was still empty. He motioned her through.

"Now what?" she demanded stubbornly.

Ryder placed one hand at the small of her back. He noticed she responded as skittishly as if he'd placed his gun there. "Through those doors," he said softly, leaning close to her ear. "And into the courtyard. You know not to call attention to yourself."

"I think you and the gun will do that nicely."

"It's dark," he said. "The uniform I'm wearing has a captain's insignia—something Harry didn't notice—and my gun is going to be under my jacket. You walked in with a valise, and you're walking out with one. You're going to slip your arm through mine and I'm going to escort you away from the buildings and past the guards."

"To where your horse is waiting."

He didn't correct her. His firm prod was enough this time to get her moving. When she opened the door to the stockade, Ryder followed her out into the clear night air. She didn't require a reminder to loop her arm through his. He adjusted his hat a notch lower and forced himself to accept the unhurried pace she set.

"You must think you're very clever," she said through gritted teeth.

"It's going remarkably well," he replied pleasantly. The common grounds between the buildings weren't deserted, but Ryder only felt a few glances in their direction. Mary was targeted with looks more often than he.

She felt it, too. "Not many people have seen me in my habit," she explained softly.

Ryder nodded. "I thought it might be something like—"

"Mary!" It was Rennie's strident call from the long porch of the officers' quarters that cut Ryder off. "Mary! What in the world are you—"

Ryder didn't wait to hear more. "Ignore her," he said. "And move a little faster."

"One doesn't ignore Mary Renee," she said under her breath, but she walked faster to stay with Ryder. To her sister she called, "I'll be there in a moment, Rennie. I'll explain it all to you."

Moira joined her daughter on the porch just then. "Sure, and what are you girls yelling about? I can hear you all the way—" She broke off when she saw Mary's familiar shape crossing the parade ground. Moira's hand went to her heart. "Oh, my God! She's taken it up! I prayed and prayed—"

Rennie lifted her hand. She didn't look at Moira. Her eyes were narrowed sharply in her sister's direction. "No, Mama," she said softly, puzzled and disturbed. "She hasn't. I'd swear she hasn't. Something's not right." There was sudden urgency in her voice as her vision expanded to include Mary's escort. "Get Jarret out here, Mama! Get him now!"

Moira didn't respond quickly enough to suit Rennie. She raised her voice so there was no possibility that she could not be heard. "Jarret! Come here! I need you!"

With Rennie's cry, Ryder knew he had been discovered. He grabbed Mary's arm and pulled her around the garrison. She stumbled, but he helped her keep her balance and forced her to match his long stride.

"You'd better go," she said, as they rounded the building and were thrust into the shadows. "Quickly." Over his shoulder she could see a horse tied loosely to a post about fifty yards away. It moved, dropping its head to nose at something in the dirt, and that's when Mary made out the shadow of the second mount. She raised her face to look at him, her normally serene features stricken. "Oh, no," she whispered. "You can't mean to—"

There was no time to listen to her protests. Ryder gripped her firmly and yanked her toward the mounts. He could have covered the ground more quickly alone, but he wouldn't have had the same protection. The shouts from the parade ground were louder now, and he knew the alarm had been raised. "Faster," he said tightly. "Run with me."

Mary tried just once to dig in her heels, but he pulled her so hard that she thought her shoulder would be dislocated. She thought she would have a chance to break away when they reached the mounts, but Ryder practically threw her in the saddle. She was so winded by that, in the time it took her to catch her breath he had released the reins and was mounting the other mare.

Glancing behind her, Mary saw the first soldiers rounding the garrison. There was no moon, and they did not appear as individuals in her eyes. They moved as a shadowy tide, and the sharp angles protruding from their mass, she recognized as raised weapons.

"For God's sake, don't shoot!" Jarret called out. "He has Mary with him!"

"At last," Ryder said under his breath. "Someone with sense." He kicked his horse and pulled on the reins of Mary's mount.

"Mary!"

It was her mother's voice, raised above all the others, that Mary heard. It traveled the distance more clearly than every other frantic shout and barked order. Mary squinted into the darkness and tried to make out her mother's shape even as Ryder was drawing her farther away. "Mama!" She did not mean to sound frightened or panicked, yet she did. She heard that in her voice. "Mama!" she called again. "I love you!"

"Mary!" It was a forlorn cry, and it wrenched the heart of everyone who heard it.

Ryder urged their horses into gallops to escape its eerie echo.

At the outset she swore she wouldn't ask for any show of kindness from him. She had already broken that promise to herself twice and she was fighting the urge now. The word please was already forming on her parched lips. She was actually grateful for the dryness in her throat that prevented her from giving sound to the word.

The night was impossibly dark to Mary. In New York there was always light, even on a night with a new moon gas lamps illuminated the wide thoroughfares. Recently there was talk of adding electric lights. It would be like having stars on the ground, she thought, and not such a bad idea given her circumstances of the moment. Heaven's bounty of stars were not providing the trail of light she could have hoped for.

Ryder, she noticed, did not appear to have any difficulty finding his way. She knew he was more responsible for picking their way through the rocks than the horses were. There was virtually no hesitation on his part that she could sense. Except for the fact that he still commanded her mare's reins, Ryder didn't seem at all aware of her presence. He hadn't even spoken to her since leaving the fort. On the two occasions she had swallowed her pride and asked for help, he had ignored her. The pace he was able to maintain was as steady as it was cruel. Ryder was the only one who showed no signs of tiring. The mares were being run to the ground, and Mary owed her own ability to stay in the saddle to sheer bullheadedness.

She found no satisfaction in the thought that Ryder might be right about her. "If I had any sense I'd faint," she muttered. "I'd faint dead away and make him stop or leave me where I lay." She glanced wearily at Ryder's back. If he heard he'd given no indication of it. It fired her anger. "I can't keep going like this," she warned him. There was no part of her body that didn't ache. In some places she hurt so badly that thinking about them brought tears to her eyes. She swore she felt pain in the roots of her hair. "I can't, I tell you." The second admission came out as no more than a whisper. Mary was humiliated by the pathetic sound of it, and she was actually glad that Ryder didn't respond. She thought about another Mary, her namesake, and the perilous flight into Egypt to escape Herod's wrath. That Mary had ridden a donkey across miles of desert with her child, and nowhere was it recorded that she nagged Joseph or complained to God.

Even though the circumstances of her flight were quite different, Mary drew upon that story for comfort and strength. It supported her well, giving her the stamina to go another two hours without a word to Ryder. When she finally spoke her words were preceded by a derisive sound that came from the back of her throat. "But no one abducted the Blessed Virgin," she said lowly, her voice raspy. "And I'll bet someone just left out the part where she complained." She didn't care that Ryder wouldn't understand the wandering of her thoughts; she wasn't speaking to him anyway. "She probably didn't have to beg Joseph for water either. He was kind enough to take care of . . ."

When Mary fainted it wasn't as part of any plan for revenge.

Ryder was unable to prevent her ignominious fall from the saddle. With no expression of remorse or frustration he simply dismounted and knelt beside her. Because the hard landing hadn't jarred her to consciousness he slipped one arm under her shoulders, another beneath her knees, and lifted her. Like so much baggage he laid her over her saddle, belly down. After securing her so she wouldn't slip off, he mounted again and resumed the hard pace he had set.

When Mary woke she was immediately disoriented. She knew her view was that of the ground, but it didn't make any sense. Her head throbbed with the rush of blood, and her nostrils were filled with the scent of horse sweat. As her thoughts cleared and the truth of her position became known to her, her face flamed with color. "The lowest circle of hell is too good for you, Ryder McKay."

"You're probably right."

Several things struck her at once: she had spoken her thought aloud, Ryder had replied, and his voice came from very close to her. She twisted awkwardly, trying to raise her head to see where he was standing.

"Be still," he said.

In spite of Mary's wretched weariness the urge was in her to fight his terse order. That Ryder merely waited for her struggle to end, and that he didn't have to wait long really defeated Mary. When he drew her off the saddle she sagged heavily against him. The humiliating truth was that she couldn't stand without Ryder's support.

"Shhh," he said softly.

Mary realized she was crying. She felt an arm circle her shoulders, and she was secured now by his embrace. Tears streaked her face and wet his jacket, but he simply held her until even crying was too great an expenditure of energy. "I can't move," she said weakly.

"I know. It's all right." Ryder lifted her as he had done earlier, but this time he didn't place her over the saddle. He carried her toward a dark, yawning gap in the face of the rock around them and entered it. He set her down when the complete absence of light prevented him from making another step toward the interior of the cavern. "I have to see to the horses," he told her. "You'll be safe here."

Mary could only make out his slim shadow as he returned to the entrance of the cave. She continued to stare in that direction until her eyes could no longer focus. With each blink it became more difficult to raise her lids. She promised herself she would only sleep a moment.

Ryder dropped the valise, saddlebags, and horse blankets near Mary's curled body. Uncapping one of the canteens he carried, he knelt beside her, raised her head, and let water trickle over her lips. Her mouth parted and she took it eagerly, raising her hands to tip the canteen at a better angle. "It's enough," he said, his voice low.

It would never be enough, she thought. She let him take back the canteen only because she couldn't fight him for it. She would have told him so, but there was no strength in her to form the words.

Ryder slipped a blanket under Mary's head as he lowered the canteen, then he stretched out beside her. He could feel her trembling, the effect of complete exhaustion. She made no protest when he slid one arm around her middle and drew her closer.

Outside the mouth of the cavern the first threads of sunlight could be seen on the horizon as Ryder and Mary fell deeply asleep.

It wasn't a dream. That was Mary's first thought upon waking, and her sore, aching limbs verified it. Turning gingerly on her hip, she removed the pebble that had made a dimple in her flesh and flicked it out of the way. With some effort Mary pushed herself to a sitting position, leaned back against a large rock, and took stock of her situation.

At some point during her sleep Ryder had abandoned her. She vaguely remembered him dropping the valise and pushing a blanket under her head. Both were gone now as was the canteen. That made Mary wonder about the horses that he'd said he had to "see to." Had he left with both of them or was one waiting for her?

Mary got to her feet, wobbled slightly, and picked her way among the rocks to get to the mouth of the cave. Sunlight blinded her momentarily. She raised a hand to shade her eyes before she stepped beyond the shadowed entrance.

Nothing about her surroundings was familiar. The harsh light of day brought the land into stark relief. She had known that they had been climbing throughout the night, but she was unprepared for the towering pines that seemed to erupt from ground wholly unsuitable to support them. The terrain was severe and hostile, rocks rising at odd angles and sparse grass making up the ground cover. The air was dry and the heat was already making a haze in the distance.

Mary could not see the horses nor could she find the trail Ryder had used to come or go. She didn't know if she were north or south of Fort Union, east or west of the rail line. She only knew she was higher than she had been before and that there was higher ground around her to be covered. The mountains where she found herself were totally unknown to her. It occurred to Mary that she might easily walk for days and never come across anything familiar or friendly.

She would have to be found, of course. Her survival depended upon that. Thinking what she might do to call attention to herself in this wilderness, Mary unfastened her headdress and shook it out. The black veil was coated with a fine layer of dust; the white wimple was stained with dirt and perspiration. Mary tiredly threaded her fingers through her hair, plucking out the strands that lay flatly against her temples.

"It's longer than I remember."

Mary spun around and faced the cave. Ryder was on the lip of the entrance, half in its protective shadow, half out. She had to squint to see him clearly, and what she saw made no sense. He was as relaxed as she was tautly strung, as clean as she was unkempt. Mary's hand fell away from her hair. "I thought you left."

His appearance alone stated the obvious. Ryder didn't waste words explaining that he hadn't. "You have to come in here," he said. "Out of the open."

Mary didn't move. "I don't see the horses."

"I sent them away."

"Sent them? But—"

"Come here."

Mary walked toward him slowly, painfully aware of her awkward stiffness and of Ryder's flat appraisal. When she was close to him he took her arm and pulled her inside. "I can manage," she said resentfully. "I have so far."

He ignored that. "You're not to step foot outside this cavern again. Do you understand?"

"I understand what you're saying," she said, her tart spirit returning. "I just don't understand why you're saying it."

His grip tightened momentarily. "I only care about the first. You don't have to understand my reasons to obey my orders."

Mary's mouth flattened mutinously. Not for the world would she have told him his fingers were bruising her skin. With mock civility she asked, "And what do you suggest I do about a call of nature?"

"Answer it." He released her arm. "I'll show you where." Ryder didn't lead her into the cave immediately. First he stepped out and quickly shinnied up one of the pines, cutting a small branch from a point high enough so that it wouldn't be noticed at ground level. He used it to wipe away the trail of his own footprints and then Mary's. Even the telltale patterns of her gown sweeping the ground were obliterated. Ryder replaced a stone her shoe had overturned so the sunbaked side was on top again.

Watching him, Mary understood why she couldn't find the trail. More importantly she understood the difficulty others would have finding it. Ryder was leaving nothing to chance. "No one's going to find us, are they?" she asked when he joined her.

He shrugged. "This way." Without waiting to see if she followed, Ryder began walking. When he reached the point where they had slept the night before, he picked up a lighted torch he had wedged between two rocks.

"Where did that come from?" Mary asked. Light flickered on the walls of the cavern as he held it up. She realized that his sudden appearance at the cave's entrance had been possible because he had been in the cavern all the time, not outside of it. Now, when he held the torch higher, she began to have some concept of the vastness of the place to which he had brought her.

Just beyond the area where she had slept, the cave opened up into an immense antechamber. The torchlight was not strong enough for Mary to make out more than a half-dozen separate passages emanating from the area though she suspected there were twice that many. She knew enough about the interior of such a cavern to understand there would be passages within each of the others, literally hundreds of different routes along miles of corridors, all of them leading somewhere—or nowhere. She could lose herself more easily in the cavern than she could lose Ryder.

"You've been here before," she said. There was accusation in her tone.

Ryder merely held out a hand to her to help her over the rocky ground. When she refused it he shrugged and kept going, leading her through a shallow wash of water by stepping on a series of well-placed stones. The interior of the cavern was a cool and constant temperature, but the air was clear, not damp or musty. It seemed to Mary that Ryder chose an opening completely at random yet she knew it couldn't be the case. She tried to pay attention to the entrance, the shape of the smooth rock, the formation of the stones leading up to it. The wavering torchlight played havoc with her perception, and it seemed to her that Ryder juggled the torch purposely to keep her from seeing anything too clearly.

The passage twisted and turned, narrowed and widened, and as Mary had anticipated, there were more choices to be made along the route. After only a hundred yards, she was hopelessly disoriented. She was about to ask him if he had forgotten about her physical needs, which were now reaching the stage of urgency, when he pointed to a narrow corridor and handed her the torch.

"Take the second opening on your right," he said. "I'll wait here."

"Your manners leave me breathless," she simpered. Her rolling eyes supplied the sarcasm. She took the torch and disappeared into the corridor.

"There's nowhere you can go," he called after her. "So don't bother trying. The other passages are all dead ends." He watched her back stiffen and could imagine she was gritting her teeth to bite off a retort. Ryder permitted himself a small smile, a salute of sorts to her astonishing resiliency. He leaned back against the cool walls of the cavern and waited in the darkness for her return. As always, waiting brought a pleasure of its own. He savored the anticipation of seeing her again. She would be disheveled and cranky, but her spirit would precede the torchlight.

He pushed away from the wall as she approached and took the torch. "It's only a little farther," he said. "Will your legs carry you or do you want me to?"

Mary was disappointed that she hadn't been able to conceal her limp. "I'll be—"

"I don't know why I asked," he said. Thrusting the torch back in her hands, Ryder picked her up. "Keep that thing high. Don't burn my hair."

It was tempting, but Mary did as he asked, raising it over their heads. He carried her another fifty yards, and she never sensed his breathing change. His stamina confounded her, but before she could comment on it he stopped on the threshold of another chamber.

Mary's eyes widened as Ryder slowly turned to show her the interior of the room. Five lanterns hanging from hooks embedded in the stone provided light. There was a small pool of water to the left of where they entered, and Mary could hear the faint trickle of the underground stream providing the water and carrying the runoff. Thick, colorful blankets were laid out on a wide stone shelf which made a rocky loft of a bed. The chamber had no real corners, but one area that was more angled than the other was the storage site for hundreds of cans of food, also for dried meat and staples in kegs and sacks. There were cooking utensils, stoneware jugs, wooden buckets, baskets, and tin cups stacked haphazardly among the foodstuffs. Nearby, a crate of Henry rifles and cases of ammunition rested beside a small unmarked trunk.

The chamber was not only well stocked, it was also furnished with a rocker, a three-legged stool, a faded brocade wing chair, and a cherry wood pie table. While the mix of pieces was odd, Mary recognized the quality.

She was as astonished as she was appalled. "It's true, then," she said softly.

"What's true?"

Mary hadn't been aware she had spoken aloud. She nudged Ryder's shoulder, and he set her down. When he would have supported her, she took a step away from him. "Is this where you've hidden the gold?" she asked.

He came to understand what she thought was true. She believed the contents of the chamber had something to do with the Colter Canyon raid. "There's no gold here." It was the only explanation he would make. When it looked as if she wouldn't be satisfied with that, he pointed to the well of water. "It's cold, but you can wash there. Bathe if you like. I get our drinking water from the source so you don't have to worry that it will be contaminated. There's soap in that trunk and liniment in my saddlebags."

Mary looked longingly at the water, then back at Ryder, less critically this time. There was no gold here, he'd said. Did she dare believe him? Did she dare not? "I'd like a bath," she said quietly. "And perhaps I could wash my habit." From beneath her wide sleeve she pulled out her dusty veil and wimple. "And these."

"Whatever you like."

"Are there towels?"

"This isn't a hotel."

"I'm not likely to make that mistake. I just thought—" She glanced around the room. "It seems you have all the important amenities."

He took pity on her. Her eyes were large and impossibly green, and for just a moment she had been uncertain. "In the trunk with the soap. I'll get them both for you."

Mary exchanged the torch she was holding for the soap when

Ryder brought it. She eased herself carefully onto the flat stones that ringed the small pool and took off her shoes and stockings. Looking sideways at Ryder, she raised her black skirt slightly and massaged her calves. "You already bathed," she said. "Alone." It wasn't a question; it was a hint.

Ryder hesitated.

"There's no way out," she said. "I'm not going anywhere."

His eyes narrowed on her face a moment longer. "Very well," he said at last. "There are things I can do elsewhere." Ryder picked up one of the wooden buckets and a ladle. Still carrying the torch, he left the chamber.

Mary waited, wanting to be certain Ryder was really gone before she stripped out of her habit and undergarments. When his light footfalls receded completely she believed she was safe. The pile of clothing she intended to wash was forgotten as she took stock of her bruised and battered body. There were large discolorations on her shoulder, upper arm, and hip and it wasn't until she recalled fainting that she understood their origin. The small, tender blisters on her palms and fingertips were easier to explain. She remembered the tight grip she had had on her saddle because Ryder wouldn't give her the reins.

Mary explored lower, touching her ribs, her flat belly, the faint outline of her hipbone. Where she had controlled her mount with her inner thighs, the soft skin was burned from the constant rubbing. Touching herself gingerly now, Mary winced. It would take more than liniment to ease her pain there.

Mary dipped her toes in the water, just skimming the surface. Ryder had understated the fact when he'd said it was cold. It was icy. She sat on the stones again and eased herself carefully into the pool until she touched bottom. The water cupped the lower curve of her breasts, and her nipples became almost painfully hard with the frigid temperature. In the beginning it was difficult to breathe. Mary was tempted to haul herself out, but it would have taken more strength than she could immediately muster.

The current tugged on her at the level of her ankles and feet as the underground stream rushed past. The deeper water was even colder than the surface, so Mary made no attempt to dunk herself entirely.

That is, until Ryder reappeared.

She had soap in one hand and a scrap of linen in the other. She held both aloft as she sank into the water as far as her chin. "What are you doing here?" she demanded.

Ryder didn't miss that her tone was as icy as the water. "I didn't hear any splashing," he explained calmly. "I wanted to be sure you hadn't drowned."

Mary made a sound that was both derisive and impatient. "You couldn't be that lucky."

His pale gray eyes widened fractionally. "It didn't take you long to recover your sass."

She wasn't certain she heard him correctly. "What did you say?"

"I said you were sassy."

It was a word that had never been applied to Mary before. Tart. Blunt. Sarcastic. Those were descriptions she had heard. Sassy was girlish, a little flirty. It made her feel gauche, youthful in a way that she'd never been, even when she was young. Embarrassed, Mary lowered her hands and crossed them in front of her breasts under the water. Some of the heat drained from her face.

Ryder watched her thoughtfully and revealed nothing. He approached the pool slowly until he could hunker at the edge. "This seems familiar," he said quietly.

Mary was thinking the same thing. Except for the cold. That would fade in time, she thought. Soon she would be mercifully numb to it *and* the humiliation of her predicament. Mustering what dignity her situation allowed, she stared back at Ryder and waited for him to move away. When he didn't she said, "You might demonstrate some decency."

"Do you need help?" he asked politely. It seemed the decent thing to do. He watched her lips flatten with exasperation, and one corner of his mouth lifted in an arch smile. "I've riled you again, haven't I?"

Mary didn't know which she disliked more, the fact that he

could get a response from her so easily or the fact that he seemed to enjoy it. "Will you please leave?" she asked.

"You only had to ask." Still watching her from behind a mask of impenetrable calm, Ryder rose slowly. The stiffness that plagued all of Mary's movements was noticeably absent from his. He didn't know it, but that did as much to fire her anger as his careless reply. As soon as his back was turned she pitched the bar of soap at him hard. It caught Ryder squarely between his shoulder blades before it thudded to the ground.

He spun around. Whatever retribution he planned in that brief span of time was aborted when he saw Mary's shoulder. She had risen far enough out of the water for him to clearly see the large bruise. "Did that happen when you fell?" he asked.

She followed his gaze to her shoulder, glanced at the blossoming discoloration on her pale skin. "Unless you beat me while I slept," she said. Mary almost regretted the flippant remark when his eyes pinned her where she stood. "Yes," she said. "When I fainted."

"Are there more?"

She hesitated.

"I'll drag you out of there and see for myself."

Mary raised her arm and showed him the one there. "There's another on my hip," she said. When he merely stared at her, trying to gauge her truthfulness, she added, "That's all."

Ryder nodded. His saddlebag was lying on the spread of blankets. He dumped the contents and spread them out. A brown bottle of Dr. Horace White's liniment was among the items Florence had packed for him. Ryder set it down beside the pool. "Compliments of Flo," he said. "She thought of everything."

Mary didn't try to reach it, nor did she thank him for it. As far as she was concerned the general's mother had a great deal to answer for. "May I have the soap?" she asked.

He handed it to her. "You'll be all right?"

She nodded. "Yes," she said. "Of course." Watching him, seeing a thread of tension leave his features and a certain remoteness return to his eyes, Mary realized there was no "of course" about it. Ryder really *had* come back because he was concerned something had happened to her. She wanted to tell him that he should have thought of that before he forced her to leave with him. The moment to say it passed as Ryder picked up his torch at the entrance and disappeared into the corridor. There would be other opportunities, she reflected, glancing around the room. Her eyes landed on the box of Henry rifles and the cases of shells, and she smiled. Opportunities could be made if one was resourceful.

Ryder leaned his torch against some rocks in the spring room. He filled the bucket with fresh water, took a few deep sips from the ladle, then set it aside. He would give Mary ten minutes to finish bathing and no longer. The water was too cold for her to be safe any longer than that. Her strength had already been pushed to the limit.

He could still feel the spot on his back where she had caught him with the corner of that bar of soap. She was at the end of her emotional endurance as well. He could only guess at the lengths she would go to to be rid of him and the methods she might use. He would have to make certain she understood there was no escape from the cavern. Otherwise Ryder was very much afraid Mary would die trying.

He mulled over the things he might say to her, testing them in his mind before he tested them on his tongue, and at the end of ten minutes he retraced his steps to the lighted chamber.

All of his carefully considered phrases were left unsaid. Mary Francis met him at the entrance wearing nothing but a blanket and a feral smile. She was also silent.

The Henry rifle she aimed at Ryder's chest spoke for her.

Six

"I know how to use this," Mary said, raising the rifle a notch.

Ryder nodded. "That's important information for me to have," he said. "Thank you."

Mary's forest green eyes flashed, set off by the hint of amusement she thought she heard in Ryder's tone. "You might want to know this also," she told him. "I *will* use it."

"I didn't think you'd pick it up otherwise."

This time she was satisfied with his sincerity. "You can put down the torch," she said. "And the bucket. Then I'd like you to remove your gun." Her eyes dropped momentarily to the weapon Ryder had tucked in his pants. "You can put it on the ground and kick it toward me."

Ryder dropped the torch and bucket. He raised his right hand slowly and took the Colt out. He was careful not to indicate in any way that he might turn the tables on her. The Henry rifle had a quick trigger and deadly accuracy. At her present range, she could hardly miss. Even if her intention was only to wing him, the wound could prove fatal. Ryder knew she hadn't entirely considered the consequences of killing him. If he died she had only the slimmest chance of finding her way out of the cavern. That still left her to face the mountains. She had even less chance of surviving in them.

Ryder carefully placed the Colt on the cavern's rock floor and kicked it in Mary's direction. "Now what?"

Mary's chin jerked briefly in the direction of the odd assortment of chairs. "You may have a seat," she said. "Your choice."

He took the stool. Mary followed but didn't sit. Ryder watched her heft the rifle again, and knew it was getting heavy for her. "Your blanket's slipping."

She shook her head. "I won't be so easily taken in."

"All right," he said, his eyes dropping to the upper curves of her breasts. "Then you won't mind if I enjoy the view."

Mary considered shooting him just to shake his imperturbable calm. "Where are we?" she asked.

"You don't have to point a rifle at me to get an answer to that."

"Apparently I do. You haven't answered it yet."

"This is the Cavern of Lost Souls."

How fitting, she thought. "A burial ground?"

"At one time. It hasn't been used for that for centuries. There are chambers within the cavern with human remains. It's still a sacred place to the Apache."

"Particularly the Chiricahua?"

"Yes."

"Then the cavern is well known."

He shrugged. "It's drawn up on all the geological surveys of the area."

He was being purposely and maddeningly obtuse, she thought. And he was still staring at her breasts. It was very tempting to look down to ascertain what he could see, but Mary resisted. The blanket was heavy wool, and she could feel the weight of it against her skin. She was still modestly covered even if he pretended to see right through her. "Will the search party know to look here?"

"We spent most of the night laying down false trails," he said. "This isn't the first place they'll come."

"I see."

"And if they do, it's doubtful they'll find this chamber."

Mary almost told him about her brother-in-law. Jarret Sullivan had made a good living bounty hunting before he'd married Rennie. She quelled the urge to be smug and said instead, "The Army has scouts as clever as you."

"More clever," he said modestly. "But at Fort Union they're all Apache."

"So?"

"They might lead the Army to Lost Souls if they pick up a trail, but not one of them will enter."

"Because it's sacred ground."

He nodded. "The Apache are superstitious about the dead, even fearful. They won't come in here."

"But you did."

Now Ryder raised his eyes and regarded her frankly. "I'm not Apache."

Mary felt the pull of his pale, frost gray eyes. "Not half?"

"By blood, not a quarter. Not even an eighth. Scots-Irish on my father's side, French on my mother's. And that's generations ago. My parents were born and raised in Ohio."

Mary's weight shifted from one foot to the other. She wished she could shift the rifle with as much ease. He was an enigma to her, raising more questions in her mind than he was answering, and she was already tiring. Mary backed up to the wing chair and stepped behind it. The high back gave her support for the rifle and steadied her aim. It also provided adequate cover. If the blanket slipped now, she would be the only one who knew it. "People at the fort think you're a friend of the Chiricahua."

"That's probably because it's true," he said. "Did that make you assume I was one of them?"

"I . . . I don't know. I suppose I thought it would explain some of your actions."

Ryder's features remained impassive, but tension was tightening his jaw line. A tiny muscle began to tic in his cheek. "What do you know about my actions?"

"I know you abducted me," she said.

He dismissed that with an abrupt slash of his hand. "Before you came to see me in my cell," he said tersely, "what did you know of my actions?"

"I thought you were honorable," she said. "And perhaps you still are, but I don't know who you honor any longer. If the

Colter Canyon raid was your doing it may be that in order to
honor your friends you had to betray your country."

"I seem to remember you saying something about helping
me if I had asked. If you believe I had a part in the raid, then
wouldn't you be betraying your country?"

How was it possible that she had the gun and he still had the
upper hand? "If I thought you were responsible for the raid I
wouldn't have offered my help."

"Exactly."

His logic confounded her. "That was then," she said. "I don't
know what I think about your notions of honor now. You haven't
behaved honorably toward me."

Ryder didn't deny it. "No," he said. "I haven't."

Mary hadn't expected his easy admission. Her brows drew
together as she studied him. "Then why—"

"I sacrificed you to protect Florence. I suppose you would
see that as more proof of my divided loyalties." Ryder leaned
forward on the stool, resting his forearms on his knees. His
posture was relaxed, casual. "I'd rather you put the rifle down,
Mary. I don't mind explaining things to you, but not this way."

She was struck by the fact that he had used her name. She
couldn't recall that he had done so before, and now he did it
with a certain deliberateness, as if there were meaning and some
expectation attached to its use. "Just tell me this," she said.
"Would this rifle be enough incentive for you to lead me out
of here?"

"No," he said quietly. "But I think you already know that."

Mary sighed and lowered the weapon. She let Ryder take it
and return it to the crate with the others. "I didn't like holding
it on you," she said.

"I didn't imagine you did." He picked up his Colt and placed
it on top of a flour keg. "And I don't think I'll need this. Why
don't you sit down?"

Mary adjusted the blanket, giving it a yank upward before
she rounded the wing chair. She thought she saw Ryder smirk,
but the expression was so brief and so faint that she warned

herself she could have imagined it. "I could have shot you," she told him.

"I was convinced."

She sat in the wing chair, drawing her legs under her. When her thighs rubbed, she winced and sipped the air to catch her breath.

"What is it?" he asked.

"Nothing."

It was such an obvious lie that Ryder's lip curled derisively. "Should I get the gun?"

"Oh, if you must know," she said impatiently, "I'm tender from riding all night."

"Tender?"

Mary's mouth flattened. Just how plain did he want her to speak? "It feels as if someone's set fire to my thighs."

Ryder watched as Mary's complexion suffused with enough color to rival the red-gold in her hair. She was staring hard at him, daring him to mention it. "I'll make a salve for you." Ryder didn't tell her it would mean leaving the cavern. He would have to do it while she slept, but judging by the faint drooping of her eyelids, he wouldn't have to wait long. "It will help."

She didn't thank him for his offer. "What did you mean about Florence Gardner?" she asked. "About sacrificing me to help her?"

"I thought you understood her part in the escape."

"I understand she arranged for me to see you, hid the key in her Bible, hid a gun in the valise, and saw to it that you had fresh horses."

"That's right. You know that because you were there. How do you suppose it looks to everyone back at Fort Union?"

Mary considered that for all of a second. "But you *abducted* me!"

"Really?" he asked calmly. "Or did you come willingly? Harry Bishop will have no record of receiving an order from General Gardner for your admission into the stockade. He let you in because you're a nun. Florence herself couldn't have gained entry that night. You were the one who carried in the valise, which we have with us, so who's to say it wasn't yours? You didn't call out for the guard while I changed into uniform, and you didn't try to warn him when he walked into the cell area."

"But you—"

"I know," he said. "That's the point. *I* know." He saw her shoulders slump as she pressed one hand to her forehead. "You escorted me across the parade ground, and when your sister called to you, you told her you'd explain everything later. You didn't ask for help, and when we ran, we ran together. There were two mounts waiting for us, not one. Both were saddled, so there's no suspicion that I wanted one for riding and a fresher one for later. For all intents and purposes this was no spur of the moment abduction. Some people are probably already questioning your timely arrival at the fort, wondering if this wasn't arranged weeks ago."

"I never told anyone I knew you," Mary said. But she was frowning, recalling that it wasn't quite the truth. She had mentioned his name to Jarret.

"Florence knows we've met before, and she'll make certain others find out. She'll be reluctant to tell, of course, because everyone knows she's my strongest advocate, but her hesitation will only make her more likely to be believed."

Mary rubbed her temples, trying to think. "And if I hadn't come to the fort?" she asked. "What was your plan then?"

"There was no plan."

Her hand dropped away from her face. "No plan?"

He shrugged. "I would have hanged." Ryder picked up the liniment at the pool's edge and held it up. "Did you use any of this?"

"There wasn't time."

"Too busy thinking about Henry rifles." He approached the wing chair, pulling the stool along as he went. "Sit up," he said.

It wasn't until his terse command that Mary realized how small she had become in the chair. With her long legs curled under her, her head bent, her shoulders hunched in defeat, she had finally taken on all the attributes of surrender. Rallying, she straightened. "What are you going to do?" she demanded.

Ryder was pouring liniment in his palm. He corked the bottle, set it down, and rubbed his hands together. The friction heated the oil so that when he placed his palms on Mary's bare shoulder warmth penetrated skin to bone. He watched her close her eyes with the pure relief of it. Her lashes fluttered briefly, then lay still, fanning out to cover the shadows beneath her eyes. Except for those shadows her skin was pale. She leaned her head back and exposed the long line of her throat. Ryder could make out the pulse in her neck, the faint evidence of her heartbeat.

His hands moved gently to her upper arm and massaged the liniment in there. She didn't attempt to move away from him. Ryder poured more of the oil in his palm, rubbed, then settled his hands on her uninjured shoulder. This time she actually sighed.

"Give me your hands," he said.

Mary raised them limply, too exhausted to worry or wonder at the ease with which she was being manipulated. His hands slipped along her fingers with tender regard for her blistered flesh. His touch was light, deft; and she was warmed by it. As he massaged oil into the centers of her palms, she felt the sensation throughout her body, tingling and tightening her skin. An unfamiliar sound rose at the back of Mary's throat and she realized she was hearing the hum of her own pleasure.

She forced her eyes open, but her gaze was sleepy and slightly unfocused. "I think that's enough." There was no force to her words, no real threat in them. "You should stop . . ." Her voice trailed off as his hands moved over her wrists then her forearms. Mary closed her eyes again and just allowed herself to feel. Every sensation was a novel one. There was steady thrumming to her heartbeat now and a gentle roaring in her ears.

Ryder had moved from the stool to the arm of the chair. He was close enough that his breath shifted silky strands of her hair against her temple. When he picked her up her head lolled

against his shoulder. Her lips parted, but there was no protest.
He carried her to the wide stone shelf where blankets had been
laid out and put her down. She turned on her side, knees drawn
up like a child, one hand under her head, the other near her
mouth. The blanket over her slipped from her hip, and he saw
the bruise from her fall. For the last time he applied liniment
to his hands, rubbed hard, and laid them on her skin. She didn't
stir.

Ryder couldn't say the same thing for himself. He finished
the massage quickly and covered her hip. When the blanket
slipped again he covered her with another. Kneeling beside the
pool, Ryder washed his hands, then washed Mary's clothes. The
sooner he put her back in her habit, the better.

When Mary woke she was alone. In the cavern there was no
possibility of understanding day or night. She felt surprisingly
rested so she imagined she had been asleep for several hours,
perhaps longer. The lanterns were still lighted, but upon inspection she saw their oil had been replenished. Ryder, it seemed,
thought of everything. He hadn't known how long he would be
gone, and he hadn't wanted her to wake up in the dark.

Mary's clothes were hanging on a rope that Ryder had strung
from one wall of the chamber to the other. The rope was secured
by spikes he had driven into the stone. Mary didn't have to feel
her habit to know it was still wet. Water dripped from the material and landed heavily on the cool floor. Only her white cotton
shift was dry enough to put on. Mary slipped it over her head.
Her feet were cold, and when she went looking for a pair of
socks among Ryder's things, she also found a clean shirt. She
put both on, rolling up the sleeves to her elbows and turning
down the cuffs of the socks so they warmed her ankles.

Mary ran her fingers through her hair several times to separate the flattened curls. She was thirsty and hungry, and she had
no idea whether Ryder intended to feed her anytime soon. Her
eyes fell on the bucket of water and ladle he had carried in

earlier. Not bothering to get one of the tin cups, she drank from the ladle, sipping first to make sure the water wasn't briny, then taking large gulps when she realized it was fresh, clear, and cold.

With her thirst slaked, Mary turned to the problem of hunger. It was not going to be so easily satisfied. There were tins of meat, tomatoes, and corn, but nothing to open them with. She investigated several sacks until she found one filled with jerky. Mary was unfamiliar with the dried meat, but she was game. With her first bite she discovered it was as pleasurable to eat as salted wood and wasn't likely to become an acquired taste. Still, her stomach pangs began easing as soon as she swallowed. She tore off another piece and chewed hard.

As she ate Mary wandered around the chamber, taking note of its contents more closely. The blankets where she had been lying were not all Army issue. Among the layers she found a quilt with a complicated double wedding-ring pattern that had been stitched by many busy hands. There were several blankets with satin edging and one cover that was supposed to hold a feather comforter. A second survey of the larder showed it to be a curious mixture of foodstuffs. One of the boxes carried a date that revealed it originated during the Civil War, another appeared to be as recently crated as August. The tin cups looked as if they came from a standard Army mess kit, but the plates were china. Mary recognized Wedgwood and Royal Doulton among the mismatched dinnerware.

The collection of books intrigued Mary. They were a varied lot, and their frontispiece usually bore an inscription. Dumas's *The Count of Monte Cristo* was a gift to someone named Anne from her loving husband Jackson. *A Christmas Carol* was given for "all the Christmases yet to come" and signed Mother and Father. The inscription in Whitman's *Leaves of Grass* had faded after repeated readings. There was no writing to indicate their owner's opinion of Mill's essay *On Liberty* or Darwin's *On the Origin of Species by Means of Natural Selection,* only a number of dog-eared pages and frayed edges to suggest both books had been catalysts for a great deal of contemplation. Slim volumes on mathematics and heavy tomes on agriculture and mining appeared to have been frequently consulted. One book on geology also looked particularly well used.

Mary had all the books piled beside her, ready to be replaced, when she noticed the basket. She picked it up, placed it on her lap, and turned it slowly so she could inspect the work. It was exquisitely made and brightly colored. She couldn't identify the fibers and stems that made each coil, but some had been dyed to weave in bands of red, black, and yellow.

"It's Chiricahua," Ryder said from behind her.

The basket flew out of Mary's hands as she cried out and came up on her knees. Her head twisted around in Ryder's direction. "I should have shot you before," she snapped. "Just because you're aggravating." She reached for the basket and turned to face Ryder, holding it before her like a shield. "Do you have to sneak up on me that way? Can't you . . . can't you *knock?*"

Ryder hadn't thought he was being especially quiet. His steps had seemed to echo in the corridor. "You must have been deep in thought," he said.

She glared. "So it's my fault. How convenient for you."

He stared at her, fascinated. "Why you've got more fangs than a cholla."

"What's that?" she asked suspiciously.

"A desert thorn bush."

"Oh." She was somewhat appeased. "I thought it might be an animal."

"It may as well be, the way it attacks if you're fool enough to brush past it."

Mary's eyes narrowed thoughtfully. "So you're saying I'm a cholla and you're a fool."

Ryder's glance was caught on the shifting flames of color in Mary's hair. He nodded slowly. "I suppose I am," he said. Her unexpected laughter rocked him back on his heels. It was as cleansing as his earlier dip in the well and just as welcome.

She pressed her lips together to stifle her laughter, then used her hand for good measure. Mary caught her breath with some difficulty.

"Don't stop on my account," he said.

His comment had the opposite effect. Mary sobered immediately. "Where have you been?" She set the basket down and began filling it with books.

"I told you I would make a salve."

"You did that already? But where—" She stopped, realizing the truth. "You went out, didn't you?"

He nodded. "It would have been too difficult to take you."

"That didn't stop you from bringing me here. Are you afraid I might learn my way back out?"

"Only that you might gather the false confidence to try."

"You don't think I could do it?"

"I wasn't issuing a challenge," he said quietly.

The wind rushed out of Mary's sails. She bent her head and went back to her task.

"You're welcome to read those if you'd like. There're a few more in the trunk."

"I've already read the nov—" She stopped, knowing she was being churlish. "Thank you," she said. "That would pass the time."

Ryder set the mortar and pestle he was holding beside the makeshift bed. "The salve's in there when you want it," he said. "Use it sparingly. There's enough to last for several days."

Mary nodded. At least there had been no mention that he wanted to apply it himself. She laid the last book in the basket and got to her feet. "Was it still daylight outside?" she asked.

"Sunset."

She'd slept most of the day away, then. "Was it beautiful?"

Ryder had walked over to the cache of foodstuffs and was picking through the cans. He murmured absently in agreement.

Mary sat down in the rocking chair. She raised her legs so that her knees were near her chin and locked her arms around them. "Tell me about it," she said.

Now Ryder glanced in her direction, his dark brows drawn together. He raked back his inky black hair and said slowly, "Red . . . gold . . . threads of copper and orange and bronze."

Mary felt his gray eyes in an odd way, as if they were capable of touching her. "Then it was lovely," she said wistfully.

"Yes." But he hadn't been describing the sunset. Mary's hair was all those colors and a score of shades in between that he had no name for. "Yes," he repeated. "Lovely."

Mary ducked her head and rubbed her nose as he continued to stare at her. When she looked up again he was studying the cans and the moment had passed. "Are we going to eat?" she asked. "I had some jerky, but it wasn't very filling."

"We can't cook," he explained. "There's nowhere to vent the smoke and if we could—"

"It could be seen," she said. "It's all right. I understand. Canned anything is fine with me." Mary waited to see how he would open them. He made it look easy as he took up a finely honed knife from the utensils and pounded it sharply into the tops of the cans. "I suppose there's something to be said for brute strength."

Ryder glanced over his shoulder. "What's that?"

"Nothing."

Shrugging, he began emptying the cans onto two china plates. There was pressed meat, potatoes, stewed tomatoes, and corn. He handed her a plate and a fork, and sat in the wing chair, propping his legs on one rung of the stool. "You're going to be sick of this soon so enjoy it now," he said. "There's plenty to eat but not much variety."

Mary didn't care. She would have eaten most anything he'd placed in front of her. Bowing her head, she said grace softly. When she looked up, Ryder was watching her. She couldn't make out the expression in his eyes, but she refused to let him know his scrutiny bothered her. Indicating the furnishings with a wave of her hand, Mary asked, "How did all of this come to be here?"

The watchfulness of his gaze faded as Ryder tucked into his meal. "I brought it in a little at a time."

"Then you didn't find it here?"

"No."

"So this chamber's a secret even if the cavern isn't."

Now he understood what she was getting at. "That's right. No one else knows about it."

Mary considered that. Her situation didn't have to be hopeless, she thought. Ryder had found a way to this chamber; that meant Jarret had a chance.

He could practically hear her thoughts, her eyes were so expressive. "I didn't find this chamber entirely on my own," he told her. "A prospector showed me the way more than fifteen years ago. Joe Panama hid out here after I helped him escape a Chiricahua raiding party."

She brightened a little, thinking about that prospector.

"He died years ago," Ryder told her flatly.

"Oh," she said softly, disappointed. Jarret's chances suddenly seemed remote. "Then I'm not going anywhere."

"That's right. Not until I say so."

Mary bent her head and continued eating even though she could no longer taste her food. She was silent, thinking. "How long will that be?" she asked finally.

"I don't know."

"What are your intentions?"

"Intentions? What do you mean?"

"Toward me," she said. "Do you intend to kill me?"

Ryder's look was a considering one. "I may," he said deeply. "If you ask another stupid question."

Mary bristled. "It wasn't stupid. How am I supposed to know? You dragged me all over God's creation last night. You wouldn't let me stop to drink or rest. You wouldn't explain—"

His voice was calm. "There was no time," he said. "Resting would have delayed us, and I didn't know if you could have continued. It would have been hard for me, probably impossible for you."

It was his small admission that he had been tired that intrigued Mary. All through the night she had wondered if he were even human. There had never been any indication on the trail that he had suffered as she had from exhaustion and thirst. "So you ignored me until I fainted."

He would always count it as one of the most difficult things he had ever done. All he said was, "Yes."

"Then threw me over my horse like a sack of—"

"Yes." He was unapologetic.

Mary sighed. "You could have left me," she said.

"I could have." Ryder finished the last of his meal. "But you would have helped them find my trail again."

Her denial was emphatic. "I wouldn't have! I never would—"

"Your body would have."

The forest green eyes were wide in her oval face. She couldn't think of anything to say to that.

Ryder leaned forward and took Mary's plate from her nerveless fingers. "I'll put this over here," he said, getting up and pointing toward the larder. "You may want something later."

She couldn't imagine that she would, but she didn't argue. "What happens now?" she asked.

"We wait."

"Hours? Days?"

He shrugged. Ignoring her, he hunkered beside the pool to rinse his plate and utensils.

Frustrated, Mary came to her feet. At her sides, her hands were clenched. Even her toes were curled inside Ryder's thick woolen socks. "That's no answer," she said, her eyes fierce. "When can I expect to see sunshine again? When will I see my mother? My family?"

Ryder paused and glanced over his shoulder. In her cotton shift and his flannel shirt, with her stubborn, angry eyes and clenched fists, Mary was an odd combination of warrior and waif. "Do you want to be reassured with a lie or unsettled with the truth?"

"I don't want to be patronized," she said flatly. "Tell me the truth."

"Then the truth is, I don't know." Ryder returned to his work, dipping the plate in the cold water again, then shaking it off. He was unprepared for the two hands that were placed solidly on his back or the strength behind them as he was pushed forward. Ryder plunged head first into the well of icy water and when he came up, Mary paused long enough at the edge to wipe her hands clean of him before she calmly began walking out of the chamber.

Ryder hauled himself out of the water. He called to her once, but she had already disappeared into the corridor. His clothes dripped water on the stone floor, leaving a trail as he picked up a lantern and left the chamber. She was not in sight when he turned the corner.

There were three immediate passages she could have taken. Without a light Ryder concluded she had to be following the contours of the cool cavern walls. That would have led her to the very first passage.

His approach was far from silent. To Ryder's way of thinking it had all the earmarks of a one-man band. Water was squeezed between his toes and through his socks and boots with every step. It splattered loudly from the tails of his shirt and the ends of his dark, thick hair. A droplet found its way through a seam in the lantern and sizzled when it touched the flame. And for good measure, he sneezed.

Mary had not gone far into the corridor. Ryder raised the lantern when its light caught a glimpse of her cotton shift. She was leaning against the cavern wall, one shoulder pressed to the stone, her back to him.

"Go away," she said. He was close enough that she didn't have to raise her voice. His light stretched past her and cast a shadow where there had only been darkness before.

"Come back with me."

Mary's arms were crossed in front of her, warding off the cold and the abject misery that wanted to be her companion.

She shook her head. "There's nowhere for me to go. I can't see my hand in front of my face without a lantern."

Ryder stepped closer and saw Mary's entire body go rigid. She still refused to turn and look at him. "You don't want to stay here," he said.

One of her hands came up and she quickly dashed a tear from her eye. "You're right. So let me go. Take me out to the mouth of this cavern and let me find my own way back to the fort."

"You'd die out there."

She sniffed and angrily brushed away another tear. "I know," she said impatiently. "And my body would attract vultures and the vultures would attract the searchers and they'd find you because one of my bony fingers would be pointing directly at this cavern."

"Something like that," he said dryly. He raised a hand to place it on her shoulder, but she sensed the movement and flinched, drawing more into herself. He was quiet for several minutes. The only sounds in the corridor were the occasional staccato drip of water from Ryder's clothes and the muffled, throaty sob Mary couldn't suppress. "Let's go," he said finally, quietly. This time she came, turning, not looking at him, her shoulders hunched and head bent. He noticed she made certain she didn't touch him.

"I think I could learn to hate you," she said without inflection.

Ryder let that pass without comment, but his eyes followed her as she stepped around him and preceded him out of the passage.

As soon as they were back in the chamber Mary sat in the rocker and picked up a book. She held it up in front of her face as Ryder stripped out of his sopping wet clothes. She couldn't concentrate on the words in front of her. What she heard was the sound of Ryder rooting through the trunk for dry things to wear. What she saw in her mind's eye was the splendid breadth of his naked shoulders and the smooth line of his back.

Mary looked up when his shadow crossed her light. She lowered the book after he placed his index finger on the edge of the spine and pushed down. He was still naked to the waist. His dark, damp hair was tied back with a leather thong, but tiny beads of water still lay glistening on his shoulders.

There was an odd, unsettling flutter in Mary's stomach. Nonetheless she raised her eyes calmly to his. "Yes?"

"You're wearing the only other clean shirt I have."

She looked down at herself. The shirt was soft and comfortable, and it was warm. She glanced at the clothes on the line. Her habit was only a little less damp than the items Ryder had just added. "May I have a blanket?" she asked, putting aside her book.

When Ryder took one of the woolen blankets off the bed and gave it to her, she shrugged out of the shirt, handed it to him, and pulled the blanket around her shoulders.

"Your habit will be dry tomorrow," he said, putting on the shirt. It was warm from her body and, disconcertingly, held her fragrance. Ryder buttoned it and tucked the tails into his trousers. He watched Mary draw the blanket more closely about her. "Maybe you'll think twice before you toss me in the drink again."

"If all it costs me is a warm shirt, I'll gladly pay the price." She picked up her book, opened it, and effectively shut him out, though he was still blocking her light. Her breathing didn't settle into its normal cadence, however, until he moved out of the way.

Mary had no idea how much time passed. She read two chapters of *An Investigation of the Laws of Thought, on Which Are Founded the Mathematical Theories of Logic and Probability*. It was slow going, but it engaged her mind fully and for a few hours she didn't dwell on her situation. It was a call of nature that finally made her rise from the rocker and stretch.

Ryder was sitting cross-legged on top of the blankets when Mary got to her feet. He put down the gun he was cleaning as she picked up a lantern. "Where are you going?"

"The water closet," she said primly. "That *is* allowed, isn't it?"

"It's allowed." He came to his feet. "With an escort."

"Oh, for God's—" She clamped her teeth tightly and left the remainder of her thoughts unspoken.

Ryder noticed that Mary had no difficulty finding the route back to what she euphemistically called the water closet. Her sense of direction was as good as he feared it might be. He let her take the lantern in with her, but when she returned he took it from her and made her wait in the dark passage until he finished. She was waiting in the exact spot in which he left her when he got back, seemingly paralyzed by the unpenetrable blackness that had surrounded her. She blinked several times with the introduction of his lantern light. The blanket had slipped over her left shoulder. Ryder lifted it to cover her again, then placed his hand at the small of her back and nudged her forward.

Mary sat back in the rocker, but she hadn't had a chance to pick up the book before Ryder was towering over her. She raised her chin defiantly. "What is it now?"

"Give me your hand," he said.

"Why do you—"

"Give me your hand."

"Right or left?" she asked sharply.

He grabbed her wrists and squeezed until her fingers uncurled. Her left hand was empty. In her right one was a small, sharp stone. He picked it out of her palm before her fingers could close over it, held it up to examine it. The sharpest point of it was shiny and warm where it had been rubbed against another stone. Ryder didn't need to return to the passage to know that Mary had used the stone to mark the cavern wall.

He tossed the stone out of the entrance to the chamber. It ricocheted in the corridor before it landed on the floor. "You're determined to give me trouble, aren't you?"

Mary didn't deny it. "Let me go," she said, massaging her

wrists. "Take me to a place where I can be found. I won't tell anyone where you are."

In answer, Ryder pulled a length of rope out of his back pocket. "Right hand," he said.

"What are you—"

He took her right hand and secured the rope around the wrist. Instead of tying her other hand with it, he attached the free end to his own wrist. When Mary jerked against her bonds she immediately tightened the knots. She tried to slip the rope off, but it wouldn't go over the ball of her hand. Her struggle made the blanket fall off her shoulders. She couldn't even reach it without pulling him with her.

Pride made her stop. A physical fight with Ryder wasn't dignified, and more importantly, she had no chance of winning it. "I suppose you think you have a reason for doing this," she said.

"I'm tired," he said. "I want to sleep. And I don't trust you." He bent, picked up the blanket, and gave it to her. "We're going to lie down, then I'm going to get some rest. I don't care if you do or not, but while I'm sleeping you'll stay by my side."

"This is ridiculous," she said, very low. She tried to hold her ground when he moved toward the designated bed, but he dragged her along with little effort, blowing out the lanterns along the way. Only one was left lit and he placed it on the slab of stone just above the blankets before he lay down. Mary was crouched uncomfortably beside him. "I don't want to sleep here."

"Then stay awake," he said. "You can sleep anywhere you want after I've had some rest." Ryder turned on his side. The movement of his arm forced her closer.

Mary was cold. She couldn't even rub her bare arms without disturbing him. "All right," she said with little grace, "but I need a blanket over me. I'm freezing."

Ryder sat up long enough to fix the blankets so some were under them and some could serve as cover. This time when he lay down it was so he could place his arm around Mary's waist.

He felt her stiffen, but she didn't pull away, not even when he fit himself to the contours of her curved body. "Warmer?" he asked.

Mary couldn't find her voice. Aware of him to the point where she could be aware of nothing else, Mary could only nod. Her limbs ached with rigidity, but she couldn't make herself relax, couldn't imagine that she would be able to fall asleep.

"You have a great deal of courage," he said. His voice was thick, husky, just a shade louder than a whisper. His breath was warm, and it touched the back of her neck. "Perhaps too much."

"I don't know what you mean."

"Too much courage can make you foolish. Trying to mark the passage with a stone . . . that was foolish. And earlier . . . with the Henry rifle . . . that was foolish."

"I suppose it seems that way to you."

He wanted to shake her, make her see sense, but he was too tired. Except for the few hours of rest he'd grabbed when they'd first reached the cavern, Ryder had had almost no sleep in more than two days. Waiting for his sentence, then waiting for it to be carried out, had not been the stuff of dreams. "I don't want to hurt you, Mary," he said quietly. "I don't want to be responsible for your getting hurt."

"You're threatening me."

Ryder echoed her earlier words as he closed his eyes. "I suppose it seems that way to you."

Mary woke thirsty. She sat up and scooted forward before she felt the pull of the hateful tether. Ryder was still sleeping and didn't appear to be aware of the tug on the rope they shared. Mary looked at him, her smile scornful. She'd hardly dared moved because he'd made her believe he'd know it right away. The truth was a little bit different than that.

Asleep, he wasn't nearly so intimidating. His strong profile had softened. The lips, slightly parted, and the thick sweep of lashes made him seem young, even vulnerable. His dark hair had dried. An inky strand of it had escaped the thong and lay across his cheek. Mary was tempted to touch it, to push it aside. She resisted.

Instead she bent her head close to her wrist and began working the knots with her teeth. Not wanting to take unnecessary chances, she was careful not to disturb Ryder by pulling too hard on the rope. The knots were tight, but Mary was able to work them loose gradually. Eventually the loop around her wrist was large enough for her to slip her hand through.

She rubbed her wrist where the rope had burned her skin, then slid to the edge of the stone loft and eased herself down soundlessly. The bucket of fresh drinking water was near all the other foodstuffs. She dipped the ladle and drank from it. The water was cool and refreshing. A few droplets slipped past her lips to her chin. She wiped them away with the back of her hand.

Her eyes fell on Ryder's saddlebags. Putting down the ladle, she reached for them. She sifted through the contents. Liniment. A small pouch of tobacco. A deck of playing cards. Peppermint sticks. A sewing kit. Comb. Brush. A flask of alcohol. Three carefully folded bandanas. Mary took everything out and began packing the bags with jerky. She filled his canteen with water and set a sack of dried navy beans beside it.

After taking off the thick woolen socks she was wearing, she pulled on her stockings, then her shoes. When she took clothing from the line, it wasn't her habit she removed but Ryder's damp shirt and pants. They were ridiculously large for her slender frame, so Mary determinedly rolled up the sleeves and the bottoms of the trousers. She knotted two of Ryder's bandanas together to make a belt for herself. The third bandana she wrapped around her head.

Mary then checked the lanterns, taking oil from several of them to fill one completely. She lighted it and immediately extinguished the lantern that Ryder had left burning. Hefting the saddlebags over her shoulder and carrying the lantern and the sack of navy beans, Mary walked boldly out of the chamber, plunging it into darkness.

* * *

Ryder couldn't see anything when he opened his eyes. The blackness of the chamber was total. Without light there was no chance that his eyes could adjust; there was nothing to reflect color or shape. He sat up and felt the blankets around him. Shaking his head to clear it, he swore softly when he realized Mary was gone. There was nothing attached to the rope. It dangled uselessly from his wrist.

Ryder tore it off and tossed it aside. He'd been more tired than he knew. Mary shouldn't have been able to get away from him, yet she had. He was soft, he thought. Months of confinement in the stockade had dulled his senses, and he hadn't counted on Mary's single-minded desire to escape him. At best he had considered her anger would become resignation. He wondered what prompted her to take so many risks. Coming to his feet, he decided it was something to think about.

Feeling around in the dark, Ryder finally put his hands on one of the lanterns. It took him long minutes to find the supplies and even longer to find matches. The sudden flare of light almost blinded him. There was enough oil left in the lantern to give him thirty minutes. To be safe he added more from a container hidden among the supplies.

Barefoot, carrying only the lantern, Ryder left the chamber in search of Mary. He didn't bother with any of the immediate side passages. He was confident she could get as far as the water closet without any difficulty. How she would go on from there, he wasn't as certain. She would have had to make a choice in another thirty yards and when Ryder came to the juncture he paused, looking for signs.

He lowered the lantern when something near the edge of the passage caught his eye. Ryder hunkered down and ran his fingers along the oddly shaped pebbles that were clustered together. They were all small, smooth, and similarly contoured. He picked one up and rolled it back and forth between his fingers.

"I'll be damned," he said softly. "Beans."

It was easy after that. Mary's trail was clearly marked. Ryder knew she had done it so she could retrace her own steps if necessary. It was good thinking except for the fact that she was being followed. He collected the beans as he went, filling his pockets.

He was amazed at the number of times she chose the right route. Ryder's map was in his head and in the nearly imperceptible markings on the stone walls. He had also been through the corridors hundreds of times over the years and was familiar with the pattern of twists and turns. Mary, on the other hand, was just plain lucky.

Following at a safe distance, Ryder waited for her luck to run out. When he saw the choice she had made after the long serpentine passage, he knew it had finally happened. He picked up the mound of navy beans at the entrance and went inside. The tunnel narrowed and angled upward. It was not dissimilar to the passage that ran parallel to it, but it would end abruptly in a spacious chamber with a single inaccessible exit that opened fifty feet overhead. The diameter of the opening was less than twelve inches. On the surface it appeared as a shadow among some rocks. From inside the chamber it seemed no larger than a saucer in the daylight; at night it was all but invisible.

Mary was moving carefully among the rocks in the chamber, looking for a way out, when Ryder appeared at the entrance. He glanced at the vaulted ceiling. It was night now. A lone star pinpointed the opening.

"Mary." He said her name softly, but it was enough. He saw her stiffen then stop in her tracks. "Come here."

She turned slowly and shook her head.

"There's no way out."

Even though his voice was a mere whisper she could hear him clearly. She opened her mouth to tell him he could go to hell.

Ryder placed a finger on his lips then pointed upward.

Mary glanced overhead and her breath caught in her throat. The roof of the chamber was alive with movement. Her knees threatened to give way as she realized what she was seeing.

Bats. Hundreds of them. Mary dropped the sack of beans and

raised her hand to stifle a scream. She needn't have bothered.
The worn, threadbare sack broke and the beans tumbled out,
rolling along the rocks with the clatter of spilled coins in a
banker's vault. There was a flurry of movement and a high-
pitched squealing like nothing Mary had ever heard. Something
fluttered in front of her face and then again at the periphery of
her vision. She dropped to her knees as the bats soared and
dove and whistled around her head.

Some bats took flight through the opening in the chamber.
Dozens more flew past Ryder's head and out the passage. Ryder
crouched, shielding his face and hair, then went for Mary. She
was frightened but uninjured. He picked up her lantern, protected
her with his body, and herded her out of the chamber. A frenzied
tornado of bats swirled around them. They dipped and rushed.
Their thin wings beat the air frantically. One flew past Mary's
mouth. She cried out and held onto Ryder tightly. He half
dragged, half carried her to the entrance, where he picked up the
second lantern and led her quickly through the tunnel.

Mary had no opportunity to catch her breath or whisper her
thanks. Ryder's features bore no expression. Only his gray eyes
were stormy as he gripped her hand and led her swiftly through
the passages back to their chamber. Once there he practically
flung her inside.

Mary stared at him, waiting for the force of his anger, steeling
herself to give as good as she got.

He set the lanterns down, then turned to Mary. He studied
her raised chin, the fiercely defiant eyes. She had pulled the
bandana off her head and was twisting it between her hands. It
was the only sign that she had more fright in her than fight. He
wondered what she expected from him.

He spoke calmly, deliberately. "Take off your clothes."

Seven

Though he had said them quietly, Ryder's words seemed to echo in the chamber. *Take off your clothes . . . your clothes . . . your clothes . . .* Mary stared at him, not moving.

Ryder took a step toward her. There was nothing menacing or threatening in his approach, yet it prompted Mary to throw out a question as her first defense.

"Why?" she demanded.

His approach halted. He stared at her for a long moment. Her complexion was markedly paler now, and her hands had stopped twisting the bandana. Tension kept her body rigid and rooted to her spot. "I believe I've already told you that you don't have to understand my orders to obey them."

Mary sucked in a breath as if she'd been slapped. The first wave of anger had to pass before she trusted herself to speak. "There's something you should understand about me, Mr. McKay," she said quietly. "I obey no man unquestioningly. Blind obedience is for my God alone."

Ryder felt heat rush into his face as Mary's green eyes narrowed on him coldly.

Mary was satisfied with his reaction. "Now tell me why I should take off my clothes."

He held up a hand and began ticking off the reasons. "They're damp. They're mine. They don't fit you. They look ridiculous."

Mary stared at his hand. Four fingers had already come up and now the thumb was slowly being raised. "And?" she asked, her eyes going from his hand to his face.

"And I want you naked."

She blinked. Astonishment silenced her.

"You wanted to know," he said simply. As Ryder took another step toward her, Mary's hands flew to the first button of her shirt. He was careful not to smile as he walked past her.

Mary watched Ryder go to the clothesline and begin removing her habit and shift. She expected him to toss the items in her direction, even held out her hand to catch them.

Out of the corner of his eye Ryder saw the movement. He turned, his arms full, and looked at her outstretched hand questioningly. "Yes?"

Confusion showed in Mary's drawn brows. "Aren't you going to give me those?" she asked.

Ryder raised one thumb and wiggled it. "Reason number five. I want you naked."

She gaped at him.

Ignoring her, Ryder opened the trunk and tossed in her habit and shift. He plucked the towels off the line, folded them, and laid them on top. He found the valise, removed the clothes he had worn in the stockade, and added them to the items in the trunk. Glancing around the chamber, he saw a few more items that Mary might make use of and put them away as well. When he had gathered everything he closed the lid and sat on it. He looked in Mary's direction, his arms folded in front of him, his expression expectant. Her hand was still closed over the uppermost button of her shirt, and there was a dazed look to her luminous green eyes.

"Mary," he said calmly. "I want you to remove your clothes."

What was it, she wondered, about the way he said her name that was so compelling? She actually had to think about what he was asking before she could respond. "You have to give me something," she said. "Let me wear the shirt."

He shook his head. "It's still damp. I don't need you getting sick on me."

"My shift."

"No."

Mary closed her eyes for a moment. "A blanket at least," she said. "Please, Ryder."

He pretended to think it over. He had always intended to give her one, but he needed her cowed first. Ryder didn't like himself much for doing this, but he didn't regret it either. "A blanket," he said, as if granting a great boon. "Now get undressed."

Mary nodded slowly. She had undone two buttons and the bandana belt around her waist when Ryder interrupted.

"Are you doing this show for my benefit?" he asked.

She frowned. "What do you mean?"

"I mean, this isn't a Chicago stage. Throw a blanket over the line and get undressed behind it." His comments had the desired effect. He watched Mary flush to the roots of her fiery hair, confused, off balance, and embarrassed. "Go on," he said. He left the trunk, picked up a blanket from the bed and tossed it to her. "Use this."

Mary's hands tightened around the blanket. She glared at him, but kept her jaw clamped and her thoughts mostly to herself. He was welcome to interpret the expression on her face in any way he wanted.

Ryder sat in the wing chair, his long legs stretched casually in front of him, while Mary fixed the blanket over the line. Her head was visible to him as were her legs from knee to ankle, but Ryder didn't bother looking in her direction. Instead he leaned his head back and closed his eyes.

As she undressed Mary looked over the rim of the sagging line at Ryder. He wasn't gloating. There was no smirk to wipe off his face, no gleam to cast out of his eyes. He merely looked bone weary. It moved her in a way that was as unexpected as it was unwelcome. Compassion for her captor made no sense, yet it was the emotion that tugged at her thoughts, clouding them.

"I'm finished," she said.

Ryder opened his eyes and raised his head slowly. Sleep had been a very near companion, but he was alert now, watchful. Mary was standing in front of him, wearing the blanket that had been slung over the line and carrying an armload of his clothes. Ryder stood and took them from her. "Go lie down," he said. "I'll join you in a moment."

She sat on the edge of the stone bed, her feet dangling over the side while Ryder put the clothes away. There was no key to lock the trunk, but he effectively sealed it by placing the case of Henry rifles on top. Mary saw the effort he exerted to lift the case and knew she could never remove it, at least not quietly and quickly.

Ryder blew out one of the two lighted lanterns and carried the other to their bed. "I said lie down."

Mary eased herself back on the blankets, her body stiff. "Are you going to tie me again?" she whispered.

"It didn't work the first time." He put the lantern beside where he would lie and stretched out himself. "That's why you don't have any clothes now." Turning on his side, he drew Mary close to him and slipped an arm across her waist. He could feel her breathing quicken as her body was brought flush to his. When his hushed voice came again it was close to her ear. "If you try to escape again I won't even give you a blanket."

"If you catch me."

He wouldn't permit her small show of bravado. "I'll catch you, Mary," he said. "I'll always catch you."

She fell asleep wondering why she heard those words more as a promise than threat.

He let her have her clothes when he woke. It was a pattern that was repeated over days that were maddening in their sameness. There was neither morning nor night in the chamber. They slept when they were tired and rose when they were rested. Their inner clocks didn't always work in concert, but Mary was forced to follow Ryder. Anytime he was ready to sleep she was made to undress and lie beside him. Her clothes were placed out of her reach in the trunk, and he always slipped one arm around her waist before he closed his eyes.

She told herself she should fight against sleep on the principle of having no choice as to when or how she took it. She never did though. When his arm stole around her middle she accepted it, drew comfort from it, and, in her secret heart, began to look forward to it.

During what passed for their days Mary read. Sometimes Ryder would disappear for hours, but she never tried to follow him. There was only one way out of the cavern from their chamber so their paths would have crossed. She envied him for being able to take his fill of sunshine and starlight, but she never asked to accompany him. She couldn't bring herself to make the request and have it refused.

Mary suspected that Ryder's reasons for leaving the cavern had to do with watching for search parties and gauging the safety of their position, but he never volunteered any information and it was again a matter of pride to her to remain silent on that. He always returned with something for her. The gifts were usually laid in her lap like an offering. She would lower her book and try not to look too pleased, but she was largely unsuccessful. He brought her a handful of nuts one time, small sweet berries at another. On a third occasion he gave her a rough piece of turquoise which he later polished into a smooth stone half the size of her thumbnail. When she thought herself unobserved Mary would take the stone out and study it, not certain what to make of Ryder's odd thoughtfulness.

He let her explore some of the deeper recesses of the cavern with him. Routes that led in the opposite direction from the entrance were open to her as long as he was with her. She knelt at the source of the spring that supplied their chamber's cold water and drank from her cupped hands. He showed her another chamber where at the very center her own whispered voice would echo hollowly in her ears. Mary would hike up her skirts and clamber over rocks and tenuous stone bridges while Ryder followed with a raised lantern.

It was an unusual prison, she thought. Spacious beyond belief, yet more confining than the convent. Sometimes when she first woke it was difficult to breathe.

For other reasons she had that sensation now. The weight of Ryder's arm pressed the rough blanket to her skin. He drew her closer as he prepared to sleep.

"What is it?" he asked.

She was not prepared for the question. By some mutual, though unspoken, agreement, they rarely exchanged words once they were sharing the bed. It seemed that speech was too intimate, too penetrating and personal. It was better to save it for the waking hours when they had all their faculties and defenses. Mary continued to stare at the play of shadows on the chamber wall and didn't answer.

She wasn't relaxing beside him as she usually did. Ryder raised himself on one elbow and looked down at her. She was staring, dry-eyed and vaguely anxious, at the far wall. "Your heart's racing like a rabbit's," he said.

"Give me a moment," she said quietly. "I'll be all right."

Ryder lifted the arm that was around her waist. The touch of his fingers on her cheek, then her forehead, was light and tentative. Her skin warmed under his fingertips.

He shouldn't touch me, she thought. It isn't fair.

She spoke because words right now would be less of an invasion than his touch. "How long have we been here?" she asked.

Ryder's fingers slipped away from Mary's face. They dragged lightly through her silky hair before his palm came to rest on the curve of her hip.

Mary's breath caught in her throat, but she didn't ask him to remove his hand. For his part he didn't seem to be aware of its position; for Mary's, she could be aware of nothing else. "How long?" she asked again.

"Twelve days," Ryder said.

"So long," she said more to herself than to him. Mary sighed. "Christmas came and went. Did you know that?"

He had known. He had brought her the turquoise. "I didn't realize."

She merely shrugged as if it weren't important, but tears gathered in her eyes.

"Mary?"

She wished he wouldn't say her name. It always seemed to prompt the response he wanted even when she wanted a different one. "It isn't fair," she said finally. "It isn't fair that my family doesn't know I'm safe, that they spent Christmas wondering about me, worrying. Isn't there some way you could let them—"

"No," he said. "There's no way."

"And the new year. We'll spend it here and they won't have any idea that I'm not injured . . . not dead."

"No." Ryder removed his hand from her hip and let his arm fall around her waist. "But you're right. It's not fair."

She hadn't expected that. His admission didn't change anything, not really. The fact that it made her feel better was troubling in its own right. "You could let me go," she said.

He didn't bother responding to that. "Go to sleep." Ryder stretched his other arm out above his head and lay down.

"I want to see the sun again," she said softly.

Ryder didn't answer, but he was awake a lot longer than Mary, thinking about it.

"Do you want to come with me?" Ryder paused in the stone archway as he spoke. He had not planned to ask. It was not like him, but the words were simply there, on the tip of his tongue, and then they were given sound. He could not call them back. He only hoped she had not heard him.

Mary lowered her book. Ryder was not even looking at her, and she suspected the invitation was reluctantly offered and already regretted. That didn't bother her. She didn't ask him to repeat himself or wonder aloud if he was serious. Dropping her book into the basket, Mary came to her feet. "Yes," she said. "I'd like that."

By the time she reached the exit, Ryder was already striding down the corridor. Lantern light made a slow sweep of the walls as the lamp swung in his hand. Mary stayed close enough to follow the light, but didn't try to come abreast of him. He was making it patently obvious that he didn't want the company.

She was so intent on following that light that when Ryder stopped she almost ran into his back. Glancing around, she saw they hadn't come very far. The corridor forked and to the right was the chamber used for nature's calls. Mary's disappointment was deep. She was certain he had intended something else when he'd made his offer. She had expected a trip to the outside, not a trip to the privy.

Ryder placed the lantern on the ground and turned to Mary. "You'll have to wear this," he said.

She looked at him in confusion until he raised one of his bandanas in front of her eyes. "A blindfold?" she asked.

He nodded. "Do you agree?"

"Yes," she said quickly. "Oh, yes."

The alacrity of her reply, the eagerness in her voice, struck Ryder like a physical blow. Her face was raised to him, and her eyes were already closed in a gesture of offering. Long lashes fanned the curves of her lids. Her mouth was set in a faint smile, anticipation warring with impatience. She had the ripe, expectant expression of a woman inviting a kiss, not a blindfold.

Ryder's head bent.

Mary opened her eyes.

They stared, hardly breathing. Time passed. An eternity, a few heartbeats. It was all the same.

Ryder drew back first. Mary swayed slightly, her slender body pulled forward by his withdrawal. He steadied her with firm hands; then he put the blindfold around her eyes, picked up the lantern, and took her hand. "This way," he said.

His voice was a little rough, a little husky, and it vibrated through Mary, unsettling but not unpleasant. She gripped Ryder's hand. "You won't go too fast?" she asked.

"No, Mary. Not too fast."

* * *

At the entrance to the cavern Ryder finally let Mary remove the blindfold. She tore it off quickly, squinting as she anticipated the sunlight that would shower her face. Her eyes widened slowly, and she was horrified by the depth of her disappointment.

"It's night," she said. And not just any night, she thought, but one so thick with clouds that starlight and moonshine couldn't penetrate.

Ryder tucked one end of the bandana into his waistband, then moved to stand behind Mary. He nudged her closer to the lip of the cavern, resting his hands on her upper arms. "Give it time," he said quietly. "Night doesn't last forever." When she nodded he could feel strands of her silky hair brush his chin. If they had been intimate he would have kissed the crown of her head then or lowered his mouth to her ear. His eyes fell instead to the habit's collar which framed her slender neck and the black fabric that shrouded her shoulders.

A gentle breeze swept the mouth of the cavern and lifted the fragrance of her hair to his nostrils. Ryder breathed deeply. She never wore the veil and wimple anymore; she hadn't since the day they'd arrived at the cavern. He'd never wondered about it. Now, with the subtle fragrance of Mary's soft hair filling his senses he had cause.

"You don't wear your veil," he said.

In an immediate, self-conscious gesture, Mary's hand went to her hair. She tugged at the curl near her temple and tucked it behind her ear.

Ryder's hand closed over hers and drew it away. He let her hand fall, then again placed his own on her upper arm. "There's nothing wrong with your hair." *Quite the opposite.* "I just wondered about the veil."

She shrugged. "It seemed too much," she said vaguely. His palms were warm on her arms, and where her back touched his chest she could feel his heat. Mary crossed her arms in front of her as another breeze eddied through the entrance, whistling in the chamber behind her and raising a soft sighing sound from the pine trees ahead.

"You're cold," said Ryder.

"A little."

He rubbed her arms lightly. "I should have brought a blanket."

"No, it's all right." She turned her head to the side, raising it slightly to see him better. "This is enough," she said. "To smell the pines . . . the fresh air . . . even if there's no—" Mary broke off as a crescent of light appeared on the horizon. Almost immediately there were bands of mauve and deep lilac running along the underbelly of the clouds. The vision blurred as tears washed Mary's eyes.

Sunshine scattered its bright light across the plateaus and mountain peaks and carved out an arc that crossed the mouth of the cavern. Mary and Ryder stood in the center of it. Her solemn face was raised in greeting, in thankfulness. He was watching her.

Ryder handed Mary the bandana. She stared at it, stricken. "Already?" she asked hoarsely. "Can't we stay—"

"For your tears," he said. "We can stay."

Mary gave him a discomfited, watery smile but her eyes radiated her pleasure. "Thank you."

Ryder took his bandana back and wiped her tears himself. The backs of his fingers brushed her cheek when his hand fell away. He turned her around to face the sun before her pleasure prompted promises from him that he shouldn't make and couldn't keep.

The clouds lifted, spread, and claimed the sky like a sheer white shroud floating in a cerulean sea. The first rays of heat had just radiated from the ground outside the cavern when Ryder touched Mary's shoulder lightly and said it was time to go. She nodded in understanding, but she didn't move and Ryder didn't force the issue.

"The Apache call this time of year ghost face," he told her.

"Ghost face," she repeated softly. It fit. Sunshine was falling on a mostly barren land. Evergreens brought color to the landscape, but the shrubs were bare and the low vegetation was brown and scrubby. "That's a proper name for winter in this part of the country."

"Not winter exactly. The Apache divide the year into six seasons, not four. We've just finished earth-is-reddish-brown."

"Autumn," she said.

"Late fall," he corrected her. "When your survival depends on the availability of wild plants you're particular about naming your seasons."

"And spring?"

"Little eagles is March and April; many leaves is May and June."

"How do you say those names in the Apache tongue?" she asked.

Ryder told her.

Mary listened to the unfamiliar language, trying to catch its cadence and intonation. "What do they call summer?"

"Large leaves." He gave her the Apache word and smiled at her attempt to repeat it. "Early fall is the season of large fruit. The Apache reckon a month as a moon and a year as one harvest. There are thirteen moons to one harvest and six seasons."

"How is it that you know so much, know the language, yet aren't one of them?"

Ryder's long fingers raked his dark hair. He looked over the top of Mary's head at the vastness of the land beyond the cavern's mouth. "I never said I wasn't one of them," he said finally.

Mary turned, frowning. "But you said—"

"I said I wasn't Apache, not by blood or birth." His pale gray eyes watched her carefully, gauging her reaction. "I'm Chiricahua," he said, "by choice."

The subject had been closed and remained so. Dozens of questions had come to Mary's mind and all of them were unasked. Ryder had placed the blindfold around her eyes and led her back to the chamber, his manner less solicitous than it had been on the outgoing journey, his tone more brusque. Mary did not know what she had done to elicit this response, yet it was clear to her that Ryder thought she had done something. She wondered about it throughout the day, but any overture she made was summarily rebuffed.

Mary couldn't know that it was merely her acceptance of Ryder's disclosure that had brought about the change. Confusion warred with the mask of calm indifference he usually wore like a mantle. He had expected distaste, even shock. It wasn't an unfamiliar response to his words, and he knew how to deal with it. If she had been fascinated as someone of Anna Leigh Hamilton's ilk might have been, he'd have known how to brush her aside. Mary wasn't even accusing. His admission could have prompted her to rethink her position on the Colter Canyon raid, could have swayed her opinion of his guilt or innocence.

Instead she hadn't judged him. Her clear, intelligent eyes were curious, not condemning; and her lovely face held the placid purity of an angel's.

In spite of her habit, Mary Francis Dennehy was a very dangerous woman.

That night when Ryder lay down beside her he didn't put his arm around her. Mary missed it immediately, missed the weight and security, the way he bound her to him with the proprietary embrace. She told herself she shouldn't be so aware of him, that she shouldn't listen for the sounds of his even breathing or the hushed words that sometimes escaped his lips as he slept. She shouldn't care if he slept or not, shouldn't concern herself with his thoughts or his displeasure, shouldn't wonder if he didn't trust himself to touch her or if he just didn't want to.

Mary turned on her side to face him. His eyes were closed and his cheek rested on an outstretched arm. The lantern had been turned back so that only a thin layer of light marked his profile. His lashes and brows were every bit as dark as his hair which was pulled back in a leather thong. His features were strong, almost predatory, and the illusion of sleep softened them only by the narrowest margin. Months in the stockade and almost two weeks in the cavern had leached color from his skin. Even so, he was still darker than she, and when he was able to bathe in sunshine again he would be as bronze as he had been on the occasion of their first meeting.

"I know you're not sleeping," she said. When he didn't open his eyes she went on. "I've been lying beside you these past thirteen nights. I think I know when you're sleeping."

His pale gray eyes opened, their expression steady yet watchful. "I'd think you'd know when I want to sleep."

"I do," she said. "And right now you only want to ignore me. Some people might take the hint."

Ryder's sigh was telling. "Obviously you're not one of them," he said dryly.

"Obviously not." She hesitated. Now that she had his attention she wasn't certain what she wanted to do with it. "I don't know why you're angry with me," she said at last. "I don't know what I've done."

"I'm not angry with you."

Mary studied his face, the enigmatic gray eyes, the impenetrable calm he wore like armor. She had penetrated it at least once, she thought, no matter that he had drawn it on again. "But you're angry," she said, then reconsidered. "At least you were."

"So it had to be about you."

He made her sound very self-centered, and that didn't set well with Mary. "Doesn't it?" she asked.

Ryder raised himself on one elbow. "There are two of us here. It could be about me. Don't you ever get angry with yourself?"

"Well, yes, but—"

He leaned forward, placed a finger on her lips and stopped her objection. "Enough. Go to sleep."

Mary waited for him to remove his finger. "I can't."

"Can't. Or won't?"

"I say what I mean," she said tartly. "I can't and neither can you." She didn't tell him why. Mary simply turned over, her back to him again, and reached behind her for his arm. She brought it across her waist then adjusted her position in a way that had become familiar to her over the last thirteen days.

"Mary." He said her name like a warning.

"It's all right," she said. "We both can sleep now."

Fifteen minutes later, when Mary was breathing quietly and evenly, Ryder realized she was half right.

"What do you mean you're not going to wear it?" Ryder asked. He was holding her habit out to her, but she continued to let it dangle at the end of his hand.

"Just what I said." Mary's voice was flat, stubborn. "There's nothing wrong with your hearing."

"Well, you can't go around all day in that blanket." By his count she had adjusted it four times across her breasts, and it was in danger of slipping again. They had been awake less than an hour. One misstep on the trailing hem and she was likely to lose the entire thing.

"Why can't I?" she demanded. "You think it's good enough for me to sleep in."

"It's supposed to deter you from sneaking out while I'm sleeping."

"Maybe that was your original aim, but I don't think it's true any longer."

"Meaning?"

"Meaning I think you really do want me naked."

Ryder stared at her. Her bold words were at odds with her flushed face, a flush, he could see now, that started just below the edge of the blanket cutting across her breasts. "I'm trying to give you your clothes," he said. "So that argument doesn't—"

Mary stamped her foot. Her toes caught the hem of the blanket and it was tugged lower. She managed to catch it before the tips of her breasts were exposed, but it was a narrow save. Though her flush deepened, she held her ground. "I'm tired of suffering alone, Ryder McKay."

He regarded her curiously, his head tilted to one side. Still holding the habit, he sat down slowly on the trunk lid. "Perhaps you'd better explain. I wasn't aware you were suffering."

Some of Mary's bravado faded at his calm request for an explanation. Was the man as stoic as he would have her believe? Or merely bluffing? Hands down Mary Francis was the best poker player in her family and her edge had always been the serenity of her expression. Now, watching Ryder McKay's carefully guarded features, Mary considered she might finally have met her match. And wasn't that just the point?

"Perhaps suffering is overstating it a bit," she admitted slowly. She bit her lower lip, thinking. "Uncomfortable would be more accurate. It isn't right that I'm the only one who has to be uncomfortable with this arrangement."

Ryder glanced around. "Not what you're used to certainly, but it's—"

He was deliberately misunderstanding her. "That's not what I'm talking about," she said. "I'm talking about sleeping next to you, your arm around me, your lips against my hair, your—"

"Mary." The caution was back in his voice.

She ignored it. "And none of it seeming to matter to you while it cannot help but unsettle me." She pointed to the habit he still held. "Do you think that makes me less of a woman, that somehow I have no woman's needs or desires? Do you think you can touch me with no consequence to my mind or my body?" Mary saw that she had engaged his complete attention. "And you," she added, scoffing, "now, you hide behind it, thinking yourself quite safe because there will be no response from me. You believe nothing can come of it so you find it all very easy to torment me. Well, I'm not going to make this easy for you. I'm not wearing that habit any longer."

Ryder's gaze dropped from Mary's face to the habit. He stared at it, thinking about her last words, wondering that derision and triumph both edged her tone. He got to his feet and came to stand in front of her. He held the habit out to her again. "Last night it was you who forced closeness on us," he reminded her.

"Take this. I wouldn't have you break your vows on my account."

"You think too highly of yourself," Mary said. He understood little about her vows and nothing about her. She took the habit and promptly tossed it aside. "You don't mean so much to me. It's not my heart you've engaged." Her green eyes flashed, and her stance was challenging. She could hardly speak any plainer.

Ryder's hand went to the bridge of his nose. He closed his eyes a moment as he massaged away the beginning of a headache and tried to remember how the argument had begun. He could hear her saying "I won't wear it" when he handed her the habit. Why hadn't he said, Suit yourself? Why had he let her draw him in?

All Ryder had to do was open his eyes. The answer was there in the bare curve of her shoulder, in the length of calf opened by a split in the blanket, and in the eyes that seared him with their brilliance. The habit protected her. She was right about that. It protected her from him, and it protected her from herself.

"Why are you telling me this?" he asked quietly.

A strand of red-gold hair had fallen across Mary's cheek. She brushed it back impatiently. "Because you can no longer depend on me to be the conscience for both of us." She tugged at the blanket again, raising it a notch and trying to secure it better; then she turned her attention back to him. "I just thought you should know."

"I wasn't aware I had asked you to be my conscience."

"You didn't." She pointed to the discarded habit. "You expected that to stand for something. It doesn't. Not anymore."

Ryder glanced at the habit, then back at Mary, his dark brows drawn. "What do you mean?"

Mary raised her chin and faced him squarely. Against her will she felt her breathing quicken. "I left the order in September," she said. "I'm no longer a nun. I haven't been one for months."

The silence was powerful. For long moments Ryder only stared at her. The word "liar" lay on the tip of his tongue, but he didn't like the taste of it. As far as he could see there was nothing for her to gain by lying to him and perhaps a great deal to lose. "You deceived me," he said deeply.

She tried to shrug it off, but her cheeks were warmer than they had been a moment ago.

"For the second time," he added.

Now Mary's eyes dropped away. "I remember," she said.

"Did you think I wouldn't mention it?" he asked. "You took some pleasure in pretending to be something other than you were the first time we met."

"I took some pleasure in being mistaken for being me," she corrected softly. Mary glanced at him. "I don't expect you to understand, but it's the truth." Honesty compelled her to add, "And yes, I did enjoy your discomfort when you found out what I was."

Ryder remembered that quite clearly. If he closed his eyes he could see her sitting on the warm rock by the watering hole, clutching her knees to her chest, her posture protective but her smile completely smug. Uncertain of his reaction, she was not looking quite so confident now. Her bright eyes were faintly anxious, and there was no smile. Only the way her arms were crossed in front of her was familiar.

"Find something to wear," he said finally. "I don't care what." He turned, picked up a lantern, and left the chamber.

Mary stared after him, unable to call him back, uncertain if she wanted to. When his light vanished in the corridor, Mary bent slowly and picked up her habit. She folded it carefully and placed it in the trunk. Her clothing options were limited. She had the cotton shift and undergarments she had worn beneath her habit and she had his extra shirts and pants. Mary slipped the shift over her head and pulled on the drawers. She used one of Ryder's heavier shirts as a jacket, rolling up the sleeves until the cuffs rested partway between her wrist and elbow. Her stockings and shoes were not as warm on her feet as Ryder's socks, but Mary decided the less she wore of his, the better. His curt order that she should get dressed hadn't precisely been an invitation to share his belongings.

Mary shook out the blanket she had worn and laid it over the other blankets on the bed. She smoothed the edges and pressed out the wrinkles with her hand. She wondered if he would make her wear it when they slept again. Her hand trembled slightly. Perhaps this would be the night he would tell her to sleep in nothing at all.

Mary yawned widely. Belatedly she raised her hand to cover her mouth. The book she had been pretending to read slipped from her other hand and fell closed in her lap.

"Perhaps you should lie down," Ryder said. He was sitting cross-legged on the floor of the chamber, several maps from the trunk unrolled in front of him. He hadn't bothered looking up.

"Aren't you tired?" she asked. It was impossible to know the passing of time with any certainty, but Mary suspected it was already very late in a day that had been interminably long. Ryder had stayed away for most of it, and though Mary didn't know what business he had had outside the cavern, she had felt as if she were being punished. She was tempted to say as much when he finally returned, but nothing in his manner invited conversation or comment. He had eaten his meal in silence. Afterward he had knelt in front of the trunk, emptying it of everything until he could lift the false bottom and retrieve the maps. He hadn't even glanced in Mary's direction to see if she was interested or irritated by the trunk's hidden treasure. It was as if she had ceased to exist in any way that was important to him.

It didn't make sense.

Mary dropped her book back in the basket and stifled another yawn. She stood, her fingers and toes curling as she tried to stretch without bringing attention to herself. She was careful not to disturb Ryder's maps as she stepped around them, but the hem of her shift slid across his knee when she passed. The tug on her shift stopped her in her tracks. She turned and looked down. Ryder was holding a handful of her shift in his fist.

"Yes?" she asked. The contrast of his skin against the white fabric, the intensity of his grip, held her focus. Suddenly Mary found it difficult to draw a breath. He didn't say anything but the pull on her was inexorable, as real as if his hand had twisted in her shift and yanked her down. She felt her knees give way and then she was sitting beside him. His gaze shifted from his hand to her face, and the cool gray eyes studied her with a predator's awareness. Mary held herself very still. Even when his hand released her shift, she felt very much his captive.

"I'm not tired," he said lowly.

"Oh." Mary had forgotten that she'd asked.

"I wanted to be." His hand was raised, and it now rested on the curve of her neck. When his thumb made a slow pass across her skin, her pulse jumped beneath it. "Why did you tell me, Mary?"

She swallowed. His fingers lifted and drifted across her cheek. He touched her ear and tested the texture of her hair at her temple.

"Is this what you wanted?" When she didn't say anything, his hand closed over the back of her neck and he drew her closer. "Or this?" His head bent and his mouth touched hers, lightly at first, a mere whisper of warmth against her lips. "This, then." The pressure this time was more deliberate. His hand tightened, held her steady, and his mouth closed over hers. He felt her try to draw in a breath, but it was his air she drank. Her lips were soft, the space between them narrow. He widened it with his tongue, the touch tentative, a mere taste. The sound she made was small, almost a whimper. Ryder did not mistake her response for arousal alone. He could sense her fear.

Instead of withdrawing, he deepened the kiss. His fingers wound around her hair and kept her close while his tongue explored the sweet recesses of her mouth. He leaned his weight into her gradually so that she was eased to the cool stone floor with hardly any awareness of how she had gotten there. His body unfolded beside her, stretching until one of his legs had captured hers. It was only then that he raised his mouth. The centers of her eyes were dark and vaguely unfocused. Her lips were parted and faintly swollen, richer in color than they had been before the kiss.

"My God," he said huskily. "You've never even been kissed before."

Mary was surprised by her own indignation. "Yes, I have," she said a little sharply.

"Oh?" He kissed the corner of her mouth, nibbled along the length of it. Her lips parted again, and he teased her with his tongue before he asked, "Who?"

"Jordan Reilly."

Her answer had come too quickly to be a lie, yet Ryder suspected there was something she wasn't sharing. He lowered his head and kissed her hard, wringing an arching response from her. Her breathing was quick and shallow when he drew back, and of their own accord, her hands had come to rest lightly on his shoulders.

"He was eight," she admitted after a moment. "I was only—"

She never finished. Ryder's mouth slanted across hers and Mary felt his urgency whip through her, lashing her with his heat and hunger. There was anger as well, and it was less easy to understand. Her fingers tightened on his shoulders. The weight of his body against her was unfamiliar, but she accepted it. Her arms eased around him and her fingers threaded in his thick, inky hair.

Ryder broke off suddenly. He pulled away from Mary's grasp and sat up. "You'd let me, wouldn't you?" he said harshly.

Mary sat up. Confused by the accusation in his tone and a little wounded, she flushed. Still, it was not in her to deny the truth. "Yes," she said simply. "I would."

"Why?"

She didn't answer the question. Instead she asked, "Why does it make you angry?"

Ryder's smile was grim and humorless. "I didn't know you realized I was."

"I could . . ." She hesitated. "I could feel it in your kisses. I'm inexperienced. Not naive." She drew in her breath and said again, "So why are you angry?"

Sighing, Ryder got to his feet. He ran a hand through his hair. "I'm not angry with you," he said. "You haven't done anything except make me want you, and you did that a long time ago." He shook his head slowly. "I shouldn't have brought you with me. It was a mistake to think I could keep my hands off you."

Mary stood. Ryder was already turning from her when she asked quietly, "Why do you want to?"

"One doesn't miss what one hasn't had."

"That isn't true," she said. "I know."

Ryder turned around. "We're not talking about the same thing," he said. "Not at all." She wanted to satisfy her curiosity. She had no idea of the need that was driving him. "Go to sleep now. I have work to do."

She almost reached for him, but she sensed he would push her away. She walked past him, careful not to brush him, and went to the bed. Drawing off three of the blankets, she tossed them in Ryder's direction; then she lay down. He put out all the lanterns except the one he needed for reading the maps. "I still have all my clothes on," she told him a shade defiantly.

Ryder leaned over the maps. Without looking at her he said pleasantly, "Shut up, Mary."

Knowing only that something had changed, he came awake suddenly. He was on his feet in the next moment as he sensed Mary's absence from the chamber.

She stood in the arched entrance holding a bucket of spring water in one hand and a lantern in the other. "Did you think I left?" she asked curiously.

Ryder raised one hand to the back of his neck and rubbed. Tension seeped out of him slowly. "You did leave."

"Only to get some water." She hung the lantern inside the entrance and carried the bucket over to him. "You were sleeping very soundly. I made a racket and you didn't stir once."

"Liar."

It wasn't said unkindly, and Mary didn't take offense. "All right," she admitted. "I *was* quiet, but you have to admit you only just missed me. I've been gone at least two minutes."

"So long," he said dryly. It bothered him more than he cared to admit. If she had wanted to, she could have gone quite a distance in two minutes. "Why didn't you try leaving? Aren't you still anxious to get away from here?"

Mary set down the bucket. "I thought about it," she said. "I think about it a lot. But I find myself in something of a predicament. If I try to go you'll probably drag me back and then you'd make me sleep in only a blanket again, right next to you, and then we'd both have a hard time sleeping. Probably we would kiss, and maybe even more than that would happen, and you would blame me for that, thinking I planned it all—heaven knows, I've given you good reason to think that—so it didn't seem to me I'd be able to convince you otherwise and—" She paused to take a breath. "And there you have it. There just wasn't any sense in trying to get away."

He was staring at her, fascinated. She was laughing at him, he knew she was, but there was no smile on her lips and only innocence in her forest green eyes. "Is that right?" he said softly.

She nodded serenely and turned to go. "Would you like some breakfast?" she asked. "I thought I'd—"

Ryder caught her hand and pulled her back. She was brought flush to his body in a swift movement. His arms circled her waist quickly, trapping her. "What if I changed my mind?" he asked. "I did a lot of thinking, too."

Mary blinked. Her face was tilted toward his, and it seemed his mouth was very close. "You did?"

He nodded and bent his head. His lips touched her just beneath her ear. "I've decided . . ."—Ryder's mouth grazed her cheek—"the next time . . ."—he kissed her temple—"you leave this chamber"—he traced the edges of her parted lips with his tongue—"I'll drive a spike in the stone and chain you to it." His hands closed around her waist as he set her from him.

Mary was still feeling the edge of his tongue on her mouth. The words registered slowly. She wavered on her feet a little unsteadily as a sweet ache swept through her.

"Now don't flirt with me anymore," he said. "I can make you hurt a lot worse than you can make me." Ryder only hoped she would believe him.

It was something of a standoff for two more days. Ryder spent very little time inside the chamber, and he never offered to take Mary out again. When they were together their conversation was cool and polite. They studiously avoided any subject that could be construed as personal and were careful not to touch. Mary slept alone on the stone pallet of blankets while Ryder made his bed on the floor.

It was a satisfactory arrangement for neither of them. On the third morning Ryder was finally prepared to announce there would be a change. He placed his hand on Mary's shoulder and shook her awake.

"Go away," she said sleepily.

"Get up."

"Why?" It was a good question, she thought. Why bother getting up at all when there was little to make one day different from another.

Ryder almost repeated what he thought about her taking issue with his orders, then thought better of it. "Because we're leaving."

That got Mary's attention. "Leaving?" She sat up and threw her legs over the side of the stone loft. "Leaving the cavern, you mean?" she asked eagerly.

He nodded and let his hand drift away from her shoulder.

"Where are we going?"

"A day's walk from here."

"That doesn't tell me anything."

Ryder shrugged. "I could tell you the name of the place, but it wouldn't mean anything to you." He pointed to the pair of trousers he had laid across the back of the wing chair. "Get out of your shift and put those on. You can wear my shirt and my hat. You won't be able to tolerate the sun without one."

"Aren't we taking anything with us?" she asked.

"Water and jerky. It will be enough."

"All right," she said. "I trust you."

He didn't let that touch his conscience too deeply. "Get dressed," he said. "I'll wait for you in the corridor."

Mary was ready quickly. She gave a soft gasp of surprise when Ryder held up a bandana intended to cover her eyes. "What does it matter if I see the way out? We're not coming back."

Ryder tied the blindfold tightly. "I never said that," he said.

"But—" When she tried to tear at the bandana he caught her hands. "What are you—" A rope was twisted around her wrists until they were bound securely in front of her. "I don't want to fight with you, Mary. Not today."

Her struggle was with tears, not with her bonds. "I'm not fighting you," she protested.

"You will." He could have pulled her along by the leading string he had tied to the ropes, but he dropped it and looped his arm in hers instead. "I expect you'll fight me most of the way."

"Why? Why would I do that?" She could feel herself holding back already, stiff and unyielding as he tried to urge her forward. "What are you going to do to me?"

Ryder surprised her by simply taking her in his arms and holding her until she calmed. She felt his breath on her face a moment before his mouth closed over hers. The kiss was warm and gentle and sweet.

"I'm going to marry you," he said.

Eight

John MacKenzie Worth found he could tolerate the ignominy of his position. What he could not tolerate was being ignored.

Moira tried to calm him. "Perhaps none among them speaks any English," she said quietly. Her eyes darted from her husband to the Chiricahua warrior guarding them. She absently massaged the chafed skin of her wrists. The leather thongs that had bound her on the journey to the Apache encampment had left their mark on her delicate skin. Smiling tentatively at the guard, she was met with a blank stare. "They don't appear to want to communicate with us at all," she told Jay Mac.

"And I don't like it," he blustered. In frustration he tried to free his wrists. There was no give in the leather, and his attempt merely restricted the circulation in his hands. Being bound was doubly frustrating because he only had himself to blame. Given the choice between cooperation and conflict, Jay Mac had chosen the latter. He wriggled his bound feet and found the result the same.

"Lean against me," said Moira. "It will ease the strain in your back." When Jay Mac stubbornly refused to move, Moira scooted closer and leaned into him. "Then let me lean on you," she said, linking her arm through his.

Although Jay Mac knew precisely what she was doing, he was placated. He turned his head. Threads of gray mingled with the deep red strands of Moira's hair, and a fine layer of dust from their harrowing ride covered all like a veil. He placed a kiss on the crown of her head. "I love you, Moira."

The edges of her mouth lifted, and she gave his arm a gentle squeeze.

Her calm fascinated her husband. He had always known she was possessed of strong character, but the well of peace she was drawing upon now was deeper than he had ever suspected. "I wish I hadn't let you accompany me this morning," he said. "I could have inspected the progress on the line alone."

"Don't be absurd. Where would I rather be than with you? If you had been captured without me I wouldn't know that you were safe. Think about Rennie and Jarret and the babies. Would you really want me to be going through the agony of not knowing as they're doing now?" She closed her eyes momentarily, and her voice lowered to a whisper. "As we've all done since our Mary was taken?"

Jay Mac wished he could put his arms around her. The catch in her voice that she hoped he wouldn't notice wrenched his heart. "I should not have been attending to business," he said, determined to lay blame for their predicament on his shoulders alone. "I should have remained at the fort with you and Rennie, waiting for Jarret to return."

"Jay Mac—"

"At least I should have accepted an Army escort."

"Should. Should. Should." Moira sighed. "You should have been a priest, and none of this would ever have come about."

"But I'm a Presbyterian."

"My point exactly," she said with a note of triumph. "You are what you are. And I love you for it." Moira's gaze wandered around the Chiricahua encampment as she spoke. Two women had leaped to help a fallen child. Another, with a cradleboard on her back, looked on fondly as the child hugged the skirt of one of her rescuers. It was human nature to protect one's own, she thought, and the knowledge of this bond she shared with her captors gave Moira an extra measure of peace. "You dropped everything in New York to come out here when you received our telegram. And you've rattled every official and every commander you could think of to elicit some help in finding Mary. You did what you could, Jay Mac. It's the waiting around that you're no good at. I was relieved when you decided to go out to the mine and look at the construction Rennie's put together. And, yes, I was quite happy to be asked to go along, because I'm no better at waiting than you are. I'm only more quiet about it."

That raised a faint smile. "You're good for me, Moira Mary," he said softly.

"Of course I am." She snuggled closer, wishing he could put his arms around her. "What do you think they intend to do with us?" she asked, surveying the encampment again. There was a lot of activity among their captors. Everyone in the camp seemed bent on some purpose. Even the conversation had an air of excitement about it.

"Hold us for ransom probably," Jay Mac said. "Exchange us for guns or money for guns."

"That doesn't make sense," Moira reasoned. "If the charges against Ryder McKay are true, they should be well armed."

Jay Mac had thought about that, too. But if he and Moira weren't being held for ransom, then . . . It wasn't a train of thought he wanted to pursue. "Perhaps this isn't the band that got the gold from the Colter Canyon raid. Or perhaps they don't want us to see their store of rifles and ammunition."

Moira didn't know what to think about that. She watched a group of women in consultation with one another over a meal preparation. Their congenial arguing dissolved into giggles as one of them looked toward Moira and Jay Mac and made some comment. "You don't think they're having us for dinner, do you?" she asked.

Jay Mac saw the unmistakable crooked smile on the mouth of their guard though it was quickly erased. Jay Mac no longer harbored any doubts that at least one of their captors understood English. That smile was not in response to the Apache woman's jest, but to Moira's interpretation. "No, dear, I don't think they plan to have us for dinner, at least not the way you're thinking. But it's clear they're preparing something."

Jay Mac took the count of the encampment to be one hundred, give or take a dozen. The site they had chosen was protected by a natural fortress of pale pink rock. Although the rocky walls were high, they had not boxed themselves in a dead end canyon, and lookouts had been posted above the camp to raise the alarm if the band was threatened. Although the Chiricahua looked settled, Jay Mac had learned enough from General Gardner to know that the bands moved quickly and easily from one location to another. In the years before the Spanish and the English had come, the Chiricahua moved in concert with their six seasons, going where the plants and game were most plentiful. Now they moved to flee an enemy as well.

Moira thought about what Jay Mac had said. "I think you're partially right, dear."

"How's that?"

"They're not preparing something." The purposefulness of the activity caught her attention again: the briskness of a warrior's stride, the discussion among the elders, the busy hands working beads into a fringed leather skirt. A joyous anticipation hung in the air and was given sound by fits of high-pitched laughter from the children. "They're preparing *for* something."

Ryder did not remove Mary's blindfold until they had walked from the cavern for two hours. The going had been slow, as much because Mary's steps were necessarily halting as because of the terrain. Covering their trail had slowed their progress also.

In all that time Mary had said nothing. When Ryder had announced his proposal he had effectively rendered her speechless, and she had remained that way throughout the first leg of their journey. It had occurred to her not to cooperate, to fight him just as he supposed she would, but perversely she didn't want to give him what he expected.

Ryder took the blindfold and tied it around his forehead. His dark hair was free of the thong, and it fell loosely past his shoulders. He watched as Mary squinted under the sudden glare of light. He shielded her face with his hands, protecting her eyes. It was the most natural gesture in the world to place his lips softly on her brow. He drew back after a moment. "Are you never going to talk to me again?"

"I wouldn't give you the satisfaction," she said. Her voice sounded unfamiliar to her own ears, and the words fairly stuck in her throat.

Ryder stared back solemnly, then raised a canteen to her lips. He didn't need to persuade her to drink. She took the water with the youthful greediness of a child. When she had had her fill he let the canteen fall to his side and wiped her damp mouth with the pad of his thumb.

Mary pursed her lips and thrust her bound hands forward into Ryder's hard, flat belly. He raised both eyebrows at the force of the blow, but she knew he wasn't hurt. Ramming her fists into his abdomen was like punching a brick wall: she was more jarred by the impact than he was. "You can remove this rope now. I'm not going to be yanked across the countryside on a leading string. I'll go where you go because I want to, not because you have me on a tether."

Ryder's frost gray eyes were remote as he considered her words. "Then you agree we should be married."

Mary hesitated. "I didn't say that. I said, 'I'll go where you go.' That will have to satisfy you for now." She waited until he removed the rope before she added, "And for the record, you didn't ask me to marry you."

His eyes narrowed as he tried to fathom the twists and turns of her thoughts, but her features were once again cloaked. An expression of complete serenity made Mary as unreadable as she was beautiful. "For the record," he said, "I'm not taking any chances."

Mary didn't reply, following him instead as he began walking ahead of her, but taking chances was exactly what she thought he was doing. How did he think he was going to engage her cooperation in front of a priest?

At first she considered that he would be taking her to a town to have the ceremony performed. The longer she pondered it, the more insanely dangerous it seemed. Mary imagined that Ryder could hardly hope to bring her into public without attracting notice. If they weren't identified immediately he must know she would make sure they were discovered. Ultimately she dismissed the possibility of a town wedding.

It occurred to her now that Ryder had a mission as his destination. The Southwest Territory was dotted with Spanish missions, especially near the border. It was not difficult to determine that they were heading south. Perhaps they were even in Mexico already, she thought, and wondered how hard it would be to escape Ryder's side in a foreign country. Was she better with the devil she did know than among strangers who might have no sympathy for her situation or wouldn't even believe her?

Ryder had told her they were a day's walk from their destination. She wondered if he counted the day as twenty-four hours or until sunset. After walking so far he must expect to spend the night. Would it be at the mission? The thought of sleeping in a real bed again, with a feather tick and pillows, a comforter pulled up to her neck, made Mary sigh aloud. The idea of sleeping in a real bed with Ryder's body fitted against her own made her knees grow weak.

She stumbled.

Ryder caught her before she fell. He helped her up and steadied her. "You did better when you were blindfolded," he said.

She drew back and brushed herself off. "Yes, well I can see a little too clearly now."

After a brief, quizzical, over-the-shoulder glance, Ryder started walking, this time shaking his head in bemusement.

The pace he set was not hurried and Mary was not tired when he stopped. He studied the ground as she leaned against a rock and took off her shoes. Fine grains of sand and pebbles no bigger than the heads of pins were shaken out. She stared at the debris with no little astonishment. She would have sworn she was carrying Gibraltar in both shoes. Mary curled her toes, wiggling them to restore circulation. "I'm not tired," she announced. "You don't have to rest on my account."

Ryder was hunkered beside a grouping of stones. "I'm not resting. I'm reading." He picked up the stones, smoothed the ground underneath to remove their depression, then placed them carefully among other rocks, making certain the sun-dried side was still facing up. "You sound almost eager," he said, glancing at her. "You'll be happy to know we're nearly there."

Mary stopped wiggling her toes. "But you said a day's walk."

Ryder shrugged. "They've moved again."

She frowned, her brow furrowed.

"It's all right," he said. "They're still expecting us."

Mary eased herself away from the rock and straightened. "What do you mean, 'They've moved'? And who's expecting us?" Militancy was back in her stance and her eyes were issuing a challenge.

Ryder ignored both. "Put your shoes on. There are a few miles left, and most of it's downhill." As he turned to go he thought he might get one of the shoes squarely in the middle of his back. He was grateful for Mary's restraint. He wondered what conclusions she had drawn about their destination. Whatever they had been she was discovering them wrong. Her confusion was quite real, however. It forced Ryder to think about how much longer he could count on her cooperation. He was certain now that she had been plotting her escape.

It wasn't as surprising as it was disappointing.

Jay Mac stiffened slightly as the guard approached. Moira rose to her feet at the Chiricahua's gesture but stood protectively beside her husband.

"It is time to go," the guard said. "They are waiting." He withdrew a knife from the soft buckskin folds of his bootlike moccasin. His flat expression didn't change when he saw that Jay Mac did not flinch, but he was impressed. "You will follow me." He cut the bonds on Jay Mac's wrists, then the ones on his ankles.

Jay Mac got awkwardly to his feet. His palms and soles tingled with restored circulation, but he gave little notice to the discomfort. His arms went immediately around Moira. He could feel her heart beating madly as he pressed her close to his chest. Believing they had lived their hearts and that nothing had been left unspoken, they exchanged no words. Jay Mac broke the embrace reluctantly. It was easy to read the guard's expression now. It was one of repugnance. "It appears they don't approve of public displays of affection," Jay Mac muttered.

Moira smiled, resting her head momentarily on her husband's shoulder. "Imagine how he'd react if you kissed me properly. We'd probably be able to escape."

The guard was not amused. "This way," he said.

Jay Mac squeezed Moira's hand. "At least they want us together," he said quietly.

"What is it?" asked Mary. She was looking at the garments hanging from the end of Ryder's extended arm as if they might bite her. The truth was, they looked lovely and were treated to her suspicious stare because of that. The leather had been bleached until it was pale as eggshell and had been worked over and over until it was soft as butter. The beadwork in the fringe along the neck, arms, and hem was all turquoise and silver. "I mean," she corrected herself, "I know what it is, but what am I supposed to do with it?"

"Put it on."

Mary didn't reach for it. Instead her hands went behind her back and she actually retreated a step. "Oh, I couldn't," she said, shaking her head. "It must belong to someone. It looks very valuable. You should put it back where you found it."

"You're not usually so slow to the mark," he said calmly. "Is it that you really don't want to see?"

She merely stared at him, bewildered.

He explained patiently. "It does belong to someone. You. I found it because it was left for me to find."

Her hands came from around her back. "For me?"

He nodded. "I thought you might like a change of clothes."

Now Mary reached for the buckskin shirt and skirt eagerly, holding them up in front of her. "Beautiful," she whispered, awed. The weighted fringe on both pieces swayed and jangled as the beads rubbed together. The leather was soft to the touch, and she raised a sleeve to her cheek. "They look as if they will fit me."

Ryder simply shook his head. She was determined not to see any part of the picture that wasn't painted especially for her. "Of course they will fit. They were *made* for you."

That brought her head up. She stared at Ryder wonderingly. "You?"

"No, not by me."

Mary raised the fringe along the neckline gingerly. The tiny beads sifted through her fingers, cool and clear. "Like droplets of water," she said softly.

"Yes," he said. Some visions did not have to be explained. He saw it in her eyes now, the knowledge that these garments had not been an undertaking of a few days, but of months, and that they had been fashioned after a likeness he held clearly in his mind's eye. "Put it on, Mary."

It would be as if she were in the pool again, she thought. She would wear this garment as if it were the water and she were naked save for its cloak. And she would remember how he had looked at her when he thought of her only as a woman and how he had held her, comforted her, when she thought a woman was all she wanted to be. She had fallen asleep in his arms, exhausted by the despair that clutched her heart, yet strangely rested from his sweet succor. When she had awakened he was gone. She had never expected to see him again but she knew she wouldn't forget him.

This garment was proof that he had not forgotten her.

"I'll show you where you can wash," he said. Ryder led her

through a copse of pines to a narrow mountain stream. It was only a few inches deep but the water was clear and cool. He knelt and washed his own face and hands. "When you're done we'll follow this stream to the bottom, and then it will be done."

Mary opened her mouth to ask a question, but Ryder was striding away. She watched him disappear into the shadows of the pines. It occurred to her he was giving her a chance to run. It also occurred that he was extending his trust. On the heels of that thought she considered that perhaps he was merely taking her compliance for granted, that in his arrogance he thought her cooperation was assured.

She gazed after him, staring at the spot where he had vanished from view, holding the fringed, pale, butter yellow skirt and shirt in front of her. It became clear that her decision would not be made because of what he wanted, but because of what she wanted. Carefully laying the gift aside, Mary knelt beside the shallow stream and folded her hands. It was not water that she raised to her lips but prayer.

Mary was not the only one who changed clothes. Ryder shed the last vestiges of the military and replaced it with garments that had been left for him. A long-sleeved buckskin shirt replaced the flannel one, and he added the breechcloth by looping the long strip of buckskin over his belt in the front, then drawing the long end between his legs and tucking it under his belt in the back. He pulled on the moccasins, tugging them up to his knees, then gathered the discarded clothes and bundled them.

For the first time in his life Ryder could find no peace in waiting. On this occasion anticipation was not a welcome companion. If Mary ran he would find her and bring her back. She could never get far enough away that he couldn't get her quickly, but he had no taste for the task. He did not want it to be against her will, yet he wanted it. Marriage was the condition he had placed upon their union. Mary did not seem to expect it or even particularly want it. She hadn't tried to bargain her body for a ring and a commitment, nor had she tried to seduce him like Anna Leigh Hamilton to appease curiosity.

The stillness that surrounded him now was an agony. He strained for some sound that would indicate Mary's presence by the stream. The pounding of his own heart left him deaf to sounds he could have heard in a windstorm. Unable to tolerate it another moment, Ryder shot to his feet and quickly retraced his path to the water.

Mary turned when she heard him, her smile more uncertain than eager. The remote, guarded expression on Ryder's face did not inspire confidence, and the clothes he wore startled her. She was reminded again of the predatory nature of man and of this man in particular. Mary wasn't certain she wanted to be in his sights now. Her eyes dropped away from his, and she fingered the fringe at her neck in order to have something to do with her hands.

He had steeled himself to accept that she would be gone, and now the expression was engraved on his features. It wasn't until her eyes fell away that he felt himself relax and the frost lift from his lightly colored eyes.

The pale leather outfit clung softly to her slender frame. When she moved the beads glanced off one another, shifting and sparkling like a curtain of raindrops. The sun was just setting, waves of oranges and reds, like a tide of color in her hair, skimming the surface of each strand so its own rich hue was reflected more brilliantly. The fringe at the hem of her skirt almost touched her feet, and it was movement there that caught Ryder's eye. Barefoot, Mary was curling and uncurling her toes in a nervous gesture that kept the fringe swinging in time.

"A moment," he said. He was gone and then he was back, producing a pair of moccasins that were as soft as the shirt and decorated with the same beads of turquoise and silver. "Here," he said, handing them to her. "I should have given them to you before. I wasn't thinking." It wasn't quite true. He *had* been thinking, but only of how she would look in wedding raiment that was like shimmering water. In the end his vision had not done the truth justice.

Mary accepted the moccasins but looked at them doubtfully.

"I think they're going to be too big." The toe of the buckskin boots would extend well past her own toes, and the tips of the moccasins turned upward. She glanced at the moccasins Ryder was wearing. The toes of his had the same distinctive upward turn.

"They are as they are meant to be," he said.

Which was to say that when Mary put them on, the fit would be perfect. The rawhide soles protected her feet as her own shoes hadn't been able to do. "Thank you, Ryder."

It seemed to him that the use of his name was deliberate, as if she understood it was not the way of the Apache to use a given name carelessly, that one's name was invoked when there was something of importance to be expressed. Of course, she couldn't know that, but Ryder found he wanted to believe it anyway. He picked up her discarded clothes and bundled them with his. He held out his free hand. "This way, Mary."

As always, when he said her name in that peculiar way of his, as though attaching some singular importance to it, Mary found herself wanting to honor his wish. She slipped her hand in his and walked at his side along the edge of the winding stream.

Their descent was gradual and slow. The pines dwindled in size but never disappeared, and Mary realized their elevation was still high above the desert floor. It wasn't until the stream widened and pines circled a small clearing that Ryder stopped. He released Mary's hand and tossed the bundle toward the trees.

"What are we doing?" she asked. It did not seem odd to her that she was talking no more loudly than the wind as it whispered in the boughs. "And what is that?" She pointed to the large woven basket in the center of the clearing. It was filled with water and had the dimensions of a wooden washtub. Was she expected to do their laundry? "Why are we stopping here?"

"In a moment." He knelt in front of her and removed her moccasins while she rested a hand on his shoulder to keep her balance. When he was done he removed his own.

Mary wanted to giggle, but something in Ryder's manner

sobered her. He was behaving solemnly, deliberately. He took her hand again and this time led her to the basket of water. He stepped in first, then lifted her. She caught her breath as much from his hands on her waist as from the first icy dip. "What are we doing?" she asked again. "What is this place?"

Ryder didn't answer. His fingers caught hers in a firm clasp.

Mary tugged, but she wasn't released. Her skin prickled with a mixture of cold and trepidation. "I don't think I want to—"

"Shhh. They're coming."

At Ryder's whispered urging, Mary was silent. She followed the line of his vision half expecting to see spirits arise from the grouping of trees to the left of them. What came out of the wooded area was no spirit, but flesh and blood. The man wore clothing similar to Ryder's, except his breechcloth and shirt were of cloth, not buckskin. His hair was thick, darker even than Ryder's, parted in the middle and held back by a wide red bandana. At the side it was so long it nearly reached his elbows. The sun had been this man's companion throughout his life. His skin had the same reddish-brown tint of a polished chestnut and deep lines were carved into the corners of his eyes and mouth. His manner was solemn and proud, and he acknowledged Ryder and Mary with the merest nod of his head.

"My father. Naiche." Ryder's words were quietly spoken and for Mary's ears alone. "The woman is my father's wife. Josanie."

Josanie stood quietly at her husband's side, reaching just to his shoulder. She was a score of years younger than Naiche, and her face was filled out, rounded and smooth, not engraved with harsh lines. Her dark hair, streaked with strands of gray at the temples, was coiled in a knot at her nape. Her acknowledgment was also a faint nod, but there was no mistaking that her mouth was set tightly in disapproval.

Naiche and Josanie did not approach, and Mary realized she was somewhat relieved by that. She felt a little foolish standing in the water, and she had no idea what she was expected to do or say. Following Ryder's lead, she remained exactly as she was, though it was hard not to respond in kind to Josanie's obvious disfavor. Just at the point when Mary thought she would embarrass herself with nervous laughter, she felt Ryder stiffen and grasp her hand even more tightly. Mary winced, but it failed to gain her release. Her eyes flew to his, and she saw he was paying scant attention to her but was looking in another direction entirely. Once again she followed his gaze.

She had reason to be grateful for Ryder's tight hold as her knees buckled beneath her.

Jay Mac and Moira entered the clearing followed by their guard. Their clothes were dusty, a little disheveled, but they were all in one piece in spite of their ordeal. In Mary's eyes they looked wonderful. She took her fill of them, just as they were doing to her, their eyes eating her up, counting every blessed hair on her head. Joyous laughter began to rise in Mary's throat. Her entire body leaned away from Ryder and toward her parents. This time his grip was unwelcome. When she tried to step out of the basket he restrained her.

Except for a slight nod from each, Moira and Jay Mac didn't move. Assured now that she was safe, their expressions mirrored less anxiety and more confusion and silent questioning.

Mary opened her mouth to speak, but Ryder gave a warning by tugging on her hand. He stepped out of the basket, lifted her to join him, and announced, "It is done."

Mary barely heard him, and anyway his words had no meaning for her. She wrested her hand free of his and ran to her parents. Moira's arms were already outstretched, prepared to bring her firstborn back to her breast. Mary fell into them gladly, holding and being held, feeling in a primal way the deep nurturing love of that nascent embrace.

Jay Mac stood close to his wife and placed his hand on the crown of Mary's head, stroking gently. The distinct colors in her red-gold hair blurred as tears gathered in his eyes.

"Come. You must leave now." It was the guard who spoke.

Jay Mac's tears dried immediately, but his vision wasn't clear as blinding anger created a thicker haze than tears ever could.

"Give her a moment with her mother," he snapped. "For God's sake show some compassion."

The guard looked to Ryder for direction. Ryder's face was expressionless, but the single shake of his head was clear. Raising his rifle a notch, the guard motioned again. "Come. You must leave."

Jay Mac had seen Ryder's gesture and recognized it for the command it was. Fury was etched on his features, but he did not allow pride and anger to overrule his judgment. "Let us take her back," he said, his voice deep with emotion. "She doesn't belong with you."

"She does now," Ryder said quietly. "Mary is my wife." He nodded again to the guard. "Take them." He addressed Jay Mac, though he spoke as much for Moira's sake. "It's for your safety and that of your wife. The Army will be looking for you. If you are not returned quickly they will find the camp and destroy everyone."

Only a subtle change in Ryder's expression let Jay Mac know that "everyone" included his beloved Mary. Jay Mac understood then that Mary's life depended on their return to Fort Union and the offering of any explanation for their disappearance except the truth. That did not lessen his anger toward Ryder McKay, but it made the dictate make sense. His hand moved from Mary's bent head to his wife's shoulder. "Moira," he said gently. "We must go."

Ryder stepped forward to lift Mary away from her mother, but it wasn't necessary. She kissed Moira on the cheek, straightened, then kissed her father. Her hand lingered on Jay Mac's forearm reassuringly before she came to stand beside Ryder. As her parents turned to go Mary's body vibrated with a wrenching shudder. She bit her lip to keep from crying out and prayed that neither Jay Mac nor Moira would find the strength to look back. Mary did not think she could remain with Ryder if they did.

The clearing was silent until Moira, Jay Mac, and the guard were out of sight; then Naiche approached the newlyweds and offered his congratulations. Mary, pale and dazed, only half listened as Ryder translated from the Apache. She murmured what she hoped was an appropriate reply which Ryder repeated at some length.

"Do they understand English?" she asked tightly.

"A little."

"Words like cruel bastard and heartless son of a bitch?"

"Your eyes are speaking a language that requires no words," he told her. "It doesn't matter what you say, they can see into your heart. They know you're angry with me."

"Angry?" Mary almost choked on the word. "Then they should look deeper, as well you should, because it doesn't begin to describe what I'm feeling." The coldness that clutched her inside and made it difficult to breathe also froze the fiery brilliance of her green eyes. She stared at him hard, willing herself not to shatter in front of him.

Ryder said nothing to Mary, but exchanged more words with Naiche and Josanie. After a minute the couple returned to the place where they had entered the clearing and began walking back to the encampment. It was at that point that Ryder addressed Mary. "Josanie's family has prepared to welcome us with a feast and dancing. It is not the Apache way that the husband's side should offer this. It was done because your family could not. Naiche is *nanta*—a leader—and he has brought great risk to his people by allowing us to be married here and to celebrate among them. To bring your parents here to witness the ceremony was Naiche's gift to me and his blessing. I could not have married you without their acknowledgment."

Mary stared at the ground, hugging herself. She was confused and hurt, and understood less than half of what was truly in her heart.

"Whatever your feelings toward me, I ask that you not share them with *N'de*—the people."

She shot him a narrowed glance. "Because it would embarrass you?"

"Because it would be an embarrassment to Naiche."

Mary looked away. It was growing darker and the cold seemed to press against her skin from both sides. "Very well," she said quietly. "But this changes nothing between us." Even as she said it, she knew it wasn't true. Everything had changed.

The public dance which Mary and Ryder joined when they reached the encampment was a lively affair. Mary would have liked to have watched, but her participation was expected and she was guided through the steps by giggling, good-natured women—all sisters or cousins or nieces of Josanie. They laughed helplessly, though not unkindly, as Mary performed her part in the dance, and to show their appreciation of her attempts, they incorporated her faltering steps among their own.

When it was over they admired Mary's dress, fingering the fringe and commenting excitedly over the fit and handiwork. As they did so, she realized who it was she had to thank for the garments, and catching Josanie's dark, watchful gaze, she made a slight bow in acknowledgment. Josanie's stern mouth softened slightly.

Ryder rescued his wife from her curious admirers and brought her to sit beside him near one of the small fires that were now dotting the encampment. "We can't stay much longer," he told her. "In the morning they'll move their camp. We must be long gone by then. There can be no evidence that they harbored us."

That bore the danger home to Mary. "Mama and Jay Mac will say nothing," she said. At least not to the authorities, she thought. But they wouldn't keep it from family. Jarret would learn of it, and he would come looking for her, using whatever landmarks her parents could recall to pick up her trail.

Watching her closely, her profile etched by warm firelight, Ryder asked, "What's troubling you?"

Mary cast him a sideways glance. "Nothing." She wasn't convincing, and he wasn't convinced. She was saved from another probe by the arrival of their food. Bean mush was served, with just a hint of meat to flavor it and cornbread as an accompaniment. Mary, who thought her palate had been deadened by weeks of eating tinned vegetables, found the meal spicy and satisfying. Later there were small pink cakes made with sugared yucca fruit and decorated with sunflower petals. Mary knew intuitively that these were a very special treat and it was an honor to be served them.

There was a lot of joking and teasing while the meal was being consumed. Mary understood little of the content, but the gist of it generally required no interpreter. She was startled to hear Ryder laugh out loud as he was targeted by his friends for another round of affectionate banter. The laughter started deep in his chest, rumbling with enough force for Mary to feel the vibration. It felt like tiny sparks alighting on the surface of her skin, touching her with a flash of heat before they vanished. She wasn't certain she wanted to be touched by his laughter.

She was still a little dazed by its effect when she found herself being ushered to the edge of the camp. She remained there, just as Ryder asked, while he spoke privately with his father. Several other men, men Mary had noted had carried special influence and respect among the Chiricahua, joined Ryder and Naiche. Their conversation lasted only a few minutes, but Mary gathered by the tone and gesturing that the words which were exchanged were not to be taken lightly.

She raised her eyes questioningly as Ryder returned to her side. "You've made your farewell?"

He nodded. "My father wanted to tell me where the band is going next, but the council questioned the wisdom of it. They're afraid I'll want to join them again."

"Would you?"

"I would be tempted," he admitted. He put one hand on the small of her back and urged her forward along the trail. A crescent moon lighted the path until the canopy of pine blocked it. "But they're right to be concerned that the Army could stumble upon them through me. I can wait until they're ready for me to find them."

Mary was quiet for a long time, concentrating on not stumbling over a raised root or fallen branchs. She recognized the clearing when they came upon it the second time, even though the basket of water had been removed.

It was here that Ryder picked up the bundle of their discarded clothes. He gave Mary his flannel shirt to put over her beaded shirt. "That slip of a moon makes you an easy target," he explained when she told him she was warm enough. He had no problem gaining her cooperation after that. He let her take the lead until their ascent became steep enough for her to require his assistance.

"They didn't appear to have many guns," she said, as Ryder helped her over a rocky incline.

"You noticed that." What he noticed was that she tore her hand away from his as quickly as possible. "What did you think about it?"

"At first I wondered if they had them hidden."

"And?"

"And that didn't make sense. If you need a rifle for protection you don't hide it so precious seconds are lost retrieving it. Of course, if you need the rifles to mount an attack you may hide them until you've marshaled your forces."

Darkness hid Ryder's faint smile. It was hard to believe she'd been a nun for so many years and not an Army strategist. "So what have you concluded?"

"They don't have any guns. Those people were more wary of being attacked than intent on attacking. I don't mean that they wouldn't fight," she added, concerned that Ryder might believe she thought Naiche's people lacked courage. "I know they would fight with whatever is available, just as I know that what's available isn't guns."

"What about gold?" he asked. "That's what they were supposed to have gotten from the raid."

Mary considered his question a moment before she answered. "I think if they'd really gotten the gold they'd have bought guns by now."

"Why?" he pressed.

She hesitated, letting the logic of her reasoning settle in her mind, testing its soundness against other possibilities. "Because no one who wants to travel light and fast can afford to be burdened by too many possessions."

"Perhaps they've hidden it." He helped her up again, this time bringing her flush with his body. He heard her catch her breath, but suspected it wasn't the climb that had helped her lose it in the first place. She was looking up at him, her eyes wide, her lips slightly parted as she sipped the air. He bent his own head a fraction. His voice was hushed. "What do you think?"

Mary was mesmerized by the sliver of light edging his hard profile, the way it touched the line of his brow, shaped his nose, and polished the corner of his mouth. He had asked her a question. It hung in the slip of a space between their mouths, but she couldn't remember what it was. She was having a hard time recalling that earlier in the day she was certain she hated him.

"Well?"

Mary blinked. "I don't think they've hidden it, because it's not their way. They would have wanted to make the trade quickly. The gold's really useless to them except as barter for guns."

"You have a very good mind, Mrs. McKay." He turned quickly and started up the trail again. He had no difficulty imagining the fierceness of Mary's expression. It was in her voice as she hurried after him.

"I'm not Mrs. McKay," she said sharply.

His tone was a pleasant contrast to hers. "In my eyes you are."

"Well, damn your eyes."

Ryder merely grinned.

"I mean it," she called after him. "That wasn't a wedding we had today."

"It was to me." Before she could damn him again he added, "I recall you not wanting a marriage at all."

"I didn't . . . I don't."

"Then . . ." His voice trailed off expectantly.

Mary's confusion had made her lose her pace. Now she ran to catch up, the beaded fringe jangling lightly. She pulled on Ryder's buckskin shirt from behind, used it to raise herself up, and scrambled around him, taking the high ground. In her haste she had forgotten that with Ryder it rarely mattered if she captured the high ground.

He dropped the bundle of clothes and grabbed Mary. His palms anchored her at the waist and kept her steady. She was so slender and lithe that his fingers almost met in the clasp. Her own hands skimmed his shoulders, fluttered momentarily, then rested there.

She couldn't think what she wanted to say.

Ryder helped her. "Cruel bastard?" he asked. "Heartless son of a bitch?"

Mary was glad for the darkness that hid her flaming face. It was difficult to meet his eyes. "My parents were returned safely?" she asked lowly.

"You have my word. Neither was harmed."

"There were bruises on my father's wrists. I saw them when he took my mother's arm."

"Your father wasn't very cooperative in the beginning. He had to be bound."

It was as Mary had suspected. "You didn't win a friend there," she told him softly. "In general Jay Mac likes his sons-in-law. In the past he's tried to handpick them. I don't suppose he thinks much of you now."

Ryder's smile was faint. "In Apache the word for son-in-law means he-who-lifts-burdens-for-me. There's an expectation that the bride's husband will care for her family."

Mary tried to imagine how Ryder could ever hope to fulfill that role in her family. John MacKenzie Worth controlled millions of dollars, thousands of miles of track, and hundreds of employees. Neither Moira, nor any of his daughters, had wanted for anything that money could provide. "I'm fairly certain Jay Mac won't have that expectation."

Ryder's smile deepened. "Probably not." He bent his head slightly and rested his forehead against Mary's. "Is there anything else you want to say?"

She closed her eyes briefly. "I wanted to spend more time with them. I hated you for not letting me do that."

"I know."

"I wouldn't have returned with them, not unless it was what you wanted. I had already made my decision about remaining with you."

Ryder's heart slammed in his chest, and he released a breath he hadn't realized he was holding.

"I just wanted to reassure them . . . explain."

"I know that, too."

Mary nodded. Earlier she had been too full of her own anguish to hear properly, and Ryder's explanation to Jay Mac had made little sense. She had had time to think about it as she was in the company of Naiche and Josanie and the score of others who made up the first family group. She witnessed the reverence one accorded one's relatives, the respect a husband had for his mother-in-law, the affectionate teasing between a brother and his sisters. The elders were valued for their wisdom born of experience, and the babies were lovingly protected by charms and amulets hung on the frames of their cradleboards. "It was a great honor you did me by having my parents brought to the ceremony."

In response Ryder placed a light kiss between Mary's brows. He hadn't expected her to see it that way.

"And a great risk to so many people," she added. "Why would you do that, Ryder? Why risk so much?"

"Do you really not know?" This time when his mouth touched her it was at the corner of her eye. His lips trailed along the curve of her cheek then pressed the sensitive hollow just behind her ear. He felt her breathing quicken and her fingertips leave their imprint on his soft buckskin shirt.

Ryder whispered her name against her skin, and his breath was like a brand. She leaned into him and raised her mouth. He covered it with his own, crushing her lips in a hard, hot kiss that seemed to last just this side of forever. His hands slid from her waist to her hips and then cupped her bottom, raising her just enough to cradle him in the cleft of her thighs. She moved against him, the rhythm instinctive, yet innocent.

Ryder eased her back gently and separated their bodies with a small space of air. His breathing was ragged. He could hardly hear hers. Night sheltered them, but this was not what Ryder wanted for the first time with her. "I have to take you back to the cavern," he said. His voice was a rough whisper as he struggled for control. His hands were resting on her bottom. He slid them up to the small of her back. She was still leaning toward him, and he could make out the line of her full mouth. The taste of her was on his tongue as he spoke. "This is no place for us."

"It's not safe for us?" she asked.

"Something like that."

"Oh." Mary didn't want to move. She felt his absence keenly. Her breasts were swollen now, the nipples raised; and the ache to be pressed to Ryder's chest again was physical. She removed her hands from his shoulders and, not knowing what to do with them, crossed them in front of her. It was a poor substitute for his arms, but the ache subsided fractionally. She regretted the loss of his hands on her waist. Cold seemed to penetrate her there and she shivered.

Ryder adjusted the flannel shirt across her shoulders. "You never quite get used to the change in temperature in the winter desert."

"I can adjust to that," she said under her breath. "It's people who blow hot and cold I can't tolerate."

Ryder thought it better that he pretend not to have heard. He did what he could to repair the trail they had disrupted with their scrambling, then he urged Mary ahead of him on the flatter ground. He noticed she covered the terrain with more agility than she had shown earlier in the day. Was she eager or merely determined? With Mary it was probably a bit of both.

A delicious sense of anticipation returned to Ryder, and this time he could embrace it. Ahead of him he watched Mary's lithe figure clamber effortlessly over rocks and fairly dance along the winding trails. She tantalized him with an occasional glimpse of her thigh as the skirt split with her stride and the beaded fringe swung across her white skin. His eyes followed the sway of her narrow hips and the stretch of her long legs. Sometimes she turned, spearing him with an over-the-shoulder glance that made him want to abandon common sense and take her standing up against the nearest tree.

It was hours before they reached the mouth of the cavern. There had been an ebb and flow to their foreplay, moments when they were merely intent on putting one foot in front of the other followed by an innocent helping hand that led to a lingering touch or a husky murmur of thanks.

Mary would have entered the cavern immediately but Ryder caught her, lifted her, and carried her across the threshold. The symbolism was not lost on her. She was still smiling widely when he turned to her after lighting the lantern.

His fingers brushed back the hair at Mary's temple. He watched her intently. "Do you have any idea what you do to me?" he asked.

Her smile faded. She looped her arms around his shoulders and stood on tiptoe. "No," she whispered. "But I'm hoping you'll show me."

Nine

Ryder laid his lips against her forehead, then drew back. Her mouth was hungry for a kiss but he refused the invitation. "We'll never make it back if I start kissing you now," he said.

Mary didn't know that she cared all that much. Something of her thoughts showed in the sulky line of her mouth.

Watching her, Ryder sighed. "You make it very tempting."

She smiled. "That's all right, then." Mary gave him her back and said dutifully. "You may blindfold me now."

Ryder touched the bandana at his forehead then let his hand fall away. He raised the lantern so light showered the area where they stood. The fingers of his other hand stroked the back of Mary's neck lightly. "Not this time," he said quietly. "Come. I'll show you the way."

Mary wasn't entirely certain she wanted this particular gift. It would mean that she wasn't a prisoner any longer, that she would have the route to leave him if she had the will to use it. The trust he was placing in her began to feel more like a burden. Then she remembered his warnings about finding her way out. Where would she go? She had no concept of the direction of the fort or of the distance she might have to travel. Getting from their interior chamber to the cavern's mouth was only a small part of the journey. It was a little like understanding how a lock worked but not being given the key.

Ryder understood her hesitation. His hand slipped from her nape, down her spine, and settled at the small of her back. "Have you worked it out?" he asked.

She nodded, glancing over her shoulder. "I think so."

"Good." He gave her a small push in the direction they should go. "I wasn't inviting you to leave me."

The secret to finding their chamber was all in knowing what to look for. The signs were there, and they were all the same . . . yet different. A straight line was always used to indicate direction at any juncture in the path, but the line might be only three small stones set along the edge of the route. Sometimes the line was lightly marked on the ceiling of the passageway, at other times it was hidden on the underside of a rock. A circle was used to indicate a wrong turn in the route and a diagonal line meant danger. Ryder pointed out to Mary that the way to the chamber hundreds of bats called home was indeed marked with a diagonal line.

"How would I have known?" she asked, staring at the faint marking in the arch of the chamber's entrance.

"You wouldn't. And no one else would either. These signs were for Joe Panama and later for me. They're not supposed to mean anything to anyone." Ryder's fingertip traced a light diagonal path across Mary's cheek. When she looked at him questioningly, he said, "Because you're the most dangerous thing in this place right now." Then he took her hand and pulled her along the passageway.

She was out of breath with excitement rather than exertion by the time they reached their chamber. As she took off Ryder's shirt, he placed the lantern near their stone shelf-bed and lighted another one. "I want to see you," he said.

Mary's eyes widened fractionally. She was flattered and a little frightened.

"You're too far away."

She realized that once he had released her hand she hadn't moved. She was still standing near the entrance to the chamber, hovering actually, as if bolting down the passageway was still an option.

"Shy?" he asked.

Mary had never been accused of it before. She regarded him narrowly, wondering if he was making fun of her.

"Come here, Mary."

She couldn't refuse him, not when he spoke in that gentle, amused voice, not when the tone hinted at an urgency he didn't show in any other way. She responded to the way he held back, as if denial was something to be savored before it was to be satisfied. Mary crossed the chamber floor.

She shimmered as she walked, he thought, as if she were moving through a waterfall. When she stopped in front of him, within arm's reach, the beaded fringe swayed gently. Her forest green eyes were large and luminous, the wide centers of them like polished onyx. Her face was raised to him, and desire had made her watchful and a little wary.

As his hand threaded in the silky strands of her hair, his fingers were washed with color. His thumb brushed her cheek. She closed her eyes and turned her face into his palm, placing her lips lightly against the ball of his hand. He felt that sweet touch ripple through him like a heat wave. Leaning forward he kissed her closed lids, then his mouth settled over hers.

He tasted her lips, learned the shape and texture of their soft undersides, the way his tongue could raise a shiver from her when he touched her just so. Her mouth parted beneath his, her lips pliant and eager. She explored tentatively with her own tongue, meeting him, teasing in a like manner.

Ryder leaned back against the stone shelf. His splayed, outstretched legs captured Mary between them. She allowed herself to be pulled closer and nestled against him. The kiss deepened. There was heat now. Hardness. A sense of demanding that had been missing before.

It seemed he was drawing on her air, forcing her to share his. The intimacy of the kiss stunned her senses. She felt as if she were completely open to him, that she was giving him the right to know her in a way no one had ever done before, that ultimately, and most frighteningly, he would come to know things about her that were a mystery to herself.

If he drew on her air he also drew on her heart. Its steady thrum had quickened, and when his mouth touched the cord in her neck she knew he could feel the wild pulse vibrate against his lips. Her throat arched when his mouth slipped to the base of it. His tongue tasted the hollow, and he sipped her skin in the curve.

Mary's fingers tangled in his thick hair, stroking, holding him to her. Her own sounds of pleasure rocked her as his hand caressed her breast.

Ryder placed his hands on Mary's waist as he slid off the stone bed. In the same motion he lifted her and set her upon it. Kneeling at her feet, he removed the soft buckskin moccasins. His palms caressed her skin from ankle to knee, sliding under the leather skirt and parting the fringe. She was warm and taut. As he stood again his hands went higher, raising her skirt while he moved beneath it to learn the shape of her thighs. She watched his face, then his hands, then his face again when his fingers slipped more intimately between her thighs.

Her mouth parted. A protest hovered. A plea was formed. Ryder heard none of it as his mouth covered hers. Now Mary's pleasure was partly expressed by a humming sound at the back of her throat as she returned the kiss in full measure.

Ryder cupped Mary's bottom and pulled her to the edge of their bed. Her thighs were parted and when he leaned into her she cradled him naturally. He raised her pelvis for a moment, letting her feel his arousal between her thighs, warming her to the shape and strength of a man; then he eased back down and took the bottom of her shirt in his fingers and lifted the garment over her head.

Mary's first instinct was to raise her arms to cover herself. It was the small, almost imperceptible shake of Ryder's head that gave her pause, and the warmth in his gray eyes that stopped her. She could not look down at herself, but at seeing his admiring stare, her embarrassment slowly faded, replaced by an unfamiliar wash of pride and the realization that she liked being looked at as Ryder was looking at her now.

Her breasts were full, slightly swollen even before he cupped the undersides. His thumbs passed tenderly over the coral tips and stiffened them to pebble hardness. His head bent and he touched her neck first, then the hollow of her throat and the curve of her shoulder. He forced anticipation on her as his mouth went lower, skimming her skin until he reached the curve of her breast. Mary's back arched and Ryder accepted the offering. His lips closed over her nipple, laving the tip with his tongue, drawing a response from her with the hot suck of his mouth.

Cords of heat traveled from her breast to her thighs. It seemed sparks had been struck in her fingertips and in her toes. She could not get close enough to him. Her hands slid beneath his buckskin shirt. His skin was hot and smooth. It retracted as her fingers explored. His abdomen was taut, the muscles defined. She traced the edge of his rib cage with her knuckles. Her fingers dipped just below the belt that held his breechcloth in place.

Mary felt the loss keenly when Ryder pulled back. Her small gasp sounded loud to her own ears, as if it echoed in the chamber instead of being caught in her throat. Ryder's smile was wicked, and she knew he understood and was even enjoying making her experience the pleasure and then the absence of it.

His mouth brushed hers. "All in good time." The husky voice complimented his smile. He pulled up on the back of his shirt and removed it, tossing it behind him. "Now you can touch me."

She wanted to, but it was with her eyes that she first covered the breadth of his shoulders and the smooth expanse of his chest. She stared at the firm curve of his arms and the way his waist tapered in clean, strong lines. His nipples were already hard. Mary placed her hand between them, covering the beating of his heart. It raced on at the same frantic pace as her own.

She raised her eyes to his. The smile had vanished. His features were calm, the silver eyes implacable; yet there was the unmistakable stamp of desire as he returned her stare.

Ryder slowly bent his head again and took Mary's other breast in his mouth. Her fingers clutched his arms at first, then moved hungrily over his back and shoulders. She felt herself being eased backward against the stone bed. Blankets twisted beneath her as he removed her buckskin skirt. He placed kisses on the underside of her breast before he moved lower, down her rib cage and across her flat belly.

Mary tensed. Ryder raised himself up on the bed and removed his moccasins and breechcloth. He straddled her thighs and leaned forward, stretching like a predatory cat, sleek and beautiful above her. He caught Mary's wrists and held them lightly just above her head. Her slender frame was taut, the muscles rigid, and her struggle was reactive, not intentional. Her head was turned to the side, away from him.

"Give me your mouth."

Mary lifted her face. As Ryder claimed her mouth pleasure coursed through her and she returned the kiss, their shared pleasure increasing tenfold. Her arms looped around his neck, and her back arched. Her breasts scraped his chest, the tender nipples radiating sensation, and Mary moaned softly.

Ryder released her wrists. His hands caressed her arms, her shoulders. They slipped along her back and raised her hips. His knee parted her thighs as he adjusted his position. He watched her face as he probed, watched the play of shadows on her features as she gave herself up to him. He was achingly hard for her, but his first thrust was restrained. Mary was biting her lip. He held himself still and waited.

"Ryder?" She said his name softly, uncertainly.

It was almost his undoing. He raised her hips a little more and felt her body begin to accommodate his. He thrust into her hard as she yielded to him, and this time she closed around him like a silk sheath.

Mary moved with him now and the pleasure of it was almost beyond bearing. Every sensation was outside the realm of her experience, of her imagination. Ryder leaned close to her as their bodies rocked in unison. His breath moved strands of her red-gold hair. She could feel the moist heat of it on her skin. She liked the way his body pressed into hers, the way she could accept him and hold him and keep him to her. She liked the way the pleasure kept building.

In some ways it was like being underwater, sensation washing over her in waves. The surface was there, just out of her reach, but she knew it was there because of the cascade of moonlight shimmering across it. She swam toward it, challenging the current, moving with it and through it with the sleek, undulating curves of her body.

Mary twisted, stretching, and finally cried out as she broke through, exhilarated as much by the journey as the destination. She sucked in great draughts of air as her muscles contracted and her spirit was lifted. She held Ryder close, felt his thrusts become quick and shallow, heard the tempo of his breathing change.

His features were taut, his skin pulled tightly across the bones of his face. His eyes closed at the moment of his final thrust. He arched, his hard, lean body shivering with the force of his release. He rested his face in the curve of Mary's neck and recovered his uneven breath.

The warmth of him was comforting. Mary raised a knee and rubbed her leg slowly against his skin, aware of the inward curve of his hard buttock, and the contrasting texture of his leg. The sole of her foot lightly caressed his calf. She was disappointed when he withdrew from her and rolled away, even more bereft when he left the bed altogether.

Mary watched him pad unself-consciously to the well of water in their chamber. He hunkered down, dipped a basin into it, took up a cloth, then rose and turned toward her. She closed her eyes as if she hadn't been watching him greedily all along. His deep, rolling laughter let her know she had been caught out.

Ryder sat on the edge of their bed, set the basin down, and wrung out the cloth. Mary was searching for a blanket to cover herself, but he stopped her and applied the cloth instead to her thighs, wiping away the evidence of her virginity, first from her, then from himself. Mary was mortified. When Ryder finally removed the basin and returned to the bed, she was wrapped tightly in a blanket, clinging to the last remnants of her composure and wondering if she would ever recapture her dignity.

Ryder tugged on the blanket but she held fast, refusing to shed her cocoon. He pulled a blanket loosely over himself and stretched out beside her, propping himself on an elbow. "It was my pleasure, you know," he said, bending to kiss her cheek. "All of it."

Mary cast him an uncertain look out of the corner of her eye. He appeared to be quite sincere. "I could have bathed myself. I've been doing it for years."

Lantern light flickered in Mary's hair. Ryder's fingers grazed the edge of her short curls, brushing them back, twisting them around the tip. "It was for me to cleanse the wound," he said. "I was responsible for it."

It is all in the perception, she thought. When he put that meaning to his actions it seemed to tilt her world right again. It was intended to be a kind, healing gesture, not an intrusion. Mary's eyes softened, and she edged a little closer to him. His fingers felt good in her hair. The way he played with the strands sent a parade of warm feelings marching down her spine. "I wish it were longer."

"It's as it should be," he said. "And when it's twice this length it will still be as it should be." Did she understand, he wondered, that her hair was perfection in his eyes. It rivaled silk in its texture and the dawn in its coloring. Its length neither lent it beauty nor took any away. His fingers continued to sift through the strands. "Josanie admired your coloring."

A small vertical crease appeared between Mary's feathered brows. "Then it was all she admired," she said. "She didn't appear to be pleased with your choice of a bride."

Ryder did not deny it. "Josanie holds you to different standards than I do."

Mary doubted that Josanie was alone. The welcome she was extended by the family group was not without a hint of pity. "What standards?"

"Chiricahua maidens usually marry before their eighteenth birthday. There's no place in the society for unmarried people—

the economics of the band work against remaining single—so they're to be pitied."

That explained it, thought Mary. "So I was much too old to take a husband."

"Something like that."

"You mean there's more?" How else hadn't she measured up?

Ryder couldn't help but grin at her indignation. "Well, you didn't come with a bride price. Your father didn't ask anything for you, and I didn't offer. A Chiricahua suitor showers his intended bride's family with gifts. Horses. Goats. Baskets of food. Your father and mother left the camp empty-handed. To Josanie and the others it seemed that you were worthless because there was no demand."

"Jay Mac is going to demand your head on a plate," she said tartly. "That should satisfy Josanie."

Ryder's rueful smile flickered again as he rubbed the back of his neck. He could imagine the blade Jay Mac Worth would use to do the job. It wouldn't be sharp.

"What is Josanie to you?" Mary asked with quiet, restrained curiosity. She slipped her hand into Ryder's and rubbed her thumb across his palm.

"I told you. She's my father's wife. Naiche took her in marriage when his first wife, my mother, died. Josanie was my mother's youngest sister, and it was expected that Naiche would continue to care for the family."

Mary remembered that the son-in-law was supposed to lift the burdens of his wife's family. Apparently it was a promise that extended past her death. "All my sisters are spoken for," she told him, half in jest, half in earnest. "In the event that something should happen to me and you feel obliged to remarry in the family."

"I don't hold to all the customs."

Still, Mary was glad they were all married. "How is it that you call Naiche your father?"

"He adopted me."

Mary realized that all she knew about Ryder she could write on the back of her hand. She stared at him wonderingly.

"I was seven," he told her, offering for the first time without being asked. "Part of a wagon train crossing the Southwest with my father and mother and my little sister. We were headed for California where my father had a new teaching post. He'd been a professor of mathematics in Cincinnati."

Mary recalled that Ryder had studied mathematics at West Point. Her eyes strayed to the books in the basket by the wing chair, treasures, she realized now, that had belonged to his family. She recalled the inscriptions written at the front of each book and put names to the parents Ryder was describing. His father was Jackson, his mother Anne. She could not recall anything with his sister's name.

"We covered half the distance—as far as Saint Louis—by a more conventional train," he continued. "But at that point my parents decided joining a wagon party was more practical and educational, so they signed on." He paused. The hand that gripped Mary's was unconsciously tighter now. "It was an adventure," he said very low. "Right until the very end."

Compassion touched Mary's eyes and she ignored the press of his fingers over hers. "The Apache?"

"Yes, Apache. But not what you think. Not the Chiricahua. A band of the Southern Tonto attacked the train before we reached Phoenix. My mother and Molly were killed outright, but they used hot pitch on my father to torture him, stripping his skin away in front of me."

Mary blanched. She could not close her eyes for fear the vision would become all too clear. Instead she concentrated on Ryder's face and began to understand what he masked with his expression of determined calm. How could she say she did not want to hear more when he had lived through it?

"I was abducted by the group along with two other boys a little older than me. One of them, Henry Parker, died shortly afterward when he couldn't keep up with the band. The Tonto killed him rather than abandon him to the elements." When he heard Mary suck in her breath, he added, "To them it was a kindness."

It was on the tip of her tongue to protest that Henry had been only a child, but who knew that better than Ryder, by his own account an even younger child?

"I spent less than a week at the camp before it was raided by a band of Chiricahua. I saw my chance to escape and I took it. I made certain the Chiricahua got the horses and the other small treasures the Tonto had taken from the wagon train, and I ran after them as they left camp. They ignored me at first, but I wouldn't turn back so they couldn't."

"They admired your courage."

Ryder shook his head. "I wasn't courageous. I was running from the people who had murdered my mother and sister and had tortured my father. Hatred and fear kept me running after the Chiricahua raiders, and when that wasn't enough revenge kept me going."

"It always takes courage to leave," Mary said gently. "Some people can't face the fear of the unknown; yet it's exactly what you did. No wonder the Chiricahua wanted you." Her hand slipped from his and she stroked his forearm. "What happened to the other boy?"

"Tommy O'Neil. I never saw him again. I assume he was assimilated into the tribe in the same manner I was taken into the Chiricahua fold."

"It's hard to know who adopted whom."

Ryder's small smile reflected a more pleasant memory. "Naiche and I have often had the same discussion."

An opening in Mary's blanket appeared as she adjusted her position. She didn't seem to notice the split along her thigh, but Ryder did. His eyes skimmed the length of her white leg from hip to ankle. She had the softest skin just behind her knee. He wondered what she would do if he turned her over and kissed her there, if he let his mouth trail up the back of her thigh, if he filled his palms with her lovely little bottom.

"How did you get to West Point?" she asked. "Or was that

your uncle's doing?" Mary imagined Senator Wilson Stillwell fit into the equation in some fashion. "He must be your mother's brother. Did he——"

Ryder shut her mouth with a kiss. His lips covered hers from corner to corner, teasing a response from her.

Mary was breathless when he drew back, her eyes radiant. "I won't always let you get away with that."

"But for now?" He was hopeful.

"For now it was an inspired idea."

As Ryder bent over her again he fleetingly wondered what had ever called Mary to the Church. Then her arms came around him and she turned into him, opening her chrysalis and enfolding him in her butterfly wings.

There was less time for exploring now. They both knew what they wanted. Mary's skin was sensitive to the slightest brush of his fingers. Her nipples stood erect when his mouth only hovered above her breasts. When he kissed the backs of her knees she thought she would shatter.

Her touch was no less powerful on him. Ryder felt her mouth draw on the skin of his shoulder, then she nipped it with her teeth. She didn't merely mirror the things that had been done to her, she found her own ways to please him. She liked to run her hand along his narrow hip, liked the heat of his skin beneath her palm and the way he drew in his breath when she strayed close to his arousal.

Ryder was more conscious of Mary's tenderness than she was. Desire made her insistent, and when he would have been gentle, she was greedy. She helped him this time, guiding his entry and lifting her hips to accommodate his thrust.

She whispered his name and he could not refuse her.

As Mary abandoned herself to pleasure, Ryder let her set the pace. He watched her savor each subtle sensation, closing her eyes and sipping the air delicately as if too much would overwhelm her. Her body was warm and pliant, a supple wand beneath him.

They moved as one, joined, hands clasped. His dark hair

slipped forward and shielded his face from the light. His profile was dark, predatory, and yet his touch was adoring. He held himself back as she rode the crest of her climax alone and then he came into her, filling her deeply with his pleasure and his seed.

Ryder lay back, replete. It was Mary who turned toward him. She stretched out, her bent knee resting against his thigh, her arm curved under her for support. The air in the chamber never changed from its standard seventy degrees, but it felt cooler now on their sweat-slick bodies. Mary drew up a single blanket to cover them both.

"Are you going to sleep?" she asked, watching him close his eyes.

"Mmmm."

"I thought the Apache were admired for their stamina."

Ryder raised one brow.

"I heard stories at Fort Union," she told him. "About the scouts."

He still didn't look at her. "Is that right?" he asked dryly.

Mary ran her knuckle along Ryder's jawline. There was a hint of stubble there. In the morning he would have to set out his razor and shaving cup, a reminder that he was not a smooth-faced Apache at all but a professor's son from Ohio. "They say a warrior can cover fifty miles in a single day and is so swift he can outrun a horse. A man like that could probably stay awake a little longer."

Now one of Ryder's eyes opened and he gave her a wary look. "There's stamina and then there's stamina." He closed his eye and settled back, his features relaxing as though the conversation had ended.

Mary opened her mouth to say something, then thought better of it. She watched him a while longer, studying his face in unguarded repose. Finally she placed her head in the crook of his shoulder and an arm across his chest. She slept deeply.

* * *

Leaving his drink unattended on the mantel, Jay Mac paced the floor in front of the fireplace. Low flames made logs crackle there, keeping the chilly night air at bay. His hands were thrust in the pockets of his jacket, and his head was bent. "I can't believe there's not some sign of them."

Rennie placed a hand over her husband's forearm. It was both a supportive and cautionary gesture. Jay Mac had been saying words to the same effect for over an hour, as if changing the inflection or rearranging the sentence would bring about the reply he wanted. Her father did not mean to be accusing, but Rennie could understand that, after so many repetitions, Jarret might begin to hear it that way. Her husband had been a skilled bounty hunter, tracking down criminals in the Colorado Rockies and east of the Mississippi. He was good at what he did, but it had been eight years since he had earned his living that way. Ryder McKay was challenging Jarret's skills in a manner no wanted man had. No one Jarret had ever hunted understood so well how to hide a trail or mislead the trackers. The trail had been cold more than two weeks, with no hint that it might turn hot again. To make things even more difficult, the territory was unfamiliar to Jarret. He understood the landscape of the Rockies. The mountains and mesas of southeastern Arizona could have easily been the hills and valleys of the moon.

"By all reports, including my own, he's very good at what he does," Jarret said. "Ryder McKay is not a regular Army scout. He's been used for years for special, sensitive assignments. The other scouts say that if he doesn't want to be found, he won't be, and their words are being borne out. This is coming from men who take great pride in being able to track anyone or anything." He added with a touch of sarcasm, "They weren't recruited by the Army because they're stupid."

Moira set her teacup on the table. Her voice, like everyone else's, was hushed. Fort Union's quarters were not so private as they appeared. Voices raised in arguments or excitement could be overheard in the corridor beyond or in the adjoining rooms. Jay Mac and Moira had not reported their abduction to the Army search party that found them. They'd told Lieutenant Davis Rivers and, later, General Gardner that they had wandered away from the main line in search of a better route through the foothills and had lost their way. They had been chastised for their foolishness, and Jay Mac had had to bear it in silence, making his stiff apologies sound sincere.

"What about that one scout . . . that Tonto person?" Moira asked Jarret. "I've heard there's no love lost between him and Mr. McKay."

"You mean Rosario," Rennie said. "Yes, I've heard the same thing. I really don't understand it, but it seems the Apache are not so easily categorized as one nation. The Tonto are part of the Western Apache, and they've no particular liking for the Chiricahua." She looked to her father. "Perhaps if you were to hire him, offer a reward above what you've already promised for Mary's return, he would cover the ground again."

Jay Mac paused in his pacing as he considered Rennie's suggestion. "General Gardner just might release him to me," he said, thinking aloud. He glanced at Jarret. "I'd like it better if you accompanied him. Mary would be less frightened if you were there when she's found."

"You're putting a lot of faith in Rosario," Jarret said. "I don't particularly trust him. I think his interest lies more in bringing down Ryder McKay than in returning Mary safely. Remember, most of the people here believe Mary helped McKay escape. For that alone, Rosario may not care what happens to her."

Rennie took up her sister's cause. "Mary had nothing to do with the escape."

"I didn't say she did," Jarret responded. "Only that—"

Moira's hands curved around her teacup. She looked across the table at Rennie and Jarret, then stole a glance at her husband. She could tell he was thinking the same as she. "Don't be too quick to defend your sister," she said quietly. The words were even more painful to say aloud than they had been to think. "You didn't see her with him today."

"That ridiculous ceremony," Jay Mac muttered.

Moira ignored her husband's comment. "I don't think she would have returned with us if she had been given the chance."

Rennie's eyes flew to her father's. He was not objecting to what Moira was saying. That alone was telling. "You mean she wanted to stay with him? How can that be?"

"Oh, she didn't want to be parted from us," Moira said. "At least not so soon. It was clear that she was surprised to see us and that being separated was an agony for her, but your father and I had opportunity to see her before she saw us." Moira's green eyes were awash with tears. She steadied herself to go on. "And she was . . . radiant."

Jay Mac's eyes closed. He rubbed the bridge of his nose tiredly. In his mind's eye he could see his Mary Francis clearly, shimmering in her beaded dress, the colors of the sunset glancing off her hair. Her hand hadn't been captured by Ryder's at that point. She had held his of her own accord.

"Papa?" Rennie asked. "Is this right? Do you think Mary's with him because she wants to be?"

Jay Mac came to stand behind Moira. He placed his hands on her shoulders. "I don't know anymore," he said heavily. "It makes it all the more imperative that we find her first. General Gardner's reduced the size of the search parties, but he hasn't given up. Sooner or later McKay's luck will run out. I think one of us should be there when that happens."

In unison Jay Mac, Moira, and Rennie looked to Jarret Sullivan.

Mary eased herself into the icy spring. The cold raised gooseflesh on her arms, and she sucked in her breath. There was really never any getting used to it. She quickly soaped her hair, working up a lather, then rinsed. Droplets of water were flung in an arc around her as she shook her head.

"You're like a puppy."

Mary's head snapped up and her eyes opened. Ryder was looming above her on the stone edge of the spring. He was perfectly, splendidly naked. The smile on his face was a trifle indulgent and a lot more wicked.

"I had a puppy once, you know." He hunkered on the lip of the well. "We left Copper behind in Cincinnati."

"Copper?" she asked on a thread of sound. Really, that wicked smile did strange things to her stomach. "An Irish Setter?"

"A bulldog," he said matter-of-factly. "Molly named him." He was grinning openly now, laughing at her. He raised his hands, half in surrender, half for protection as Mary showered him with water. "I didn't say you reminded me of *that* puppy!"

Mary wasn't placated. She scooped another handful of water into her cupped hands and let it fly.

There was nothing for it but that Ryder should join her in the spring. He jumped in, sending a geyser of water into the air. When he surfaced Mary was pressed to one edge of the spring hiding her face behind her hands and laughing helplessly. Pinning her to the edge, Ryder placed an arm on either side of her. He bent his head so his forehead touched hers and growled lowly at the back of his throat.

Mary stopped laughing. That husky growl could start the butterflies in her stomach as easily as his wicked smile. She cast him a wary glance through her splayed fingers. His eyes were boring into hers, not frosty now, but a slightly darker gray, more like molten silver than melting snow.

She found she was wrong about the water. One could do better than get used to it. One could learn to ignore it entirely. As Ryder's mouth closed over hers it was what she was able to do.

In his arms she felt weightless. He lifted her with ease, bringing her body flush to his. Her breasts were crushed against his slick skin, and her legs wrapped naturally around his flanks. They exchanged excited, hungry kisses. He touched her temple with his mouth, her closed eyes, and cheeks. His teeth caught her earlobe and he tickled the hollow behind her ear with his tongue. She liked the texture of his skin beneath her lips, the sweet and salty taste of him when she pressed her mouth to the taut line of his jaw and the plane of his shoulder.

His hands roamed freely, exploring the shape of her head, her face, her slender neck. His palms and fingers moved with a certain exactness, as if he would be held responsible for recreating each angle and contour. He learned the slant of her shoulders and the gentle curve of her spine. Her narrow waist fit neatly between his hands while her bottom filled them. Her long legs fascinated him, curved as they were around his body, melding her to him even before they were joined.

Mary let her fingers trip along the length of his back. His muscles bunched when she touched his shoulders. His ridged abdomen was flat against hers, and his arms held her in a secure embrace. She laid a line of kisses along his collarbone and pressed her cheek against his skin. He was stirring between her thighs, and she learned that the shape of her own body could be defined by the fit of him against her.

Ryder's fingers slipped between their bodies. His knuckles brushed her breasts and his thumb passed back and forth over her raised nipples. A flush of desire crept under Mary's skin, suffusing it with color. Her pelvis cradled him tightly and she undulated against him slowly as he drew on all her senses.

His hand went lower, this time to the juncture of her thighs, and he pressed his palm against her mound sending a shudder through her. Her fingertips whitened on his flesh as his fingers stroked and probed. Tongues of flame licked her skin. She jerked against him as his fingers dipped and entered.

He murmured against her ear. The words were unintelligible but the tone was gentling soothing, and in the end he seemed to have possession of her will. Mary's body obeyed his commands. The intimate press of his fingers made her limbs grow taut and her slender frame arch. She threw her head back and rivulets of water slid past her temples and her shoulders. She felt his eyes on her, gauging her restless response, ready to push it to another level.

And when he did, Mary's fingers unfolded as pleasure engulfed her. Her mouth opened but she made no cry. Her entire body went rigid, still. The tightness lasted only a moment before she collapsed against him, sinking into the curve of his embrace. He stroked her damp hair as her heartbeat slowed. Between her legs he was still stiff and hard. This time his satisfaction had not been physical.

Mary's eyes were closed. A little ashamed of the selfish pleasure she had enjoyed, she couldn't look at Ryder. She could feel him against her, his arousal pulsing. She would have taken him into her, had wanted to, but he had denied himself. "Why did you do that?" she asked softly. Even in his embrace the water was chilly now. She shivered lightly.

Ryder set Mary down carefully and raised her chin with his forefinger. "You're not ready to take me again. Not so soon." His thumb traced the edge of her damp lower lip. "But I did not want to deny you . . . or myself."

Mary wrested her chin away from his light grip and looked down through the crystalline water. Ryder made no attempt to shield his aroused state. "I think you did deny yourself," she said.

"That's only because you're still an innocent."

She looked at him oddly, not understanding. Rather than ask him what he meant she determined to find out for herself. Looking around, she spied the slim bar of soap she had used on her hair. Mary picked it up, ignoring the cloth that lay nearby. She raised a bit of lather between her hands, then she applied the soap and suds to Ryder's body.

"I don't think—" he began.

"You think too much," she interrupted gently. Her hands worked deftly, sliding the soap over Ryder's shoulders, massaging his chest and upper arms with slippery lather. Her fingers glided to his neck before she circled around him and rubbed down his back. His flesh rippled under her touch and defined the hardness lying beneath his taut skin. She washed the base of his spine, finding the small dimples with her index finger. She soaped his hard buttocks and the backs of his thighs, then returned to his back, slipping her palms along his tapered waist and narrow hips.

Mary slipped her arms around him from behind, resting her forehead against his back. Her soapy fingers traced the ridges of his rib cage and rubbed lather across his abdomen. Her hands went lower to the arrow of hair below his navel. That was when she dropped the soap.

And the pretense.

Made buoyant by the water, Mary slipped around Ryder again, her entire body rubbing smoothly against his. Her hands went below the surface of the water and grasped him. She could feel the coursing of the blood that was making him hot and hard beneath her fingers.

Ryder's hand closed over Mary's and he showed her how to take him. She discovered that by giving this pleasure she had denied herself nothing.

"You were right," she said quietly when he set her outside the pool. She picked up a thin cotton quilt and began drying herself.

Ryder hoisted himself out of the spring and steadied himself. Water dripped on the stones in a slowing staccato rhythm. He had a little less strength coming out than he had had going in. There was no chance that he was going to forget that dip in the spring anytime soon. "About what?" he asked.

"That I was an innocent."

Though Mary wasn't looking at him, he couldn't miss her smug smile. "Just a little full of yourself, aren't you?" he asked dryly.

"Pride is my worst fault. Sister Benedict always said so."

Ryder dried himself off briskly, hitched the damp blanket around his hips, then pulled Mary to her feet. She dragged the cotton quilt around her, tucking the ends neatly between her breasts. Ryder turned her toward their bed and gave her a pat on the bottom, urging her forward. "How is it that you ever became a nun?" he asked.

Mary stiffened at the question. She slowly pushed herself

onto their stone shelf bed. "You say that as if you think I shouldn't have. It's not very complimentary."

"I only meant—"

She held up her hand, stopping him. "I don't want to hear it. You think because I respond to you so completely I was somehow unsuited for convent life. If I carry your reasoning a little farther it's natural to conclude I should have become a whore at seventeen instead of a bride of Christ."

One of Ryder's brows kicked up. "I was trying to—"

Mary's full mouth flattened mutinously, and if it had not been so predictably childish, she would have clapped her hands over her ears. "I'm hungry."

Ryder hesitated. He had no liking for their argument and even less for the misunderstanding. However, it seemed that Mary had closed the discussion. "Very well," he said after a moment. He turned and went to their larder, opening tins of meat and vegetables. Realizing he was hungry as well, Ryder set out the portion on two plates. He handed one to Mary, but didn't join her on the bed. He sat in the wing chair, his long legs stretched negligently in front of him.

She pushed the cold food around her plate. Hunger had been a diversion, not a need. She tried to think of some way to make amends for her sharpness. She had never been very good at saying she was sorry. She lamented that pride, indeed, was her worst fault. "I can't talk about it," she said at last. "It's too . . ." She struggled for the word. "Too *personal.*"

Ryder nodded, saying nothing.

"You'd have to know my parents better, particularly my mother." She sighed. "I'm just not ready." She sighed again. This time her eyes were apologetic as she shrugged uncertainly. "I'm sorry."

Ryder couldn't pinpoint the precise thing her regret was supposed to cover, but he accepted it. "Eat up," he said gently.

Mary tucked into her food. "Tell me about our ceremony in the clearing," she said around a mouthful of peas. "Why did we stand in the water?"

"The Apache trace their origin to the Child of the Water. We were united with that blessing and the acknowledgment of both families."

"It's very symbolic, then." She liked that. Her life in the Church had been full of symbols and ritual. "Although I'm not certain my father actually acknowledged us. It's not as though he gave me away."

"His presence was enough."

She ate more, thoughtful now. "You realize I don't consider us really married."

He nodded. "It seemed like a good compromise."

Mary barely heard him. "I mean, it's more of an arrangement, isn't it, instead of a marriage?"

"If that's the way you want to think about it."

"It won't require an annulment or a divorce . . ."

"Not a church annulment," he said. "And not a lawyer's divorce." Ryder set his empty plate aside and regarded Mary steadily. An edge of frost had returned to his lightly colored eyes. "You only have to pack my things and put them outside the entrance to our home." He spread his hands to indicate their chamber and shrugged. "That's all. If you find me lazy or unwilling to provide for you, if we're incompatible, if we bicker too often, or if I'm uncommonly jealous—all of these things can end it." His eyes darkened a fraction. "As can infidelity."

Returning his stare, Mary swallowed hard. It was almost as if he was warning her. "Well, yes," she said, bemused. "Of course. Infidelity."

His smile was not a smile at all. The watchful predator had returned. "Just so we understand each other." He rose from the wing chair and rinsed off his plate in the pool. The underground current swept the debris away. "Are you finished?" he asked Mary, looking at the half-eaten remains.

She nodded, handing them over. "I suppose I wasn't as hungry as I thought I was."

Ryder put the uneaten portion back in a tin to be used later in the day. He rinsed Mary's plate and the utensils, put them

Take A Trip Into A Timeless World of Passion and Adventure with Kensington Choice Historical Romances!
—Absolutely FREE!

Enjoy the passion and adventure of another time with Kensington Choice Historical Romances. They are the finest novels of their kind, written by today's best-selling romance authors. Each Kensington Choice Historical Romance transports you to distant lands in a bygone age. Experience the adventure and share the delight as proud men and spirited women discover the wonder and passion of true love.

4 BOOKS WORTH UP TO $24.96— Absolutely FREE!

Get 4 FREE Books!

We created our convenient Home Subscription Service so you'll be sure to have the hottest new romances delivered each month right to your doorstep—usually before they are available in book stores. Just to show you how convenient the Zebra Home Subscription Service is, we would like to send you 4 FREE Kensington Choice Historical Romances. The books are worth up to $24.96, but you only pay $1.99 for shipping and handling. There's no obligation to buy additional books—ever!

Save Up To 30% With Home Delivery!

Accept your FREE books and each month we'll deliver 4 brand new titles as soon as they are published. They'll be yours to examine FREE for 10 days. Then if you decide to keep the books, you'll pay the preferred subscriber's price (up to 30% off the cover price!), plus shipping and handling. Remember, you are under no obligation to buy any of these books at any time! If you are not delighted with them, simply return them and owe nothing. But if you enjoy Kensington Choice Historical Romances as much as we think you will, pay the special preferred subscriber rate and save over $8.00 off the cover price!

We have **4 FREE BOOKS** for you as your
introduction to
KENSINGTON CHOICE!
To get your FREE BOOKS, worth up to $24.96, mail
the card below or call TOLL-FREE 1-800-770-1963.
Visit our website at www.kensingtonbooks.com.

Get 4 FREE Kensington Choice Historical Romances!

♥ **YES!** Please send me my 4 FREE KENSINGTON CHOICE HISTORICAL ROMANCES (without obligation to purchase other books). I only pay $1.99 for shipping and handling. Unless you hear from me after I receive my 4 FREE BOOKS, you may send me 4 new novels—as soon as they are published—to preview each month FREE for 10 days. If I am not satisfied, I may return them and owe nothing. Otherwise, I will pay the money-saving preferred subscriber's price (over $8.00 off the cover price), plus shipping and handling. I may return any shipment within 10 days and owe nothing, and I may cancel any time I wish. In any case the 4 FREE books will be mine to keep.

KN124A

Name_____

Address_____ Apt._____

City_____ State_____ Zip_____

Telephone (____)_____

Signature_____

(If under 18, parent or guardian must sign)

Offer limited to one per household and not to current subscribers. Terms, offer and prices subject to change. Orders subject to acceptance by Kensington Choice Book Club.
Offer Valid in the U.S. only.

4 FREE

Kensington
Choice
Historical
Romances
(worth up to
$24.96)
are waiting
for you to
claim them!

See details
inside...

ll..l..lll....lll.l.l.l..l.l.l.l..lll.l..l..lll...ll...l.l.l..l

KENSINGTON CHOICE
Zebra Home Subscription Service, Inc.
P.O. Box 5214
Clifton NJ 07015-5214

away, then got out his maps from the chest. He brought them over to the bed and unrolled them, flattening them with the side of his hand.

Mary yawned. She had no idea if it was day or night outside of the cavern or if she had slept hours after their last lovemaking or only a few minutes.

"You can go to sleep," he said. "I won't disturb you."

He began to pick up the maps, but Mary stopped him. She was tired, it was true, but she was also strangely reluctant to go to sleep. His mood had cast a pall over her. All the talk of marriage and divorce . . . it was unsettling.

"I don't mind if you look at them here," she said. She brought down the lighted lantern from another shelf and placed it beside her.

Ryder laid out the maps again.

"Perhaps I could help you," she offered.

"You're welcome to look on."

It wasn't an enthusiastic invitation, but neither had he said her help wouldn't amount to much. Mary knelt on her knees and elbows and surveyed the topographical map closely. Ryder remained leaning against the high stone bed, his eyes occasionally drifting from the contours at his fingertips to the ones Mary was unwittingly presenting to him.

"You may want to tuck that blanket a little more firmly," he said. Under his breath he added, "Before I forget which mountain range I'm studying."

"Hmm?" Mary murmured, glancing up at him.

He pointed to his own chest. "Your blanket."

Mary looked down at herself. She was practically spilling out over the top. "Oh . . . thank you." She adjusted it without embarrassment and resumed her inspection of the uppermost map.

Ryder shook his head, wondering what to make of her. With her head bent he couldn't see the small, satisfied smile that lifted her mouth.

"I assume these maps have something to do with the gold from Colter Canyon," she said. "Do you know where it is?"

"Do you mean, do I know where it is because I have first-hand knowledge, or do I have suspicions?"

"Suspicions, of course," she said, raising her eyes to his. "I don't think you had anything to do with the raid."

"I was there."

"I know. I heard that. My brother-in-law told me."

"I see," Ryder said. "What else did you learn?"

"Not much. There wasn't time. I wasn't in the fort very long before you took me away."

"Then you don't know about Miss Hamilton?"

A chill crept down Mary's spine. She brushed back a tendril of hair that had fallen over her forehead. Her forest green eyes narrowed thoughtfully. "No, I've never heard the name." With a sense of foreboding she asked, "Who is she? Your fiancée?"

Ryder was watching Mary closely, gauging her reaction. "Anna Leigh Hamilton." It was difficult to maintain an indifferent profile when he had to say her name. "Senator Warren Hamilton's daughter. The woman who says that while the Chiricahua were attacking the wagons in Colter Canyon, I was raping her."

Ten

It wasn't shock that touched Mary's features, but curiosity. She looked at Ryder and asked frankly, "Why would she do that?"

Ryder's eyes mirrored nothing of what he was thinking. "Aren't you going to ask if it's true? Don't you want to know if I raped Anna Leigh?"

Mary's brow furrowed. "Why would I ask that? I can't imagine you even *thinking* about raping her."

"Then you're the only one," he said without rancor. "Miss Hamilton was very effective in telling her story."

A short red-gold strand of hair had fallen over Mary's forehead. She blew it out of the way. "I'm sure she was. But I have another experience with you that makes it difficult to believe you would act in any dishonorable way." Her gaze dropped back to the map, and she pretended to study it. "I haven't forgotten the night we spent outside a watering hole in the Hudson Valley. You held me, comforted me, and quite against your will, I think, your body responded to mine."

"It wasn't against my will," he said softly. "I wanted you that night. I had wanted you that morning."

Mary's fingers stopped tracing map lines as a frisson of heat tripped down her spine. She closed her eyes and said words she had never spoken aloud before, words that she had struggled not to put together even silently in her own mind. "And you never acted on it. Not that morning when I would have fought you . . .

and not that evening when I would have given you anything you wanted."

Ryder had to strain to hear her last whispered words. It was no admission she was giving him, but her confession. "Oh, Mary," he said quietly. He took her wrists and pulled her toward him. The maps twisted and curled beneath her, but Ryder didn't care. When she was at the edge of the bed he lifted her down but never let her leave his embrace.

She rested her head against his shoulder. Tears pressed at the back of her closed lids. "It's not the reason I left the Church," she said on a thread of sound. "I was already struggling . . . questioning . . . If you hadn't been there that night the outcome would have been the same . . ."

He stroked her hair, resting his chin against the crown of her head. Pain shuddered through her and Ryder felt the vibration against his skin.

Mary's voice was choked now. She had to work words past the hard, aching lump at the back of her throat. "Sometimes . . . sometimes I think God sent you to me . . . to help me surrender. I was fighting His wishes . . . ignoring what He was telling me so I wouldn't . . ."

Her tears touched his chest, slipping along the outline of her cheek. Ryder didn't probe or press. He waited.

"So I wouldn't disappoint . . . my mother." Her eyes were squeezed tightly shut, but tears still ran freely from them and her breath came in small, pained gasps. Sagging against Ryder, Mary cried until she exhausted herself.

Ryder pushed the maps aside and lifted her back on the bed. This time he joined her, stretching out beside her, his arm placed familiarly around her waist. An extra blanket warded off the chill. He wiped her eyes with the corner of it.

Mary gave him a watery, embarrassed smile. "I don't know what happened," she said. "I didn't expect to say those things."

"I know."

"We were talking about you . . . I shouldn't have—"

"Shhh," he whispered. "It's good. It's healing."

Mary closed her eyes. He was right. Her heart was lighter now, her head clearer. Ryder's body was warm at her back, and the arm around her was exactly as it should be. She was asleep before she realized it was going to happen.

Ryder woke from a dead sleep and sat upright. A chill covered his body, and beads of perspiration touched his brow. He was hot and cold at once, and the premonition of danger wouldn't leave him. He could no longer tap the dream that had pulled him to consciousness, but emotions—fear and pain and loss— lingered. Something forgotten, he thought. Something left behind.

Mary was sleeping quietly beside him, undisturbed by his nightmare. The evidence of her tears and exhaustion was in her slightly swollen lids and in the shadows beneath her lashes. She was breathing softly now, easily, the serenity of her expression so markedly beautiful that Ryder knew a measure a peace merely looking upon her.

The unsettled feeling persisted, however, and he had learned at the knee of Naiche not to ignore that feeling. He moved to the edge of the bed and swung his legs over the side. Fiddling with the lantern, he increased the light so most of the chamber was visible to him from where he sat. There was nothing out of place, nothing different than it had been, yet the sensation of danger would not be put to rest.

Ryder got up and put the lantern aside. There was no terror for him in the darkness, but he lighted all the other lanterns anyway. The only shadows in the chamber were the ones he created as he moved from place to place seeking out the thing that disturbed him.

In the end he had to admit to himself it was only foolishness. It had been nothing but the cold tentacles of a forgotten dream. He looked over his shoulder at Mary. Let her sleep, he thought, but for him it was time to make a new day of it. He would dress and . . .

It came to him then, like a physical blow. The sensation of danger tightened Ryder's abdomen and prepared him to receive it. The force of it was all in his mind, and it still had the power to make him recoil.

He spun around, searching for the clothes he had bundled and carried on the journey back from the clearing. His eyes went to every level of the chamber. He could remember picking the garments up after they had left the camp and returned to the clearing. He had even given Mary his shirt for warmth. His gaze settled on the flannel shirt lying on the floor beside their bed. Ryder closed his eyes, trying to visualize what had happened to the other things. He could almost feel the weight of them in his hand, the way he had shifted the bundle from one hand to another as he'd helped Mary along the rocky path. How was it that he held it at one moment and forgotten it in the next?

Ryder's eyes opened and Mary filled his vision. Of course he had forgotten. Mary had filled his senses.

Ryder moved to the bed and laid his hand on Mary's shoulder. As if she could sense urgency in his light touch, she came awake almost instantly.

Her eyes flew to his face. "What is it?"

"I have to leave. I wanted you to know I'll be gone—"

"What? What do you mean you—"

He gave her shoulder a squeeze and said calmly, "I'll be gone longer than usual."

Mary sat up as Ryder began to dress. Feeling a little dazed by the abrupt wakening, she watched him put on the buckskin shirt, breechcloth, and moccasins he had worn in their wedding ceremony. "You don't usually tell me when you're leaving," she said. This was different, she thought. Something was wrong.

"Things are different now. I thought you'd want to know."

"Why leave at all?" A small vertical crease appeared between her brows. She hitched the quilt around her breasts as she came to her feet. "There can't be anything impor—"

Ryder stopped her by gripping her shoulders. "I left our clothes on the trail," he said. "I had them in my hand. You and

I were arguing . . . I kissed you . . . I think I dropped them then. I can't remember having them after that."

Mary understood. "Of course, you have to get them." All the work he had done to cover their trail was undone by a moment's inattention. She searched his face wondering if he blamed her or himself.

"This isn't about blame," he said, answering the question she hadn't had to ask. "It's about responsibility. I was supposed to be responsible."

"Can I help? Is there something I can do?"

"It's for me to fix," he said. "And I can travel more quickly alone."

Mary held onto those words. She could not remember time in the chamber ever passing so slowly. She had no way of knowing if Ryder had faced sunshine or starshine when he reached the mouth of the cavern, or which would have helped him more in accomplishing his task. In her mind, she allotted time for him to search for the clothes, time for him to cover his trail. She made allowances for the climate and still more for his caution.

She tried to read, but thought instead of all the things that could go wrong. What if the clothes had already been found? Animals might have scattered them. Soldiers could pick up the trail miles from where they had been searching, and their success in finding Ryder would be a tribute to coincidence and luck. It occurred to her that someone else might find the clothes. A prospector perhaps. An Army scout.

A bounty hunter.

Jarret Sullivan.

It was senseless now to wish she had warned Ryder. She had hugged the secret of her brother-in-law's bounty hunting to herself. In the beginning she had not wanted Ryder to take any extra precautions or set any traps. He was so certain his hideaway couldn't be found that she had kept the secret to serve him his comeuppance. When had the desire to teach him a lesson gone?

If Jarret had ever stopped looking for her it was a certainty he had taken up the search again. That would be the consequence of Ryder including Jay Mac and Moira in the wedding ceremony. Jarret would find whatever remained of the Chiricahua camp and from there . . .

Mary dropped her book, startled as one of the lanterns flickered, then was extinguished. She stared at it. How long did one of them stay lit before the oil was used? Six hours? A little longer? Perhaps it hadn't been completely filled. But she had done the filling herself and this lantern had only been burning since Ryder had wakened. If he could really travel faster on his own why had he already been gone six hours?

Mary's book slid from her lap to the floor as she stood. It lay there unnoticed as Mary considered her options. She could wait—Ryder would want her to do that—or she could search for him. It was what she wanted to do. She compromised, deciding she could wait at the mouth of the cavern. Armed with the knowledge of how to read the signs in the passages, Mary was confident that she could make it to the entrance safely. It would pass the time. Perhaps, she thought, she would even meet him along the way.

Mary refilled the empty lantern with oil and lighted it. Wearing a pair of Ryder's trousers, one of his shirts, and the moccasins he had given her, Mary hefted the lantern and began her journey to the mouth of the cavern.

She took her time, stopping to examine the signs carefully at every juncture. With each pause she found herself imagining that Ryder was closer. She half expected to look up and find him standing in a stone archway and watching her study his peculiar hieroglyphs. He never was.

At some junctures the signs were harder to locate. Mary had good cause to wonder at her wisdom in making the journey. She regretted not bringing beans with her again in the event she got lost, but she was of no mind to turn around. On two separate occasions she took passages that would not have been her first choice if it hadn't been for the markings. At least once she was forced to choose a route that was not clearly marked at all.

Relief washed over her when she stumbled into the wide, yawning entrance of the cavern. Weak-kneed, she sat on a smooth slab of stone until her heart quieted in her chest and she could laugh at her own foolishness.

Mary picked her way over the boulders and across the small stream to reach the opening. Putting the lantern out, she set it down and walked outside long enough to take her measure of the sun's height. Her very rough calculation was that it was late afternoon. That meant Ryder had had to make all of his journey in daylight.

She sat down again, worry replacing relief that she had come so far with no sign of Ryder. He had told her he would be gone longer than usual, and she tried to keep that in her mind. It was difficult to do with no timepiece to make a comparison. It seemed to her that he had never been gone even half so long before. Or was it merely that she hadn't cared so much?

Over the next few hours Mary ventured out of the cavern on five occasions. Although she strayed farther each time she was always aware of the foolishness of her venture. It was as Ryder had always warned her—there was simply nowhere for her to go. The realization that she couldn't do anything for him only made her feel more helpless.

After the sun set Mary stayed put. Wind eddied through the cavern's mouth and raised odd sighs and whistling moans among the rocks. The sound raised the hair on the back of her neck, and she remembered there were chambers here that had been used for a burial ground. When the pitch of the wind died she was surrounded by silence. It was more eerie in its own way than the moaning.

Mary's hand strayed to her side to finger the rosary that was no longer there. The wind picked up again, blowing life into the cavern. Mary bowed her head and prayed for all the lost souls, Ryder among them.

Her voice came to Ryder on the back of the wind. He stood

just inside the entrance and leaned heavily against the stone archway. She wasn't visible to him, but her voice was the sweetest music.

"Mary."

She thought she had imagined it at first, that it was only the wind playing tricks on her. But then it came again and Mary knew—she *knew* her prayers had been answered. Her eyes flew open and her head snapped up and she searched the yawning entrance for the dark silhouette that was no part of the landscape. "Ryder!" She was on her feet when she saw him, running to his side.

He was almost toppled by the force of her arms around him. His greeting was a groan.

Mary stepped back instantly, her eyes trying to pierce the darkness to search his face. "What is it?" she demanded. "You've been hurt, haven't you?"

"It's not so bad."

Fear made her voice sharp. "I suppose you think that's an answer to my question. You should have said, 'Yes.' I'll be the one to determine how bad it is."

"Be careful. You're beginning to sound like a wife." He sucked in the beginnings of a laugh as pain shot through him. Ryder clutched his side to limit the agony to as small a place as possible.

Mary stopped her gentle search. "Let me light a lantern," she said. "I can't do you any good in the dark. I may even hurt you."

Ryder missed her hands immediately. "What are you doing here anyway? You should be back in the chamber."

Mary struck the flint. White light nicely illuminated the sour look she gave him. For good measure it was accompanied by an unladylike snort.

His smile was lopsided. "Point taken," he said dryly.

Mary raised the lantern. "Oh, God," she whispered. Ryder's face was ashen and lines of strain were clearly etched at the corners of his mouth and eyes. Dried blood covered his fingers and streaked the front of his breechcloth. The wound that was the source of the blood ran in an ugly, jagged line for most of the length of Ryder's left thigh. He had torn part of the breech-cloth to make a bandage, but it was inadequate for the task. Some of the buckskin had dried to the wound while elsewhere blood continued to drip.

She looked at the way Ryder was still holding his ribs. "Broken?" she asked.

He nodded. "Two, I think."

Her eyes dropped to his feet. The bundle of clothing he had gone out for was lying there.

Ryder followed her gaze. "I brought back the prize."

Mary didn't comment. She couldn't help but wonder at the cost. "Let me fix a bandage for you now."

He shook his head. "I'll bleed more if you lift the bandage I've made. I want to get out of this area. We're too vulnerable."

"Were you followed?"

"No, but I won't be so difficult to track."

She understood. He hadn't been able to cover the route he had taken. Somewhere beyond the cavern there was enough of Ryder's blood for the trail to be picked up again. Mary wouldn't let herself think about that now. Ryder wasn't nearly as strong as he was pretending to be. "I need to get you back to the chamber where I can look after you properly," she said. "Should I support you or would it be less painful for you to walk unassisted?"

"I can go alone," he said. "You carry the clothing and the light. Don't forget to bring my lantern."

Mary led the way as Ryder hobbled behind her. It was difficult to keep her pace as slow as his. His normal stride would have swallowed hers; now it was only a third as long. She asked no questions, not wanting to tax his strength any further. Halfway to the chamber it seemed that Ryder's face was the same pale shade of gray as his eyes. A hundred yards from their chamber's entrance Mary had to present her shoulder and arm for his support whether it pained him or not.

Leaving one lantern and the clothes bundle behind, Mary managed to get Ryder to the bed. She realized how much he had girded himself for that effort. Once he was lifted onto the edge of the rock shelf, he collapsed.

Mary's work began at that moment. She made Ryder as comfortable as possible, rearranging the blankets under him and folding another for a pillow. At the well she filled the basin and dipped several cloths into the cold water. Laying it all aside for a moment, Mary raided the trunk for material that would make the best bandage. She settled on her own chemise, tearing it into long strips. She rifled the saddlebag that Florence Gardner had packed and found a flask of alcohol, the bottle of liniment, and a small sewing kit.

Ryder's eyes were closed when Mary returned to the bed and his breathing was shallow. She removed his bandana and put the back of her hand to his cheek. His skin was cold and clammy. She touched his lips lightly with her fingertips and began to work.

The jagged wound on his thigh required her first attention. There were other scratches and cuts, but none so deep as to call for stitching the way this longest one did. Little Sisters of the Poor had served the hospital in Queens for years. Mary was no stranger to nursing. She had been called upon to cleanse wounds and stitch them before, and she had always done it with a glad heart. It wasn't the same now. Her hands were shaking.

She pushed Ryder's breechcloth free of his thigh and began removing the dried-on bandage. The wound bled again, but she had learned from doctors that wasn't necessarily a bad thing; infection could be washed away by the blood. Mary carefully laid back the torn flesh and used Ryder's knife to cut away the dead and shredded tissue. She cleaned the wound first with soap, then inspected it. There were embedded bits of gravel that had to be painstakingly removed. When Mary had removed as many of them as she could hope to get, she cleaned the wound again, then liberally showered it with alcohol.

Ryder had been stoic until that point, centering his mind on something other than the pain. With the introduction of the alcohol, he fainted.

"Thank you, God," Mary whispered. It was beyond her how he could have withstood so much in the first place. She glanced at his face and saw the release of tension in his features. With his final collapse, she noticed that her hands were no longer shaking. Mary bent to her task, working quickly before Ryder regained consciousness.

She threaded the needle deftly, wishing only that she had one curved for sutures. "Oh, Maggie," she said softly, "what I wouldn't give for even a tenth of your skill." But her physician sister couldn't aid her now, so Mary set to work. She sutured the underlying tissue first with the alcohol-soaked thread. The wound took sixty stitches before she was ready to close the skin over it.

Ryder came awake as she was finishing the last of the skin sutures. He watched her cut off the thread and study her work with a critical eye. "Well?" he asked hoarsely. The white lines were at the corners of his mouth again.

"Mama said that needlepoint was never my strong suit," she said. "But I think she'd change her mind if she saw this."

"It didn't have to be pretty," he said.

Mary laid one hand over his forehead, brushing back his thick hair where it clung to his skin. She smiled down at him. "Oh, it's not," she told him. "But it's good."

"That's all right, then." He closed his eyes. Mary's fingers were warm where they stroked his cheek. He wanted to reach for her hand, but his arm fell uselessly back to his side.

She bent and kissed his cool cheek. Her hand found his. Tears welled in her eyes as she felt him squeeze it. In other circumstances she would have called the gesture gentle. She recognized it now as weak. "Rest," she said softly. Then she sat by his side while he did just that.

* * *

"You should eat something," Mary told him. She raised a spoon of vegetables to Ryder's lips.

He took a bite, chewed, then laid his head back down. "It's enough," he said tiredly.

"But—"

"It's enough."

"Very well." Mary gave in because she couldn't force the issue. Ryder wasn't regaining his strength with the speed Mary had hoped for. He slept in fits and starts, the pain of his broken ribs giving him little relief when he unwittingly turned on his side. What measure of comfort he could derive from sleep was erased soon upon waking. The scar on his thigh was puffy and red where it curved near his knee, and Mary was afraid she was seeing the first signs of infection.

She took away the food, rinsed the plate, then sat down in the rocker. She spent what passed for her nights in that chair, moving it closer to the bed so she would hear Ryder each time he woke. "Would you like me to read to you?" she asked.

"No."

"Then let me bathe you. It will ease the heat in your skin."

Her hands all over his body? Ease the heat? Not likely. "No."

"As you wish." Once again she acquiesced with a grace that would have astonished her family or the Little Sisters.

"I know what you're doing," he said.

"Oh?" She didn't bother looking in his direction, pretending no interest as she unrolled his maps.

"You're giving in."

One of Mary's brows shot up. She raised her face and speared Ryder with a level look. "Not fighting is not always the same as giving in."

Groaning softly, Ryder closed his eyes. That meant she was biding her time. Probably had plans to force-feed him while he was unconscious and bathe him while he slept. He turned gingerly over on his side, determined to stay awake as long as possible. "What are you doing with those?"

"Looking for gold," she said. "Same as you were."

"You don't know where to look."

She shrugged and bent to her task again. "I found Colter Canyon marked on this first map, and I've been able to match the elevation markers and topographical features to the second map. It's really just a closer view, isn't it? I suppose it intentionally wasn't marked as Colter Canyon to make it less useful to someone who stumbled upon it."

"Like you."

She ignored his sarcasm and said patiently, "No, not like me. Like another prospector. That *is* who drew this map, isn't it? Your prospector friend?"

Ryder's brows raised a fraction. He nodded his head slowly.

"Your amazement is not flattering. I *know* how to read a map, and I can put two and two together for the correct sum as well as anyone else."

At least he'd gotten a bit of a rise out of her. "Yes, you're right. Joe Panama drew the map. He explored most of this area at one time or another. He was convinced there was a mother lode of silver in these parts."

Mary could hear the strain in Ryder's voice, the small breaths between sentences that signaled he was tiring. She thought of cautioning him, but decided against it. Showing concern for his strength was a sure means of raising his ire. "Did he ever discover it?" she asked. Perhaps she could simply exhaust him with questions.

Ryder shook his head. "Not that he ever told me."

"He's dead?"

"A few years ago. He killed himself not far from here after a fall broke his back."

Mary's features softened compassionately. "You found him?"

"No," he said, watching her closely. "I was with him."

Her eyes widened. "And you let him kill himself?"

"I let him end his suffering," he said, "because I couldn't end it for him."

"He asked you to?"

"Of course." He saw Mary's brows draw together as she

struggled with this information. "Measuring one sin against the other?" he asked. "Was letting Joe pull the trigger any different than pulling it myself? What if I told you that he didn't carry a gun?" He saw her brows lift fractionally. "That's right. I gave him mine."

Something of the sorrow Mary felt in her heart touched her eyes.

"I'm not a saint," Ryder said.

"I never mistook you for one."

"If you're cataloging my sins, I have some more I—"

"I'm not judging you," she said quietly. "I was only thinking how it must have pained you to make such a difficult choice. I know what the Church teaches, but I can't help wonder how I might have decided in the same circumstances."

"You may find out," he said gravely.

At first she didn't take his meaning. Her features went from blank to horrified as she saw him tap his wounded leg lightly. "What are you saying? You want me to shoot you?"

"Not just this minute."

"Don't make light of this," she said angrily. Mary's mouth flattened and her tone became sharper. "Or me. I find nothing about it remotely humorous."

"I recall that not so long ago you held a Henry rifle to my chest and claimed you were willing to use it."

Mary did not appreciate being reminded. "That was different," she snapped.

"What was different was that I was in good health then. Now that I'm likely to die, you're not willing to help me along. You have a confusing sense of morality."

"It would have been a grievous sin if I had killed you then. It would be an equally grievous one if I did it now."

"So you're saying it really wouldn't have been different at all," he said thoughtfully. "You're very quick to change your opinion." He saw her face flush and her eyes flash. "You look as if you're giving my request more serious consideration. Perhaps the key to getting what I want is to goad you into it."

Mary bent her head and stared at the map. The lines ran together and place names blurred. A fat, heavy tear slipped past her lowered lashes and splattered on the paper.

"Mary?"

She shook her head, not trusting herself to say anything and not wanting him to speak.

Ryder forced himself to sit up, wincing as he slid his legs over the side of the stone bed. He was glad she hadn't looked up, glad that she couldn't see the pain in his expression. She would think it was all because of his leg, and she would have been wrong. He hadn't meant to make her cry. "No more tears on my account, Mary," he said. "I don't want—"

She sucked in a sob and pressed the back of her hand to her mouth.

Ryder managed to push himself off the bed. Relying heavily on his uninjured leg, he hobbled toward where Mary sat on the floor. He nudged aside the maps with the toe of his foot, putting himself in her line of vision.

"Go back to bed," she said hoarsely. "There was no reason for you to get up."

"There was every reason."

She raised her head. "You're a horrible man."

She said it as if she meant it, and Ryder had no doubt that in that moment she did. "Worse than horrible," he said.

"Don't patronize me."

"I was agreeing with you." He held out his hand to her. "Take it, Mary, or I swear I'll get down on my knees beside you." That threat had her slipping her hand into his. Ryder drew her to her feet. She was stiff and unyielding when he pulled her into the circle of his arms, but he held out, keeping her close in a loose embrace until she relaxed against him.

"You're not going to die," she whispered. Mary's tears dampened his shirt. "You're *not.*"

Ryder said nothing. It was a certainty that his life wouldn't end by her hand or with her cooperation. He regretted that he had let her think, for even a moment, he might ask it of her.

She was going to fight for him, and in the end, if her ministrations and her prayers weren't enough, he would do what he had to without any help from her.

Mary knuckled her tears aside as she felt Ryder's weight shift toward her. It was harder to know who was holding whom now. Slipping her shoulder under his arm, Mary aided him back to the bed. His face was pale, and parenthetical lines of pain creased the corners of his mouth. He didn't argue when she rearranged the blankets over him and examined his leg.

The swelling and redness had spread. Ryder's knee looked inflamed with the infection from the injury. A thin red line was now visible, snaking from the base of the wound toward his calf.

Mary knew what she had to do. "I'm going to have to cut these stitches," she said, "and clean the tissues again. It's going to hurt like hell." When Ryder didn't respond she stopped her examination and glanced in his direction. He was out cold. "Just as well," she whispered. "I can't spare any liquor for an anesthetic."

Numbing her senses to the task at hand, she began working. She sliced the lower third of the visible stitches and laid open Ryder's skin. Sanguineous, malodorous fluids seeped from the infected tissue. She cut the second layer of stitches, and more of the infection was revealed. Mary cleaned the wound, this time scrubbing it with the hard, alcohol-soaked bristles of Ryder's hairbrush. Splinters of wood came to the surface, and she used a needle to extract every one that she found. The wound bled freely again, and Mary let the bleeding run its course before she began the task of suturing.

Ryder never woke while she worked, but occasionally his body would jerk in response to the deep pain she was inflicting. All the while her lips moved in the ceaseless litany of prayer.

When she was done Mary knelt at the well and washed her hands. Having done all she could was not the same as having done enough. It was the disparity between the two that troubled her.

She sat in the wing chair, her long legs curled under her, and watched Ryder sleep. How serious had he been, she wondered, when he'd compared his situation to Joe Panama's? Did he really think she might give him a gun so he could kill himself? Was that his idea of being cruel to be kind?

Mary's head throbbed. Fingers of tension seemed to be pulling the skin tightly over her pounding temples. Bright flashes of light, created by the deep ache behind her eyes, began to cross her vision. The steady roar in her ears reached tidal wave proportions.

Mary's head fell forward. Her shoulders slumped. Only the curled position of her body kept her from sliding to the floor from the chair. Eventually her dead faint became a deep, healing slumber.

Standing unnoticed in the entrance to the chamber, Jarret Sullivan slipped his Colt back into its holster. The showdown he had anticipated and prepared for was not going to happen, at least not immediately. He turned down the lantern he had carried with him into the cavern and then set it aside. There wasn't any need for it in Ryder McKay's well-lit hideout. Jarret counted six lanterns, all of them burning with varying degrees of brightness. Mary's idea of prayer candles, he decided. He doubted Ryder would use his supply of oil so frivolously.

Jarret could see that both occupants of the room were sleeping deeply, but he had no difficulty in discerning the differences in their slumber. His tread was silent as he passed Mary's chair and went straight to the stone shelf-bed on which Ryder lay. Jarret had only glimpsed Ryder at Fort Union, but he had been given a photograph that left him with no doubt that it was Ryder McKay he was seeing.

Jarret looked for the injury that engraved Ryder's face with pain and brought beads of perspiration to his upper lip. Finding none visible, he raised the blanket and whistled softly. "Hell of a thing, you bastard," he said softly. "I could almost feel sorry for you."

Lowering the blanket, Jarret turned his attention to Mary. She didn't appear to be injured, only exhausted. There were shadows beneath her eyes and no color in her cheeks. He had never thought of her as particularly fragile, but she had that aura about her now, looking too slender and delicate in Ryder's clothes. "If he hurt you," he said under his breath, "I'll break his knees."

The threat would have been a familiar one to Mary. She had used it herself on four different occasions. Jarret first heard it when he stood up as best man for his friend Ethan Stone. Mary had been looking out for her sister Michael that time. She had given Jarret a similar warning when he'd taken Rennie in hand. Connor Holiday hadn't been spared when he'd made Maggie his wife, and Walker Caine had heard the same threat when he'd exchanged vows with Skye. Mary Francis always looked out for her sisters. She would have protected them with her life if it had come to that.

"And who's been looking out for you?" he asked softly. Jarret saw the cloths laying out to dry beside the well. He picked one up, dipped it in the icy water, and carried it back to Mary's side. He laid it gently against her brow, then wiped her tear-stained cheeks. She stirred slightly, but didn't open her eyes. When he touched her cheek with his hand she turned and pressed her face against his palm. "Ah, Mary," he said, understanding. "Who do you think I am?"

"Ryder."

The word was hardly spoken, was more an expulsion of air, but Jarret didn't mistake that it was in response to his question. Moira was right, he thought, Mary Francis felt something for the renegade Army scout.

When Jarret hunkered beside the chair his foot caught one of the maps peeking out from beneath it. He started to push the paper aside; then he saw what he was kicking and stopped. Laying the washcloth over the arm of Mary's chair, Jarret picked up the uppermost map and looked at it.

Months earlier, when Rennie had first considered expanding Northeast Rail in the territory of the Southwest, she and Jarret had poured over maps of the area. While they had studied the land around the Holland Mines most particularly, they had also examined a number of other locations. Jarret had no difficulty recognizing the map he held as marking the territory in and around Colter Canyon. The next map showed him Colter Canyon itself in more detail. He recognized some of the markings as indicating different types of ore deposits.

His dark brows were raised admiringly as he looked over it. Rennie would have paid a lot of money for a geological survey as detailed as this one. The ones she had gotten from the government men paled in comparison.

Jarret put the document aside and quickly scanned the third and final map. It was territory he didn't recognize at all, with markings that made little sense to him. Puzzled, he held it up to get a better look at it.

"Put that down or I'll shoot you where you sit."

Jarret didn't move. "In the back?" he asked Ryder.

"In the backside if I have to."

Jarret lowered the map and carefully slid it under Mary's chair with the others.

"Keep your hands up," Ryder said. His voice wavered slightly with the strain of talking.

"I've already looked under those blankets," Jarret said evenly. "The only thing you had under there worth noting was a bum leg." He turned around slowly and stood, hands at his sides. He could see clearly that Ryder's threat was an empty one. "I expected a little more from you."

Even Ryder's shrug was painful. "I got you to put those maps down, didn't I?" he asked, striving for carelessness in his tone. "You weren't completely sure."

Jarret tipped the brim of his hat back a notch, conceding the point. "You been awake long?"

"Long enough to hear you threaten my knees. Hate to disappoint you, though. I've only got one leg worth breaking." His pale gray eyes took Jarret's measure and immediately recognized a worthy adversary. The man didn't flinch under his scrutiny. "You must be one of the in-laws," he said finally. "Rennie's husband?"

"That's right," said Jarret. "How did you know?"

It was a struggle to sit up, but Ryder managed. Feeling less at a disadvantage even though he was out of breath, he said, "I always figured I had more to fear from her family than from any three units the general might send out." Ryder raked his hair with his fingers. "You must be the one who used to bounty hunt."

"Did Mary tell you that?"

Ryder shook his head, a slight smile lifting one corner of his mouth. He looked past Jarret to where Mary slept, still slumped in the wing chair. "She played her cards very close to the vestments."

Jarret's faint smile was a salute of sorts. "Jay Mac taught her well. Her sisters will tell you she's the best one at the table." His smile faded. "So how did you know?"

"She forgot about Walker Caine."

Now Jarret's dark brows knit. His eyes narrowed. "You know Skye's husband."

"For years," he said, not explaining their friendship began at West Point. "When Walker married Skye he wrote about her family. He had a line or two for you." Ryder winced as he shifted his weight. "I didn't connect you and your wife with Mary when you first came to Fort Union."

The trial had been underway then, Jarret remembered, and the testimony had been damning. "You had a few other things on your mind," Jarret said.

Ryder's rueful grin acknowledged the truth of that. "Just a few." And only a few less now, he thought. "You tracked the blood?" he asked.

Jarret nodded. "Hell of a fall you took back there. I half expected to find a body at the bottom of that ravine."

"Disappointed you didn't?"

"Glad I didn't find Mary."

"I don't suppose you and I would be talking if you had."

"That's right." Jarret tapped the butt of his Colt. "I would have killed you. No questions."

It was nothing less than Ryder would have expected. He was a little surprised that Jarret was carrying on a conversation now. "I may ask you to do it anyway," he said. "Mary can't."

"Jesus," Jarret said lowly. "You *asked* her?"

"I told her I was considering it."

"Jesus," he said again. "You had no right. Not Mary. You know what she is . . . what she was. She'd never give up. She'll kill herself working to save you."

"Do you think I don't know it?" Ryder asked quietly. His eyes strayed back to Mary's exhausted figure and lingered there. "You've got to get her out of here."

It was what Jarret came to do. However, he hadn't expected to be invited to do it. He pointed to Ryder's injured leg. "What the hell were you doing on the lip of that ravine anyway?"

"Trying to cover our tracks."

"Mary was with you when you fell?"

"God no." He closed his eyes briefly, thankful she hadn't been around when the ridge of stone had given way beneath his feet and sent him plunging over the edge. "I left something along the route, and I had to go back to get it."

"Clothes," Jarret said.

"That's right. How did you—"

"You missed a sock." Jarret raised one hand, holding off the question he saw in Ryder's eyes. "It's all right. I have it now. I cleaned up the trail, too. Just in case it led me to you. I didn't want anyone else finding it."

Ryder didn't thank him, his mind already racing ahead to the obvious question. "Anyone in particular?"

"A Tonto scout."

"Rosario."

"That's right. Jay Mac upped the ante. Rosario gets a bonus above what's already being offered for—"

"For my head," Ryder finished. "It's all right. Mary warned me her father would want my head on a platter." He forgot his pain long enough to allow himself a small, self-mocking chuckle. "Jay Mac could have saved his money. Rosario would happily turn over my scalp for free."

"So I understand."

"It's not personal," Ryder said. "Rosario hates all Chiricahua equally and that's what he considers me. That's why he's been such a good scout for Gardner. Bringing in the Chiricahua is a matter of pride. He can cut his teeth on me, but if he can bring down Geronimo he'll be a legend." Ryder shifted his weight again, this time moving back on the bed so he could lean against the stone side. The effort beaded his brow with sweat. "So Rosario's out on his own. I'm surprised General Gardner released him to go alone."

"Jay Mac was convincing. And the general thinks Rosario's with me."

"Why isn't he?"

"I lost him."

"No one simply loses Rosario. I may have no liking for him, but I respect his skills."

"I hammered him on the head with my peacemaker," Jarret explained. *"Then* I lost him."

"Why?"

"I didn't trust him."

"Because he's an Indian?"

"Because he wanted you too badly. I was afraid for Mary if she got in the middle." He glanced over his shoulder. The sight of Mary still sleeping comfortably in the chair raised a smile. "And she can't seem to help herself. I used to think it was her habit; now I realize it's just her way."

Ryder nodded, understanding. "Then, thank you," he said quietly, "for realizing what her father couldn't and acting on it."

Jarret took off his hat and ran his fingers through his hair. "Jay Mac's not thinking straight. You can't blame him. You have his little girl. I suppose you'd have to have a daughter of your own to appreciate what he's going through."

"What makes you think I don't?"

Frowning, Jarret pinned Ryder with a hard, cold look. "What are you saying?"

"I have . . . *had* a daughter," he said. It was odd to him that he was telling this to Jarret Sullivan. The words he was speaking he had meant to share with Mary. "She was murdered in her cradleboard. My wife . . . her family . . . they were all killed in the same raid."

Jarret's stare could not penetrate the mask that Ryder had drawn over his features. Here was grief so profound, Jarret thought, that it could not be made visible. "I didn't know," he said.

"Not many do."

"Mary?"

Ryder shook his head. "I haven't—" He broke off as a movement behind Jarret caught his attention. At first he didn't know what had changed. Mary hadn't shifted in the chair. Her legs were still curled under her. The tilt of her head was exactly the same. Her shoulder sloped at an identical angle. Ryder's gaze went back to Mary's face and locked on the forest green eyes that were returning his regard. The movement that had anchored his attention was the raising of her eyelids. The emotion he saw in her gaze was more hurt than anger.

Jarret followed the drift of Ryder's attention, turning to face Mary. He saw immediately that she had heard. Her expression seemed to confirm that Moira was indeed right about her daughter's feelings for Ryder McKay. "Hello, Mary," he said gently. He bent and kissed her warm cheek.

Mary blinked and the emotion that had been in her eyes for both men to see was shuttered. "Jarret." She said his name politely, as if he were an unwelcome guest, but good manners forbade her from behaving less than graciously.

To Jarret, her tone was another sign of her hurt and confusion. Mary Francis Dennehy had never been one to stand on ceremony. "How are you feeling?"

She straightened, running one hand through her hair in a negligent fashion. There was a vertical crease between her brows as she frowned, trying to shed the dregs of her heavy sleep. "What are you doing here?"

Jarret looked back at Ryder. "Trust her to come straight to the point."

Mary wasn't amused. She came to her feet, a little unsteadily at first, but she had no use for Jarret's extended hand. Brushing past him, she went to the bed. "Let me see your leg," she said. Although her tone brooked no argument, Ryder tried to object. She stared him down.

"All right," he said, giving in. Over Mary's shoulder, he could see Jarret's interest in the exchange. He pushed back the blanket and let her examine the wound.

"It's better," she pronounced.

"Wishful thinking," Ryder told Jarret.

"It *is*," she said. "Look. Some of the redness is gone. I think the poison is gone. Jarret, come and look at this."

"He's already seen it," Ryder said, even as Jarret was approaching. "He knows I'm going to lose my leg."

Mary's head swung in Jarret's direction. "Is he right?" she demanded. "Is that what you think?"

It *was* what he had thought when he'd first seen the wound. Now he saw Mary's fierce determination and remembered what it was like to fly in the face of that. "What I think," he said heavily, almost on a surrendering sigh, "is that there's something in my saddlebags that might help."

Eleven

Once Jarret was gone from the chamber Ryder was left basking in Mary's triumphant smile. "How do you do it?" he asked. "How do you get people to move in ways they're not at all inclined to pursue?"

"I'd like to think they respond to superior reasoning," she said primly. "The truth is, I bully them."

The real truth was somewhere in between, Ryder decided. Not that Mary wasn't capable of sound reasoning *and* bullying tactics, but it was her ability to make people believe in her, and in the things she believed in, that had them stepping lively to her tune.

"Lie down," she said. "All the color's faded from your face."

Ryder acknowledged that he was in no condition to gainsay her. With Jarret gone, he didn't even try.

Sitting on the edge of the bed, Mary picked up a damp cloth and wiped the perspiration from Ryder's face. "I wish you had told me about your wife," she said after a moment.

"I know." The cloth was cool on his skin, and Ryder closed his eyes. "It was so long ago," he said. "I was married before my uncle found me, before West Point. I can almost believe it happened to another person. It's the same way I feel about my childhood in Ohio. Separate places. Separate lives."

He was a man with roots in two worlds, she thought, part of both, belonging in neither. "Where is it that you find peace?" she asked.

Ryder opened his eyes and looked at Mary steadily. The serenity of her features masked the ferocity of her temperament . . . his warrior angel. "In your arms," he said, as though the answer were profoundly simple. "Only in your arms."

Mary's breath caught in her throat. For a moment she couldn't move. It was the way he said it, with that air of inevitability and acceptance, that gave truth to the words. Leaning over, she kissed him full on the mouth. "All the more reason to get well," she said, lifting her head. "So you can be there again."

Ryder murmured his agreement, his eyes closed again. Sleep was edging at his conscious mind. He felt Mary's gentle touch on his face, then his neck and shoulders. The cloth was cool, her fingertips warm.

Mary continued to wipe down his fevered skin even after Ryder fell asleep. She pushed back strands of his dark hair where it lay against his temples and brushed her knuckle across the pronounced hollow of his cheek.

"He's sleeping?" Jarret asked from the entrance. "Or did he pass out?"

"A little of both, I suspect." Mary left Jarret's side to dip the cloth in the pool again. "How did you find us?"

Jarret dropped his saddlebags on the rocker and set down his lantern. He tipped his hat a notch as he looked in Mary's direction. "There's a trail of blood a greenhorn could follow."

Mary nodded. "Ryder was afraid of that. Where did you pick up the trail?"

"Above the ravine where he fell. I went down first, just to make certain there were no bodies, then I climbed out, using the same route he did. It's pretty much a miracle he survived at all—and with no broken bones."

"Two ribs," she corrected.

Jarret just shook his head. "The man has a will of iron."

"He wanted to come back to me," she said simply. "You would have done the same for Rennie."

"But I love your sister."

Mary sat beside Ryder again. "Well?" she asked.

Jarret's eyes went from Mary to Ryder, then took in both of

them together. "I see," he said. "So that's the way it is. Do you return it?"

"If I do," she said, "I wouldn't tell you first. That's for Ryder to hear."

Jarret grinned as he removed his hat and dropped it on the rocker. "You were never one to show your hand early," he said. "Just so you know, your mother thinks she has it figured out."

Mary nodded, accepting it, but saying nothing.

Jarret sat in the wing chair and reached for the saddlebags. He placed them between his knees and began removing their contents. "How long ago did he fall?"

"I don't know." When Jarret looked at her oddly, she explained, "There's no means of telling time in here. Neither of us has a watch, and there's no sun—no moon to orient us. My best guess is that it's been a week since the accident. I just can't be sure." She began to wipe down Ryder's skin again. "Was the ravine far from here?"

"Easily eight miles."

"I've been that way once in the daylight and once at night, but I don't remember it clearly. How far did Ryder fall?"

"Didn't he tell you?"

She shook her head. "And I didn't ask. It wasn't as important to know the details as it was to have him here."

"He went down about a hundred and fifty feet." At Mary's gasp, he added, "Not all at once. He dropped in stages. The ground kept crumbling under him, and he slipped on his own blood as he tried to climb out. That gash in his leg was the result of slipping past a tree branch that was growing out of the side of the ravine."

"I thought it might be something like that." She sighed. "I suppose it would have been better if he hadn't gone after the clothes at all." At Jarret's curious look Mary explained why the clothing had been on the trail in the first place. Some of her guilt came through in the telling, because Jarret was quick to point out that the events that followed were not her fault.

"There's not much comfort in that," she told him. "So I may

as well feel guilty." Mary pointed to the items Jarret was removing from his saddlebags. "What do you have there to help Ryder?"

"Balms and tinctures," he said. "Your sister made me bring them—just in case."

"Then thank Rennie for me."

"It was Maggie, not Rennie."

"Maggie? When did you—"

Jarret held up his hand and cut her off. "Mary, did you really imagine the family wouldn't gather at a time like this? Maggie and Connor arrived hours before I left. Michael and Ethan are on their way from Denver. Skye is the only one with no chance of getting here and she won't thank you for it."

Mary's shoulders slumped a little. "It occurred to me, of course," she said softly, more to herself and to Jarret, "but all of them . . ."

"Jay Mac was here right away."

"I knew he would be." She wrung out the cloth and put it aside. "Mama is doing well?" she asked.

"For the circumstances," he said. "The more frustrated Jay Mac gets, the calmer Moira becomes."

Mary smiled faintly. "It's always been like that."

Jarret grinned, understanding. He sorted through the items he had removed from the saddlebags and carried the most important ones to Mary's side. "Maggie's instructions were hurried," Jarret explained, "but I think I know how to use these things."

Mary accepted a bottle of tincture and studied her sister's neat, handwritten label. "The wonder is she didn't insist on coming herself."

"She did," Jarret said dryly. "Connor held her back."

Uncorking the small brown bottle of white willow tincture, Mary swabbed Ryder's wound carefully. "I had to cut him open again to remove more of the infection," she told Jarret.

"Then you haven't tried cauterizing the wound."

"No. I was afraid to build a fire. Ryder would never let me."

"It's all right," he said. "I'll light a small amount of your lantern oil and heat my knife."

"I never thought of that."

Jarret put his hand on Mary's shoulder. "You've done as much as any three people," he said. "Don't blame yourself now for what you didn't think of." That said, he began working quickly and efficiently, building the small fire to sterilize and heat the blade. Flames licked at the steel, turning it smoky blue. "Hold his shoulders, Mary."

She frowned. "He's going to feel this?"

"He's going to think he's coming out of his skin."

Mary placed her hands on Ryder's shoulder and watched Jarret turn the blade to get the flat, hot side of it lined up with the wound. At the last moment she looked away. The smell of searing flesh assailed her nostrils and she squeezed her eyes tight. Under her palms she felt Ryder's immediate struggle and she heard his growl of pain. She counted a full five seconds before Jarret removed the blade.

Ryder was breathing hard. There were white creases at the corners of his mouth. He had grabbed Mary's wrist to move her hand from his shoulder, and his fingers still pressed her skin hard.

Jarret put the knife aside. "Let her go," he told Ryder.

"It's all right, Jarret," Mary said. "He doesn't—" She felt Ryder's grip ease. When she looked down at him she saw that he had passed out. "I always feel relieved when he does that."

Jarret nodded. "I know what you mean." He handed her the balm Maggie had packed for him. "Take this. I'll get the bandages. Rub it carefully around the burn, then I'll wrap it lightly. Maggie's also given me some herbs so I can make a tea."

"You'll have to use cold water," she said.

"That's all right. It will only take a little longer."

By Mary's estimation it was thirty-six hours before they were able to note any change in Ryder's condition and another twelve before they could be certain it was a change for the better. The herbs that Maggie had had the foresight to provide helped break Ryder's fever and reduce the inflammation around his wound. Mary gave thanks that when Ryder slept his slumber was no longer tormented, but was a deep, healing rest that would leave him stronger upon waking.

Mary sat beside the well, rinsing bandages while Ryder slept. Jarret lounged in the rocker, watching her. When she heard the tempo of the rocker change for the third time, she glanced over her shoulder at her brother-in-law, a question in her eyes. "If you have something to say," she said, "say it."

The rocking stopped. "Very well. Ryder's stronger now. The time has come."

"Oh? What time is that?"

Jarret studied her. Was she pulling his leg or did she really not know? "Did you imagine I'd be staying indefinitely?" he asked. Before she could reply he added, "Or that I'd be leaving without you?"

Mary frowned, her eyes narrowing. "No, I didn't think you'd be staying," she said slowly. "But there's no question that you'll leave without me. I'm not going back to Fort Union with you."

"I'm not going to argue about this, Mary."

"Good." She shrugged and wrung out another bandage. "Neither am I."

Jarret realized that not arguing did not necessarily put them on the same side of the issue. "Your mother, father, *everyone,* expects that if I find you I'll bring you back."

"I'm aware of that. You'll have to lie to them, of course. Tell them you didn't find me."

He shook his head and raked back his hair with his fingers. "I can't do that. They're worried, Mary. With good reason. There's nothing remotely safe about your being with Ryder McKay. I can't pretend that I haven't seen you. Your parents, your sisters—all of them deserve better than that."

Mary acknowledged the truth of his words with a slight bow

of her head. "Then we'll have to think of something else, something that will appease them."

"Your return to Fort Union will satisfy them."

Her chin came up and her knuckles whitened on the cloth she was holding. "No," she said firmly. "It's not going to happen. Not now. Not without Ryder." Her eyes widened and her features became still as another thought occurred to her. "You don't intend to try to take him back, do you? You didn't help me make him well just to see him hang?"

Jarret paused a beat too long in responding and had to duck the damp washcloth that was fired at his face like a snowball. He held up his hands, partly in surrender, partly to ward off another missile.

"Answer me, damn you," Mary snapped, coming to her feet. "Is that why you've been so helpful, because you've planned all along to force Ryder to go back to Fort Union?"

Jarret stood as well. His voice was deep and steady, reflecting a shade more control than Mary's. "Listen to me," he said flatly. "There are enough men already looking for Ryder. I don't have to concern myself with his capture. Do you understand what I'm saying? It's inevitable. Your father's offered a reward for him, separate from the one for your safe return. That means he's worth the same amount dead or alive." He saw Mary's complexion pale. Her green eyes were impossibly large in her face. "The one with the best chance to collect that reward is a Tonto scout who bears Ryder no special affection. I've already shared that with Ryder—which is more than I had to do or probably should have done. Ryder's accident out there enabled me to pick up his trail. It's only a matter of time before Rosario is able to do the same."

Mary took no pains to hide the small measure of relief she felt. When Jarret looked at her as if she'd lost her mind she explained. "You don't understand," she said. "While the Tonto and the Chiricahua have no liking for one another, they're still Apache, and this is sacred ground to the Apache. That scout won't come in here, not if he doesn't want to be visited by the dead ancestors of all the tribes."

Jarret let out a long breath. This information put another twist on their circumstances. "Burial grounds?" he asked.

She nodded. "Ryder and I are safe in here. If I erase his blood signs on the route to this interior chamber, even you wouldn't be able to find your way in here again."

There was more truth to that than Jarret wanted to admit. He sat down on the curved arm of the wing chair, stretching one leg out to the side, and considered what he had learned. "I doubt Ryder has plans to stay in here forever," he said finally. "Rosario will be waiting for him outside the cavern. If not Rosario, someone like him."

"Then you'll have to make certain the trail to the cavern is covered. Better yet, that it proves misleading." Her expression was earnest now. "You can do that."

"Why would I want to?"

Mary nearly stamped her foot in frustration. "For *me,*" she said. "Because I'm asking you to. If my safety means something to you, then don't let the scouts or the Army find me too easily."

"I thought we were talking about Ryder being found."

"It's all the same. If he's found, then I will be, too. I'm not going with you, Jarret. I mean it. I'm staying with him."

"God, Mary . . . What you're asking . . ."

"He's innocent," she said. There was a naked plea in her voice now. She was willing him to be convinced of her own conviction. "He had nothing to do with the Colter Canyon raid. If he served some purpose it was as a target for the blame."

Jarret's eyes darted to Ryder's still and sleeping form huddled beneath a mound of blankets. His tone was frankly scoffing. "He says he was set up?"

"No," she said, exasperated. *"I* say he was set up."

"Mary, he oversaw every detail of the transport. Except for the newest recruits, he handpicked most of the men for the journey. The route was known only to a few officers, and Ryder himself was responsible for dividing the troop. As if all that isn't enough, he has a known history with the Chiricahua. His adopted Apache father is Naiche, blood brother to Geronimo."

Mary was taken aback by all the information Jarret had on Ryder, most of which she did not know herself. Still, it did not sway her from her argument. "Who better to frame?" she asked simply. "With so much stacked against Ryder just because of who he is, it hardly provided any challenge for the real criminals."

"And the real criminals would be? . . ." His voice trailed off expectantly and one of his dark brows kicked up.

"I don't know," Mary admitted reluctantly. "That's what I plan to find out. That's why I'm not going back with you."

His look was patently suspicious now. "And that's the only reason?"

"It's the only reason I'm giving you," she said tartly. "I'll return to Fort Union with Ryder when his name is cleared. Not before then—not alive anyway."

Jarret rolled his eyes. "A bit too much drama at the end for my tastes."

Mary's expression turned sheepish. "I couldn't help myself."

He sighed. "All right, so you're not going back with me. That doesn't help me deal with your family. I owe them some explanation. God knows, they're preparing for the worst."

"That I'm dead?"

"That you're involved."

Mary's brow puckered. "Involved? How do they mean that?"

"They mean from the beginning. We all know you met Ryder before you ever came out here. Florence Gardner gave that tidbit to your mother." When Mary didn't deny it he went on. "You had also mentioned Ryder McKay to me before we ever reached the Fort."

Mary nodded slowly. It had happened just as Ryder had said it would. The odd circumstances of their first meeting gave support to their subsequent one six months later.

"There's the fact that you went to his cell and that you were wearing that habit. General Gardner believes you helped plan and carry out Ryder's escape. Your family is only a little less inclined to believe it."

Mary was silent for a long time. She stared off at a point beyond Jarret's shoulder, thinking. A chill seeped through the flannel shirt she wore. She crossed her arms in front of her to ward it off. Finally she looked at Jarret. "Then you should make them believe it," she said quietly.

Jarret's gaze narrowed. "What?"

"Make them believe it," she repeated firmly. "This way you can tell them you found me, I'm safe, and I refuse to abandon Ryder until his name is clear—for my own sake. After all, why would I come back to face charges of aiding his escape before I can prove his innocence?"

"Mary, if I take back that story you'll face charges whether Ryder's proved innocent or not. It's called obstruction of justice, and you're admitting your guilt."

"I don't care. There's no other alternative I can accept."

"But it's a lie. You didn't help him escape."

Mary's faintly sly smile touched her eyes. "Are you asking me or telling me?"

"I'm . . ." He broke off, studying her face closely. The inscrutable, serene expression was firmly in place. "Oh, hell. I'm not sure anymore."

"Good. Then you'll be especially convincing."

Jarret didn't smile as he was meant to. "I don't like it."

Mary approached him, placing her hand on his shoulder. "He didn't do it," she said quietly. "You need to believe that, Jarret. The rest will come easily."

He looked up at her, wondering how she passed on the strength of her convictions so effortlessly. "Mary—"

She shook her head, stopping him before he could muster an objection. "He's an honorable man. He respects tradition and values honesty. He married me in the Chiricahua manner because the ceremony was important to him. I didn't care if there was a ceremony at all." Mary's faint blush made Jarret understand what she meant. "He did it so there would be no shame in our being together. He did it to protect me from the consequences of my own rash actions. And without warning me at all, he risked a great deal to have Jay Mac and Mama brought there to witness the ceremony."

Mary's hand dropped away from Jarret's shoulder. Her eyes darkened and her voice took on a harder edge. "I know what he's supposed to have been doing at the time of the Colter Canyon massacre," she said.

Jarret nodded. "I wondered about that."

"Well, I don't believe it and neither should you. Anna Leigh Hamilton lied. I don't know why exactly, but I know she did. Whether by intention or coincidence, she helped set up Ryder."

"You're taking on quite a bit, Mary. What can you hope to accomplish here?"

"Not much," she admitted. "But as soon as Ryder's better we're going to find the gold."

Ryder knew instantly that something was different. Though nothing had moved, there was a shift in the air in the room that captured his attention. He sat up. The throbbing in his leg was only a dull ache now, and he rubbed the stitches absently. He was alone in the chamber. Jarret's saddlebags and bedroll were gone, but the bottles of tinctures and liniments had been left behind. There was no sign of Mary.

Closing his eyes briefly, Ryder rubbed the bridge of his nose between his thumb and forefinger.

"You're awake," she said.

Ryder's head snapped up and he stared at the entrance to the chamber. She was standing in the archway, holding a lantern in one hand and a rolled map in the other. "You're still here," he said.

Mary hung up the lantern and approached the bed. "I'm going to choose not to be insulted by that." She placed the back of her free hand over Ryder's forehead. "No fever at all. That's good."

"Hmmm." Expecting to see Jarret, he looked past her shoulder. "Where's your bodyguard?"

"Bodyguard?" Realization dawned. "Oh, you mean Jarret. He's gone back to Fort Union. I told him to wait until you were awake before he left, but he said it was better his way."

"Wise man," Ryder said.

Mary looked at him oddly. "Why's that?"

"Because I damn well would have insisted he take you with him."

That rocked Mary back on her heels. She pitched the map on the bed in anger. She had a good mind to clip him on the jaw he thrust in her direction.

Ryder had no difficulty reading the bent of her mind. There was no sense giving her a clear target. He curbed the defiant angle of his chin. "What the hell was he thinking, leaving you here?" he asked instead.

"He was thinking it was what I wanted!" She gritted her teeth. "Oooh, when I think of all the breath I wasted convincing him, I could just . . . just. Words absolutely failed her as Ryder simply stared at her, his head tilted slightly to one side, his fascination total. "Stop looking at me like that," she said, but there was no real conviction in her tone.

He didn't stop, but the centers of his eyes became a shade darker. "Like what?"

Her eyes dropped to his mouth. It was slightly parted. "Like . . . that."

Ryder took Mary by the wrists. Her fists were still clenched and he could feel the tension in her forearms. The blanket hitched around his waist parted along his wounded thigh. He brought Mary between his opened legs and placed her hands on his hips. His hands went around her back and clasped at the base of her spine.

Mary couldn't take her eyes away from his mouth. She felt her own lips part, but there was nothing she wanted to say, only something she wanted to do.

She leaned into the waiting kiss, slanting her mouth across

his. The taste of him was sweet, with the lingering coolness of mint tea. Her tongue traced the line of his upper lip and she felt him draw in a sharp breath, robbing her lungs of the same. Her hands ran up the length of his chest. Heat followed in her wake.

Ryder pressed the kiss more deeply. It had been too long to go gently. His tongue was hard against hers, and the rhythm was achingly familiar and intimate. Her fingers splayed flat on his chest, then curved at the tip. He could feel the tiny crescents of her nails mark his skin. Her mouth was warm and sweet, her response full and generous.

Mary wanted to be closer to him. She wanted to feel the press of his skin against hers, the delicious contrasts of contour, texture, and shape. When his hands moved to the buttons of her shirt she knew a rush of heady anticipation.

Ryder broke the kiss and felt the loss keenly. Almost immediately, Mary brushed her mouth against his, seeking what he was denying them both. "Take off your shirt," he said.

Mary's fingers stilled on Ryder's chest. Her eyes opened slowly and she stared at him, the centers of her eyes dark and wide.

"Take off your shirt," he said again.

There was the merest tremor in his voice and Mary responded to it. Her hands went to the throat of her shirt as Ryder's dropped away. She looked down at herself as her thumb made a pass across the uppermost button.

"Look at me." The husky order was accompanied by his forefinger under her chin, raising her face.

Color rushed to Mary's complexion as desire warred with uncertainty. His eyes held her, waiting and watchful. It was her nearly imperceptible nod that made him release her face. Mary drew in a shaky breath, and her fingers slipped to the next button on her shirt.

She couldn't see her reflection in the darkly mirrored centers of his eyes, but it was as if she could. Her slightest movement raised a response there, and she knew she was looking at powerful, naked hunger held in check. Mary's fingers fumbled on the next button.

Lantern light cast its warm glow across her skin. Strands of copper and gold were highlighted in her hair. A shadow was chased across her collarbone as she shrugged out of the shirt, first with the left shoulder, then the right. Without conscious thought she raised her arms to cover her breasts. The look in Ryder's eyes stopped her.

He didn't say anything. He didn't have to. Mary removed the rest of her clothing.

His eyes touched her everywhere, and the impact was greater than if he had used his hands. She felt them on her breasts, her abdomen, the curve of her hip, and grazing the lengths of her legs. Between her thighs she was warm and moist, and when his eyes went there she felt a tug on her womb.

Ryder took her wrist. As his thumb passed along the soft inner skin the contact was almost too much for her. Her quick, indrawn breath was like a reaction to pain. He paused, searching her face, and recognized her response for what it was. She stepped toward him, not away. His hand closed over her breast. His thumb brushed the erect tip of her nipple and she sipped the air again. Her flesh swelled beneath his cupped palm.

He bent his head. His mouth touched hers but a moment before its sweet warmth was on the curve of her neck, then her shoulder. She arched, aroused by the slow, inexorable journey of his mouth to her breast. His lips caught the nipple. The damp edge of his tongue bathed the tip.

Mary's fingers tangled in his hair, holding him to her as ribbons of pleasure uncurled just beneath her skin. He drew out her response, and when she didn't think she could stand it any longer he showed her that she could. Mary felt herself being lifted to the edge of the stone shelf, and now Ryder was standing in front of her. The blanket that had covered him lay on the floor. He cupped her bottom and brought her closer to the edge of the stone bed, hooking her legs on either side of his hips. His mouth took hers again, and this time the plunging force of his tongue was matched by his hard, swift entry. Mary's gasp was trapped by his mouth. He was in her deeply, completely. She was raised against him, accommodating the heat and hardness of him, holding him to her as surely as she was held.

"Please," she whispered against his mouth. But she could not have said what she was asking for. It was only when Ryder began to move inside her that she realized this was what she had been wanting. It did not bother her that he knew it better than she.

The force and rhythm of his body seemed to rob her of breath and thought. She could only feel.

She felt the heat of his skin, the strength of his arms, the steady rise of pleasure. Not as a single sweep, but as a force that ebbed and flowed, and never abandoned her. She felt the press of his hands, the imprint of his fingers. The shape of his mouth was a brand on her shoulder. Where he rocked between her thighs she felt the hot, darting lick of delicious tension.

Ryder's senses were filled with Mary. He breathed in the fragrance of her skin, her hair, and her sex. He tasted her sweet mouth and the faintly salty flavor of the curve of her shoulder. Her skin was smooth and warm to his touch. His head was filled with the small cries of pleasure at the back of her throat. Mary was in his vision even when he closed his eyes.

The climax was sharp and searing. He shuddered against her powerfully. Mary held him, her legs tightening against his hips, her hands clutching his shoulders. The thrust of his body shattered the last of her defenses. She embraced her release as she embraced him. Pleasure vibrated between them.

Ryder eased Mary back on the bed. She lay there, looking up at him, relaxed and replete. The smile on her face was faintly smug, certainly satisfied. She stretched lazily as he climbed onto the bed beside her. His kiss was tender, and Mary fairly hummed with the sweetness of it.

"You're looking a shade too full of yourself," he said, propping himself on one elbow.

Nothing changed about the placement of her lips. She

couldn't help herself. "A little while ago I was a shade too full of you."

Ryder blinked. He could have convinced himself he had misheard her if it hadn't been for the tide of red sweeping over her face. For once she looked as if she wanted to call back her words. At the same time she was practically daring him to mention them. Instead he simply stared at her, fascinated by the contradiction.

The intensity of Ryder's expression, his darkly searching gaze, held Mary still. She tried to imagine what he was thinking when he looked at her like that, when he peered all the way to her soul.

Ryder picked up a blanket and drew it over them. "You should have gone with your brother-in-law," he said after a moment.

Of all the things she had thought she might hear, this comment was not among them. "That subject is closed," she said flatly.

It was as if she hadn't spoken. "Why didn't you?"

Mary's mouth flattened, and she simply refused to answer.

Ryder sighed. "Very well." Ignoring her small, stiff response when he touched her, Ryder tucked a strand of Mary's hair behind her ear. "We're not going to stay here much longer," he told her.

She frowned, not understanding. "But Jarret is going to cover your trail. He promised. Rosario won't—"

He cut her off, shaking his head. "I'm not worried about Rosario. And I believe Jarret will do as he promised, but he'll be tempted to return just to be certain you're safe."

"No. You're not—"

"It's what I would be tempted to do," he said. "He'll make one trip and then another, then another. It's only a matter of time before he's followed and we're found out. Rosario won't come in here, but there are plenty of Gardner's soldiers who will."

Mary considered that. Ryder was probably right. Jarret would feel a powerful obligation to assure her safety. She hadn't considered that when she'd sent him away alone. She hadn't meant to endanger Ryder with her presence; her intention had been exactly the opposite. Her forest green eyes clouded as she considered the consequences of her actions.

Ryder had no liking for the anxious, reflective look in her eyes. "What is it?" he asked.

"I should have left," she said, worrying the inside of her lower lip. "I'm sorry. I didn't understand."

Ryder wasn't sure that she did now. Her agreement didn't necessarily mean she had surrendered to his point of view. "I think you'd better explain yourself," he said.

Mary sighed. Couldn't he just accept that he was right? Did he have to hear the whole of her error? "I didn't realize I was endangering you by staying behind. It makes sense that you would want me out of the way now."

Ryder listened to the explanation and nodded slowly. It was just as he thought. She couldn't imagine that he had wanted to protect her. "I'm the one endangering *you*," he said. "You should have left to protect yourself. That's all I meant." One side of his mouth lifted as he watched her try to take that information in. She was working up to another argument. "You really are a perverse creature," he added.

She bristled predictably. "What's that supposed to mean?"

"It means that not so long ago you were fighting to make me let you go. Now you're arguing with me about staying."

"That's entirely different," she said immediately.

"Entirely."

Mary looked at him suspiciously. Was he agreeing with her or only pretending to agree? There was a faint edge to his tone, but his expression was shuttered. "You're maddening, do you know that?"

"Maddening? Is that good or bad?"

It was on the tip of her tongue to say bad. That, after all, was the easy answer. The truth was more complicated than that. Could he really hold her attention so completely if he weren't a little maddening? His calm intrigued her. His humor undid her. His logic gave her pause. From the very first he had challenged her. Mary made a small concession. "Being maddening is not entirely bad," she said.

"Be careful," he chided her. "You almost complimented my character."

She nudged his hard belly gently with her fist. When she would have drawn back he placed a hand over hers and held it there. Her fingers unfolded and lay flat against his skin. When his hand fell away hers remained. She traced the edge of his rib cage. There was still some faint bruising from his fall, but he appeared to be on the mend. "There's no pain here?" she asked.

"Hardly any."

"And your leg?"

"Much better." He raised one brow when her eyes narrowed. "Do you doubt it?"

He was referring to the way he had taken her, of course. With her legs anchored around him Mary had felt the strength in his thighs. "No," she said after a moment. "I don't doubt it."

Ryder liked the breathy, husky quality of her voice when she said that. He lowered his head and touched her mouth. The kiss lingered sweetly. When he pulled back he adjusted his position to accommodate her. Mary rested her head in the crook of his shoulder and laid an arm across his chest. He wondered how often or how long she had slept during his illness. Jarret's presence had eased the physical tasks of taking care of him, but had not lightened the emotional burden.

"Thank you," he said quietly. When Mary didn't acknowledge him he thought she had fallen asleep. It was only when he glanced down and saw wet, spiky lashes and the tears on the curves of her cheeks that he knew otherwise. "Mary?"

She knuckled her damp eyes and gave him a tentative, watery smile. "Relief," she said, explaining her tears. "And gratitude."

He nodded, understanding. His fingers sifted through the curling ends of her soft hair. "I hadn't imagined you would know so much about healing," he said.

Mary remembered how often she had prayed for the skill that was her sister Maggie's. It didn't seem to her that she knew so very much. "I've always worked in a hospital," she said. "That's what the sisters of my order did."

"Tell me about it."

"The hospital?"

"If you want to start there."

She shrugged. "There's not much to tell."

"I don't believe that," he said. "How did you choose your order?"

"I don't know that I did choose it," she said. "At least not consciously. It was the place that called me. My mother used to make visits to the sick every Wednesday. When I was still very young she would take me to the hospital the Little Sisters operated. Usually I would sit beside her while she read to the patients or wrote letters for them. Sometimes I would get them water or help them with their pillows."

Mary turned a little in his arms. "Jay Mac used to argue with Mama about going. He was afraid she would contract some disease. He thought giving her money for the charity would keep her away but she always delivered it in person and stayed to tend the sick anyway. It couldn't have been easy for Mama to cross Jay Mac, but she did it once a week for years."

"And took you with her."

Mary nodded. "Every week."

"Until you entered the order. Then she stopped."

Mary raised her head and looked at him. "How did you know?"

"Just a guess."

No, she thought, it was more than that. He had the uncanny ability to listen to her and hear more than she could hear herself. It was like having an echo that was clearer and stronger than her own voice. "I suppose," she said slowly, "that once I was there she didn't feel the need to go as often." Mary laid her head on Ryder's shoulder again. "Mama was going to be a nun, you know. That habit I was wearing when I visited you in the stockade wasn't mine. It was hers. She never told me that it had been something she had imagined for herself."

"Didn't she?"

"Not in so many words. She never seemed to regret her life with my father."

"Perhaps that's because she didn't."

Mary was silent for a long time, thinking. "No, you're right," she said at last. "Mama didn't regret the choices she made, but she never quite gave up her dream either."

"She gave it to you."

"She forced it on me." Even to her own ears her tone sounded harsh and unforgiving.

"You didn't want to go to the hospital with her?" he asked.

It wasn't as simple as yes or no. Mary let her hand be taken by Ryder. His long fingers laced with hers as she stared off to the side, seeing nothing but the memories in her mind's eye. "I was interested in the hospital," she said quietly, "but I was fascinated by the sisters. They moved with such poise and purpose and they were such a mystery to me. Kind. Gentle. Brisk. Reserved. I didn't understand their reservation then. I thought it was characteristic of the habit. It was years before I realized that they disapproved of my mother. She was a whore, you know. At least that's how they saw her. And I was the bastard daughter." Mary smiled a little crookedly as tears hovered, then were suppressed. "My mother didn't go to mass after she became Jay Mac's mistress, but she endured the weekly censure of those nuns."

"To help others?"

"To make amends for the choices she made. In some way I was part of it, falling in with plans that were never quite my own. There was satisfaction in helping others and I was intrigued by the nuns, but the truth is, if my mother had been going to a racetrack once a week I would have liked that just as well." She felt Ryder's fingers tighten on hers. "I wanted to be with her, that's all." Mary's short laugh was humorless, and she shook her head. "That I can be so selfish—"

"Mary," Ryder chided her. "I don't think—"

"No," she said. "It's true. I was the firstborn and for a while I had her to myself. I was the first Mary. Then the others came and I had to share her as well as my name." Mary felt as if poison was spilling from her heart. "The time at the hospital was so special to me. I knew it pleased her to have me there, and she never took any of my sisters. I think I might have threatened them if they had ever expressed an interest. It was just me and Mama, and if I had to share her with the patients it didn't seem so bad because she approved of me helping." Mary took a dry, aching breath and spoke so quietly that Ryder had to strain to hear her. "And when I followed the sisters around I could see that she liked it even better." She took her hand out of Ryder's and raised herself up, drawing the blanket around her breasts. "I'm not a very good person, Ryder. I think I've always been a fraud. Certainly I've been a liar."

Ryder reached up and touched Mary's cheek. A strand of hair clung damply to the curve, and he pushed it back. "You're too hard on yourself, Mary."

She shook her head. "No, I'm—"

"No one has ever expected as much from you as you've expected from yourself. If you're a deceiver, then you're a completely decent one. The years you spent in the service of your Lord weren't a pretense. You helped others. You were generous with your spirit. You championed those without a voice and ministered to those who had a need. That was no lie you lived. Compassionate . . . fierce . . . confident . . . serene—you *are* those things."

She wanted to believe him. She wanted him to believe what he'd said.

Ryder watched her struggle, saw the doubt surface in her eyes. He sat up, leaned against the stone shelf behind him, and drew Mary into his arms. She curled against him, hugging her knees to her chest. As she had on the night of their first meeting, she fit perfectly in his embrace. "Our paths would never have crossed if you had made different choices in your life," he said.

"I'm selfish enough to admit I'm satisfied with the ones you made." He closed his eyes and rested his cheek against her hair. "I like to believe that God was saving you for me. God knows, you saved me."

Mary's watery smile was imprinted against the knuckles she pressed to her mouth. Huddled in the security of his arms, she slept the deep untroubled sleep of a child.

"Tell me about Anna Leigh," Mary said. She gave up the pretense of reading and closed her book, dropping it back in the basket. Ryder was sitting on the edge of the stone bed. He had the rope handle of the bucket slipped over his foot, and he was raising and lowering the weighted wooden pail to strengthen his injured leg. There were beads of perspiration on his upper lip as he strained to lift it again. "I think you're doing too much," she said. "Stop that and tell me about Anna Leigh."

He paused—the bucket up in the air—and completely ignored Mary's disapproving look. "You're bossy."

"My sisters say the same thing. It's never bothered me." When it appeared that he wasn't going to pay her any more heed than her sisters, Mary took action. Jumping out of the chair before he guessed her intent, she removed the bucket from his foot and dumped the water back in the pool. She hugged the bucket to her to keep it out of his reach and returned to the wing chair. "You'll thank me later."

Ryder didn't doubt it. For as near as he could mark the passing time he had been working the leg back into shape for three days. This was his second session today, and he knew he had overdone it as soon as he got to his feet. Hobbling to the rocker was painful. Having to hobble in front of Mary only exacerbated the ache.

"Smugness does not necessarily become you," he said, easing himself into the rocker.

"As if I care this much for my looks." She snapped her fingers to punctuate her point.

It was true, he thought. She was rarely troubled by how she appeared. She had no practiced gestures or studied expressions. While an air of serenity marked her features most often, she also could be beautifully animated. Well, not always beautifully, he amended. Right now her expression was downright sour. "All right." He stretched his leg. He massaged the injury lightly through his trousers. "What do you want to know?"

"Why was she with you in the first place?"

"You mean why was she accompanying the troop or why was she with me?"

If anything, Mary's mouth became a trifle more puckered. She sighed impatiently as if his question were unreasonable. "Both," she said shortly.

"Well, as long as you're clear . . ." His comment didn't provoke a smile, and he finally recognized how serious she was. He wondered what had been going on in that fine mind of hers. She must have been mulling over some part of the situation for more than a week. "Anna Leigh accompanied the troop because her father insisted. I assumed at the time that she did it in part just to show me she could. We had a disagreement the night before the wagons left, and she wanted to prove she had the upper hand."

"What sort of disagreement?"

"She wanted me, and I didn't want any part of her. I wasn't kind."

Mary didn't want to know the details. "You humiliated her?"

He nodded. "And she told me she was coming along the next day. I thought it was a spur of the moment decision on her part, but I've wondered since then if it might have been planned all along."

"Why?"

"Well, her father was adamant about her accompanying the wagons. Even when General Gardner and I explained the dangers, he insisted."

"That seems odd, don't you think?"

"Anna Leigh was very used to getting what she wanted. I

think that tradition started with her dear papa." He continued to rub his leg absently. "I stayed away from her the next morning. When I reported that I sensed trouble to the lieutenant, he ordered me to take her with me. I was obliged to follow orders, but she knew I didn't want her along. She hampered my climb back up to the ridge, and at the top she insisted on stopping to drink. The trouble was, she wanted my canteen. Complained that her water was tainted. I thought it was another tactic to slow me down and make me pay attention to her. I traded canteens and drank some from hers to prove she was lying."

Mary's eyes narrowed fractionally. "She wasn't?"

"No," he said shortly. "She was telling the truth about that. Whatever contaminated her water laid me out. It probably would have killed her if she had ever done more than sip it."

"Oh, I doubt she would have done that," Mary said frankly.

"How would she have known it was bad if she hadn't tasted it?"

Mary sat back in her chair. "Because she poisoned it, of course."

Twelve

Ryder considered Mary's conclusion. "You think Anna Leigh deliberately poisoned her own drinking water?" he asked. "Why would she do that? What did she have to gain?"

Mary's eyes widened. "Besides revenge?"

He nodded.

"Goodness," she said softly. "I am coming to admire Miss Anna Leigh Hamilton more at every turn. If I'm right, then she's really quite good at what she does." She leaned forward in her chair and explained patiently, "She poisoned her water to achieve exactly the end that happened."

"To create an opportunity to accuse me of rape?" he asked.

Mary shook her head. "That's been your mistake all along," she told him. "You've made Anna Leigh's motives too personal. What happens if you consider she had a larger purpose?" Mary did not have to wait long for Ryder to make all the same connections she had. The intensity of his thoughts was there in his eyes. "That's right," she said, satisfied. "She was the diversion. No one could have expected you to be pulled away from your duty by Anna Leigh alone. Certainly not Anna Leigh, not after her experience with you the night before. That's why she used some sort of drug in her water."

"She couldn't have known I would drink it."

Mary recognized Ryder's pride was making him resistant to hearing her explanation. "I'm sorry, Ryder, but I think she could. Anna Leigh was armed with the fact that you already had determined she was spoiled and manipulative. She used those very qualities to make you think she was lying about the water. And it worked."

Ryder stared at the far wall of the chamber, his half smile rueful. He considered how much Anna Leigh had learned about him the night before the Colter Canyon raid. He had shown her that he did not suffer fools gladly, that he was not above humiliating someone to prove his point, and that he had little patience for feminine wiles. Anna Leigh Hamilton hadn't lost any sleep over how to dupe him. He had built the trap for her.

Ryder's light chuckle was humorless. "I showed her."

Mary smiled gently. "It's probably little consolation, but I imagine you're not the first man she's taken in so completely."

"It's *no* consolation."

"Then how about this? I could be wrong."

He looked at her. "You've set about convincing me of one thing, and now you want to change your tune?"

"There's no proof," she said. "That's all I'm saying. It's always been your word against hers."

"There was a little more to it than that," he said. "Anna Leigh presented herself to the search party with a torn blouse and a few scrapes and bruises. The evidence, such as it was, was on her side. It seemed to offer an explanation for my absence during the raid."

"Can you remember any of it?"

"Nothing much after I drank the water. I was sick almost immediately and lost consciousness soon after. When I came around it was all over. Anna Leigh had started walking back the way we came. She was found by Lieutenant Rivers and Private Carr. They hauled me out of the shelter and threw me over a saddle. I was in chains long before I understood the charges."

"So the trial centered around the supposition that you had been derelict in your duty, rather than that you'd been prevented from doing your duty. Is that the way it was presented?"

"That's right. Anna Leigh told her story once and it was all anyone had to hear."

"You must have had your advocates."

He nodded. "Character witnesses mostly. No one who could really refute Anna Leigh's story. The prosecution found a couple of scouts who had seen me with her the night before." He paused remembering how he had taken Anna Leigh to a more secluded part of the compound, how he had forced her back against the wall of the soldiers' quarters as if she were a whore, and how she had left angrily when she'd realized he didn't want her. He knew how it had looked to the witnesses. They hadn't had to lie. "Their testimony was very damaging," he said quietly.

"Rosario?"

"He was one of them, but he spoke the truth about what he saw. There was no need for him to embellish the details to make a case against me."

"Then we'll have to find proof that undoes the case."

"That would be the gold itself."

"Perhaps." She rested her chin in the cup of her palm, thinking. "If we assume Anna Leigh's role in your conviction was larger than a means of petty revenge, then we have a lead we didn't have before. Finding the gold doesn't necessarily take us to the people who organized and carried out the raid, but following Anna Leigh may take us to the gold."

"Anna Leigh Hamilton is long gone from the Arizona Territory," Ryder said. "She left with her father after she gave her testimony."

"Then the gold might have left with her."

Ryder looked doubtful.

Mary's tone strove to be more convincing. "We've been pouring over the maps as if they held the answer. They may have at one time, but now—so many months after the raid—the gold could have been moved."

"Mary," he said patiently as if she hadn't understood what he was saying the first time. "Anna Leigh is in Washington with her father."

"So? We should go to Washington."

It sounded very simple when she said it like that. Ryder felt it was incumbent upon him to point out the obstacles in their path. "This cavern is safe," he said.

"We can't stay here forever. You said that yourself."

"I was thinking we'd move somewhere in these hills, not to Chesapeake Bay."

"That's when you were still thinking you could find the gold." She leaned over the wing chair and pulled out the maps that were stored beneath it. She passed them to Ryder to emphasize her point. "You've been over every inch of them. Joe Panama might have known about prospecting for gold and silver, but he didn't draw these to find hidden treasure. That bottom map describes this cavern, doesn't it?"

Ryder was not surprised that Mary had worked it out for herself. "You're very good," he said quietly. She could have left him at any time while he was sick; still, she had elected to stay behind and care for him. "So you know where we are."

She nodded. "Colter Canyon."

"Close enough."

"Do you think the gold was brought here?"

"Not to this cavern, but somewhere close by. I've been over most of the area since we've been here. There's nothing to follow any longer. If the gold's here, then no one's come to claim it. If it's not, then it was removed in the months after the raid."

"While you were on trial. Another diversion." She leaned forward and said earnestly, "There must be someone who can help us."

He didn't take issue with her repeated assumption that his problem was hers as well. He would save that argument for later. "I don't know," he said heavily.

"Florence Gardner?"

He shook his head. "I won't ask her."

Mary recognized his firmness on that front. "Very well," she said. "What about Wilson Stillwell?" She raised her hand, holding off his objections. "Hear me out, Ryder. You may not have any great feeling for the man, but he *is* your uncle and he *is* a senator. He came from Washington to be present at your trial. That says something about his commitment to family."

"He didn't want me to embarrass him," Ryder said. "That's why he made the trip."

Mary ignored that. "I don't know the history between you two, but he is in a position to help you. It's a terrible toll your pride is exacting if you refuse to ask him for anything."

The frostlike chill was back in Ryder's pale eyes. He said nothing.

"If we can get to Washington, will you ask him for help?"

It was the way she phrased the question that lowered Ryder's guard. "Yes," he said. "If we can get to Washington."

"Then it's settled," she said, satisfied. "Good." She stood, stretching her arms and yawning widely.

Watching her, Ryder rolled up the maps and tapped them lightly on the arm of the rocker. As far as he was concerned nothing was settled. "You'd better explain what you mean."

She covered her mouth to suppress another yawn. What was it he didn't understand? "As soon as you're well enough to travel we'll start for Washington. I can't say it plainer than that."

"You're going to have to," he said. "How is it that you propose we get there? Walk?"

Mary waved a hand dismissively. "Of course not. We'll take the train." When she saw that he was still looking at her oddly she realized he still didn't know how it could be accomplished. He was probably thinking it would require money. "Northeast Rail goes all over this country," she told him. "And my father owns Northeast Rail."

Ryder dropped the rolled maps on the floor and came to his feet. "Absolutely not."

Mary flinched at his tone. When she recovered from her surprise, she asked calmly, "Why not?"

"No."

It was not an answer. "Surely it's my decision."

"You're my wife."

She blinked at that. "It's still my decision. They're my family."

"They're *my* family."

That announcement took some of the wind from Mary's sails. She suddenly realized she wasn't looking at the problem from Ryder's perspective. He had already told her that in the Chiricahua culture it was the role of the son-in-law to provide. What she was suggesting was flying in the face of that tradition. "I wasn't thinking," she said finally. "I didn't realize what it would mean to you. This changes things."

"Good," he said. *"Now* it's settled."

She nodded. "I'm divorcing you."

Ryder's head snapped back as if he'd been struck. "You will not."

Mary was already moving toward the trunk. She threw back the lid and began gathering his clothes. "Didn't you say all I had to do was leave them outside our home?" She rooted through his possessions with the single-mindedness of a puppy uncovering a bone. "Should I put them in the passage or drop them at the mouth of the cave on my way out?" Shrugging off the hand that Ryder placed on her shoulder, she continued to go through his belongings. "I want there to be no mistake about my intentions."

"Mary, you can't divorce me for no reason," he said.

She stopped long enough to cast him a sideways glance. "Since you don't think saving your life is a good reason, let me give you another one. You're provoking." She bent to her task again. "Don't you dare smile behind my back. I'm not doing this for your amusement."

Ryder scooped up the clothes she had gathered and pitched them back in the trunk. "I can keep it up longer than you," he said.

Mary's mouth flattened as she stared at the work he had undone. "All right," she said. "I won't divorce you." She stood and began unbuttoning her shirt.

His expression didn't change, but Ryder did sigh. "What are you doing now?"

Raising defiant eyes, Mary continued to release the buttons.

"When you wanted to keep me around before, you kept me naked. I'm merely anticipating your orders."

"Now who's being provoking?" he asked. "And you're doing it deliberately."

Mary shrugged. Her shirt slipped off her right shoulder. She let it be and removed the belt holding up her trousers. Thrusting it at Ryder, she said, "In case you want to tie me."

What he wanted to do was gag her. Unconsciously he wrapped the ends of the cloth belt around each of his fists and pulled tight.

"Or strangle me," she said, eyeing the garrote.

Ryder looked down at his hands and saw what he had made. Unraveling the ends, he tossed it away impatiently.

Mary could see she was engaging him in a battle he didn't want to fight. Careless of the consequences, she shimmied out of the trousers. Tossing back her head, she let her shirt slip off both shoulders. "Well, Ryder? This is what you want, isn't it?"

It was as if lightning seared his eyes. He didn't look anywhere but at Mary's face, and when he acted it was without telegraphing his intentions. In a single sweeping motion he lifted her off her feet and tossed her over his shoulder.

She was robbed of breath for a moment. She pummeled his backside. He walloped hers once. Shock held her still.

The blessed silence almost caused Ryder to change his mind, but he was already at the pool. She tried to hold on to him as his intent became clear, clutching at his shoulders and arms, but he peeled her off, tipped her into the well, and jumped back to avoid the splash of icy water. He was already walking away by the time Mary surfaced.

She shook off thick droplets and knuckled others from her eyes. When she could see clearly she glared at him. "Bastard!"

Ryder sat down in the wing chair and stretched out his legs in front of him. One dark eyebrow was raised. "You just stay there until you cool off."

Mary was damned if she was going to do that. She hauled herself out. The icy water had raised bumps on her skin and her teeth had begun to chatter. Belatedly realizing Ryder had another motive for dropping her in the water, Mary gave him a sour look as she reached for a blanket to cover herself. "Satisfied?" she asked, drawing it around her.

Ryder had no difficulty recognizing the trap in that question. He pointed to the bed. "Sit down," he said. "Over there."

Mary recognized that he was insisting on some distance between them. "Are you concerned about my safety or yours?"

"Sit down, Mary. Now."

She sat. The silence between them built to a point at which it was almost tangible. Mary refused to show what a struggle it was to meet Ryder's predatory stare.

"Tell me about your plan," he said finally.

She took a deep breath and let it out slowly. "You can't keep me here, Ryder. Not easily, anyway. I'm leaving you, and I'm going back to my family. It's not an idle threat. I've studied those maps every bit as much as you have, and I already know how to get out of this cavern. The journey back to Fort Union is more straightforward than I could have believed. You must have taken the most roundabout route imaginable to make your escape from the stockade."

Ryder acknowledged the truth of it with a slight nod of his head.

Mary tucked the corner of her blanket more firmly between her breasts. "You'd better be prepared to make me your prisoner again because I'm done being your wife." Her voice was clear and firm, leaving no doubt that she meant what she said. The blanket that Ryder had maneuvered her into taking was beginning to look more like armor.

"I wasn't thinking so much about your plan to leave me," he said, "as I was about your plan that we should leave together."

"Oh."

Ryder crossed his ankles and folded his arms across his chest. "Oh," he said softly. "I'm prepared to listen."

Mary twisted some water out of her hair and untangled the crown with her fingers. "Rennie and Jarret are still working at

Holland Mines. It makes sense to go there rather than try to make contact at Fort Union. With their help, we can get to the station at Tucson. That's where the private cars will be. There's the one that my mother and I used to come out west and I'm sure my father brought another for his journey. Rennie and Jarret have yet another for their own use. We only need to ask for one to take us to Washington. Rennie's in charge of all of Northeast's operations in this area. She can arrange it easily."

"If she will."

"She will," Mary said with serene confidence.

"Then we wouldn't have to ask your father's permission."

"No, we wouldn't. Does that make it more palatable?"

Ryder had to admit that it did. "It might work."

"You'd still have to ask for your uncle's help. We'd need a place to stay and assistance in finding Anna Leigh. Senator Stillwell could be invaluable to us."

"We *still* have to get to Holland Mines," he reminded her. He would think about his uncle later. Mary was so certain of her family's help it didn't occur to her there might not be aid from the other quarter. "There are troops all over this territory looking for us. That hasn't changed. It was a risk taking you to the Chiricahua encampment, but this is a greater one. We'll be crossing more open ground, and all of it will be on foot." He leaned forward and rested his forearms on his knees. "Besides, this may be for nothing, Mary. Have you considered that? Anna Leigh Hamilton may not be the key."

Mary had thought of it. "I don't have any other ideas," she said simply. "It's better to go off in the wrong direction, than to have no direction at all."

They left two days later, but mistimed their departure and had to cool their heels in the mouth of the cavern until nightfall. Mary wore trousers and a blue chambray shirt. A bandana was tied around her forehead. Her upturned moccasins were laced to her knees. Ryder wore the uniform he had escaped in. They traveled light. No blankets. No change of clothing. He carried a Henry rifle in one hand and had a Colt at his hip. The saddlebags, filled with extra ammunition, maps, medicine, bandages, and a polished turquoise stone, were slung over his shoulder. Mary carried the canteen, its straps slung diagonally across her chest, and the pocket of her right moccasin concealed a knife.

They covered the ground at Ryder's half speed. Mary's stamina was a marvel to him but no match for his. Even with his recent injury still plaguing him at odd moments, he had to slow his pace to let her keep up.

She never complained, and she didn't waste her breath asking questions. Her trust in him was absolute. He felt this as a boon and a burden. They walked all night, resting only to drink. It was only when the sun was clearly overhead that Ryder indicated they would stop.

Mary looked around for shade and saw it in the narrow natural hollow of one of the red rocks. She immediately began to go in that direction.

"No," Ryder told her.

She stopped and glanced over her shoulder. "There's shade there. It will be cooler."

"Apache don't rest in the shade because it's so obvious. We'll rest there, among the mesquite and yucca." When Mary didn't argue, but obligingly turned around and followed him, he once again felt the enormous responsibility of her trust.

They were up again at sunset. A patrol from the fort passed within a hundred yards of them a few hours later, but not one man in it glanced in their direction. Mary and Ryder stayed concealed in the rocks until Ryder was reasonably certain the danger had passed.

"They weren't looking for us," Mary whispered as Ryder helped her up. Her voice was husky. She hadn't spoke a word for hours.

"That was just a routine patrol. No scouts. They weren't

searching for us, but they would have been happy to stumble on our trail."

Mary realized that Ryder had not exaggerated the dangers. She fell in step behind him and found comfort in a familiar litany of prayers.

Ryder found fresh water for them as the moon was on the rise. Mary filled the canteens and splashed her face while he kept watch. Out of the corner of her eye she glimpsed his still, waiting expression. He seemed prepared to sense even the slightest shift in the current of air.

"I'm ready," she said.

He reached for her, touching her hair with his fingertips. Her features were so perfectly composed, her manner so tranquil, that he took a measure of her peace for himself. Ryder nodded once. "This way."

They arrived at Holland Mines when it was still dark, but there was no means of approaching that would not create a stir. Tents were set up near the perimeter of the track that led to the mine's adit. They were all fairly uniform and nondescript. No lantern light emanated from under any of the canvas. There was no way of knowing if any of them was being used by Rennie or Jarret or some other member of Mary's family.

No one stirred in the camp. A guard was posted near the adit, but his head lolled to the side at such an uncomfortable angle that Ryder and Mary knew he was sleeping. A dozen horses and burros shifted listlessly in the corral.

"Where is the track being laid?" Ryder asked.

"It's coming north from Tucson," she whispered. "They work from the point of the completed section so they can carry supplies and timber as they go. Rennie is having this area graded and prepared." Mary massaged the back of her neck and rotated her head slowly. "If Rennie and Jarret aren't here now, they will be in the morning. We'll just have to wait."

Ryder had been thinking the same thing. He looked around, examining their location again to make sure it was safe from a casual observer in the camp. In the morning, when the miners and track laborers began rising, he and Mary couldn't afford to be vulnerable.

Satisfied, he leaned back against a rock and stretched his legs. He patted the ground beside him and waited for Mary to scoot back and join him. Her head fit nicely into the curve of his shoulder. "Sleep," he said.

Her eyes already closing, she didn't require the soft command. There was no casual drift into sleep. This time she was overpowered by it.

Ryder's hand relaxed on the Henry rifle at his side. The night sounds around him were familiar and unremarkable: the gentle snuffling of the horses in the corral; the rustle of the scrub grasses; the soft, even cadence of Mary's breath. Small animals like the burrowing owl and the raccoon moved out of their homes to investigate the mining camp's easy pickings.

Leaning back his head, Ryder stared at the clear night sky. After so many nights spent in the confines of the cavern, this vast canopy of light gave him enormous pleasure. The heavens held the constellations of his father's teachings, characters of ancient Greek and Roman legends. They also held the stars of his Chiricahua upbringing. The same grouping of stars lent themselves to different myths depending on one's perspective.

It was Ryder's destiny, his gift and his burden, to be in one place and absorb two views. In this moment he enjoyed it as a gift.

Mary came awake abruptly. Her eyes opened wide above the hand that was clamped hard over her mouth and nose, but the sharp edge of her panic was dulled as she recognized it was Ryder who held her. A warning for quiet was clear on his face. She nodded slightly, communicating her assent and understanding.

Ryder removed his hand slowly. He pointed to the ground, then her, indicating she should stay where she was. She looked at him questioningly, but agreed. Her expression became more anxious when he pointed to himself then toward the camp. He shrugged out of his Army coat and gave it to her, but when she would have put it around her shoulders, he stopped her. With quick economic gestures, he told her to sit on it.

Turning away from Mary, Ryder crouched behind the rock that served as their cover. He felt Mary's tug on his belt, but gave it no attention. His hand gripped the Henry rifle now and he raised it, not to fire but to have it ready.

The Chiricahua raiders were at the corral. Ryder counted four men, all on foot, slipping around the posted perimeter. The horses were not alarmed in the least by the quiet, calming movements of the trespassers. In the distance, out of the line of his vision, Ryder could hear the more agitated sounds of other horses, the high-strung shuffling and nervous energy of animals ready to be urged into a wild run. Ryder's best guess was that the raiding party included a dozen more warriors who were only waiting for the corralled horses to be released before they attacked.

Ryder slipped out from behind his cover and cautiously worked his way down to the camp. The raiders were preparing to swing open the corral gates. Ryder's rifle was useless in this situation. If he fired it would rouse the mining camp, but it also would bring a volley of shots from the waiting warriors.

Cupping his hands around his mouth he mimicked the cry of the great horned owl. All four Apache raiders stopped in their tracks. The owl's cry was an omen of danger and death, and they acknowledged this by pausing in their work. Ryder released the cry again, softer this time, capturing the eerie fierceness of the night predator, then he raised his rifle overhead and stood.

The raiders, made hypervigilant by the night stalker's cry, saw Ryder emerge from his hiding place as if he had risen from the dust. Their momentary rush of fear was transmitted immediately to the animals, and the horses and burros began to snort and bray. Keeping his weapon lifted above his head, Ryder

walked quickly toward the corral before the restless animals
woke the camp's guard or alerted the more distant warriors.

Mary's heart was lodged firmly in her throat as she watched
Ryder stride boldly across the open ground. It was a good place
for her heart, she thought absurdly, because that kept her from
making a sound. She found she could not draw a full breath
until he made it to the corral without incident.

It was unnerving to watch the action and have no role in the
outcome. Mary could see that Ryder was speaking to the raiders
at the same time he was drawing them away from the corral.
She was aware of the animals quieting and of silence returning
to the encampment as Ryder and the raiders disappeared behind
the curtain of night.

Minutes passed and he did not reappear. Mary's legs ached
from her crouched position, and her promise to stay where she
was tore at her conscience. It had never been her way to do
nothing, but in this instance she had no clear idea of what she
could do.

In a heartbeat the decision was taken out of her hands.

Ryder carried his rifle at his side. Surrounded now by the
raiders, it was no longer necessary to hold it overhead. After
some arguing with him and among themselves they led him to
the band of warriors who had been awaiting their signal. Ryder
had no difficulty finding the great Geronimo among them.

Geronimo's broad face was cut by deep creases, carved by
the weather in much the same manner the earth was carved by
sun and storms. The silver medallion he wore on a rawhide
thong around his neck flashed briefly in the moonlight. He allowed his mount to advance a few steps, bringing him out of
the phalanx of skittish animals.

"Ryder." Geronimo pronounced it with a guttural harshness
that could not be mistaken for a greeting. "You interfere."

"My wife's family may be among those you intend to murder
in their sleep," he said.

The Chiricahua leader did not blink. He stared at Ryder stonily, unmoved by this information. "Naiche is my brother, and you are his son. That is why no one moves to kill you now. You may go and we will forget this trespass in our affairs."

"I will bring you the horses," Ryder said.

Geronimo's mouth flattened. "The animals were ours, and you stopped the raid."

"I stopped the bloodshed." Ryder saw the truth of his words in Geronimo's flinty eyes. "My wife's father is powerful among his people as you are powerful among so many. There will be great retribution for taking the lives of his loved ones."

"Your wife's family brings the iron horse," Geronimo intoned gravely.

Ryder's chest tightened. He hadn't realized Geronimo knew that Mary's family was connected to the railroad. This did not favor Ryder's ability to bargain. "Yes," he said.

"You are a traitor to your people," the chief said.

Ryder knew Geronimo meant the Chiricahua. "The white leaders say the same," he said. "But I have betrayed no one. I live in one world and I remain true to all people as I am true to myself."

"How will you fight tonight?" Geronimo asked. "On whose side?"

"On my side," Ryder said, returning Geronimo's hard stare. "I will fight you to prevent more bloodshed, and I will fight my wife's people to bring you the horses."

Geronimo was silent, in no hurry to make his decision. "My heart is sad for you," he said finally. "For I think you live in no world and trust no one." There were whispers among the warriors as they anticipated their leader's decision. "Bring us the horses." There was the slightest pause, and then Geronimo spoke Ryder's name in the Apache tongue, "One-Who-Rides-The-Wind."

Ryder acknowledged this with a slight bow of his head before he turned. The irony of the similarities in his Christian and Chiricahua names had never been lost on him, but now the connection seemed more important than ever. Once again he was bridging both cultures, two lives.

Ryder returned to the corral alone. He climbed over the fence and dropped inside. Leaning his rifle against the fence, he began to run a leading string around the horses, tethering them together so they wouldn't stray when he released them. The animals were calm under his gentle direction. The horses lined up docilely, and the burros meekly went to another corner. Ryder was ready to raise the rope on the gate when a familiar but unexpected voice stopped him.

"I'm not going to let you do that," Rosario said lowly.

Ryder did not drop the rope, but some small movement he made indicated his intention to go for his gun.

Rosario stepped out of the shadows of the nearby mining machinery. "And I'm not going to let you do that." The Tonto scout was shielded by Mary's body. He held a knife to her throat.

Ryder's face gave no indication of the jolt that went through him. He let the rope fall back into place. "Let her go." Though Rosario had spoken English, Ryder gave his order in the Tonto dialect of the Apache tongue. "You only want me."

"I will have both."

"You will have nothing." Ryder practically spat the words. "You hide behind a woman. There is no honor in that."

Rosario recognized the ploy: attack his pride and force him to give up his captive. "It means nothing coming from a man who has no honor," he said tightly.

The blade was no longer cold on Mary's throat. The edge of it had drawn blood once, and she could feel the trickle against her skin. She was afraid and she was angry, but anyone who knew her would realize in which direction the scales of emotion were tipped. "For God's sake, speak English," she snapped. "If I'm going to die over it, then I'll damned well know what the argument's about."

Ryder didn't flinch. Rosario, he saw, was taken back by her tone and her vehemence: The knife was pressed more firmly against Mary's throat, the blade turned in just a fraction more lethally. "He doesn't want me to release the horses," Ryder told her. "And he isn't willing to release you in exchange for my promise." He looked past Mary to Rosario. "You're condemning everyone here to death."

Rosario's head cocked to one side, but he said nothing.

"You saw the raiding party, didn't you?"

He nodded. "Less than twenty men."

"You fool. Geronimo is with them. It makes them a hundred strong." He saw Rosario's confusion. "And they'll run over this camp if I don't give them the horses. No one will escape. Least of all you. You could have had the great Geronimo. You settled for the easy coup instead."

Mary felt her captor's anger rise and knew the moment she was going to be pushed away so he could face Ryder. Prepared as she was, the vigorous thrust still sent her sliding forward onto her knees. Her palms scraped the ground as she came to a halt. Catching her breath, she looked up and saw Ryder vaulting over the corral to attack Rosario.

Mary scrambled to her feet and removed the knife from her moccasin pocket. Ryder and Rosario were circling each other. Rosario's knife was darkened on the edge by Mary's own blood. Ryder was without a weapon save his Colt, and it was useless because he didn't want to fire it and precipitate the bloodbath he was trying desperately to avoid. Mary tossed her knife onto the ground between the men.

Rosario was small of stature, lithe and quick. A bandana held back his long ink black hair, but his locks swirled about his shoulder as he stabbed at Ryder to keep him from retrieving the weapon. Ryder easily removed himself from harm's way, feinted left then dove right, capturing the hilt as he somersaulted forward. He came to his feet again easily, this time on the other side of Rosario.

Now that Ryder was armed, Mary turned her back on the combatants. Nothing she could do there could affect the outcome, but she must save the camp. Raising the looped rope on the gate post, she let the corral gate swing open and grasped the leading string of the first horse to sidle up to her. With a firm, commanding tug, she led the animal out of the corral. Tethered together as they were, the others had little choice but to follow. Out of the corner of her eye she saw Rosario's arm make a wide sweeping arc, saw Ryder duck the lethal pass. Mary pressed on.

She didn't know where she was taking the horses. She was aware of the general direction in which Ryder had gone when he'd left the corral with the four Chiricahua raiders. She supposed, correctly, that they would find her.

A band of six warriors stopped her, blocking her route with the animals. Giving herself to God's care and grace, Mary faced them squarely. She held up the leading strings in a tight fist. "These are for you."

No one moved. No one commented. They simply stared at her. Mary was a woman outside the realm of their experience. Her shirt and trousers gave her an appearance they were not accustomed to in a white woman. The upturned moccasins, similar to their own, identified her as the one Ryder had married. They wondered at her cropped hair and oddly serene expression as she faced them. She did not cower in terror or raise her fist defiantly. If she was afraid she had learned to accept the fear and absorb its strength for herself.

One warrior moved forward. "She is One-Who-Rides-The-Wind's woman."

Mary did not understand what was said, but there seemed to be general agreement among the other warriors. "These horses are a gift for the great Geronimo. My husband and I wish to make him this gift."

The warrior who had come forward now reached for the leads and took them from Mary's hand. "What do you know of Geronimo?" he asked in English.

Mary held her ground, but it was difficult with the horse and the men towering over her. "I know he has the mark of a powerful man," she said clearly.

"How do you know this?" was the deeply graveled reply.

"He is both feared and respected by his enemies."

The warrior considered this a moment, then he translated for his band. There was another general murmur of agreement. "And would you tell him this if you met him?"

Mary shook her head. "Respect and fear would shut my mouth."

There was deep, rich rumbling laughter when this was translated. "A cunning fox would have to steal her tongue to shut her mouth," he added in Apache and laughed at his own humor.

Mary did not have to understand the language to know she was the object of their joking. It was clear they had no intention of harming her. Having made her gift, she was anxious to get back to the corral and Ryder. "I must go," she said. "My husband is—"

"Is going to turn you over his knee."

Mary spun on her heels as Ryder's voice came to her from behind. Moving past the horses, she launched herself into his arms and planted kisses over his face. Only half aware of what she was doing, she patted him down, exploring for puncture wounds.

"I swear I am, Mary," he said between kisses. "Right over my knee."

The warrior holding the horses nodded approvingly and offered his opinion in Apache.

Still holding Ryder's dear face between her hands, Mary drew back slightly. "What did he say?" she asked.

"Geronimo says I should beat you now and save myself years of agony."

Mary blinked. "Geronimo?" Her hands dropped from Ryder's face, and she turned quickly in the direction of the band of warriors. They were already moving away, the great man himself leading the captured horses. She stared after him, awed by her close encounter, amazed at her own temerity. She closed her eyes and made the sign of the cross.

Ryder lifted Mary against him in a hard, solid embrace. "I can't turn my back on you for a moment." He kissed her forehead, her cheeks, her ear. "God," he whispered against her hair. "Thank God."

"Does this mean you're not going to beat me?" she asked when he set her down.

A wash of moonlight highlighted her mouth. Ryder's decision was easy. He kissed her. Mary gave herself up to it, forgetting all her questions and losing herself in the taste and texture of that kiss. "Oh," she said a little dazedly when he lifted his head. "Oh, my."

Ryder smiled. "I'll take that as a compliment."

His dry tone was enough to sober Mary. She stepped back and turned her gaze in the direction of the mining camp. "What happened?" she asked. Since Ryder was alive there was only one answer she expected. It wasn't the one Ryder gave her.

"Rosario's trussed like a calf for branding."

Mary's forest green eyes held her astonishment. "You didn't kill him?"

"Not yet. Jarret's deciding his fate."

"Jarret! Then he and Rennie *were* in the camp."

Ryder nodded. "He'll probably never know for certain what roused him out of his cot or what made him decide to take a look around, but he had a lot more to do with saving my life than I did."

Mary tried to take it all in. "Is the entire camp awake?"

"No. Just Jarret. Even the posted guard's still sleeping. Jarret wants to kill him more than Rosario." Ryder took a bandana from his pocket and wet one end of it. Lifting Mary's chin, he cleaned the thin trail of blood from her neck. "Jarret clipped Rosario with the butt of his Colt and tossed him into one of the mining carts. We pushed it into the mine, then I came to get you. Jarret was going to keep Rosario in one of the abandoned shafts until we make our escape. If he sees the blood on your neck he may just push Rosario down it."

Though he spoke lightly, Mary knew it was the truth. She supposed Jarret's interference had a great deal to do with saving Rosario's life, too. The flinty look in Ryder's eyes told her that he could easily take the scout's life for what he had done to her. "I'm fine," she said. "Really." Mary laid her hand over Ryder's wrist and forced him to stop attending her. She pushed his hand gently away. "Rosario came up behind me," she told him. "When you went to the corral. I didn't go looking for trouble." It was important to her that he know the truth.

"I believe you." And he did. Rosario had probably been following them at some distance from the time they left the cave. Ryder blamed himself for not being more observant. "Let's go. Jarret's waiting for us." He thrust the bandana back in his pocket and took Mary's hand. "He has some place in mind for us to hide."

The hiding place turned out to be the same abandoned portion of the mine where Jarret had made Rosario a prisoner. Jarret's torchlight flickered over the unconscious scout as he led Mary and Ryder deeper into the shaft. Mary saw that Rosario, bound and gagged, was not likely to stir anytime soon. "You won't let him die," she said to Jarret. When he didn't answer her she tugged on his shirt. "Don't ignore me, Jarret."

"As if I could." He stopped because he had reached the end of the horizontal shaft. He thrust the torch into a crevice between the timber uprights and the rock wall. "No," he said plainly. "I won't let him die. But he has to stay there until we decide what's to become of the two of you." He pointed to the blankets he had already laid out on the ground. "It's the best I could do on short notice. You weren't exactly expected."

"And certainly not invited," Ryder said, giving Mary an arch glance.

Jarret said, "Oh, I know whose idea this was. It has that masterful Dennehy touch all over it. I'm only surprised you went along with it." He sighed and his voice lost the sarcasm that had marked it. "Never mind. I *do* understand." He raked back his hair in a weary gesture. "Get some sleep. There are a few hours left before sun up. You may as well rest until then. There's going to be quite a commotion in camp once I tell the miners their horses are gone."

He left the torch behind and made his way out by touch alone. Mary and Ryder heard him swear softly as he tripped over Rosario's body. To her shame, Mary had to control the urge to laugh.

"It's all right," Ryder said, quelling his own smile. "Rosario didn't feel a thing."

"I was thinking more of Jarret's toes. He was barefoot, did you notice?"

Ryder had noticed. "I don't suppose Jarret's had much cause these days to sleep with his boots on." He helped Mary down on the blankets, smoothing them out on the edges. He didn't even have his coat to lend her for a pillow. "Put your head on my lap," he said.

"No," she said. "You put your head on mine."

Ryder recognized the flat, dogmatic tone. If he argued with her they would both spend the night sleeping sitting up. He valued his own rest more than winning an argument with Mary. "Very well." He let her settle back against the wall, then lay down. When her fingers began to sift through his hair he closed his eyes. Her touch released the tightness in his scalp and the tension at the back of his neck. His mouth relaxed, then his shoulders.

Hours later Mary raised a finger to her lips as Rennie and Jarret entered the area from the mine passage. The torch Jarret had left behind had long since burned out, but Rennie was carrying another. Mary squinted to adjust to the onslaught of light. "Is it morning already?" she asked softly, loath to wake Ryder. He had slept deeply, rarely stirring.

Rennie knelt beside her sister. She touched her face as if to assure herself it really was Mary—and in one piece. "Are you all right? What are you doing here? Don't think for a minute that I believe all that nonsense Jarret reported after he found you. I know you didn't help plan Ryder's escape. You told me about finding Mama's habit, remember? You weren't pretending to be hurt or angry. It was all very real. You didn't plan that."

Mary rolled her eyes. She had forgotten how wearing Rennie's energy could be. "Of course I didn't plan to wear it, you ninny. That just came about because it was the better idea." She saw that she had momentarily confused her sister. "Stop trying to guess at things it's better you don't know. What does it matter what I've done when I'm here to talk about what I intend to do?"

Rennie's mouth clamped shut.

"That's better," Mary said firmly. She glanced down at Ryder. His eyes were open, and there was a barely suppressed smile on his lips. "See?" she told Rennie. "He's awake now, and I'm certain it has something to do with your chattering."

Ryder pushed himself upright. "I distinctly heard two jays squawking."

"Jays!" Mary said.

"Squawking!" Rennie said.

Jarret hunkered down in front of Ryder and handed him a tin plate with scrambled eggs, corn meal, and bacon on it. "As long as you're eating you can't get in the middle of it."

Ryder saw the wisdom of it immediately. He tucked into his food and let the Marys carry on.

Rennie passed the next plate from Jarret to her sister. "You're safe enough here. The miners have no reason to come down this passage, and Jarret and I weren't followed in. Most of the men left when Jarret raised hell about the horses being gone. They're walking to where the track is being laid, hoping to get a ride into Tucson where they can get new mounts and raise a ruckus about the Apache raid."

Jarret added, "They know they're lucky to be alive, but they still want to ride out. They don't think the Army's doing enough to stop the Chiricahua. At least not the band Geronimo's leading."

Ryder's brows rose a fraction but he said nothing. Mary stared at her plate.

Rennie looked from one to the other. "So it was Geronimo." Unconsciously her hand went to her hair as if to check the placement of her scalp. "The men were right."

"I didn't tell them anything," Jarret explained. "Around here these days it's a matter of two and two is four. The only thing that puzzled the men is why they're still alive. I didn't tell them that either, but I suspect it has something to do with you." He leveled a hard look at Ryder and saw once again that the man did not flinch easily.

It was Mary who spoke, giving the details of last night and then including in her story their departure from the Cavern of Lost Souls.

Rennie put her arm around Mary's shoulders. The affection between the sisters ran deep, and admiration formed another bond. "I could not imagine being half so brave as you," she said, real awe in her voice. She shook her head slowly trying to take it in. "To exchange words with Geronimo. What was it like?"

Mary's smile was modest. "Not half so bad as exchanging words with Mama."

Thirteen

Ryder and Mary spent the day waiting for night. The details of the escape had been mapped out at breakfast and the arrangements made by lunch. That left little besides anticipation and apprehension to fill the time until dinner and departure.

Rennie thought the tension was almost tangible. "Here," she said, dropping a valise at Mary's feet. "I've brought you both a change of clothes. It's time you were out of trousers, Mary. You'll raise suspicions dressed like that, not reduce them."

Mary had come to appreciate the advantages of trousers. Her agreement was reluctant.

"Do as your sister says," Ryder said. "She's right."

"I know she is," Mary snapped. "That's why I agreed."

Rennie looked over her shoulder as her husband entered the area. Her eyes warned him about the emotional climate. Jarret nodded, understanding. "I have horses for you to ride," he announced. "A half dozen of the miners just returned, and they have two horses between them. I told them Rennie and I wanted to ride to Fort Union, and they'll let us have them. We'll ride out and meet you just beyond sight of camp. You'll be on your own after that. One of the private cars has been brought as far north as the track's been laid. You shouldn't have any trouble there." He pointed to the clothes Rennie had brought. "Once you're wearing those, there'll be enough resemblance to fool people at a distance. You only have to stay inside and give your orders through the door, just like we planned."

"Won't your workers think that's a little odd?" asked Mary.

"Why would either of you stay inside the car and shout your orders through a closed door? That's very strange behavior."

Rennie's mouth pursed in exasperation, and she gave her older sister a frank stare. "You can't be that naive, Mary Francis." Just to make certain she understood, Rennie added, "Some mornings Jarret just can't get out of bed."

Jarret came up behind his wife and slipped his arm around her middle. With a low, playful growl he nuzzled her ear. "That's right. Blame it on me, you lusty wench."

Rennie flushed to the roots of her hair. She poked Jarret in the ribs with her elbow. "Let's get out of here so they can change. I think Mary's been made to understand, thank you very much. And you have to give our prisoner something to eat anyway."

"Very well." He let her go and pointed to the things he had carried in and dropped just inside the entrance. "I collected the saddlebags, Army jacket, and canteens that were left up in the rocks. If you want any of those items, fine. If you don't, I'll take them to our tent later and eventually get rid of them."

Ryder nodded. He knew Jarret was trying to eliminate their trail and also reduce the chances that he and Rennie would be pegged as accomplices. "You haven't been to the fort yourself today?" he asked.

"No. There's been plenty of activity between Fort Union and the mine, though. Since word reached the fort of the raid, they've had patrols all over the place. Jay Mac and Moira and the rest of the family know we're fine here."

"It's a wonder Jay Mac didn't come himself to make sure," Mary said. "That would be just like him."

Rennie nodded in agreement. "We understand that General Gardner won't give any civilians permission to leave the fort right now. Ethan and Connor can't be any happier about that than Jay Mac. That's why we're returning to the fort as soon as you're safely off." There was a small catch in her throat. Tears glistened unexpectedly in her eyes. "And I want to see my babies."

Mary flew to her sister's side and embraced her. "Of course you do. Dear, dear Rennie, how will we ever thank you?" She looked to Jarret over Rennie's shoulder and held out her hand for him to take. "And you," she said, squeezing his hand gently. "You've done so much. There's no repayment ever that will be—"

Jarret shook his head. "Finish this business in Washington," he said. "And invite all of us to your next wedding." His glance at Ryder was significant. "There'll be hell to pay otherwise."

Ryder nodded once, acknowledging the point. It was clear Mary's family thought she deserved a more conventional ceremony. "If she'll have me," he said quietly.

Rennie took control of the embrace with her sister, holding Mary by the shoulders and giving her a steady look. For once, she didn't say anything. She was satisfied with what she saw. She released Mary and took her husband's arm. "Let's go. I'm as anxious to be gone from this place as they are."

Mary and Ryder changed clothes quickly once they were alone. Her gown was a serviceable blue and white gingham, while he exchanged his Army uniform for jeans, a clean white shirt, and a brown leather vest. One of Rennie's bonnets covered Mary's short curls, and Ryder tucked his long hair under the hat Jarret lent him. When the transformation was complete they bore a more than passing resemblance to Rennie and Jarret.

Ryder actually began to have some confidence that their scheme just might work.

They passed Rosario as they were leaving the mine. He was still bound and gagged and sleeping peacefully. Rennie and Jarret had fed him well but they had also drugged his food. Ryder didn't spare the scout a glance, though Mary said a brief prayer over him.

Mary and Ryder were able to leave the mine without incident. Crossing the camp unnoticed was more difficult, however. The miners and track laborers who had returned were milling about, not so eager for sleep as they had been the night before. They sat in small groups of two and three around several different fires. Someone was playing a fiddle, and the mood was such that even that happy instrument was given a mournful sound.

"Thought you had already left," a miner called to them as they crossed the encampment.

Ryder simply raised a hand. The gesture worked as well as a verbal response.

"Mrs. Sullivan," someone else begged for attention. "You promised you'd give me those plans tonight."

Mary could hear the footsteps behind breaking into a new rhythm as the Northeast laborer tried to catch up with them. Thinking quickly, she pulled on Ryder's sleeve and stopped him. She could tell he was questioning her judgment, uncomfortable with having a face-to-face confrontation with anyone.

Mary slipped the saddlebags off Ryder's shoulder. "Go on," she encouraged him. "I'll be there in a moment." As Ryder strode away she quickly opened the bag and withdrew one of the maps. She had no idea which one she was handing over when the laborer finally caught her, but she kept her head low and thrust it into his hands. "Just as I promised," she said in a credible imitation of Rennie's huskier voice.

"Thank you, Mrs. Sullivan." He took the paper she gave him, tipped his hat, and let her go, satisfied with the exchange.

Mary's own heart was slamming hard in her chest when she came up behind Ryder. She returned the saddlebags.

"Don't take a chance like that again," he said tightly. He was furious with her and didn't care if she knew it.

"What would you have had me do?" she asked in the same harsh whisper. "Run away? That would have raised a few eyebrows and called attention to us."

It didn't make it any easier that she was right. He wasn't used to being impotent in challenging situations. "I could have given him a map, the same as you."

"He *asked* for me. Rennie is the one who is the engineer, after all." Mary clamped her mouth shut before she said something she would regret.

Without their being aware of it, their angry tandem stride

kept anyone else from calling out or approaching them. In a few minutes they were beyond the mining camp and the light from the fires dotting it.

Rennie and Jarret were waiting for them in the prearranged location. Rennie gave her sister a brief hug, then began counting instructions on her fingertips. "It's already arranged for the car to leave as soon as you arrive at the work site. Don't forget to tell them in Tucson that you want to go to Santa Fe, not to California. That will be different than the route they're used to Jarret and me taking. I'll telegraph ahead to Santa Fe and lay out your journey from there. After you're safely on your way we'll be able to communicate by telegraph—though I think caution is in order. Perhaps Pittsburgh would be a good place to send messages. If the rest of us stay here a while longer, no one will suspect that we've arranged for you to leave. If Jay Mac will only cooperate it will be brilliant. We'll confuse the Army."

Jarret and Ryder exchanged glances, but both of them were wise enough not to comment. Confusion, they had both learned, was a peculiarity of all the Marys' plans. They had no doubt that Mary Margaret and Mary Michael would fall in easily, even approve. And if Mary Schyler had been around the whole thing would have only become more elaborate.

Farewells were kept brief to ease the ache on both sides. Jarret and Ryder shook hands. Rennie kissed Ryder on the cheek. Mary embraced both her sister and her brother-in-law.

When Mary could steel herself to look back at Jarret and Rennie, night hid them from her view.

Out of the corner of his eye Ryder saw Mary hastily brush away a tear. He doubted it was from sadness. Tonight Mary was more likely to cry out of gratitude. He understood perfectly.

Their arrival at the work site was uneventful. A guard waved to them and sauntered over to take their horses when they dismounted. Mary simply leaned against Ryder in a posture of weary affection, and conversation was effectively eliminated as the guard saw they seemed eager to retire.

The private car that Rennie and Jarret used was really more of a work station. It had fewer creature comforts and more utilitarian items. Earlier in the day Rennie had removed all the essential items she needed to continue her work on the rail line, leaving the car bare of the charts and surveys that normally were scattered across every flat surface.

The wide desk still held a heavy glass paperweight that served only an ornamental function now. A small armoire, bolted to the floor and the side of the car, was filled with clothing and personal items—a razor, strop, shaving soap, and combs. Clearly Rennie's intention had been for Mary and Ryder to freely use whatever they needed.

Mary ran her fingertips across the dresses and shirts hanging in neat array. "She thinks of everything," she said softly.

Ryder was looking at the bookshelves that were built in under the bed. "Everything," he agreed.

Mary followed his line of vision, trying to decide if he was looking at the narrow, neatly turned-down bed or the leather-bound volumes below it. Either way, she supposed, his agreement fit.

Ryder slipped the saddlebags off his shoulder, propped his rifle in one corner, and unfastened his gunbelt. He hung the latter over the chair behind the desk, then crossed the car to the bed and sat down. There was a large basket on the middle of the covers. He opened its hinged lid and saw it was filled with food for the first leg of their journey. Ryder placed it on the floor and leaned back on his elbows. One corner of his mouth lifted in dry amusement as he watched Mary flit around the car examining one thing and then another. She made a point of checking all the lamps for oil as well as to be certain they were secure. She drew open the curtain that shielded the commode, wash basin, and toiletries from view. Availing herself of a glass of water from the keg below the washstand, Mary also familiarized herself with the contents of the oak cupboard.

"You can't be that interested in bath salts and lavender soaps," Ryder said.

"A lot you know," she retorted, closing the cupboard and pushing the curtain back in place. "After weeks and weeks of cold dips in that well, I'm looking forward to a warm bath in scented water." To prove her point she went over to the copper hip bath and stepped inside it. Just fantasizing what it would be like filled with steaming, fragrant water brought a flush to Mary's skin. She hugged herself, closing her eyes. "Mmm," she murmured. "Can't you imagine it?"

Ryder could—quite well. The vision of Mary up to her neck in bubbles—and nothing else—was very clear in his mind's eye. He even adjusted his vision so the bubbles only came as far as her breasts. If he looked carefully he could make out the tips of her coral nipples peeping through. It was easy to conceive of time passing and the bubbles disappearing in tiny bursts. The steam would have made the ends of her hair curl damply, and droplets of water would cling to her white shoulders. The hollow of her throat would hold the scent of lavender. Her complexion would glow with a thin film of water, like dew on the petals of a flower.

In his mind the hip bath suddenly became large enough for two.

"Ryder!" Mary called his name sharply.

He blinked and sat up straighter. "What?"

"You know what. Stop intruding on *my* imagination."

A touch of ruddy color crept under his complexion, betraying the tenor of his thoughts. He didn't apologize for them though. "Well, as long as you're going to avoid this bed, I may as well live on dreams."

Mary raised her brows skeptically and unfastened her bonnet. Stepping out of the tub, she sent the hat sailing across the car toward Ryder. He caught it and fell back on the bed as if laid low by a weapon. "Very amusing," she said dryly.

Lifting one corner of his mouth was as much amusement as he could muster.

Watching him, Mary shook her head bemusedly. He could make her heart turn over with so little effort that sometimes it stung her pride. She constantly battled being too easily led, surrendering so much of herself that she would not know where she left off and he began. He did not seem to have the same concerns. Ryder could give himself up to any moment and still come away whole.

She asked him about it later. They were lying comfortably in the narrow bed, the crisp sheets and covers in a tangled disarray about them. He had made love to her with such sweet passion that Mary's skin still tingled. "How do you do it?" she asked, leaning over him, her forearms crossed on his chest. He was so utterly at peace now, his features calm and untroubled, it was difficult to equate him with the man whose taut body had rocked her only minutes earlier. Tension had engraved the lines of his face then, working a muscle in his jaw, straining the cords of his neck. She had held him, running her fingers along his back, feeling the rigid musculature beneath her palms. He had filled her and she had tightened around him. She had actually been able to feel her body respond to his thrust as if it could halt his withdrawal. There was an ache between her thighs now, a sensation of something lost. Mary could sense the shape of her own body because of the absence of his.

She didn't want an answer to her question any longer. She wanted him again. Inside her.

Mary moved so that she was lying fully along the length of his body. She saw his eyes widen a fraction, then darken with pleasure, surrender, and arousal. Her mouth touched his and she kissed him hard, drawing it out deeply as her tongue speared his. Her breath came in tiny gasps. He drew in air with no less difficulty, as selfish of the intensity of the kiss as she.

Mary's sensitive breasts rubbed his chest. Her nipples grazed his skin, and the contact was like a current running between them. The sensation was almost greater than her tolerance, the pleasure so furious and heated that it bordered on pain. Between her thighs she was warm and wet and ready for him again.

She raised herself up, pushing on her hands. His hands cupped her breasts as she moved to center herself over him. It wasn't possible that he should be ready for her again, not so soon. It had never happened before, and Ryder had not expected it, but at this moment it didn't seem to matter what was possible. He responded to her urgency, to the heat and passion that filled her and spilled onto him. Her supple body moved against him like liquid fire. Her hand closed over his rigid member and she eased herself onto him. It was no vaguely sleepy-eyed, suggestive glance that riveted Ryder's attention. Mary's look captured the deliberateness of her actions, the self-awareness of her body and its movements against his.

It was exciting beyond reason.

His hands slipped away from her breasts and slid over her waist and abdomen. He thrust his fingers between their bodies and stroked her as she rocked. She cried out. No words, just a hoarse cry of elemental passion. Her head was flung back; her pelvis tilted forward. The line of her body was a sensual curve.

Ryder's entire frame arched as Mary forced his release. He caught her as she collapsed against him, trembling. Tendrils of damp hair clung to her temples and her skin glowed. He could feel her heart pound, ease, then pound again. His fingers flicked her hair away from her brow. He cupped the side of her face, turned, and eased himself out of her. "Don't move," he said huskily. If she touched him again he would simply come out of his skin.

Mary didn't. She lay very still as blood roared in her ears and her breathing calmed.

Ryder turned on his side and propped himself on one elbow. Only one lamp in the car was still lit. Its light flickered weakly as the car jerked once and then began to move. They were finally underway, just as Rennie had promised. No questions. No complications.

Ryder amended his last thought. Perhaps one complication . . . and he was looking at her now. "Suppose you tell me what that was about," he said.

Mary was staring at the paneled ceiling of the private car.
Intricate scrollwork engraved each of the mahogany panels, and
her gravely serious eyes traced the edges.

"Mary?"

She was worrying her lower lip now, struggling to come to
terms with the enormity of her own thoughts. "Why is it when
you say my name, I feel compelled to answer?"

He smiled slightly. "The Apache do not use a person's given
name frivolously. It is reserved for more important moments,
and the person called upon is obliged to grant favor when their
name is used at such times." Ryder gathered the sheet and quilt
that had been pushed to the side and drew the covers over them.
"You may not be aware of it, but you use my name in much
the same way."

"I do?"

"You do. I find myself responding as if it were Naiche or
Josanie or any other Chiricahua asking a boon." He considered
her a moment longer, waiting for the answer she had yet to give.

It was his patience that undid Mary. From the very first she
had known he would always be able to outwait, if not outwit,
her. He even seemed to enjoy the wait while she could not
forbear it. "I love you, you know."

Ryder was silent, watching her.

"I didn't know what it would be like to act on it or say it. I
was afraid, I suppose. I thought it would make me part of you
in a way that would be intolerable for me. And yet I have never
doubted you loved me, even though you've never said the words.
I watch and experience your expressions of love and marvel
that you seem to be unchanged by them, that you are not different, only richer."

Ryder let his fingertips drift lightly across Mary's collarbone,
then rest on her shoulder. "Because you have always been part
of me," he said. "From the beginning. Not from the moment
we met, but from the moment we *were*. There has been a place
for you in my heart, under my skin." He touched his temple.
"Here, in my head. The spirit of you has always been here, and

when you are with me in the flesh it is deeper and truer and . . . richer."

Mary felt as if something inside her soared and took flight; yet there was no sense of loss. It was the difference between something being set free and something escaping. One could be celebrated, the other mourned. She turned and was captured in his arms. Her smile took his breath away as she settled contentedly against him.

"Go to sleep," he said when she looked as if she might want to talk.

"But—"

"Mary."

Her eyes closed dreamily. "All right," she said. "Since you said it like that."

In Tucson their car was coupled to a Northeast train headed to Santa Fe. From Santa Fe they traveled northeast to Topeka. Their transit was smooth. Rennie had made good on her promise to telegraph the directions ahead, and Ryder and Mary were largely undisturbed.

They read a great deal, sometimes spending entire evenings together without exchanging a word. Mary found a deck of cards in the armoire and proceeded to relieve Ryder of his shirt and a good deal more with her expert poker play. Meals were brought to them, but left on the balcony of their car as per Rennie's instructions and the DO NOT DISTURB sign Mary hung over the door. The porters and conductor accepted their reclusive behavior without any overt curiosity. It made Mary wonder if her sister and brother-in-law spent as much time making love as she and Ryder.

She quickly dismissed the thought as unseemly, and when Ryder asked why she was blushing she tossed a pillow at him rather than answer.

In St. Louis they dared step off the train and took dinner in a hotel restaurant where no one knew them or suspected they were fugitives. They ate catfish and new potatoes, asparagus with cream sauce, cold potato soup, and salad. They sampled three different wines, then finished the meal with fruit, cheese, and coffee flavored with a sweet vanilla liqueur.

After their meal they strolled in the park and took a carriage ride along the river. It was a pleasure to be among people who only gave them cursory glances and went about their business. They could have been any couple sharing the romantic glow of St. Louis's gaslight, and for a few hours they pretended that's all they were.

They returned to the train unnoticed by the employees of Northeast Rail. Their car was already coupled to the line that was headed east to Columbus. Mary and Ryder settled into the routine they had enjoyed since leaving Tucson. There was a fraction more restlessness in each of them following the brief respite, but neither commented on it.

As their car passed through Ohio, Mary was conscious of Ryder sitting close to the windows and watching the landscape roll by. It was still the heart of winter. The engine carrying them across the flat farm land had to plow through the great drifts that had blown across the tracks.

"In my mind it's always summer here," he told her.

Mary sat on his lap as he tipped back the chair against the lip of the desk. "What was it about summer that you liked?"

"Fishing with my father," he said without hesitation. "Stealing green apples from Mrs. O'Reilley's backyard. The Fourth of July."

"Hmmm. I love parades, too."

He shook his head. "Fireworks. My friends and I would tie a string of 'crackers to—" He stopped. Mary was looking very disapproving. "Well," he said sheepishly. "The cat never got hurt."

"That's awful, Ryder McKay."

"I suppose you never did anything like that."

"Of course I didn't," she said with righteous indignation. "I didn't have to. I had four younger sisters to torment."

* * *

Mary trimmed Ryder's hair as the train approached Wheeling. She was reluctant and he was insistent. It was only when he started to cut his hair himself that she relented. To suit herself, she left it long enough to brush his collar in the back.

She returned the scissors to the desk drawer then stood just to Ryder's left as he examined her work in a handheld mirror. Mary smoothed the ends of his hair with her fingertips. "Well, Sampson?" she asked. "Will it suit?"

Ryder turned the mirror so it contained both their reflections. "Admirably. I look like thousands of other Easterners."

She cocked one eyebrow. "Hardly." Slipping an arm through his and laying her head on his shoulder, Mary said, "I'd still notice you in a crowd."

He smiled at that. "Are you trying to seduce me, Delilah?"

"Just want to see if you have any strength left."

Ryder put down the mirror, lifted Mary off her feet, carried her to the narrow bed, and tickled her helpless. Laughter marked their lovemaking this time and Mary embraced the sheer joy of it.

Still smiling, albeit a little weakly now, Mary lay back. "Have you thought about children?" she asked.

Ryder stopped punching the pillow under his head, no longer caring if it conformed to a comfortable shape. He sat up and studied her face. Was that smile just a little smug? he wondered. A bit secretive? "Are you—" He stopped. It wasn't possible. At least not that she would know. She had had her flow just after they left Tucson. It had been the source of some embarrassment to her and a disappointment to him. The truth be known, he *had* thought about children. "I want children," he said quietly.

Mary lifted her hand and touched his forearm, stroking it lightly. She heard the faint echo of grief in his words. "Tell me about your daughter," she said. "What was her name?"

He told her the Apache word. "It means One-Who-Smiles.

It was her baby name. The Apache are given a name at birth and take another when they are older. It's part of the passage from child to adult." Ryder looked away from Mary, his gaze becoming more distant with the rush of memories. "Her little face was as round as the moon, and her eyes were dark, like her mother's. Her hair was every bit as black as mine and softer than cornsilk. It seemed she was born smiling. That smile was contagious, like laughter, and the old women in the tribe always remarked on it. She was interested in everything around her, curious to the point of being in trouble several times a day. She was the child who would go too close to the fire, or climb too high, or wade too deep. She *had* to touch a cactus spine to be certain it was as sharp as she was warned. Everyone indulged her, though. I think it was her smile. She won us all over."

When Ryder glanced at Mary again he saw there were tears in her eyes. He touched the corner of her eye with the pad of his thumb. "Dear, dear Mary," he said softly. "Yes, I want to have a child. You've made room in my heart for one again."

He held out his arms and made room for her there.

There were telegrams waiting for them in Pittsburgh. The porter slipped them under the door of their private car soon after their arrival. All of them were addressed to Mr. and Mrs. Sullivan, but Mary suspected that from the volume of messages, Rennie and Jarret had told the rest of the family what she was up to.

Mary found a letter opener in the desk and sliced the first telegram open. She sat on the edge of the desk to read.

"Well?" Ryder asked. He was stretched out comfortably on the bed, reading a Wilkie Collins mystery, but when Mary remained silent for so long, curiosity drew him away. "Is it Rennie?"

She shook her head. "This one is from Mama," she said slowly. She read it aloud. " 'You must love him. I pray you know I understand.' " Mary looked up. There was a soft smile lifting the corners of her mouth. "I think this means she's come to terms with my decision."

Ryder closed the book and set it aside. "It sounds as if she's come to terms with her *own* decision," he said. When Mary looked at him oddly, he explained. "I only know what you've told me, but it seems that your mother was not so certain of the choices she made. She hid it from herself, so it's no surprise that she was successful in hiding it from everyone she loved. Well, perhaps not everyone. You, more than the others, seemed to suspect that her long affair with your father had deeply personal ramifications. She did find solace in the fact that you had made your vows with God."

"And when I told her I was leaving the sisters . . ."

He nodded, reading the expression on her face, knowing what was in her thoughts. "It opened the Pandora's box of uncertainties. Moira had to revisit her decision all over again." He pointed to the telegram. "I think she's telling you that if she were to do it over, her choice would be exactly the same."

Mary read the telegram again, then folded it slowly. "I think you're right," she said. "In fact, I'm quite sure of it."

As pleasurable as it was to bask in the glow of Mary's satisfaction, Ryder's attention turned to the other telegrams. "I doubt your father's message will be so welcoming."

Mary plucked another telegram at random and sliced it open. "This is from Maggie. She wishes us success and hopes you are doing well. She's even given me the name of three medicines to try if your leg is not completely healed." Mary shook her head, amused. "It seems Rennie couldn't wait to fill them all in on the details. It may as well have been her who found us in the cavern as Jarret. And I'm certain my sister embellished that business at that mining camp. Maggie asks if it's true that I stood toe to toe with Geronimo."

Ryder laughed. "What else do you have there?"

Mary opened another. "From Ethan and Michael," she said. " 'WIRE US IF YOU NEED HELP.' " She grinned. "Ethan's a federal marshal. That could help us."

"It can't hurt."

"And don't forget that Michael's a reporter. She knows how to get a story published. That could mean a lot when it comes time to publicly clear your name."

"You have quite a few family connections."

"More than you know," she said serenely. Michael's godfather was a judge. Rennie's, a bishop. Maggie and Skye had godparents in politics, and her own godfather was the director of one of the largest financial houses in New York. She told all this to Ryder and added, "Jay Mac wanted to see that we were all protected from some of the censure society coldly reserves for bastard children. His foresight didn't make us respectable, but it did make us respected—more or less." She paused. "Why are you smiling?"

"I'm imagining you as a child, bloodying the nose of someone who dared to whisper you were a bastard. And God help the person who said it about one of your sisters within your hearing." He saw by Mary's pink cheeks that he had hit the mark perfectly. "You may have tormented the other Marys—and I'm sure they tormented in turn—but I'll wager that when it came to society's cold censure, the five of you closed ranks so tightly cannonshot couldn't have breached your defenses. I should think that in time Jay Mac discovered all his protection was superfluous."

Mary nodded. "Poor Jay Mac," she said without a hint of pity in her voice. "He loves us all to distraction."

There were two telegrams left unopened. One of them, Mary knew, had to be from her father. Her hand wavered between them. She picked the one on the left and opened it. Her sigh was audible. "It's from Rennie and Jarret," she said, glancing at the last line first. She scanned the contents quickly, then went over it again, filling Ryder in. "The search for us has all but been called off. Rennie says General Gardner thinks we left the area a long time ago and isn't willing to commit so many men to our capture. Rennie is battling him on it, of course." She glanced at Ryder. "Can't you just picture her insisting that

Gardner muster all his forces for another search and all the while she knows we're somewhere east of the Mississippi?" Mary went back to reading. "Rosario's dead," she said, her voice deep with regret. "Apparently he tried to escape and fell into one of the vertical mine shafts."

Privately Ryder wondered if there were more to the story than Jarret or Rennie cared to share. For himself, Ryder had no regrets, but he watched Mary struggle with this news. "Do they write anything of Geronimo?" he asked.

Mary inhaled deeply and let the breath out slowly, composing herself. "Only that he still evades capture. There have been no more raids on the mining camp." She frowned. "This is strange. Rennie wants to know about the map. She's interested in it and wants to survey. What's she talking about?"

Ryder shrugged. "Hell if I—" He stopped, his brows drawn together, remembering. "When we were leaving the mine . . . the man who stopped you, thinking you were Rennie . . . didn't he want a map?"

"Oh, God, yes. I forgot. I gave him one of the ones from your saddlebags."

Ryder jumped off the bed and went straight to the wardrobe. He took out the saddlebags, opened them; and removed the two remaining maps. The map that showed the largest geographical area was still there. So was the one that charted the caves and passages of the Cavern of Lost Souls. "You gave him Joe Panama's map of Colter Canyon. And he gave it back to your sister."

Mary was relieved. "Well, that's not so bad. For a moment I was afraid Rennie had taken it in her head to survey the cavern. I don't think she should go around blasting a burial site, do you?"

"I was thinking the same thing." He folded the maps and put the saddlebags away. "At least there's no harm in her having Panama's map. She's welcome to it." He gave Mary a knowing look. "As if either one of us could stop her."

"Welcome to my family." She put aside Rennie's telegram

and picked up the last one. "Do you want to open it?" she asked hopefully. "He's your father-in-law."

"Pass." He did walk over to Mary's side. She made room for him on the edge of the desk, and he read over her shoulder when she unfolded Jay Mac's telegram.

HAVE YOU LOST YOUR MIND STOP ON MY WAY STOP HAVE SHOTGUN STOP

"Your father does not mince words," said Ryder.

"It *is* succinct."

"At least he hasn't notified any authorities. He could just as easily have turned me in."

"That's not Jay Mac's way," Mary said, sighing. "No, I'm afraid he wants to kill you himself."

"That's how I read it, too."

They were silent for more than a minute, simply staring at the neatly phrased telegram, before they burst out laughing. Not that there was anything remotely funny about John MacKenzie Worth's questioning his daughter's sanity or stalking Ryder with a loaded shotgun. It was just that the tension needed a release, and Ryder and Mary could find it in the most unlikely of places.

Mary replaced the telegram carefully in its envelope and wiped the tears that had gathered at the corners of her eyes. "If Jay Mac's coming, then you can be certain he's not alone. The cavalry is coming with him."

The same thought had occurred to Ryder. It didn't matter that none of the other telegrams mentioned it, the rest of the family would be there if for no other reason than to prevent Jay Mac from committing murder. "I suspect the Marys are about to close ranks," he said.

"Be thankful we're closing them around you."

He leaned toward her and kissed her cheek. "I give thanks every day."

* * *

It wasn't until they reached Baltimore that Ryder told Mary about his uncle. He didn't expect anything to dissuade her, so he simply put off the unpleasant task until time ran out.

Mary had bought a newspaper at the Baltimore station, and she was reading it, her eyes intent. He took the paper out of her hands when calling her name had absolutely no effect on her concentration.

"What is it?" she asked. She was not successful at masking her annoyance. "I was reading that, you know."

Ryder folded the paper and tossed it on the desk. It slid across the surface, teetered on the far edge, then fell to the floor. Mary started to rise to get it, but he stopped her. "I want to talk to you," he said.

It was his grave tone more than the words themselves that had Mary sitting again. She looked at him curiously, her annoyance vanishing.

"I know you've put a lot of stock in my uncle's help," he began. "Indeed, you can't imagine that he wouldn't come to our aid. That's easy to understand when you've been privileged to have your experiences. Wilson Stillwell—that's how I think of him, not as Uncle Wilson—we've never been on close terms. He was my mother's stepbrother. They were the same age and not particularly close themselves although they were raised together from the time they were eight. When my mother married, Wilson was already in the state legislature. By the time my sister was born he was a congressman and except for obligatory visits back to Ohio for campaigning and fund-raising, we rarely saw him."

Ryder ran a hand through his hair. "He never took much interest in us or we in him. It's not anything anyone's ever regretted. It's just the way it was . . . the way it is."

Mary was silent, waiting for Ryder to make his point.

"I know you think he was present for my trial because he cared what happened to me. Given your experiences, that's a reasonable assumption. But it's not an accurate one. He was a character witness at my trial; he testified on my behalf."

"Surely that—"

He held up his hand. "He needed to do it to absolve himself. Wilson Stillwell wields a lot of power in the Senate. He sits on a number of important committees and has the ear of the President. He was largely responsible for my assignment to the Colter Canyon patrol. He saw that I got good assignments, that I came to the attention of people who could further my career. In fact, he had a lot to do with my favored status among the Army commanders."

"I don't believe that," Mary inserted quickly. "If your status was favored it's because you earned it. I'll never believe anything else. Anyway, if there weren't some feeling on his part, why would he want to give you important assignments or see that you enjoyed any privilege?"

"To absolve himself of more guilt." Ryder sat in the chair behind the desk, turning it so he could stretch his legs out to the side. The curtains in their private car were drawn back. Sunshine filtered through the weather-stained windows and touched the side of Ryder's face, highlighting his austere, angled features. "I hold Wilson Stillwell responsible for the death of my daughter, my wife, her family, and the thirty other Chiricahua who were massacred at Antler's Ridge."

It was a horrible accusation, one that Mary did not fully understand, but she had little doubt that Ryder held it close to his heart.

"When my family was murdered by the Tonto, and I was abducted, there was no search, there were no reprisals by the Army. I find no fault with that. Someone, somewhere, had decided the killing should stop. After all, the raid on our wagon train was a retaliation by the Tonto Apache for a previous Army attack on one of their camps. The only point I want to make is that my uncle saw no reason at that time to have the raid investigated or to put any pressure on anyone for revenge. Instead, he used it. He accepted that we had all been killed and mourned our passing very publicly. It served his purpose very well; he closed the narrow margin that separated him from his political opponent and took a seat in the Senate."

"You cannot be so cynical," she said softly.

It made sense to Ryder that she would see it as cynicism whereas he only saw it as truth. "Years later, when I began to go on raids, and a rumor surfaced about a gray-eyed, white boy living among the Chiricahua, my uncle decided it was expedient to look into the matter."

"You can't fault him for that. It's natural that he would want—"

"He was running a close campaign for reelection. This time he was the incumbent and likely to be unseated. It would have been humiliating for him. The investigation was a way to get attention off policy and the scandal-ridden administration and to play on public sympathy." Ryder's smile did not reach his eyes, his grin was humorless. "The Army found me," he said. "Captured me, to be more specific. I ran away. Not once, but on three different occasions. I could not have made it more clear that I had no desire to return to my uncle or any other way of life. I had a wife, a daughter, and a family. They were more real to me than an uncle I could barely remember.

"I said as much to my uncle when he came West to convince me himself. He didn't recognize me, couldn't even be certain I was his nephew, but I couldn't keep the recognition out of my own eyes and it was enough for him. I was more of a trophy than I was his kin."

Mary's hands were clasped tightly in her lap. She bit her lower lip to keep from offering any measure of unwanted sympathy.

"That was before I ran the third time. I was twenty years old. I had been a man—a warrior—for years, and Wilson Stillwell convinced himself I didn't know my own mind. Or he was convinced I was wrong." His jaw tightened, and Ryder's voice took on an unpleasant edge. "Or he believed that his own needs were more important than mine."

He caught himself and straightened in the chair, drawing back his long legs and leaning forward. He rested his forearms on his knees. "The last escape was the easiest, I realized that later. But then I was confident, a little arrogant in my ability to fool all of the whites. I forgot what I had learned about caution or listening to the warnings in my own head. I forgot to embrace the waiting and struck out when it seemed easiest."

Mary knew now what she was going to hear, and she braced herself for it.

"I was followed. Most unusual for the Army, they waited. They waited through the celebration of my return until a raiding party was formed days later. They let the men leave. Then they struck the unprotected camp. It was deliberate, and it was savage, and it was done at my uncle's behest. He couldn't get me to leave my family so he took them away from me. That's the kind of man he is, Mary. Don't ever forget that."

She was staring at him, her eyes revealing horror. Ryder wondered at the source of that emotion. Was she horrified by what he told her, or horrified that he believed what he was saying? She considered herself worldly, but she liked to think the best of others. She would have a difficult time accepting that he was not so inclined to give the benefit of the doubt. Ryder knew it would be her nature to try to change his mind rather than alter her own beliefs.

"You must be wrong," she whispered. "You must have misunderstood."

He merely shrugged. An argument could accomplish nothing. He had armed her with the same knowledge he had, the knowledge that evil could be embodied in a man who craved power. She would have to make of it what she would. "When I was captured again, I remained," he said quietly. "I was numb with grief, too tormented to suspect the truth then. That came to me over time, over years of watching my uncle and learning what he had to teach me that he did not mean for me to learn. He sponsored me at West Point. I lasted two years, but it was long enough to distinguish myself as a troublemaker. I didn't fit in, and I didn't much try to. With the exception of Walker Caine, I had no friends and no desire to find any.

"There were professors who thought I had promise academically, but I wasn't interested in following in my father's footsteps. Some of the men there thought I had promise in other areas. That's when Wilson brought me to Washington and I began to take on special assignments."

Ryder raised his chin a notch and said flatly, "And *that's* when I read the confidential accounts of the Western Campaigns and satisfied myself as to my uncle's duplicity."

Mary took in an uneasy breath. His eyes were so cold, so hard, it was difficult to look at him and recall he was capable of any kindness. "What did you do?"

"I confronted him."

"And?"

"He denied it. It was no less than I expected, but this time I saw the recognition in *his* eyes. He knew I knew, and it was enough for me."

"Yet you took the assignments. You accepted his help."

There was no regret in Ryder's eyes. "The assignments were dangerous," he said frankly. "Of course I accepted them."

It was then Mary realized he had only been trying to kill himself. The enormity of what he had been contemplating, the grievous nature of that sin, chilled Mary to the bone. She hugged herself.

Ryder was watching her carefully. Her face was pale, the skin almost porcelain with its cool delicacy. Had he become a monster in her eyes? She could no longer be thinking that she understood him so well. She must be thinking that she didn't know him at all. "I survived," he said, shrugging as though it were of little account. For many years it hadn't mattered. He'd felt more anger about surviving than any sense of gratitude.

Mary came up out of her chair. "How dare you say it like that," she said sharply. Her eyes pinned him in place, flashing. "How dare you think—" She couldn't go on. She had no words to express what she felt and anyway anger closed her throat.

Her hands, now dropped to her sides, were clenched tightly. If Ryder had tried to touch her in that moment she would have driven one bloodless fist into his jaw and knocked him senseless.

He came to his feet slowly, but he didn't approach her. He saw the intent in her posture all too clearly. "It was like that then," he said. "Not now."

"It doesn't matter. Your life was as precious then as it is today. You were careless with it because you thought there was nothing to live for. Life is its own purpose, Ryder. It has meaning in and of itself." Tears glittered in her eyes. "You must never love me so much as you loved your wife. I won't allow you. I won't—"

His arms came around her. Mary struggled briefly, but he had her in a secure embrace and in the end she quieted and leaned limply against him. "You have no say over how much I love or how well," he said, stroking her hair.

Her damp cheek was pressed to his shirt. "I would not want you to end your life because I was no longer in it," Mary whispered hoarsely. "There would be no peace for me if that was a decision you could come to."

Ryder kissed the crown of her head. He breathed deeply of the fragrance of her hair. "Sweet Mary," he said softly. "I would survive because I know you'd pass up the chance at heaven just to get even with me in hell."

She raised her head and gave him a brilliant, if somewhat watery smile. "No one knows me half so well as you."

It didn't seem there was any point in discussing things further. They were only one hour out of Washington. There were better ways to pass the time.

Fourteen

They agreed they should stay in a hotel. A day ago Mary would have insisted they see Wilson Stillwell immediately upon their arrival. In light of Ryder's disclosure, she was willing to wait.

It was raining when they disembarked. They were clearly seen by two porters and the conductor as they left the private car. Mary merely smiled as the Northeast employees watched them with some confusion, scratching their heads and then talking excitedly among themselves.

"We've been found out," Mary said. She hefted a valise in each hand while Ryder carried a trunk. "Let's go before they rush to help us and ask more questions than we care to answer."

Ryder flagged a hack just outside the station. He gave the driver the address of a boarding house he knew was suitable for Mary and reasonably priced. The funds loaned to them by Rennie and Jarret would go quickly if they weren't carefully managed.

Mary leaned back on the cushioned seat of the hack and removed her bonnet. Water dripped from the brim and splashed the hem of her dress. She was grateful for the arm Ryder put around her shoulders to warm her. It seemed there was nothing colder than a rainy day in winter.

Although the ride from the station to the boarding house was not overly long, Mary was drifting off to sleep by the time they arrived. Ryder paid the hack driver the fare and a little extra to help with the baggage so he could assist Mary.

The Monarch Hotel had a grander name than its appearance warranted. It catered to boarders rather than overnight guests.

The clientele appreciated the homey atmosphere which was really just deterioration of the furnishings and neglect of the structure over time. Not that the hotel was rundown. It was just that things weren't replaced or repaired quickly.

The lobby was small, furnished with a few overstuffed chairs and an Oriental rug that was worn in the center and frayed at the edges. The clerk's large oak desk was polished but scarred, and the potted plants that decorated the lobby's perimeter looked in need of watering.

The book the clerk turned for Ryder to sign was a massive tome. It contained the signatures of some of the most famous and infamous politicians of the past forty years. Beside him, Ryder felt Mary shake off sleep as her curiosity was aroused by the registry. "Later," he said. "Mr. Stanley here will let you look. They're very proud of this book at the Monarch."

"Indeed we are," the clerk said. He adjusted the glasses on the tip of his nose and looked over the rims at the new guests. "I didn't think you'd remember me, Mr. McKay. It's been a long time."

"A few years, Doc."

Doc Stanley wasn't a doctor at all and he had never professed to be one, but in his years at the Monarch he had often functioned as the house medical expert, pulling teeth when he had to, bandaging an injury, or setting a fracture. One guest had used the title in a half-joking manner, and it had stuck for the better part of forty years. Most people didn't know his Christian name any longer. Doc turned the registry around, flipped through it quickly, and pointed to a line halfway down the page. "Three years and four months," he said. "There you have it. Not so long ago after all."

Ryder looked at Mary. "As you can see, Doc Stanley's memory is longer than mine. He remembers everything and everyone, and if he were the profiteering kind, he'd be a very rich man from what he knows."

The clerk shrugged, scratching behind his ear. "If I started blackmailing my boarders, who'd come around anymore? A man's got to have principles."

"Of course." Ryder reached in his pocket. "How much to be certain Senator Stillwell can't find me here if he learns I'm in town?"

"Twenty dollars."

Ignoring Mary's small gasp of outrage, Ryder gave it over.

"Room three hundred," Doc Stanley said, palming the gold piece. He pointed to the stairs. "Your bags and trunk will be right behind you." He gave Ryder the key to the room. "Hope you and—" The clerk hesitated, looking from Ryder to Mary to Ryder again.

"She's my *wife*," Ryder said dryly. He pointed to his notation in the registry. "Mr. and *Mrs.* McKay."

Doc's cheeks reddened, but he didn't apologize to Mary for his mistake. It wouldn't be the first time someone had tried to pass off a lady friend as a wife. "Well, I hope you and the missus enjoy your stay."

Ryder linked his arm in Mary's and moved her out of the lobby before she gave the clerk the cutting edge of her sharp tongue. "You really don't want to cause a scene."

"That man thought I was a whore."

"More likely he thought you were my mistress."

"That hardly makes it more palatable."

"It's not so terribly uncommon here." When Mary didn't reply, Ryder glanced at her and saw she was studying her left hand, turning it this way and that. When she became aware of his attention she let her hand drop quickly to her side and didn't offer an explanation of her actions or what she had been thinking. They were already at the landing on the third floor so Ryder let it pass. He opened the door to their small suite of rooms and ushered Mary inside. "Why don't you lie down and rest?" he suggested. "I'll take care of our things when Doc brings them up. After that I need to go out and get a Washington paper and make a few inquiries."

Mary frowned. A nap sounded wonderful, but she was wor-

ried about Ryder's plan. "Shouldn't I do that?" she asked.
"You're known in Washington. Doc Stanley recognized you after more than three years. He must be aware you're a wanted
man. Your escape from Fort Union would have made the papers
here, especially with your connection to Senator Stillwell."

Ryder was not concerned. "Doc won't say anything. He's
close mouthed about what goes on here."

"You bought his silence for twenty dollars. A man like that
can be encouraged to speak for twenty more."

"You're wrong. No matter how it sounded, it was a gift, not
a bribe. Doc has much more to lose by speaking out than he
does to gain." Ryder cupped Mary's face and kissed her lightly
on the forehead. "Trust me on this. It's something I know."

After a moment's thought Mary nodded. She was used to
trusting family, but she found it more difficult to extend that
same level of confidence to outsiders. Ryder's experience was
almost completely the opposite. "Very well," she agreed. "I'm
out of my element."

"I doubt that," he said, grinning. He turned her around and
gave her a little push toward the bedroom. There was a knock
at the door at the same time. "Go on. That'll be Doc with our
bags and trunk."

Mary disappeared in the bedroom. The four-poster bed took
up most of the space. A wardrobe was crowded diagonally into
one corner and a chest of drawers occupied another. Mary had
to turn sideways to slip past the large armchair and cheval glass
to get to the French doors. She tried the handle and discovered
the doors were nailed shut. Pressing her face close to the rain-
streaked window panes, Mary could make out a small balcony
in a state of disrepair. The stone balustrade was chipped and
the balcony floor itself was crumbling. Mary sighed. The French
doors were going to remain closed to her as long as the balcony
was unsafe.

She drew the curtains, blocking out the gray skies and muf-
fling the incessant tapping of the rain. After turning up the gas
lamps, Mary removed her cape and unfastened her gown. She

was hanging both these items in the wardrobe when Ryder entered with their valises.

"Is it satisfactory?" he asked, gesturing to the room at large.

"Yes, of course it is." She smiled a little at his desire to please her with the accommodations. "Ryder, I don't know what you think I'm used to, but our chamber in the Cavern of Lost Souls was an improvement over my cell at the convent."

He hadn't thought of it that way. He had been recalling her family's summer home on the Hudson and the private railroad cars that were available to all family members for travel anywhere in the country. Ryder had never seen the Worth mansion in New York, but he had no difficulty imagining its grandeur.

Mary shut the wardrobe doors and sat on the edge of the bed. Raising one foot on a faded brocade stool, she began to remove her shoe. "I'll be quite content here," she said. "As long as it's safe for you."

"I don't know that I'll ever get used to it," he said. "That you come from so much and accept so little."

"You're speaking of material things," she said. "And those aren't so important to me. But my home was filled with love and laughter and lively conversation. So was the convent. If you think I can live with less than that, you're mistaken."

Yes, Ryder thought, Mary's spirit had to embrace all those things. He saw she was struggling with the buttons on her shoe. He knelt at her feet and undid them himself, removing the shoes. "It might be easier if you only wanted a life of luxury," he said. "I'd just find a gold mine."

She chuckled. "See, you've made me laugh. It won't be so difficult for you to satisfy my every whim."

He tickled the bottom of her foot until she managed to get it out of his grasp. Promising to be more respectful of the other foot, he removed the shoe when she finally allowed it. Ryder turned down the bed while Mary slipped off her stockings. He stayed around to tuck her in, pressing a brief kiss to her soft mouth.

She was sleeping by the time he let himself out.

* * *

The first thing Ryder did was stop at the front desk and talk to Doc Stanley. While Doc would have cut off his own arm before giving up information on any boarder at the Monarch, he was free with whatever he considered common knowledge in the town. For Doc, common knowledge was rarely what was reported in the papers. He dealt more in rumor.

Ryder listened to the report without asking many questions. He did not want Doc to speculate concerning his own purpose in returning to Washington. After thirty minutes, he had heard enough to know where he wanted to begin.

By the time Ryder walked from the Monarch to the library he was soaked. Droplets of water splattered noisily on the marble floor as he removed his coat. He made less commotion walking over fallen, dried leaves in a forest than he did walking from the entrance hall to the librarian's desk. His water-logged shoes squeaked on the cold, green-veined Vermont marble.

After that initial disruption, the librarian was not particularly disposed to help Ryder. She brought him what he wanted, but her expression was frozen in disapproval. Ryder did not attempt to win her over as there was nothing to be gained by it. She looked at everyone that way, treating the library as if it were her private domain and each patron was an intruder. She would have been happier if the stone lions on the steps outside the building had actually been guard dogs.

Ryder sat alone at a long reading table. The library was not crowded, and as near to closing time as it was, more people were leaving than coming in. The newspapers stacked around him accounted for most of what had been written in the Eastern papers about the Colter Canyon raid, the trial, and the escape. Ryder read the stories as objectively as he could, trying not to react to every misinterpretation of the facts as though it were intentional. Ignorance explained more of the mistakes in the reports than any deliberate twisting of the facts.

There was a general lack of understanding about the differences among the Apache tribes. Everyone was painted with the same brush, and much was made of Ryder's connection to the Apache as a whole rather then the Chiricahua specifically. The reports did not know quite what to make of Ryder McKay. He was an enigma: a white man who turned his back on his upbringing to live among his captors and then turned his back on the people who had adopted him to begin hunting them down. There was still another twist as he was found guilty for aiding the enemy at Colter Canyon.

Out of town papers printed a few lines about his alleged assault on Anna Leigh Hamilton. She was only referred to as the daughter of a Washington politician. In the Washington papers she wasn't referred to at all—at least not in association with his trial.

Anna Leigh Hamilton was quite frequently mentioned in the society pages. She hosted large gatherings for her father's friends and small, intimate dinners for his cronies. Accompanying her father, she was invited to every important function in Washington, and from Ryder's quick perusal, it seemed there was something deemed an important function almost every night of the week.

Ryder read what he could until closing time, then scribbled a few notes about things he had yet to look at or wanted to come back to. He and the dour-faced librarian left the vaulted building at the same time.

The offices of the War Department were closed, but Ryder was well aware he couldn't simply walk in there and ask to look at their files. His face was known to too many people, most of whom would consider it their duty to arrest him or find someone who would. He mulled over that problem on his way back to the boarding house.

Overcast skies brought night on early. Gaslight was reflected in pools of water on the sidewalks and cobblestone streets. Ryder walked quickly with his head down, paying scant attention to the traffic or the pedestrians. He had learned that the easiest way not to be noticed in the open was not to openly notice others.

When he returned to the Monarch, Ryder paused long enough at the front desk to ask Doc to have dinner sent to their room. The boarding house had a large dining area on the second floor to accommodate guests in a family-style setting, but Ryder wanted no part of something so public. When Doc assured him all would be taken care of, Ryder bounded up the steps, anxious to talk to Mary about his plans.

She was in the bathing room which adjoined their bedroom. He knocked politely, and the door, which had not been latched, swung open wide enough for him to poke his head through.

It was clear Mary hadn't heard him. She was sitting in a copper hip bath, her head tilted back and resting against a folded washcloth. Her eyes were closed and her complexion glowed with the sheen of steamy water.

Ryder stepped inside the room and began to shrug out of his coat. He might have made it to the bath without her hearing him if he'd only thought to remove his shoes. Water squished between the leather sole and welt as loudly in the tiled bathing room as it had in the marble library. When Mary turned on him, her eyes narrowed with annoyance, he was reminded that the librarian still had something to learn about expressing disapproval.

"I take it you're not inviting me in," he said.

It was so obviously the truth that Mary had to laugh. She flicked water at him though she could see it had no impact. He was already wet. "Have you been walking all this time?" she asked, concerned. "You'll catch your death. Why didn't you take a hack wherever you went?"

"We have limited funds."

"I'll wire New York for money."

"No. We'll do fine. I don't want to borrow more from your family."

"It's *my* money," she said. "Jay Mac set up a trust fund for me years ago. He only stipulated that I couldn't turn the money over to the church. As a consequence, I've never touched it. Now, are you going to be stubborn about it?"

He sat on a small, three-legged stool and removed his shoes and socks. "I don't suppose there's any sense in it," he said at last.

"That's right." She smiled. "Come here. I'm feeling very generous." Too late she realized what he was going to do. She only had time to cry out his name, half in shock, half in laughter, as he stepped into her bath wearing everything but his shoes and socks. Water sloshed on the floor and ran in thin rivers between the tiles. The towel Mary had set nearby soaked up some of the spillover but not nearly all of it. "I don't know that I was feeling *this* generous," she said, trying to be stern. "What are you doing?"

Since Ryder was picking up the soap, he thought the answer was obvious. He ran the bar across the sleeve of his jacket from shoulder to cuff, then across his chest, paying special attention to the pleats in his white, tailored shirt.

Mary could never have predicted he was capable of something so spontaneous or ridiculous. She found the well of love she had for this man was capable of deepening. Leaning forward, careless of the water she splashed over the sides with her movement, she took the bar of soap from his hand and let it float away. "Let me help."

She undid him as much with her husky voice as she did with her fingers. Ryder only helped by lifting his hips so she could get him out of his trousers and drawers.

Intent as they were on touching and teasing it was not immediately apparent that they could *not* make love in the hip bath. The cramp in Mary's foot and the one in Ryder's calf made that clear. Slick as seals, they slipped out of the tub and onto the floor. Their legs tangled as they rolled. Mary lost the tussle and ended up on her belly beneath Ryder. He moved the red-gold hair aside at her nape and kissed her damp neck.

The playful aspects of their lovemaking faded as desire became hunger and the hunger became urgent. Ryder reared up behind Mary, pulling her with him, his hands on her breasts and his mouth on her shoulder. His breathing was harsh and uneven. He stroked her skin with his palms. Her breasts swelled and her nipples hardened. She arched, pliant as he molded her. His hands slid over her hips and caressed her thighs. His fingers dipped between her legs. His exploration was intimate and demanding, and Mary let him touch her in any manner he wanted because it was what she wanted too.

He pushed her forward, lifting her hips, and entered her from behind, driving into her with enough force to make her gasp. On the next thrust she pushed back against him and seemed to take him rather than his taking her.

The rhythm was primal. Blood roared in Mary's ears and had the sound and pulsing beat of ancient drums. She responded to his every touch, to everything he did to her. Her skin was all nerve endings and sensation. She had no clear thoughts; she was all feeling.

Mary's climax rocked her forward, arching her body like a bow. Ryder came into her, held her, and shuddered with his own release. They went limp together, easing themselves down on the wet tile.

Mary hid her face in the curve of her elbow. When she felt Ryder tap her lightly on the shoulder she turned her head and gave him the benefit of one open eye and a single raised brow. "Don't ever interrupt my bath again," she said, weary with pleasure. "I won't survive it."

"May I take that as a compliment?"

She nodded and closed her eye. "This floor's cold." Still, she made no move to get up. Ryder helped her a little later, after he found dry towels in the washstand. He sent her off to the bedroom and cleaned up the mess they'd made.

"Someone's knocking at the door," she called in to him. "Are you expecting anyone?"

"It's our dinner," he said. "I'll get it. You're not decent."

"I'm decent," she mumbled. "I'm just not dressed." Mary flopped back on the bed. The towel unraveled at her breasts, and she was tugging it closed as Ryder came into the room. She regarded him skeptically. "You're not precisely prepared to receive company either."

In short order Ryder pulled on a dry shirt and clean trousers. He was tucking in the shirt, on his way to the door, when he called back to her. "Get dressed. When we're done eating, we're going out."

"Out?"

Ryder didn't reply. He opened the door. Doc was standing on the threshold with a large tray of covered dishes. Ryder took the tray.

"I don't do this for just anyone," Doc said.

"I didn't expect personal service." Ryder balanced the tray in one hand and began searching his pocket for money for a tip.

Doc shook his head. "Don't trouble yourself. I came on another matter, too."

"Oh?"

"Mrs. Anderson—she's the boarder below you—came to me with a complaint. Seems there's a regular waterfall coming from your suite into hers. You wouldn't know anything about that, would you?"

Ryder's expression didn't change. "My wife was taking a bath," he said. "I'll have to ask her."

Doc looked at Ryder's wet hair and the shirt that was clinging damply to his chest and drew his own conclusions. He cleared his throat, hiding his smile, and said, "You do that."

Ryder shut the door and carried the tray to the table by the window of their sitting room. He lifted the lids and waved some of the fragrance of their hot meal in the direction of the bedroom. "Can you smell that?" he asked. "Dinner's ready."

"I heard everything that man said," she called back. "I'm never coming out."

Ryder smiled. "Suit yourself."

He arranged the dishes on the table and sat down. He hadn't finished unfolding the napkin in his lap when Mary joined him.

"My stomach's growling," she explained defensively, taking the chair opposite him.

"I didn't say anything."

She ladled mushroom soup into her bowl. "You didn't have to. No one who uses silence as effectively as you has to say much of anything. I swear you could have wrung a confession from Saint Joan." Mary spooned some soup, raising it to her lips. The aroma was delicious, and the first taste proved it was every bit as good as it smelled.

They ate in silence for several minutes, moving from the soup to the crisp salad with vinaigrette dressing. Mary asked, "Where are we going?"

"To the theater."

"The theater?" She could not have been more surprised if he had said they were going to jump in the Potomac. "There's a play you want to see?"

"Not exactly."

She waggled her fork at him. "I know how to use this weapon."

He laughed. "All right. I was at the library this afternoon, catching up on what Washington knows about the Colter Canyon affair. While I was going through some of the most recent papers I saw an opening night notice for *Much Ado About Nothing.* It's anticipated to draw quite a crowd because Yvonne Marie is playing the role of Beatrice. I may not have seen anything but saloon-hall dramas these last few years, but even I've heard of Miss Marie."

"I shouldn't wonder," Mary said tartly. "She has her picture on cigarette packages. I've seen them."

He arched one dark brow. "Really."

"We had patients at the hospital who swore her picture, if held close to the heart, had healing powers. It was not a notion well received by Mother Superior."

Or Mary either, he suspected. "Well, tonight she's live at the Regent Theater and I'd like to be there." He served Mary her portion of the broiled trout and parsley potatoes.

"I rather despise myself for saying this," she commented, "but I really don't have anything to wear."

Ryder's gray glance slid smoothly over Mary's dark green gown. It was embellished with ivory lace at the throat and cuffs, and she had found a brooch among her sister's things to enhance the high neckline. "You look fine to me."

She grimaced. "That's because you haven't been to anything but saloon-hall dramas. Someday I'll explain how insulting that comment is."

He changed the wording a bit. "You look beautiful, and you'll be fine for what I have in mind."

Mary rolled her eyes. "That's only marginally better."

"Trust me."

"I have to," she said. "I have no idea what you're up to."

What Ryder had in mind did not involve stepping foot in the theater. Mary sat back in the carriage, propped her feet on the seat opposite her, and sighed dramatically. "And I did so want to see Miss Marie perform Beatrice," she said.

Ryder patted her foot absently as he continued to stare out the carriage window in the direction of the Regent's front entrance. He had a good view of the six double doors that led into the theater. While carriages waited in a very civilized line along the wide avenue to pick up the theater patrons, none blocked the entrance, and therefore, none blocked Ryder's line of vision from across the street.

"I can't imagine what you think you'll see," Mary said, stifling a yawn. "It will be at least ten minutes before the final curtain."

"People are enamored of the theater to different degrees," he said. Ryder put Mary's feet on his lap and massaged her ankles. "Someone may always leave early."

She hummed her pleasure as his fingers worked over her ankles and feet and didn't bother to disagree with him. Once the play was ended there would be a well-bred, mannerly rush to the street to exit the entertainment hall, but leaving prior to the first round of applause was simply not done.

This last thought was barely a complete sentence in her head when the doorman stepped forward to open the doors on the right side of the entrance. Mary caught the movement out of the corner of her eye, and she sat up straighter, removing her feet from Ryder's lap. She leaned closer to the carriage window and immediately had to clear the condensation of her breath on the glass.

"Washington," she said, low, reminding herself of their location. "This wouldn't happen in New York." She heard Ryder chuckle under his breath, but she ignored him as two couples exited the theater. Both of the men were wearing Army uniforms. Mary didn't know enough about insignia to identify their ranks. "Do you know them?" she asked.

Ryder didn't answer her. He was frowning, studying the soldiers with a narrowed, incisive gaze.

As Mary watched, the doorman went to the curb and waved for a hack. A hansom detached itself from the long line of waiting cabs, and the driver smartly guided his horse and hack to the entrance. Her view was blocked by the carriage momentarily, and when the hansom moved on, the doorman was once again a solitary figure outside the Regent Theater.

Mary leaned back again, turning her attention to Ryder. He was no longer looking across the street, but his eyes, though trained in Mary's direction, were not seeing her either. "Ryder?" she asked. "What is it?"

He didn't answer immediately, and when he did, the reply was cryptic. "The unexpected," he said.

Mary had no patience for that. Her foot connected with his shin. She nodded, satisfied that she now commanded his complete attention.

"You kicked me," he said accusingly.

"I nudged you," she said. "There's a difference."

"Tell that to my leg." He rubbed it a moment. "I thought I

recognized one of the men, that's all," he said. "I'm probably mistaken."

Mary wasn't convinced that Ryder would make that sort of mistake. For some reason she couldn't divine, he wasn't prepared to tell her more. She decided to share what she knew instead. "Neither of them were high-ranking officers," she said. "Nor have they been in Washington very long."

Ryder regarded her with interest. "How do you surmise that?"

"The hansom that was summoned for them is rented, just as ours is. The carriages lining the street on the other side belong to their owners. If those men were more permanent residents of the city, and if they could afford it, they would have had their own carriage meet them at the entrance. It makes a more proper presentation, and even in Washington, perhaps most *especially* in Washington, presentation is as important as substance."

"What else?" he asked, intrigued.

"Neither one of them has been an officer long," she said. "Their uniforms are slightly faded, but the insignia is new. It was much brighter under the theater lights than even their buttons."

"And?"

"And they didn't go to West Point," she said with assurance. "They would have learned some manners there if they hadn't been taught any at home. They should not have left the theater early. Illness alone might provoke that action, but you could see very well that none of the party was ill." Mary's smile was a trifle smug as she concluded, "And the women they escorted were as rented as the hacks."

Ryder was not surprised she had noticed that.

"It's really not appropriate to hire a . . . a . . ."

"An escort," Ryder supplied. "I think that's the word you're searching for."

"It's not," she said honestly. "But it will serve. As I was saying, it's not appropriate for an opening-night performance. Husbands quite properly escort their wives to an event like this.

They don't even take their mistresses unless they want to embarrass them or publicly humiliate their wives. It's simply not done. Now, tomorrow evening is an entirely different matter."

Ryder's lip curled derisively as he considered the mores and mandates of polite society. "How does one learn these things?" he asked with a touch of sarcasm.

"My point exactly," Mary said. "One learns by living with them. These rules aren't written down anywhere. They're rarely spoken of. Yet they often are accorded more respect than the Ten Commandments, and they are enforced with more exacting punishments than the plagues God visited upon the Egyptians. Those two men who just exited don't know the rules or they didn't care enough to observe them. Now, if you thought you recognized one of them it only makes sense to me that you met the man in the West." Mary gave Ryder a firm, questioning glance. "So? Are you going to tell me something more than you have or do I—"

Ryder held up his hand as all the double doors in front of the Regent were opened with considerable flourish. The opening-night patrons began to spill onto the sidewalk almost immediately. "You can wait here or come with me," he said, as a handsomely gilded carriage approached the front doors and blocked their view. "But if you come, stay by my side and don't draw attention to yourself."

"As if I would."

Leaning forward quickly, Ryder kissed her quickly on the cheek. "You can't help it, Mary. Cover your hair." He opened the door of the hansom, jumped down, and held out his hand to her.

Mary raised the hood of her cape before she took the proffered hand. Ryder told their driver to move on, circle the block, but not take another fare. He assured the man they would be making the return to the boarding house with him and they would pay for his time. Mary was going to remark on the wisdom of this, in light of their reduced funds, when she felt Ryder tug on her arm to get her to cross the avenue.

The pace was more frantic now as hansoms vied with each

other to collect their owners and the hired hacks moved in to snare the patrons who didn't have their own means of transportation. Ryder and Mary dodged horses and hansoms as they crossed the wide thoroughfare. They slipped behind a hack just pulling up to the sidewalk, then took their place as part of the crowd. Ryder wove Mary skillfully through the throng until they were able to stand just beyond the gaslights on the shadowed perimeter of the theater.

Mary did not know who he was looking for or what to expect, but she was able to identify a number of people in the sea of faces. "That's Alvin Schafer," she whispered to Ryder. "And his wife Carolyn. Over there, in the blue, just coming out now. He's a social reformer, and very well connected politically. I've heard him speak in New York. They take up the cause of orphaned children in the cities."

Ryder was only listening with half an ear. He gave the couple a cursory glance and continued to scan the faces in the swarm in front of the theater.

"There are the Dodds." She stood on tiptoe to get a better view of the pendant at Mrs. Dodd's throat. "Why, I believe that's paste," she said, astonished. "She must have sold the original and had a copy made. I can tell you, the original is not half so large as that garish item. And look at the way she refuses to close her cape. She's inviting everyone to ogle it."

"Perhaps they don't have your discerning eye," Ryder said dryly. "Or perhaps she's inviting a thief." He glimpsed Mary's questioning frown. "If it's insured, then she would be reimbursed for its loss."

Mary was left to wonder at it as the Dodds disappeared into their waiting carriage without incident. She pointed out several other people to Ryder and received little comment in return. It was obvious to Mary that he was searching for a very particular face in the crowd.

"There's Warren Hamilton," she said, as the senator exited the theater. There was no mistaking the sharp features of the Massachusetts' politician. In most cartoons Mary had seen he was unimaginatively represented as a hatchet. In person, it seemed the cartoonists had been kind. "Is that who you've been—" Mary stopped because she felt Ryder stiffen as the senator stepped to one side and revealed the presence of the young woman on his right. "Oh," she said, her voice hushed. *"She's* the one we've come to see."

Ryder placed a hand on Mary's shoulder as she came up on tiptoe and began to crane her neck in order to catch a better glimpse of their quarry.

Feeling a bit like an unruly puppy who has just been ordered to heel, Mary nonetheless shrank back into the shadows. She had seen enough to form an initial impression. Anna Leigh Hamilton was acknowledged as a beauty for very good reason. The woman's sunshine yellow hair caught the eye, and her flashing eyes and smile held one's gaze. She cut a dainty figure on the arm of her tall, angular father. She was as ebullient as he was sober, as generously proportioned as he was spare. His impatient air faded only when he cast an indulgent smile in her direction.

Ryder retreated a step backward into the safety of deeper shadows when Anna Leigh glanced in his direction. She did not see him, but looked past him instead, trying to spy the location of the carriage that was meant for her and her father The doorman also saw her look and immediately stepped forward to search for Senator Hamilton's carriage himself.

"She's a princess," Mary said softly. "Everyone does her bidding."

Ryder nodded. "Let's go. I've seen enough. She's here and we can follow—"

Mary laid her hand on his forearm, stopping him. "Wait," she said. "Isn't that your uncle?"

Wilson Stillwell emerged from the theater, accompanied by two gentlemen. Mary recognized neither of them, but she was struck by the fact that they nodded politely to Anna Leigh and addressed her father while Wilson Stillwell made no acknowledgment.

"Your uncle has as little time or regard for Miss Hamilton as you do," Mary said. "He cut her and her father dead."

"I doubt that it was on my account," Ryder said dryly.

Mary sighed. "You might give him the benefit of the doubt. Miss Hamilton maligned you, and your uncle is responding to it in the only way left to him."

Ryder did not argue with Mary's interpretation. Certainly she was correct in that Wilson Stillwell had made a direct cut. Ryder was just unsure of the motivation. He tore his attention away from his uncle and surveyed the thinning crowd. He and Mary could not afford to stay much longer as they would be noticed by the doorman who had returned to his post. "Come on," Ryder said. "Our driver's circled the block for the third time. We need to go."

Mary let her arm be taken. She was briskly escorted across the avenue just in time to meet the hack as it completed its final tour. As Mary clambered into the cab, she vaguely heard Ryder give the order to their driver to follow Senator Hamilton's carriage. She had her face pressed to the hansom's window as Ryder settled himself in the seat.

"What are you still looking at?" asked Ryder.

Mary did not pull back, turning her head sideways to keep her vision trained on the same point when the hansom began to move. "Your uncle's not gotten into the carriage with his companions," she said. "I believe he's going around to the side of the theater. Why yes, there he goes. What do you suppose he intends to—"

"Miss Yvonne Marie," Ryder said.

"What?" asked Mary. Then, "Oh. I see. He wants to make the actress's acquaintance." She turned away from the window. "He's never married?"

"Briefly. Years ago. My aunt died in childbirth. The child died a few days later. He never remarried."

Mary was genuinely moved. "How sad for him. Then you're all he has."

"It may explain Wilson's actions," Ryder said tightly, thinking of his own dead wife and child. "It doesn't justify them."

"No," she said quickly. "Of course it doesn't."

Ryder sighed. "I'm sorry." He patted the space beside him, and Mary came across the swaying carriage willingly. "I know you had hopes that he could help us."

That comment surprised her. "I haven't given up. Perhaps he still can. You saw how he was with Senator Hamilton and Anna Leigh. He might be willing to help if for no other reason than to get his own revenge. I've not seen or heard anything that makes me think we shouldn't ask."

Ryder slipped his arm around Mary's shoulders. He gave her something else to think about. "I need to get into the War Office records," he said. "I'd be pleased to entertain some ideas as to how that could be accomplished."

"I'll do it," she said immediately. "What are you looking for?"

"Out of the question." He leaned forward as the hansom slowed to take a corner. Ryder looked out the window, marked the street, then relaxed and settled back. "I want to see the transfer orders and records for anyone connected to Fort Union."

"You could find those things there?"

He nodded. "Every document finds its way to the War Office sooner or later."

Mary considered what Ryder might be after for a moment. "This has something to do with those men who left the theater early, doesn't it?"

Ryder smiled, not at all displeased that she had put it together. "No one will ever accuse you of being slow off the mark," he said. "Yes, it has to do with them. The taller one was vaguely familiar, but I recognized the other one. He was a private when I last saw him. I can't think of any reason for those stripes he's wearing now except that he was one of the two men who brought me in."

Mary's eyes widened. "You mean at Colter Canyon?"

"Patrick Carr," Ryder said. "He accompanied Davis Rivers up to the ridge to search for me and Anna Leigh after the raid."

"I met Lieutenant Rivers," Mary said slowly, trying to place the time and situation. "It was my first day in Arizona. The lieutenant and a small party of soldiers accompanied my family and me from Tucson to Fort Union. I don't recall ever seeing Carr."

"You weren't at the fort very long," Ryder reminded her. "And he may have already been transferred back here." His dark brows were drawn together as he tried to make sense of it. "His part in the trial was done a while back, but it's still surprising that he would have been brought East. No one moves privates around like that."

"But you saw that he's an officer now."

"A sergeant," he said. "It still seems unlikely that he should find himself in Washington. And the promotion was accomplished rather quickly. He was still a private when he testified against me."

Now Mary was frowning as well. "What can it mean?"

"That's why I have to get into the War Office," he said. "Apply yourself to solving that problem. I'm known to too many people there to simply walk in and ask to see enlistment and transfer rolls."

There was no time to give it any thought as their hansom slowed again. They looked out together and saw that Senator Hamilton's carriage was leaving the street to enter a wide, semicircular drive in front of a gray stone mansion. Ryder slid back the communicating panel and ordered their driver to keep going down Jefferson Street. When they were out of sight of the Hamilton residence, he had the driver stop. He got out of the carriage, helped Mary down, and paid the driver. "We won't be needing you any further," he said, adding a generous tip for the man's time.

"Now what?" Mary asked when they were alone on the street. In the distance she could hear the approach of another carriage. "Do you have any plan?" The words were drawn out of her

rather breathlessly as Ryder was pulling her off to the side
where a row of sturdy, bare-limbed oaks lined the avenue like
palace guards. He took her behind one of them so they were
completely out of sight of any passersby. "What are we doing?"
she asked, leaning back against the tree. The bark was wet from
the earlier rain and droplets of water fell from the limbs overhead. She wiped one away from where it splattered her cheek.
"Ryder?"

"We're waiting."

"Waiting? But—"

He pressed a finger to her lips. "Shhh."

Mary stilled instantly and listened with all of her senses. The
night air was cool and crisp, and it seemed to sharpen the occasional dropping of water, the rhythmic click of carriage
wheels, and clop of horses hooves. She became aware that the
carriage in the distance wasn't coming any closer, but had
turned. Sound and rhythm were altered as the equippage moved
over gravel instead of wet cobblestones. She looked up at Ryder
and saw he was looking intently in the direction of Anna Leigh
Hamilton's home. There was almost nothing he could see from
such a great distance. His view was obstructed by the iron fence
bordering the property and the row of hedges that lined the
driveway. But they both could hear Anna Leigh's clear melodious voice raised in greeting. The words were not clear, but the
intention was, and her guest—only one voice was raised in reply—was invited inside.

The carriage left immediately and passed within a few feet
of them. It was a hired hansom and offered no means to identify
who had arrived in it.

"Apparently we were not the only ones following Anna Leigh
and her father," Mary said. Her eyes narrowed on Ryder's face.
"But I think you suspected that."

Ryder nodded. "I saw the hack when I looked to see where
we were turning." He pointed to the house. "I'm going over
there to look around. I want you to wait here." Even in the dark
Ryder had no difficulty seeing that Mary's mouth was pursed

to one side in obstinate disapproval. "All right," he said, giving in because there was so little choice. "But you follow me—follow me quietly."

Mary saluted smartly.

"Very amusing," he said in a tone that made it clear that wasn't so.

She shrugged unapologetically and gave him a small push in the direction of the house, then became his shadow.

The carriage that had deposited Anna Leigh and her father at their front door had been taken to the rear of the house. Crouching low, Ryder led Mary along the hedgerow until they had to cross the driveway openly to reach the front porch. This was accomplished quickly, the light spilling from the house marking their path. They stole across the low, wide porch silently, stopping when they reached the first lighted window.

Ryder gestured to Mary that she remain where she was while he ducked and crept beneath the window to stand on the other side. His first look inside was brief, and it appeared their stealthy approach was all for naught as the room on which he peered was empty.

Disappointed, Mary sighed audibly.

In the next moment she cried out, startled this time by the sudden movement of the interior curtains and the subsequent crash of a vase. Ryder's disapproving look had no impact on Mary because her eyes were squeezed shut in anticipation of being found out. She felt herself being swiftly dragged to Ryder's side of the window where he held her tightly. She did not mistake that he had comforting her on his mind. He wanted to make certain there were no more outbursts. His hand was hovering very close to her mouth, ready to clamp it if she squealed again.

From inside the room there was another noise, and since Ryder hadn't made a move to leave the porch, Mary opened her eyes a fraction. A fat tabby cat sat on the interior sill and peered at its own reflection in the glass. Mary grimaced as she realized her sigh had caused the cat to jump and in turn to frighten her.

The tabby was supremely uninterested in the broken vase or the pools of water on the hardwood floor. She licked her paws, preening beautifully.

As interested as she was in the cat, Mary didn't see the approach of Anna Leigh until the young woman's hands closed around the cat and lifted her off the sill. Mary would have jumped back if Ryder hadn't held her. She wondered why Ryder didn't move until she realized that the gaslight inside the house made the windows reflect only the interior of the room back to the occupants.

Mary looked through the delicate web of lace curtains to the door that was opening a little wider. She saw Anna Leigh turn away from the window, still stroking the cat. "It's only the cat," she said. Her voice was a trifle muffled through the glass but perfectly understandable. "She's broken a vase. It didn't wake Papa, did it?"

For the first time Mary realized the person standing just outside of her vision in the doorway was not Anna Leigh's father. She squinted, but couldn't make out the shadowy form. Was it a servant? she wondered. Or Anna Leigh's guest? And who would the senator's daughter be entertaining after her father had retired for the night?

Anna Leigh raised the tabby and rubbed her cheek against the soft fur. "Clumsy cat," she said affectionately. Then to the person in the doorway: "Oh, I think I do hear Papa. Tell him what happened and that everything's all right. There's no need to trouble anyone. I'll clean it up myself."

The reply was inaudible, but Anna Leigh seemed satisfied with it. She put the cat down, shooed her away, and knelt to begin picking up damaged flowers and shards of glass.

Mary winced in automatic sympathy as Anna Leigh cut her fingertip. Anna Leigh dropped the flowers and several pieces of glass to nurse the wound. Simultaneously the door to the library opened fully, and now the voice could be clearly heard, rich and resonant, a man's voice, too intimate and too concerned to belong to a servant.

Ryder's hand closed over Mary's mouth as the man stepped into the room. Ryder was prepared. He had recognized the voice almost immediately. He had heard it giving long, damaging testimony at his trial. Mary's acquaintance with it was brief, so he was not surprised that she needed to see Anna Leigh's guest to identify him.

Lieutenant Davis Rivers crossed the library floor quickly and knelt beside Anna Leigh. With his bright blond hair so close to hers, the strands were almost indistinguishable. His handsome features were boyishly expressive in their concern, sweet and disarming. He took Anna Leigh's hand, examined the wound, and kissed the break in her skin himself. There was a drop of blood on his lower lip when he drew away.

Ryder pulled Mary back from the window, but not before she glimpsed Miss Anna Leigh Hamilton lick her own lips lasciviously and launch herself into the lieutenant's arms.

Fifteen

Ryder's sleep was restless that night. The Colter Canyon raid made up the tapestry of his troubled dreams, and in none of them was a solution revealed. He always woke at the same point: Anna Leigh Hamilton standing above him, accusing him of rape, while Lieutenant Rivers consoled her and Private Carr prepared a rope for hanging.

He was not surprised when he woke late, only that Mary had let him sleep. He imagined that she had been anxious to do something about what they had learned last evening. She was not one for cooling her heels. After leaving the Hamiltons' they had argued about going to his uncle. Ryder was not ready to do it; Mary was adamant that it was time.

Stretching, Ryder rose from bed. He felt soft and sluggish, and regretted now that he hadn't taken his blankets to the floor and tried sleeping there. He paused at the French doors to examine the sky. It was clearing, with large patches of blue highlighting the distinct presence of the sun. Evidence of yesterday's dismal rain was on the glazed streets below, and a collection of icy water droplets ran along the edge of the stone balustrade.

Ryder turned away, hopeful the change in weather was a portent of changes elsewhere. He glanced in the sitting room on his way to wash. Mary was curled under a mound of blankets on the sofa. Obviously his restlessness had disturbed her as well. Ryder resisted the urge to put her back in bed and instead took his time completing the morning rituals of washing and shaving and dressing. When he finally stepped into the sitting room it was to discover that Mary hadn't stirred.

Ryder nudged the pile of blankets gently and succeeded in uncovering two pillows and Mary's night dress—but no Mary. He threw the blankets down angrily and searched the room for a note. Had she merely gone for breakfast? Or had she gone, as he suspected, to see Wilson Stillwell? Was he reacting to an assumption and not to fact?

When Ryder could find no note he went straight to the front desk to see Doc Stanley, the logical place for Mary to have left a message. Doc had seen Mary leave two hours earlier, but she had given him no note for Ryder.

"She didn't stop to chat," Doc said, adjusting his spectacles. "Asked me to get a hansom for her and that was that."

"Did she give you the address to tell the driver?"

"No. Told that to him herself, and I didn't catch it. Never occurred to me that you didn't know where she was going this morning."

It hadn't occurred to Ryder that Mary would strike off on her own, but he didn't say as much to Doc. "Yes, well, she's an independent sort."

"The worst kind," Doc said sympathetically. "Mark my words, the very worst kind."

Ryder ordered and ate breakfast in the second-floor dining room. From time to time he glanced up when someone entered, but he never really expected to see Mary on the threshold. He considered trying to follow her, but the thought was fleeting. He was less clear on her destination after talking to Doc than he had been beforehand. The fact that she hadn't asked for directions gave him hope that she hadn't gone to his uncle. He had never told her where Wilson Stillwell lived, and the man's address wouldn't necessarily be known to every hack driver in Washington. As far as he knew Mary's familiarity with the city was what she had gained the previous evening, and her list of acquaintances was probably confined to the people she had pointed out at the Regent Theater. How could any of them be of assistance to her?

Ryder finished his coffee and returned to the room. The door was ajar, and he distinctly remembered closing it. He entered cautiously.

"Where *were* you?" Mary asked, coming to her feet. "I was worried. Doc said you were looking for me, and then I couldn't find you. Didn't you think to tell him you weren't coming straight back to the room? How was I supposed to know where you might have gone?"

Ryder finished stepping into the room and closed the door behind him. "It won't work," he said. "Those are *my* questions and you know it."

Mary's posture lost a bit of its militant stance as Ryder called her on her attack. "I *was* worried," she said.

"I believe you." He simply looked at her then. Silent. Waiting.

Mary did not hold up well under that sort of scrutiny. "I wish you would use thumbscrews," she said after a few moments. "I really can't tolerate that expectant silence." When Ryder's features remained unchanged Mary sighed. "Very well. I'm sorry I didn't tell you I was leaving, but I know you would have wanted to come or would have argued with me about going at all and I just don't believe it would have been in your best interest to do so."

As an explanation it didn't begin to suffice. Ryder gave her an arch look, warning her she would do well to be more clear.

Mary pointed to the valise by the door. "Would you hand me that?" she asked. "I can explain everything."

Ryder gave her the valise, glad that he hadn't realized she had taken it with her. It would have only increased his concern tenfold.

Pushing aside the blankets on the sofa to make room for herself and the valise, Mary sat down. She opened the case and began setting pots of creams and dyes and powders out on the end table. "You asked me to apply myself to finding a way for you to get into the War Office," she said, continuing to empty the valise. A pair of spectacles was added to the array of pots along with hairpieces of assorted lengths and colors. "And that's what I did. I have a collection of items here that can be used to make a credible disguise. I have also had some instruction on using these things. It's not so simple as it may seem. The face paint has to be applied carefully if one is going to pass the disguise off at close quarters. I was assured, however, that I have a knack for it, so you needn't worry that you'll look hopelessly out of place when I've finished with you."

Ryder sat down himself now. He looked at the odd assortment of pots and jars and hair on the end table, then to Mary. Her expression was one of serene pleasure. "Mary," he said finally. "Where exactly was it that you went?"

"To the Regent Theater," she said, as if it were obvious. "It came to me this morning that the one person who could help us was Miss Yvonne Marie herself."

Ryder knew Mary's plan had a better than even chance of succeeding when Doc himself didn't recognize them as they passed through the lobby. She flagged the hansom, while Ryder, looking remarkably frail beside her, leaned on her arm.

"You're still going to be a handsome old man," Mary said when they were settled and the carriage was underway. She leaned forward, "Here, let me straighten your mustache. I told you not to fiddle with it until the glue dried."

Ryder suffered her attentions with little grace. "It tickles."

"That can't be helped." Mary patted the graying mustache in place so that it fit smoothly above his upper lip. It was a full, thick mustache, and the ends brushed his lip when he talked or smiled. She had already warned him he would do well to do little of those things. Sitting back, Mary studied Ryder's appearance again and pronounced herself satisfied. She had used a grease pencil skillfully to create age lines at the corners of his mouth and eyes and across his forehead. Yvonne Marie had showed her how to blend the pencil marks into the skin to emphasize the weathered appearance. Mary had used a gray hairpiece to cover most of Ryder's own healthy hair and had added touches of gray to Ryder's temples to merge his coloring with the desired one. A pair of wire-rimmed spectacles rested on his nose, and side whiskers had been added to give fullness to his face. His eyebrows had been lightened with the same paint and powder mixture she had used for his temples. "You're holding yourself too straight," she said. "Can you round your shoulders a little?"

Ryder complied. "Better?" When she nodded, he asked, "If I have to be an old man, why don't you have to be an old woman?"

"It would be too much," she said practically. "We don't need to invite scrutiny." A rich, chestnut-colored wig covered Mary's brighter red-gold hair. Her eyebrows had been darkened, and she had added touches of color to her face to lend her complexion a deeper shade of peach. Mary smoothed back the coiffured red wig with a delicate touch. "It feels as if I'm wearing a helmet," she said. "I was seventeen the last time I had this much hair piled on my head."

It would have suited Ryder if Mary had changed nothing about herself and had remained behind, but she had presented a convincing argument that her presence would be a diversion of sorts and thereby make him less likely to be carefully questioned or watched.

Ryder watched Mary fix her hair and retouch her lips with a bit of rouge. She was actually looking forward to this, he thought. The hours spent in Miss Marie's company this morning had certainly had their influence. It wouldn't have surprised him now if Mary announced she was taking up the stage. "Did you really tell Miss Marie the patients clutched her picture to their chests?" he asked.

"Of course I did," she said. "It's true. Well, perhaps 'clutched' is overstating their attachment to those cigarette photographs, but they *did* collect and admire them. Miss Marie was touched."

"I'm certain you made sure she was."

"She helped us, didn't she? What's more, I was able to discover she recalls your uncle. Senator Stillwell did indeed make her acquaintance last night as you suspected. She remembered him being very pleasant and offering her a proper congratulation on her performance."

"My uncle has a glib tongue. If he's polite, he has reason to be."

"Miss Marie was impressed with him," Mary said, then added gently, "it wouldn't hurt to keep an open mind about your uncle."

Ryder made a small, cantankerous grunt befitting the old man he was supposed to be. The subject was closed.

At the War Office, Mary did almost all of the talking. She introduced herself as the widow of Samuel Franklin, Ryder as her father-in-law. They were interested, she said, in records from the War Between the States, most especially in anything to do with the battles at Shiloh and Vicksburg. She explained she was trying to locate a journal her husband had begun when he'd enlisted and that was not returned with the rest of his belongings after his death. Her tone was quiet, her manner dignified. She let the fabricated facts speak for themselves and didn't attempt to push or cajole anyone into making exceptions for her.

Ryder watched her entrance everyone she spoke to. As a result of her performance very little attention was paid to him.

They were given a room off the main records room. It was small and windowless, a cubbyhole really, but it was furnished with a table and chairs and two oil lamps. In the beginning the Army clerks brought the records into the room, but as the afternoon wore on and Mary never found what she pretended to want, they allowed her to search in the larger room herself. While she pored over letters of commendation and enlistment ledgers from a war that was about a score of years in the past, Ryder made free with more recent files that accounted for most of what had happened in the Western Campaign.

The clerks never noticed he was looking at papers different from the ones Mary perused. On one occasion they found him in the wrong area of the records room, but it didn't raise their suspicions. Thinking he was lost, they simply turned him around and shooed him in the direction of the right stacks. Their manner was solicitous but vaguely condescending, and Ryder abided it only because it served his purpose.

Mary scribbled notes as she read. Except for the things Ryder asked her to take down most of them were nonsensical. She would have preferred to read the same accounts as he, but she knew her role was to divert suspicion and she had to be satisfied with that.

On the way out she made a point of thanking everyone who had been so kind to her. She was particularly gracious to the clerks, calling them by name. When Ryder began to make impatient noises about leaving, she apologized for him but allowed that it had been a long afternoon and had dredged up many memories.

Outside the War Office Mary heaved a sigh of relief. "This is one widow they won't forget anytime soon. That's good, don't you think?"

"Very good. *You* were very good."

"Don't kiss me," she said quickly, looking up at him. "At least not the way I think you want to."

"It shows, does it?"

She nodded, glad that it did. It boded well for the future when he really was an old man. Taking his arm, Mary led him down the stone steps. "Let's walk awhile," she said. "An afternoon of sitting in close quarters has done me in. I'm as stiff as you're supposed to be."

Feeling the need to stretch his own legs, Ryder agreed.

"Well?" she asked when they had gone only a few feet. "You're going to tell me, aren't you? What did you learn? Certainly nothing I read was of any help."

"And it wasn't supposed to be," he said. "Do you really want to know now? I'll only have to repeat myself when we get to my uncle's."

Wilson Stillwell's Washington home was a large white clapboard Victorian house with blue shutters and gingerbread molding. Unlike the Hamiltons' fenced-in property, this senator's grounds were separated from his neighbors on either side by a low, neatly trimmed hedge. There was no circular drive at the front of the residence. Carriages would deposit their passengers on the street and guests would follow the walk to the front door. The view from the street was cheerful and bespoke a comfortable and unfussy elegance.

The interior was much the same. Mary and Ryder were shown to the front parlor to wait as the senator was not home when they arrived. Rather than return later they elected to stay. Once the housekeeper left them alone, Mary wandered about the room, trying to learn something of the man from his furnishings.

"The housekeeper didn't see through your disguise," she said, picking up a delicate jade figurine. There were a number of Oriental carvings in the room, most of them jade, a few ivory, all of them quite exquisite.

Ryder stretched out in a mauve brocade wing chair. "She's never seen me before," he said. "That's why."

Mary glanced at the mantel which was crowded with photographs. "I don't know about that," she said. She replaced the figurine and went over to the mantel. Picking up an ornate, gilded frame, she studied the photo within for several moments. "This is you as a West Point cadet."

Ryder nodded. "It's all for appearances, Mary. It's what he thinks makes the best impression on his constituency. He wants to show good taste but not to excess. He would abhor Hamilton's mansion."

Sighing, Mary replaced the photograph and looked at the others. She recognized Ryder as young boy in a family picture with his mother and father. His sister Molly was still a babe in arms. Ryder's appearance, a blend of his father's hard profile and his mother's coloring, was very solemn as he stared at the camera. She could imagine even at that early age he had had no trouble remaining still. There was a wedding photograph of Wilson and his wife, another of Ryder's parents. The last frame didn't hold a picture at all but a lock of baby-fine golden hair. "His daughter's?" Mary asked, holding it up for Ryder to see.

"That's right. A poignant touch, isn't it?"

Mary gave him a sour look. "This sarcasm of yours is not becoming. I can't think of one reason your uncle would be moved to help us if you continue to act in such a manner."

Ryder drew in a breath and let it out slowly. "I'll do better," he said quietly.

The housekeeper chose that moment to return. She carried a tray with tea for Mary and wine for Ryder. She served both, waited for their approval, then left as silently as she had come.

Mary eyed Ryder's wine glass suspiciously. "You don't drink," she said. "Why did you choose that?" Ryder had specifically asked for Montrachet and had even noted the year he wanted. Mary thought it a strange jest on his part until the housekeeper appeared with the bottle.

"My uncle's secret vice," he said, raising his glass. "His wine cellar is where you can find the excess that appears nowhere else in this house. In the short time I lived here he had it expanded twice to accommodate his growing collection. He's very particular about the temperature and the light down there, and he has one servant who's responsible for seeing that the bottles are uniformly and regularly turned. Do you want to see it?"

"I'll let him show me," she said. "You wouldn't do it justice."

Ryder sipped his wine. "It's a remarkable vintage."

"And completely wasted on you," Mary said. "You asked for that to be spiteful."

He couldn't disagree. Recalling that he'd promised to do better, he put the glass aside. Petty revenge really did have a bitter taste, he decided. Getting to his feet, he went to the fireplace and laid a log on the meager fire the housekeeper had laid. After brushing off his hands he began removing the mustache, side-whiskers, and hairpiece that Mary had carefully applied. He gave them to her to put in her reticule, then took out a hand-kerchief and began to wipe away the face paint and grease-pencil lines.

The front door opened and closed, and there was a hushed exchange in the hall before the pocket doors to the parlor were parted. The housekeeper gaped when she saw Ryder standing at the mantel, removing the lines from his face, and Mary on the settee critically eyeing a helmet of hair on the end of her fist.

"It's all right, Mrs. Shanahan," Wilson Stillwell said. "I know these people." He gave her his hat and coat. "Nothing to drink for me," he said when he saw the bottle of wine Ryder had ordered. "Just bring a glass. I can see my nephew has already made a good choice." He stepped inside and closed the pocket doors behind him. "Ryder," he said shortly, nodding once. "Un-expected hardly describes your presence here."

"Wilson," Ryder said with equal terseness. He finished re-moving the face paint and stuffed the handkerchief back into his pocket. "This is Mary McKay."

Mary made quick work of thrusting her chestnut wig into her reticule. Her cheeks were flushed as Wilson Stillwell made a stiff bow in her direction. "Senator," she said, injecting warmth into her voice. "I'm pleased to meet you."

"McKay?" Stillwell said, not returning her sentiment. "I un-derstood you were one of Jay Mac Worth's . . ." There was a slight pause. "Daughters," he finished.

Mary's eyes narrowed, and she raised her chin a notch. She understood that hesitation because she had heard it before when people wanted to make certain she knew that they knew she was a bastard.

"She's my *wife*," Ryder interjected.

"Wife? When did this happen?" Wilson Stillwell had a sternly grave face that darkened slightly with displeasure. In spite of that, his austere visage was handsomely molded and his blue eyes glittered like ice chips.

"It doesn't matter," Mary said, coming to her feet. "We haven't come for your blessing or even your approval. We've come for your help. If you can't offer that, then we've already wasted too much time. Yours and ours."

The senator seared Mary with his brilliant blue eyes for a moment, studying her stiff back and proud stance. He raked his hair back in a gesture that was reminiscent of one Ryder frequently made and nodded slowly, appreciatively. "You have a lot of your father in you," he said in the manner of giving a compliment. "Go on. Sit down. If I've offended, then I apologize." He glanced behind him. "Where's Mrs. Shanahan with my glass?" he asked of no one in particular He pointed to the unfinished glass of wine on the tray. "Are you going to drink that, Ryder?"

Ryder shook his head. "Help yourself."

"Indeed," Wilson Stillwell said deeply. "You certainly did." He sat in the chair that Ryder had recently occupied and looked from his nephew to Mary and back again. "I was at the fort when you made your escape," he said. "I even stayed a week to see if they would apprehend you. When it became clear Gardner's men weren't up to it, I left. I told the general you wouldn't stay in the territory, but even I couldn't have predicted this." He raised his glass to his sternly set mouth. "An explanation seems in order."

Mary held her breath, wondering if Ryder would comply. The request was reasonable. Something in the way it was stated made it seem less so, however. Jay Mac had never suffered fools gladly, and Mary suspected the same was true of the senator, yet there was a distinction in their manner that widely separated the two men. Jay Mac did not shy from confrontation, neither was he deliberately provoking. She wasn't certain the same could be said for Wilson Stillwell.

Mary listened with half an ear as Ryder gave his uncle a review of the events that had led to their visit. She watched the senator take in the information while revealing little of his thoughts. When the housekeeper arrived with the glass, he sent her out with a dismissive wave of his hand, never taking his eyes from Ryder, for all appearances mesmerized but reserving judgment.

She could not recall ever having seen a political cartoon of the senator. His handsome, even features did not lend themselves well to caricature. There was no single attribute that could be easily emphasized except perhaps the eyes, and it would be difficult to capture their piercing brilliance in a black-and-white line drawing.

Wilson Stillwell was a little better than average height, his posture and demeanor adding inches in the perception of others if not in fact. His hair was brown and would have been nondescript if it weren't for the threads of iron gray at his brow and temples. His mustache and side-whiskers were both neatly cropped. As Ryder had noted, his uncle was not given to any excess the public could see. Although his build was on the lean side, his shoulders were broad, and they gave him the effect of sturdiness and dependability. He asked sharp, incisive questions of Ryder. Mary had no trouble imagining that the senator could hold his own in a debate.

"So you've been in Washington a little more than twenty-four hours," he said. He reached for the black lacquered cigar box on the table at his side and removed a cigar. He drew it under his nose once, more out of habit than to appreciate the aroma, then cut off the tip and lit it. "And you're only now getting here." He drew on the cigar deeply, then exhaled slowly, with obvious relish. "Are you going to tell me what caused the delay?"

Certain that Ryder would say he wasn't convinced he should have come at all, Mary did not allow him to answer. "We were gathering evidence to present you," she said. "It was important to us that you know Ryder's innocent."

"I think I know something about my nephew's character."

Which, Mary realized, was neither an endorsement or an indictment. She did not take issue with the statement, preferring to get to the heart of their findings at the War Office. "We're convinced we know who orchestrated the raid at Colter Canyon," she said with quiet confidence. "Your help now could be invaluable."

One of the senator's brows rose. He looked through a haze of blue-gray smoke at Ryder. "Is that right?" he asked. "You know? And that's why you've come here?"

"Yes, sir."

"Well?" Stillwell's eyes narrowed fractionally. "Let's hear it. And for God's sake, sit down."

Ryder hesitated. He had no liking for the command or the tone. It was only when he saw the gentle encouragement in Mary's eyes that he left the fireplace and sat in the chair opposite his uncle. "Mary and I spent most of the day at the War Office," he said. "I was interested in the records of assignments, transfers, and discharges for Fort Union and we—"

"Why?" asked Stillwell.

"Because the short time we've been in town we've already seen two men who escorted the gold wagons through Colter Canyon." There was a slight indication of surprise on the senator's part as he exhaled sharply. Ryder continued. "It made me curious as to who else might be around."

"And?"

"I can't say with any certainty that they're here in Washington," said Ryder. "But to a man, they've received transfers from Fort Union or were discharged from the Army."

The senator's brows pulled together as he squinted at Ryder. He lowered his cigar slowly. "You're saying," he said deeply, almost growling, "that no soldier who survived the Colter Canyon massacre is still stationed at the fort. Is that right?"

Ryder and Mary nodded in unison. Mary's look was more expectant than Ryder's.

"Well," Stillwell said impatiently, "what's so blasted unusual about that? The Army thought they could be more useful elsewhere after their experience. Hell, I'd have put in for a transfer myself."

"And it's doubtful it would have been granted," Ryder said. "One man. Two. Maybe a half dozen could have been expected to be permitted to transfer, but not *all* of them. And they were fresh recruits, newly assigned to the post just before the gold shipment was supposed to take place."

"Do you see?" Mary asked eagerly when Stillwell didn't respond. "They were assigned to the fort for just one purpose—to be part of escorting and protecting the gold."

"Of course I see," he said. "But what does it mean? They were assigned, did their job—poorly, I might add, or the Apache raid wouldn't have been so successful—then they were transferred. You two have drawn some conclusion other than the one I have settled on."

Mary shifted to the edge of her seat and asked earnestly, "Senator Stillwell, do you believe Ryder's innocent of the charges leveled against him?"

There was no hesitation. "Of course I do."

Satisfied, she nodded once. "It's Ryder's contention that there were no Apache involved in the massacre."

The senator's attention turned to his nephew. "You've said that before, but you've lacked evidence to support it."

Ryder rested his forearms on his knees. "It was impossible for me to prove it wasn't a Chiricahua raid," Ryder said frankly. "I wasn't allowed to return to the canyon after my arrest. I believe investigators who did go saw things that were placed there purposely to support the stories of the surviving soldiers. Only one Army scout—Rosario—was permitted to comb the area, and he had his own reasons for concealing the truth."

"And the truth is . . ." Stillwell sounded both impatient and expectant.

Mary broke in. "The truth is that the *massacre* was a surprise attack by the new recruits against the old ones."

Complete silence followed her announcement. The senator exhaled very slowly, his narrowed eyes moving thoughtfully from Ryder to Mary, then back to Ryder. "Did you put that idea in her head?" he asked at last.

"I gave her the information," Ryder said. "Mary's quite capable of putting things together on her own."

"You realize what you're saying, don't you? You're talking about brother against brother here. A bloody little civil war right in Colter Canyon, Arizona."

"That's what it was," said Ryder. "Except it had no purpose other than greed."

Stillwell stubbed out his cigar. "They sure as hell weren't able to execute this plan all on their own."

Ryder nodded. "You're right. This kind of operation—the dates, the assignments, the route—demanded help from someone who had access to all that information. I was one of those people."

"Except that Ryder didn't have the authority to transfer men in or out of Fort Union," Mary said. "He could have suggested certain men to General Gardner, but that was the extent of his influence."

The senator's frown deepened as he tried to take it in. "Then you're saying Gardner put this attack together and framed you?"

Ryder shook his head. "I'd never believe that. It was someone who could wield more power than the commander."

"But who—"

"Warren Hamilton," said Ryder.

Stillwell was in the process of raising the glass of Montrachet to his lips. He paused in midmotion, stunned. "Hamilton?" he said softly. "That doesn't seem—"

Mary nodded understandingly. "We know. It will be hard for anyone to believe, and that's why we need your help." She began to click off points on her fingers. "We know these things: Senator Hamilton is a member of several committees that oversee expenditures to the War Department; he has been supportive of the Western Campaign from the outset; he has financial interests in Holland Mines; he was influential in helping Northeast Rail secure a land grant for the railroad in that area; he was at the fort at the time of the raid; and"—Mary drew a quiet breath and let her fingers fold back into a loose fist—"and his daughter was instrumental in supporting the charge of treason against Ryder."

"My God," the senator said again, softly this time. He straightened a little and added flatly, "You realize, of course, that most of your points could be made about me. I wasn't at the fort at the time of the raid, and Anna Leigh is not my daughter, but other than that . . ." He drank some of his wine. His eyes were fixed on a point beyond Ryder's shoulder. He was a man caught in his memories. "Until the debacle at Colter Canyon and his daughter's ridiculous charges, I counted Warren Hamilton among my friends. We served together . . . had the same outlook. And when we didn't"—he smiled slightly—"we enjoyed wrangling like two young bucks." He came out of his reverie and looked hard at his nephew. "I don't believe it. What was his motive?"

"His share of the gold. It was a rich prize."

"Perhaps, but I don't think he would risk so much for it. It doesn't fit with the man I know—or knew."

Mary's shoulders sagged a little. "Then you won't help us prove it?" she asked.

"I didn't say that." Stillwell refilled his wine glass. This time when he sipped, it was apparent he was deriving more pleasure from the experience. "Warren Hamilton," he said slowly, drawing out the name as if it were the first time he had ever heard it. "It just doesn't seem possible. You may be headed in the right direction, but I think you've jumped a track or two. Why don't you let me make a few inquiries into this. I'd be happy to—"

Mary stood now. "No," she said clearly, forcefully. "Forgive me, Senator, but for too long this has been left to other people. Every day that Ryder and I spend in Washington is dangerous. There's no telling at what point one of us will be recognized and turned in. If that were to happen much of what would follow would be out of our control. That's an unacceptable risk. We need your help now, and we need you working *with* us, not on your own."

Stillwell considered Mary thoughtfully, then looked to his nephew. "You agree with her?" he asked.

Ryder nodded. "I can tell you that from the beginning she wanted to come here. I didn't. But yes, in light of what we know now, I agree with her."

The senator's expression didn't change. Ryder's statement was not an unexpected response. "Give me something else," he said at last. "I do believe you're innocent, but I'll be damned if I'll believe Warren Hamilton is behind this. You must have something more."

Ryder and Mary exchanged glances, and Mary gave Ryder an almost imperceptible nod of encouragement. "Last night," Ryder said, "Mary and I waited outside the Regent Theater." He saw his uncle stiffen slightly. "Yes, we saw you there, and we saw you intentionally not acknowledge them. It's what gave Mary hope that you could be persuaded to assist us."

"Go on," Wilson Stillwell said.

"After the performance we followed Anna Leigh and her father home. We had no intention other than to see where and how they lived."

"Then you observed for yourself that Warren Hamilton does not need money."

"On the contrary," Ryder said. "I observed someone whose particular way of living requires a great deal of money."

"You saw what you wanted to see."

Mary's hands curled into fists at her sides. "We saw," she said pointedly, "Anna Leigh and her father greet Lieutenant Davis Rivers moments after they arrived home." Wilson Stillwell merely stared at her, his features nearly expressionless. "Davis Rivers," she repeated. "The man who was promoted after the raid for capturing Ryder was a guest in the Hamilton home."

"It doesn't prove anything," Stillwell said carefully. "It doesn't—"

"More to the point," Mary interrupted. "Rivers and Anna Leigh Hamilton are lovers." At first there was no reaction that she could detect on the part of Wilson Stillwell; then Mary glanced at the hand holding the wine glass. His knuckles were white on the delicate stem of the crystal.

"You know this?" the senator asked.

"We saw enough to be confident of our conclusion." She added primly, "It would have been unseemly to witness more than we did."

Wilson Stillwell set his glass aside. He raised one hand slowly to his face and rubbed his brow hard with thumb and fingers as he thought. The lines on his forehead deepened. His eyes were almost closed now. "He'd do most anything for her," he said, more to himself than his guests. "I always knew she was his weakness. He could never tolerate a word being said against her. Too much like his wife, she was, in looks if not in character. Warren never could get past one to see the other." He sighed heavily and his hand dropped away. He studied Ryder for a long moment. "She's a better motive than greed," he said finally. "I don't think you'd ever have convinced me Hamilton would have done it for the money . . . but for her—for Anna Leigh—he might very well have sold his soul."

"I think he did just that," Ryder said quietly.

Mary went to the fireplace and poked at the logs. Fire crackled and spit at her. She brushed the hem of her skirt, but didn't move away. She was cold to her marrow. "We can't know how the plan was first conceived or who may have suggested it. I don't even know how much that matters now. It seems clear, however, that Senator Hamilton was in a position to orchestrate it."

Ryder went on. "I was assigned to Fort Union to organize the delivery of the gold shipment. I was responsible for almost every aspect of that mission, and you were influential in getting me that appointment."

Stillwell chuckled humorlessly. "Hamilton suggested it. Said it would be a feather in your cap . . . and in mine." He topped off his wine glass and said under his breath, "The bastard."

"The records at the War Office indicate that Davis Rivers was an attaché to General Norman Dalton here in Washington before his assignment to Fort Union. His transfer and that of about thirty-five other men can all be traced back in one way or another to Warren Hamilton."

"Hamilton can't make the transfers you suggest. No senator can. That's the province of the Army."

Mary regarded Senator Stillwell frankly. "Are you saying that you don't have enough influence to see the thing done?" she asked. "A word in the right ear? A promise to the right person. A favor extended?" Mary saw immediately that she had him. For the senator to deny it would be admitting that his leverage and authority was not as extensive as he wanted others to believe. If he admitted that he had the power and prestige to accomplish such a task, then he was also saying that someone like Hamilton could do the thing as well.

Stillwell regarded Mary consideringly. "You're a very clever young woman," he said at last. "Perhaps too clever for your own good." Out of the corner of his eye he saw Ryder shift slightly and recognized that he needed to tread carefully. "But, yes, you're correct. I could arrange it if that were my desire. It's not easy to admit that Hamilton carries as much in the way of clout as I do, but it's true nonetheless. There are ways it could be accomplished."

Satisfied, Mary returned to the settee. "Then a reasonable conclusion is that Senator Hamilton helped arrange the assignments of a group of men who had no real purpose at Fort Union except to steal the gold shipment."

Ryder's long fingers intertwined and became a single fist. "In carrying out their mission, they murdered an equal number of men assigned to escort the wagons, planted evidence to make it seem as though it were a Chiricahua raid, stole the gold, and arranged very neatly for me to assume the blame."

"Miss Hamilton," the senator said softly.

Ryder nodded. "Mary suspected her part in this long before I did. The senator's daughter was instrumental in making certain I was unavailable at the time of massacre."

Stillwell's lips compressed. He sighed heavily. "Why weren't you killed?"

"I might have been if it weren't for Miss Hamilton's successful playacting and her sordid account. I think it was decided it was better to have someone to accuse for the mission's failure than to leave an open-ended investigation into the matter."

"Ryder was the perfect choice to take the blame," Mary said.

"He certainly was," Stillwell agreed. "My God, he certainly was."

"The hangman was supposed to silence me."

Wilson Stillwell's mouth curled upward in a humorless smile, but his eyes alighted appreciatively on Mary. "And he would have if it hadn't been for Mary here."

"More or less," Ryder said enigmatically, refusing to explain her real role in his escape or that of Florence Gardner. His quick glance at Mary cautioned her as well.

The senator raised his wine glass again and sipped. "Obviously there's something you don't wish to tell me," he said. "I have no problem with that, but do you know where the gold is?"

Ryder shook his head. "We don't think it's in Arizona any longer. It was Mary's idea to follow Miss Hamilton in the hope she would lead us to it."

"Well, she led you to Lieutenant Rivers and to her father. I'd say Mary's instincts are good ones. Who can say where the gold might turn up?" He leaned back in his large armchair. "I've heard quite enough to make my decision." He sipped his wine again, then regarded them both over the rim of his glass. "How is it that I can assist you in bringing Hamilton and his slut of a daughter to justice?"

Mary blinked, taken aback by an underlying viciousness in the senator's almost genial tone.

"Do I shock you, Mary?" he asked matter-of-factly. "Did you think I wouldn't take this information so personally? I don't know what my nephew's told you about our relationship, but I can assure you I take this all very, *very* personally. Not only was Ryder cruelly maligned, but I was unwittingly duped into offering myself up for public ridicule."

Mary suspected it was the latter situation that Wilson Stillwell found most difficult to accept. Still, it no longer mattered why he wanted to help, only that he did.

"I do not suffer fools," he said lowly. "And neither will I be made one. No one does that to Wilson Stillwell. *No one.*"

Mary had an urge to look at Ryder, but she resisted. There was a fierceness about the senator's announcement that she found unsettling, even dangerous. "It's good of you to offer your help," she said evenly. "Ryder and I both appreciate it."

Mrs. Shanahan parted the pocket doors to the parlor and announced that dinner was ready. The senator rose, took Mary's arm, and escorted her to the dining room. Ryder followed with interest, watching Mary's reaction to his uncle. There were small signs, imperceptible to someone who didn't know Mary as well as he did, that she was not eager to be in Wilson Stillwell's company, that she didn't like linking arms with him or matching her step to his.

The senator seated her at the long walnut dining table, then took his place at the head. Ryder sat on his uncle's right. Each time Mary turned to him, a question in her forest green eyes, his own expression was carefully guarded.

Clams were served first, then cream of potato soup. More Montrachet filled their glasses, but before a servant carried in the tender bass fillets, Stillwell ordered Amontillado and Rauenthaler be brought up from the wine cellar. The fish course was followed by cucumbers and thin slices of rare roast beef and more wine.

"Ryder tells me you have a fine collection of wines in your cellar," Mary said. Dinner did not lend itself to important conversation. Although she wanted to do nothing more than finish the discussion that had begun in the parlor, she held back, following Ryder's lead. "What I've tasted thus far is certainly proof of that."

"I imagine your father has a similar cellar," Stillwell said modestly.

Mary shook her head. "Nothing like yours, I'm sure. He appreciates a good wine, but admits he has no real taste for the distinction between them."

"It can be learned," Stillwell said. He savored the Rauenthaler. "I'd be proud to show you the cellar."

"And I would be honored to see it."

The conversation proceeded in just that fashion, simple exchanges with no consequence or purpose except to fill the silence between the sorbet and the salad. This situation lasted until coffee was served.

Stillwell drew another cigar from the lacquered box that was presented to him and lighted it with relish. Ryder declined a second time.

"You haven't explained," Stillwell said, "what it is I can do for you. You understand that simply going to the papers with what we have won't be enough. The fact that you're my nephew, Ryder, means that whatever I say in support of you will be critically examined. I feel certain that Hamilton will be able to provide explanations for the assignments and transfers, and it will become my word against his. That won't do at all. The papers will also be very cautious in regard to Miss Hamilton. You can't level accusations at her pretty head without proof."

"We know," Ryder said. "That's why we think nothing less than Senator Hamilton's confession will serve."

Stillwell hadn't expected that. "His confession? You think that cagey old bird is going to give it to you?"

"No," Mary said. "But he might to you."

"Tell *me?*" The senator was astounded.

"With us listening," Ryder added. "And some other people who have an interest in this."

"Reporters, you mean," Stillwell said.

"Them. But also one or two commanders from the War Office. General Hatcher comes to mind as someone who's consistently fair and willing to listen. You could pick someone else, of course. It doesn't matter as long as you think he'd be fair and impartial, and would act accordingly."

Wilson Stillwell rubbed his chin with the back of his hand. "Let me see if I understand this. You want me to coerce a confess—"

"Not coerce," Mary interrupted. "Confront and cajole. *Dare* him into telling you the truth."

"In front of witnesses," Stillwell said, unconvinced.

"No," said Ryder. "He wouldn't be able to see the witnesses. You could do it right here, in this house, in this room. The witnesses only need to assemble on the other side of the door and—"

Holding up his hand, the senator shook his head and effectively silenced Ryder. "It won't work."

"Then another place," Mary said. "It doesn't have to be here."

"No, that isn't what I meant," Stillwell responded. "Here is fine. In fact, here is very good. I can arrange that with no difficulty, but Warren Hamilton won't step foot in my home. The general public isn't aware that his daughter is the young woman mentioned in the Colter Canyon affair, but he has to be careful to maintain appearances. People who do know would find it odd that Hamilton came here, what with my connection to Ryder, so he wouldn't come and he would be suspicious if I invited him."

"Then we should find a way for you to go to him," said Mary. "Meet in some neutral place where he would be less suspicious."

Stillwell shook his head. "You're focusing your sights on the wrong target."

Mary tilted her head to one side, puzzled. She glanced at Ryder and saw that although his eyes had narrowed slightly, there was a glimmer of understanding in them. He was beginning to nod his head, slowly at first, then more firmly as his uncle's idea took hold. "What?" asked Mary, impatient that she alone did not understand. "What are you both thinking?"

"He's right," Ryder said. "Warren Hamilton is the wrong target. It's Anna Leigh who can give us what we want."

"Exactly," Stillwell said. There was pride in his voice as he spoke the single word, pride that his nephew had come to the same conclusion and had seen the wisdom of it.

Mary darted between Ryder and his uncle. "How in the world will Anna Leigh be persuaded—"

Drawing deeply on his cigar, Stillwell said, "Miss Hamilton will come here. That's not a problem."

Mary frowned. "But how—"

"Let me worry about that. It can be arranged. Will you trust me?" His brows rose fractionally when Mary's answer was not immediately forthcoming. He looked to Ryder questioningly.

"Yes," Ryder said. "I believe you can do it."

Mary caught herself blushing at her rudeness. "Yes, of course. I didn't mean that I didn't trust . . . it's just that . . . Well, I'm surprised . . . That is . . ." She trailed off because the senator was paying her no attention. He was staring at the flower arrangement in the middle of the table, clearly not seeing it, but working out things in his own mind instead.

"Yes," he said quietly, blowing a wreath of smoke above his head. "It can be arranged with perfect ease. Not only Miss Hamilton, but I think we can include the lieutenant as well. Two birds with one stone, as it were."

Mary wouldn't have been surprised if he had licked his lips. The tips of her fingers whitened as she gripped her coffee cup but this was the only sign of her uneasiness.

"You mentioned General Hatcher, Ryder," Wilson Stillwell was saying. "I think he's a good choice for this. I know him, of course, but he's not a close acquaintance. That would make him seem to be less on anyone's side save that of the truth. I'll have to give some thought to which reporter I would trust with this story. There's Marcus Asbury. He's good. And Des Richards. They're with rival papers, but that could be to our advantage. Get the word out more quickly. The *New York Chronicle* has a reporter in town. I could interest him in the story."

"That's certainly sufficient to our needs," Ryder said. He looked to Mary. "Are you satisfied with that?"

She nodded slowly, wondering at her own reticence. "It makes sense. How soon can it be arranged?"

Senator Stillwell did not bother to consult clock or calendar. "I need only twenty-four hours," he said. "I'll have the players here. The two of you will have to write the script."

Sixteen

"You're very quiet." Ryder stroked Mary's silky hair. The red-gold ends of it curled around his fingertips. They brushed her shoulders and fell sleekly past her nape.

"Mmmm," she hummed softly, fitting herself more comfortably against him.

They had declined Senator Stillwell's offer to stay in his home and had returned to the boarding house. Neither of them had spoken about the encounter. Indeed, neither had had much to say about any of the day's events. They undressed in silence, slipped into bed, and fell asleep wrapped in their own thoughts instead of each other's arms.

Sometime in the middle of the night that changed, though who reached for whom would never be established with any certainty. The truth was, it didn't matter. The need was mutual, the desire was shared, and they woke completely simultaneously only moments before a shattering climax.

Neither fell back into sleep, although both made a pretense of doing just that. For a long time Mary lay on her side, staring toward the French doors. Blue-white moonlight was filtered through the gauzy lace curtains. Occasionally some raucous sound came from the street below: an outraged bellow as one drunk assailed another, the cacophonous clatter of milk cans being rushed for delivery. Mostly it was quiet enough to hear the soft tread of a boarder in the hallway or the plaintive mewling of a stray kitten.

"Talk to me, Mary." Raising himself on one elbow, Ryder

touched her bare shoulder. Moonlight covered his hand. "What are you thinking?"

"Only that it will be over tomorrow." She turned onto her side, toward him. Their knees bumped. "Or most of it will be. Have you thought of that? Of what it will mean to us?"

"It means we can stop hiding and running and wearing ridiculous disguises."

"I'm serious."

His smile was gentle. "So am I," he whispered. He moved his hand a fraction and kissed the warm curve of her shoulder. "I have some money put aside, not much, but enough to buy land around Flagstaff. I have a friend there, a retired general, who's encouraged me to settle near him. He'd be the one selling off a portion of his land. It's beautiful country, Mary. Mountains. Clear, cold streams. Good grazing for cattle. We could have a ranch there. We'd never be rich, but we'd be self-sufficient."

"We'd be very rich," she said, but she wasn't talking about money.

He found her hand under the covers and threaded his fingers between hers. "It's what I want," he said. "But what about you? Can you see yourself living like that?"

"I can't see myself living any other way," she said quietly. Her meaning was clear. Sharing a life with him interested her more than any particular lifestyle. Still, she had her own dreams, and she knew they were no less important to Ryder than his. "I'm going to teach someday," she said. "If there's a school in Flagstaff."

He laughed softly. "If there isn't, there will be." He'd build her one, he thought, and they would fill it with their own children if no one else had any use for it. Ryder squeezed Mary's hand. "It's going to work out," he said. The small vertical crease between her brows didn't disappear. "Mary? What is it?"

"Your uncle seems almost eager to bring down Warren Hamilton."

So it wasn't their distant future she was thinking about now, but their more immediate one. "He explained that to you. He doesn't like being made a fool."

"None of us do," Mary said. She laid her free hand over his, absently stroking the back of it. "I don't know . . . It's just that . . ." Her fears were vague ones, difficult to put into words. "How will he ever persuade Anna Leigh to come to his home?"

Ryder shrugged. "Is it important? He said he could do it, and I believed him. Did you?"

"Oh, I believed him. But does it make sense?"

"That you believe him?"

"No," she said a bit impatiently. "That he should be able to do it." She removed her hand from his and lay on her back. "If Warren Hamilton would think twice before he stepped foot in your uncle's home, why wouldn't his daughter?"

The easy answer was that Anna Leigh was a flighty, cotton-between-the-ears, young woman. It was also the wrong answer. Anna Leigh Hamilton had already proved that she was sharp and deviously single-minded in pursuit of something she wanted. Nothing good could ever come of underestimating her. "My uncle must know something we don't," Ryder said at last.

It was the same conclusion Mary had come to. "I know," she said softly, almost distantly. "But what?"

It was agreed that Mary and Ryder would arrive at the senator's house just before dinner, at eight o'clock. Wilson Stillwell had promised that all other parties would arrive shortly thereafter.

Mary dressed with care, but with no enthusiasm, for their engagement. Her dinner dress was ecru satin, with pearl buttons from the rounded neckline to the waist. Three large satin rosettes enhanced the right side of the draped skirt. The sleeves were three-quarter length, pointed toward the wrist and decorated with seed pearls. She had spent the afternoon thinking about the impending meeting and letting out the hem a half inch. Now the dress looked as if it had been made expressly for her and not her sister.

Mary made a quarter turn in either direction, critically eyeing the dress and her handiwork. She smoothed the beaded front and straightened the sleeves. French-braiding her hair had given her green eyes a faintly exotic look, and pinching her cheeks had added color to her complexion. When a tendril of red-gold hair fell over her forehead, she blew it out of the way in exasperation.

Behind her she heard Ryder's deep chuckle. She stepped to one side so she was no longer blocking his reflection in the mirror. He was wearing a crisp white shirt, black trousers, and a tailored two-tailed coat. "No one would ever know you're equally comfortable in buckskin and moccasins," she said.

"*I* know," he said pointedly, drawing nearer. "I have something for you."

"Aaah," she said knowingly. "Finally an explanation as to where you were all morning."

"Not quite. This has nothing to do with that." He reached inside his coat pocket, withdrew a small velvet-covered box, and held it out to Mary. In way of explanation, he said, "Doc just delivered it a few minutes ago."

Mary's eyes held Ryder's in the mirror for a moment before she turned to accept the gift.

"If you don't like it I can—"

She stopped him with a telling look and a single arched brow; then she opened the hinged box. The polished turquoise stone that Ryder had given Mary in the Cavern of Lost Souls now rested in an exquisite silver setting on a bed of black velvet. "Oh my," she said on a slender thread of sound. "How did you . . . when did you? . . ." It was difficult to complete a thought.

Ryder gently took the box from her, removed the ring, and raised her left hand. He slipped it on and the fit was perfect.

"Oh, Ryder . . . it's lovely."

In spite of Mary's obvious pleasure he felt compelled to point out, "It's not a diamond."

She raised herself on tiptoe and kissed him full on the mouth. "Who wants a diamond?" she whispered.

"I thought . . ." He hesitated. "I noticed you looking at your hand when we registered here at the boarding house." He saw Mary's flush as she recalled the incident. "You didn't say anything, but I saw it wasn't right that you didn't have a ring. Not here, not among these people." Ryder lifted her hand and studied the fit of the ring. The silver setting was a delicate complement to the large blue-green stone. "I should have thought of it before Doc brought it to my attention. My uncle noticed it, but he had better manners than to stare as pointedly as Doc. I didn't want you to be embarrassed again."

Mary removed her hand from his, laid her head against his chest, and embraced him hard. "I'm not embarrassed to be your wife." She tilted her head back, offering him a slightly wicked smile, and tapped him lightly on the chest with her forefinger. "And with or without this ring you're my husband."

He wasn't likely to forget it or to want it any other way. Ryder set Mary away from him and looked her over from head to toe. "Beautiful," he said. Then he basked in the warmth of her smile.

For a moment.

She added an arch look and said, "If this ring isn't the reason you were gone all morning, then exactly where were you?"

His cool, frost-colored eyes flickered for a moment with something like amusement. Nothing changed in the shape of his mouth. With grave import he said, "Scouting for the cavalry, my dear."

Mary and Ryder were shown to the dining room immediately upon their arrival. Wilson Stillwell was at the sideboard, pouring himself a glass of wine. Mary accepted a sherry for herself while Ryder declined to drink at all.

"As I remember, your father didn't drink either," Wilson said.

"He didn't have anything against it," said Ryder. "He just didn't particularly like it."

"Can't understand that myself." The senator raised his glass and touched the rim of it to Mary's. "To our success."

"Success," she murmured. She sipped gently, wanting as clear a head on her shoulders as she could manage. "I take it that Miss Hamilton has accepted your invitation."

"And Lieutenant Rivers. There was never any doubt."

Again Mary felt a surge of disquiet. Why was there no doubt? she wondered. How could Senator Stillwell be so certain of Anna Leigh and Davis Rivers? She glanced at Ryder to see if any measure of concern could be detected on his features. He appeared completely at ease with this information. "They'll be here soon?"

"The invitation was for dinner," Stillwell replied. "Fifteen minutes after the hour."

"What about General Hatcher?" asked Ryder. "And the reporters you mentioned."

Stillwell nodded. "All taken care of. I spoke personally with Hatcher this morning and with all three reporters this afternoon. Believe me, they were eager to come. I had to tell them very little to whet their appetites. Mrs. Shanahan is expecting them at the back door. She has been instructed not to show them into the hall until after Miss Hamilton and her escort arrive." Stillwell finished his glass of wine. "You understand you'll have to speak up. It isn't as easy to hear from the hallway as you might think. I experimented myself today with Mrs. Shanahan."

"You seem to have covered everything," Ryder said.

"As promised." He started to pour himself another glass of wine, but stopped when he heard the arrival of his other guests. "That would be Miss Hamilton and the lieutenant," he said, putting down his glass and bottle. He looked from Ryder to Mary. "You both know how you want to handle this?" he asked. "I've left that up to you."

"I was certain you had," Ryder said. "We're prepared."

Detecting an undercurrent in Ryder's words, Mary shot him

a sideways glance once the senator's head was turned. Not only did Ryder not respond to her overture, he very pointedly ignored her. Mary had an urge to poke him in the ribs with her elbow. It took a great deal of self-control to resist.

When Senator Stillwell left the dining room he did not close the doors completely. Mary and Ryder were able to hear him greet his guests and to follow the innocuous conversation that followed. Mary winced as she heard Anna Leigh Hamilton's practiced, trilling laughter. It was so obviously affected that she was surprised the woman had such success with it.

Senator Stillwell parted the doors with a grand flourish and ushered his guests inside. His mouth was curved in a narrow, satisfied smile as he stepped into the room.

"I believe you all know each other," he said calmly. Shutting the doors behind him, the senator intentionally ignored everyone and went straight to the sideboard to pour himself a glass of wine.

Anna Leigh stared at Ryder. "My God," she said softly. She placed a hand to her heart as if to keep it in place.

Mary thought this last gesture was overdone. She regarded the younger woman skeptically. Anna Leigh's slender hand was arranged artfully over her low-cut neckline in order to bring attention to her breasts rather than hide them.

"McKay," Rivers said stiffly. His eyes went to Mary next, and his acknowledgment of her presence was equally stilted. "Miss Dennehy."

Mary noticed that with their sunshine yellow hair and striking blue eyes, Anna Leigh and Davis Rivers were like a pair of perfectly matched bookends. The lieutenant's boyishly handsome features complemented Anna Leigh's dainty beauty. It struck Mary suddenly that their attraction for each other had a great deal to do with how much each was in love with his or her own image. She was hard pressed not to comment on it.

Anna Leigh's hand dropped away from her bodice as her gaze narrowed on Mary. "So," she said, drawing out the single word thoughtfully, "you're the fallen angel who came to Ryder's aid.

You were a nun, weren't you?" She did not ask the question to encourage a response. She knew the answer. She looked Mary up and down critically. "I don't suppose that after being without a man for so long you minded being raped by a half-breed savage."

Mary didn't hesitate. She crossed the short distance to Anna Leigh in less than a second and slapped her so hard the younger woman was knocked sideways against the wall. "You ever say anything like that again," Mary warned, "and I won't use the flat of my hand." Out of the corner of her eye, she saw that Lieutenant Rivers was preparing to restrain her. She leveled him with a cold stare. "Keep your hands to yourself or I'll put you on the floor beside your bitch."

The lieutenant's face flushed with color. In spite of that he drew in a breath and puffed like a banty rooster, prepared to take issue with Mary. She was not backing down.

"I think you'd better see to Miss Hamilton," Ryder said significantly, catching the lieutenant's eye. "She appears to have been bloodied in the first round."

Rivers hesitated, rocking on his feet slightly as he held off the forward motion that would have had him toe to toe with Mary. He let out his breath slowly as if he were finding control rather than being deflated, and went to Anna Leigh's side.

Mary turned her back on the lieutenant as he drew out a handkerchief. She could see that Ryder was not pleased with her performance, but she was unapologetic. She came to stand at his side again and said quietly, "It *had* to be done."

Still standing at the sideboard, the senator raised his glass in the direction of both couples. "I take it that we're off to a fine start," he said. "Salute."

With the lieutenant's assistance, Anna Leigh straightened. She pressed the handkerchief to the right corner of her mouth. The tears that made her blue eyes glisten were no artifice. Mary's slap had been a stinging blow, and her cheek felt as if it were on fire. Anna Leigh looked to Rivers and said calmly, "Kill her."

"Oh, for God's sake," Stillwell protested. "Haven't you any more imagination than that?"

Mary's brows rose a little at that. She could have sworn the senator was enjoying himself. What about the reporters and General Hatcher? she wondered. Had enough time elapsed for them to be positioned on the other side of the door? Were they finding this exchange as entertaining as Senator Stillwell? Mary looked to Ryder for direction and saw nothing in his implacable calm that supported her own disquiet.

Lieutenant Rivers made no move to carry out Anna Leigh's order. He was not wearing a weapon, at least not one that was visible to the eye, but he gave no indication that he was likely to have obeyed her in any event. "Be quiet," he said calmly, recovering some of his own presence of mind as he faced Ryder. "What is it you want, McKay?"

Ryder's answer was simple. "The truth about Colter Canyon."

"The truth?" Rivers scoffed. "You were there."

His eyes straying to Anna Leigh for a moment, Ryder said, "No, I wasn't."

Before the lieutenant could reply, Anna Leigh interrupted, "Are you going to just let this go on?"

At first Mary thought Anna Leigh was speaking to Rivers, but when the lieutenant didn't answer Mary followed the direction of her militant, expectant look.

"A little like leading sheep to the slaughter," Wilson Stillwell said almost apologetically.

Mary's initial confusion was compounded as she turned and saw that the senator had exchanged his glass of wine for a gun. It was slowly borne home to her that his weapon, like his comment, was not intended for Anna Leigh and Lieutenant Rivers. He was aiming both at her and Ryder.

Wilson Stillwell jerked the Colt revolver once, indicating the lieutenant should approach Ryder. "See if he's carrying a gun," he ordered. "And for God's sake be careful."

Rivers crossed the distance in a few strides. Mary, who had

moved protectively in front of Ryder, felt his hands gently come around her waist and move her to one side. Then he let her go and raised his arms, permitting Lieutenant Rivers to pat him down.

Rivers completed his check efficiently, then straightened and stepped back with almost comical quickness. "There's no gun," he told Stillwell.

One of the senator's brows arched as he regarded his nephew. "I'm surprised. I expected you not to leave anything to chance."

Lowering his hands slowly, Ryder said, "We all make mistakes." He placed one hand lightly on the small of Mary's back in a gesture that was at once a warning and a protection. "I couldn't anticipate things would go quite this way."

Stillwell smiled. "No one could, nephew. No one could." Keeping his revolver aimed at Mary and Ryder, he said, "Show them to the cellar, Lieutenant. Anna Leigh, open the doors for them. You may as well assist in the capture. All the glory can't be mine."

Anna Leigh removed the handkerchief from her mouth. The bloodstained cloth had hidden a superior, malicious smile. She looked from the handkerchief to Mary. "A pleasure," she said sincerely. "A real pleasure."

Mary's only satisfaction was that Anna Leigh winced when her smile became a bit too fulsome and had to quickly bring the handkerchief back to her lips.

"This way," Davis Rivers said tersely. "Miss Hamilton. The doors."

Anna Leigh drew them open and stepped into the hallway. Rivers took a step backward and gestured for Ryder and Mary to follow Anna Leigh. Mary didn't move until the hand at her back increased its pressure slightly and she understood that Ryder wanted her to go. Shoulders set squarely, her hands curled into fists, Mary expressed her protest with her body as she left the room. Once she was in the hallway she saw there were no reporters and no General Hatcher. Mrs. Shanahan and the other staff had evidently left as well.

"You too," Rivers said to Ryder.

Ryder paused to regard his uncle with pale, expressionless eyes. He moved on only when Wilson Stillwell was the first to look away.

Anna Leigh demonstrated her familiarity with the house as she marched down the hallway and chose to open the second door on her right. Throwing the bolt, she waved Mary toward the dark entrance. "This way. It's the wine cellar. You're not afraid of the dark, are you?"

There was enough light from the hallway for Mary to make out the narrow stairs that led below. She looked over her shoulder at Ryder. He nodded slightly. "No," she said. "I'm not afraid of it."

"You should be." Anna Leigh was poised to give Mary a smart push at the top of the stairs when she glimpsed Ryder's cold, taut expression. She had no doubt that if she touched Mary he would kill her. It didn't matter that his uncle had a gun pointed at his back and was prepared to use it. Ryder had the look of a man who was prepared to accept that. Anna Leigh let her hand drift back to her side. She stepped out of the way to give Ryder room to follow.

Mary raised her gown and began to descend the stairs carefully. The edge of each step was slightly damp and there was no rail for support. Ryder was right behind her, proceeding into the dark, yawning cavity with similar caution.

Without warning there was a cry above them. Mary recognized Anna Leigh's high-pitched squeal, then Lieutenant River's guttural shout of surprise. Even though Mary knew what to expect, she froze on the stairs. Ryder grabbed her by the waist and lifted her, abandoning caution in favor of getting down the stairs as quickly as possible. He took them blindly, two and three at a time, moving only a heartbeat faster than the two bodies that came tumbling after them.

Anna Leigh's long scream rose and fell in pitch as she was bounced and jolted and scraped by the hard edges of the steps.

In contrast, after his first hoarse cry, the descent of Davis Rivers was eerily quiet.

Ryder lost his balance when his feet hit the cool brick floor of the wine cellar. He protected Mary from the worst of the fall by twisting so that he hit the floor first. For a moment he couldn't breathe. Mary was sprawled on top of him, her elbow planted solidly against his ribs. She tried to scramble off, but Anna Leigh somersaulted down the last three steps and landed hard on top of them both. Davis Rivers followed at a slower pace, his body slipping limply down the stairs as if it were a corrugated sliding board.

Ryder had a glimpse of his uncle silhouetted at the top of the steps before the door was shut and the wine cellar returned to complete darkness.

Mary raised her head slowly, trying to make out Ryder's features. She expected his silver eyes would glow in the dark. They didn't. "If this is how your uncle gives tours of his wine cellar," she said, "I don't think I approve."

Ryder managed to draw a rattling breath and to chuckle at the same time. He had no difficulty finding her face. He patted her cheek lightly. "You've gained some weight."

She snorted. "Anna Leigh's on top of me." Mary unceremoniously shifted her position and pushed the younger woman off her. "Better?" she asked as Anna Leigh's landing caused the beauty to emit an unladylike grunt.

"Almost," Ryder said. "If you would just take your elbow out of my ribs."

"Oh!" Mary pushed herself upright and off Ryder. She blinked, trying to adjust her eyes to the darkness. It wasn't possible. The blackness around them was every bit as deep and penetrating as it had been in the Cavern of Lost Souls. That experience had prepared her for this. She didn't fight against what she couldn't change.

Ryder sat up, drawing his legs toward his chest. He had some pain in his right knee, but nothing was broken. "You're all right?" he asked Mary.

"A few bruises. I'll be fine."

"Miss Hamilton?"

There was a small groan in response.

"Not doing as well," said Mary. She reached out in the direction of Anna Leigh's whimpers, found the other woman's shoulder, and gave it a firm shake. "Rise and shine, Miss Hamilton," she said sweetly. "The senator's decided you're no better than the rest of us."

Anna Leigh found enough strength to push Mary's hand off her shoulder. "Get away from me."

Mary was happy to oblige. She brushed her hands off smartly. "She's as good as she ever was," she said to Ryder.

"Don't start a catfight," he warned her. "I can't see to separate the two of you." Before Mary could take issue with that, Ryder asked, "What about Rivers?"

"I don't know where he is."

"I don't think he ever made it to the bottom." He held Mary back when he felt her start to move. "I'll check on him," he said. Ryder got stiffly to his feet. "Don't let me step on you."

Mary pulled in her arms and legs, giving Ryder a wide berth as he searched for the stairs. She heard him stub his foot on something. Anna Leigh's shrill expletive helped her identify what it was. "Get out of his way, Miss Hamilton," said Mary. "He's trying to help *your* friend."

Anna Leigh pushed herself upright, curling her legs under her. "What's happened to Davis?" she demanded. "Is he—"

Ryder didn't let her finish. "He's out cold. Not dead." He dragged Davis off the steps and laid him on the floor. "He's right here, if you want to tend to him," he told her.

Anna Leigh wasn't of a mind to minister to her unconscious lover. Going to the origin of Ryder's voice, she crawled to the steps and stood. Before Ryder knew her intentions she was scrambling up the stairs to the door. She tried the handle first, and when it wouldn't turn she began pounding on the wooden panels. "Wilson!" she cried. "Let me out of here! Wilson!" She paused long enough to listen for a response. When none was forthcoming she began again. "You can hear me! I know you can! Let me out!"

The pounding continued for several minutes. It was interspersed with strident demands to be released. As Anna Leigh's banging became weaker, her demands turned to tearful pleas. Eventually she just slid down the length of the door and cried quietly.

Ryder wasn't moved, and he didn't expect that his uncle was either. "I don't think he cares much what happens to you," he said.

Anna Leigh stayed where she was at the top of the steps. "Shut up."

Mary got to her feet and brushed herself off. The brick floor of the wine cellar was too cool for sitting on. "Ryder?"

"Here, Mary." He held out his hand. After a few misses, she managed to find him. They sat down together on one of the lower steps. "I suppose you want an explanation."

"I suppose I do," she said tartly. "You seem to know a lot more about what's going on here than I do."

He called up the stairs to Anna Leigh, "You'll be certain to correct any mistakes I make, won't you?"

She sniffed. "Go to hell, half-breed."

Ryder felt Mary stiffen. "Let it go," he said. "It's a compliment, not an insult." They both knew Anna Leigh hadn't meant it that way, but Ryder learned of Mary's acceptance from her small sigh.

"Very well," she said softly. "But you can't protect her forever."

He gave her hand a small squeeze. At their feet he heard Davis Rivers stir once. The lieutenant grew still again. He wasn't going to wake anytime soon. "You don't understand either, do you, Anna Leigh?" Ryder said politely. "I believe you and Rivers here thought the senator was going to give you some of the credit for my capture. The lieutenant might even have received another promotion out of it. No one else can say he captured Ryder McKay twice."

Although Anna Leigh was silent, Ryder suspected he had her full attention. "Did he tell you why he changed his mind before he pushed you down the steps?" There was no answer. "No? Well, I suppose there wasn't time."

Anna Leigh waited, but Ryder didn't say anything else. She ticked out thirty more seconds in her mind before she finally screamed in frustration, "You bastard! What do you think you know!"

The silence had been so complete that Mary actually jumped at Anna Leigh's outburst. She had no difficulty understanding it. She was on tenterhooks herself.

Ryder didn't raise his voice but spoke in a matter-of-fact, conversational tone. "The senator knows about your affair with the lieutenant, Miss Hamilton."

It was on the tip of Anna Leigh's sharp tongue to call him a liar when she realized there was no explanation for how *he* knew about the affair. Calling him a liar would only confirm his statement. Perhaps he was only guessing. "What are you talking about?" she asked with deliberate coolness. "What affair?"

Mary had no patience for the woman's prevarication. She turned her head in Anna Leigh's direction. "Don't try to be too clever," she said dryly. "It only undermines you. Ryder and I saw you with the lieutenant at your home. There was no mistaking that you're lovers."

Anna Leigh raised her hand to her mouth, but not in time to stifle her gasp.

"The question in my mind is," Ryder said casually, "whether you were lovers before you were involved in the Colter Canyon raid or if it came later in the celebration of the success of your scheme." When Anna Leigh didn't answer, Ryder went on. "I suspect it was later. Perhaps since you returned to Washington. It would have been difficult for you to act on any attraction you felt for each other at Fort Union. Too many observers, including my uncle. The news about you and Rivers came as a surprise to him. He never suspected that you'd taken another lover."

Mary blinked widely. "Another lover!" Her voice blossomed with surprise. "You mean *your* uncle and *Anna Leigh*."

Ryder's affirmative response was drowned out as Anna Leigh began pounding on the door again. "Wilson! Let me out of here! They're wrong about me and Davis. They lied to you! Wilson!" The door rattled with the force of her blows, but it didn't budge. No answer came from the other side. "I'm telling you, Wilson! Ryder and the bitch lied. I'm not having an affair with Davis. I'm not!"

Mary waited for Anna Leigh's pounding to subside, then she said, "The senator might find your protests more compelling if you didn't use the lieutenant's Christian name."

Anna Leigh practically hurled herself down the stairs. Her move was so unexpected that Ryder had to push Mary aside in order to take Anna Leigh's flailing blows himself. He grappled with the Hamilton woman for several seconds before he managed to get her arms crossed in front of her and to force her wrists back. She quieted once she realized Ryder was securing her with her own arms. The more she struggled, the tighter his hold got.

As soon as she was calm and Ryder was certain Mary was out of Anna Leigh's immediate reach, he set Anna Leigh down hard on one of the bottom steps. "Stay there," he said. "Until I tell you to move. I won't be so gentle the next time you try to attack Mary."

Anna Leigh tossed her head disdainfully. It was an ineffective gesture in the dark cellar.

"Do you understand, Miss Hamilton?" he asked.

"Yes," she said tightly.

"Mary?" Ryder said.

"Hmmm?"

"Behave yourself."

"All right," she said pleasantly.

Ryder stepped over the lieutenant's body again to move away from the stairs. He found Mary, took her hand, and led her out of Anna Leigh's reach once more. His shoulder bumped one of the wooden wine racks. "Here," he said. "Sit right here. You can lean against the rack."

Mary thought better of protesting that the floor was cold. She bunched her train and bustle under her and sat down. Her fingers idly traced the shapes of the smooth bricks by following their edges as Ryder spoke to Anna Leigh again. Mary's nails began to chip away at loose bits of mortar.

"It doesn't appear my uncle is going to let you out," he said. "I think Mary's right. He doesn't believe your story."

"He'll change his mind," Anne Leigh said. "You'll see."

Mary gave her credit for the confidence she forced into her tone. Only the slight quaver at the end betrayed the woman's fear that it was misplaced.

"Tell me about Colter Canyon," Ryder said. "It will pass the time."

"Oh?" she said archly. "You mean there's something you *don't* know."

"There are a few things," Ryder admitted easily.

Anna Leigh felt blood trickle from her lip again. She dabbed at it with her handkerchief, cursing Mary silently. "Why should I?" she said sullenly. "What do I gain?"

"Your freedom."

She hadn't expected that. "You mean you can get out of here?"

"Yes."

"Then do it," she demanded. "What are you waiting for?"

Ryder didn't answer immediately. He felt Mary lean her head against his thigh. He stroked her hair lightly. She had trusted him so completely, had been so certain of his ability to protect her that she had been fearless in facing the senator's gun. If she weren't so curious for the truth about Colter Canyon, Ryder believed she was nearly comfortable enough to fall asleep against his leg.

It was different with Anna Leigh. Even in the darkness, Ryder could sense her agitation. "Waiting is not always a means to an end," he said quietly. "It has its own rewards."

Anna Leigh snorted. "What does that mean?" she asked sharply. "Some Apache nonsense, no doubt."

Mary felt Ryder's shrug and smiled to herself. Anna Leigh would never understand about the waiting. "You'd do well to answer him, Miss Hamilton," she said. "Ryder's rarely in a hurry. We'll grow very old here. Just as Senator Stillwell intends."

Ryder doubted that was all his uncle intended, but he didn't point it out. "Colter Canyon," he said. "In exchange for your freedom."

Anna Leigh carefully stretched her right leg. She could just touch Davis Rivers's body with her toe. She nudged him several times, but got no response. There would be no help from that quarter. He hadn't even armed himself, so there was no weapon she could steal. More disgusted than distressed, Anna Leigh drew back her leg. Her skirt rustled softly. "What is it you want to know?"

"How my uncle planned it," said Ryder.

Anna Leigh's short laughter was without humor. "Wilson said you suspected it was my father's scheme. What changed your mind?"

"My uncle did."

"Wilson? How?"

"When he said he could arrange for you and the lieutenant to come here. He could offer no explanation. Only the certainty that it could be done. Mary said from the beginning that it didn't make sense. She was right . . . and wrong. Mary's only mistake was her refusal to change her premises. It didn't make sense if my uncle was innocent, but if he was involved . . ." His voice trailed off and he let Anna Leigh and Mary draw their own conclusions.

Mary raised her head, disappointed that she hadn't guessed it for herself. "Then it was Senator Stillwell who arranged for your assignment—on his own, not with Warren Hamilton's encouragement."

."That's right," Ryder said. "He lied about that and a few other things."

"Your uncle's very good at lying," Anna Leigh interjected bitterly. "I'm not so easily fooled as your dear Mary." The last three words were iced heavily with scorn. "You were right. He deceived Davis and me this evening. We did expect to be part of your capture, not our own." She leaned back against the step behind her. "Your uncle and I were lovers for almost a year before Colter Canyon was ever mentioned. I knew Wilson had power and influence in Western policies and the Indian campaigns, but I had no idea he could implement something as stunning as the Colter Canyon raid." There was the subtle rise of excitement in her voice as she went on. "Watching him maneuver people like pawns . . . he was brilliant. I've never seen anything like it." She suddenly seemed to recognize that enthusiasm and admiration were not called for. Now she spoke with more deliberation, carefully modulating her voice. "He didn't confide his plans right away. He wasn't so certain of me in the beginning of our relationship. That took some time on my part . . . a bit of maneuvering equal to his. I never knew the full scope of what he intended. Never guessed that he meant for so many soldiers to die."

Mary felt Ryder's hand on her shoulder, cautioning her against interrupting. She doubted Ryder believed Anna Leigh was so innocent. She certainly didn't. But he wanted to hear all from her.

"My father could never have engineered such a plan," she said. "I don't think it would have been a completely moral judgment on his part. He just wouldn't have had the stomach for it." She paused. "Or the brains, for that matter."

Mary's own stomach became a trifle queasy as she listened to Anna Leigh speak with such disrespect and disregard.

"Wilson Stillwell called in all debts to put his plan together. Most of the men he had assigned to Fort Union felt they owed him some favor. Of course that was only a small reason they joined him. There *was* the gold, after all." She drew her legs up, hugging them as the cool dampness of the cellar sent a shiver through her. "My father and I were there as part of Wilson's plan," she said. "Not that Papa was aware. As far as he knew his reasons for being there were perfectly legitimate. I understood that Wilson was setting up another scapegoat in the event that you did not take to the role so obligingly."

Ryder's deep chuckle was mirthless. "I was everything you could have hoped for."

Protected by the unrelieved blackness, Anna Leigh smiled, remembering. "Yes," she said. "Yes, you were. I really was intrigued by you, you know. I'd heard so much about you. Some from the women at the fort, much more from your uncle. He thinks of you as a half-breed. He really does. All those years among the Apache. It's as if you're one of them in his mind." Anna Leigh's head tilted to one side. She brushed away the tangled hair that clung to her neck. "It's hard to say how different things might have been if you hadn't pushed aside my attentions. You might have been killed during the raid. Who knows, I could have saved your life."

"But then, if my uncle's plan had unraveled, if it had been discovered the Chiricahua were not behind the raid, your father stood to take the blame. I think you saw a way to make certain I stayed alive and was fingered with the responsibility."

Anna Leigh was silent for a moment. "My father had been critical of Washington's policies on the Indians of late. He was recognized among his peers to be more sympathetic. Wilson and my father . . . they were known to argue publicly—and privately. I think Wilson saw Papa as a patsy for his scheme long before he recognized you were a better choice." She tossed her disheveled hair defiantly. "And what if I did help Wilson to see it? Better you than my father."

"You could have turned everyone in," Ryder said with quiet conviction. "But then, there *was* the gold."

Anna Leigh sighed. "I suspect you know me too well," she said. "Betraying your uncle wasn't something I could do."

Mary couldn't help herself. "You seemed to have changed your mind."

Anna Leigh's voice was sharp. "He's the one who deceived me," she snapped.

"I was referring to your affair with Lieutenant Rivers," Mary said. "That's the betrayal that made him push you down these stairs. Senator Stillwell wasn't very interested in what we had uncovered about Colter Canyon until we mentioned your tryst with the lieutenant. That engaged his attention. He saw us as a way to get back at you."

Anna Leigh shrugged. "If he thinks about it he'll know it didn't mean anything. Why would I care for Davis when Wilson can give me so much more? I have no intention of being a lieutenant's wife."

"Even with all the gold you have?" asked Ryder. "That certainly would smooth out life's little bumps."

"All the gold?" Anna Leigh said scornfully. "What do you suppose was my portion when it was all said and done? Not much, I can tell you. Wilson had the ore shipped and processed into bullion. That's not something that can be readily used as legal tender. It will be a while before anyone can spend it."

"But in the meantime you can dream about what it will buy."

"Your uncle took the lion's share, and the rest was split between all the men."

"That's only fair," Ryder said, his voice suddenly taut. "They had to kill their *brothers* for it."

Anna felt the vibration of Ryder's tightly strung anger as if it were a wave in the cool, moist air. She found herself recoiling to avoid a slap that never came. "They knew what they had to do for it," she rejoined. "They accepted the assignment. Most of them welcomed it. You know for yourself that none of them flinched when the time came. No one was left alive who could say what had happened in Colter Canyon except for the men who had done the deed." She raised her chin. The brilliant sparkle of her blue eyes was lost in the darkness. "And none of them are talking."

"You certainly are," Mary said. She rested her head against the wooden wine rack and closed her eyes. So it was true, she thought. Anna Leigh had confirmed the horrible truth of Colter Canyon. One bluecoat against another. Not for flag or freedom, but for gold. Her nails continued to trace the mortar maze between the bricks in the cellar floor. Struggling for control she opened her eyes again. "But then I suppose you still believe the senator will come to his senses and take your side." Anna Leigh didn't have to respond. Mary knew it was the truth. She touched Ryder's thigh. "We have all the answers," she said. "What do we do now?"

His response was long in coming, as if he were shaking off the sadness. Mary swore she could see Ryder's slowly emerging smile when he finally said, "Celebrate, of course, and wait for the enemy to charge."

Bemused, Mary let herself be drawn to her feet and led between the tall racks of wine.

"Where are you going?" Anna Leigh called a little uncertainly. She squinted, trying to see. "Are you leaving me?"

Ryder ignored her. Running his free hand along the wall of bottles, he asked Mary, "Is there something in particular you'd like to try?"

Mary frowned. "Ryder, you know I don't drink much."

"I wasn't thinking that we'd drink it."

"Well then, what are we—"

"Break them," he said. "Break them all."

"And wait for the enemy," she whispered slowly, understanding. "Ryder McKay, I like the way you think." She took a bottle by the neck and removed it from the rack. "I'll start with this."

Ryder found her face, cupped it, and kissed her swiftly and sweetly on the mouth. "Be careful," he said. "I'll be at the top of the stairs."

She nodded. "I thought you would." She heard him tell Anna Leigh to get out of the way; then he climbed the steps.

Mary had to knock the first bottle of wine against the floor a few times before it broke. The sound was not as satisfying as she'd hoped it would be. The thud was too dull and the bottle didn't shatter easily. "I don't think he'll hear that," she said.

Anna Leigh groped around in the darkness until she came upon Mary. "Here, let me try." She gripped one bottleneck and pitched it hard in the direction of where she knew a wall would be. It shattered nicely. "You have to know where to throw it. I've seen Wilson's cellar before."

"How nice for you," Mary said dryly. Anna Leigh's assistance now wasn't going to make her a fast friend. Mary hefted a bottle and tossed it. It broke easily. She tossed another, then another. Anna Leigh joined her and they pitched the bottles in unison. Overhead they could hear the heavy thud of running feet. Senator Stillwell was pounding down the hallway to save his beloved collection of vintage wines. "He's coming!" Mary whispered.

"Yes," Anna Leigh said. "He is."

The last thing Mary saw was the sliver of light at the top of the stairs as Senator Stillwell threw open the door. She remembered thinking it was a good thing the bottle Anna Leigh brought down squarely on her head didn't shatter.

"Look out, Wilson!" Anna Leigh cried. "It's a trap!"

Her warning came too late. The senator had already launched himself headlong onto the stairway, his revolver drawn. Ryder rose from his crouched position and drove a fist hard into his uncle's midsection. Wilson Stillwell groaned and lost his balance. The force of his headlong plunge knocked Ryder off his feet and for the second time in the space of an hour, Ryder twisted and dove down the length of the stairs.

Stillwell's gun was discharged as it thudded against a step, its bullet exploding a magnum of Moet et Chandon. Anna Leigh screamed as she was struck in the face by champagne and shards of flying glass, and she screamed even louder when she tasted blood mixed with the bubbly.

Ryder wrestled the senator to the floor, taking a surprisingly stiff blow on his chin as they both grappled for the gun. Stillwell caught it once with his fingertips, but sent it skittering along the bricks when Ryder reached for it, too. The door at the top of the stairs began to swing shut slowly, cutting off the hallway's gaslight.

With the return of complete darkness Wilson Stillwell got lucky. His roundhouse punch connected with Ryder's temple, knocking Ryder sideways and further wrenching his knee. The senator threw himself in the direction where he'd last spied the gun and began flailing around for it. Ryder caught him by the legs and pulled him back. Stillwell's aggressive chin got a solid thudding as he was dragged belly first across the brick floor. He groaned as Ryder straddled him and yanked his arms behind his back.

"Now what?" Stillwell said tersely, one side of his face pressed uncomfortably against the floor. "You don't have anything for tying my hands."

Ryder had realized that as well. "I'm prepared to improvise," he said.

Without any more warning than that, he raised himself high enough to turn his uncle over, then he knocked him out with a hard right hook.

Suddenly there was light at the top of the stairs as the door was opened again. Not certain what he could expect, Ryder rolled off Stillwell and sprang to his feet. Anna Leigh's screams had subsided into hoarse sobs. Out of the corner of his eye he saw Mary lift her head weakly and search out the lump on her scalp. Nearby Lieutenant Rivers was finally stirring. Only his uncle was singularly still.

The figure filling the doorway above took a step down to let more of the light behind him filter into the wine cellar. He made a quick but thorough survey of the carnage, then looked Ryder squarely in the eye.

John MacKenzie Worth slowly raised his shotgun. "Give me one reason why I shouldn't use this on you."

Ryder didn't blink or miss a beat. "I was hoping you'd save it for the wedding, sir." At the top of the stairs, directly behind Jay Mac there was more commotion. Some of the voices he recognized, others he didn't. That gave him hope. He hadn't expected to know them all, though some were tantalizing familiar.

Jarret Sullivan pushed his way through the throng clogging the entrance, and Rennie followed closely on his heels. Moira shouldered her way into the fray and looked over her daughter's shoulder. "Jay Mac," she said firmly. "Put down that gun."

Ryder released a breath he hadn't realized he'd been holding. "Finally," he said softly. "The cavalry."

Epilogue

New York City, July 1885

It wasn't a shotgun wedding. Judge Halsey, in spite of a life-long friendship with Jay Mac, his position as godfather to Mary Michael, and his role in the marriages of all the Dennehy women, absolutely refused to allow the weapon in his chambers. Jay Mac, not one for accepting defeat easily, carried the shotgun as far as the courtroom and left it propped in the hallway against the wall.

The judge's chambers were really not big enough to accommodate the crowd gathered in them. He only permitted them access because they were all related to one another and didn't seem to mind the squeeze. It was the first reunion of the entire family since Mary Margaret's graduation from medical school over a year ago—and their numbers seemed to be swelling. Certainly the bride was.

The Honorable Judge Halsey thought he detected a slight roundness to Mary Francis's abdomen that hadn't been evident when she'd first approached him about the wedding ceremony. She had come to him in March, he recalled, just after Senator Wilson Stillwell's dramatic prison suicide had ended his sensational impeachment proceedings and criminal trial. Mary had told Halsey then that she was in no hurry for the marriage to take place, that in her eyes, in her mother's and the Marys' eyes, and she was certain that in *God's* eyes, she was already very much married to Ryder McKay. This formal ceremony was to appease Jay Mac and New York civil law. Judge Halsey didn't doubt that the former was more influential than the latter.

The judge looked around his private chambers now. He saw that Moira Dennehy Worth was quite content to preside at her husband's side over their brood of children and grandchildren. Jay Mac kept his arm around his wife's shoulder and occasionally, when his eye would catch one of the grandchildren in some antic reminiscent of his own daughters, he would whisper in Moira's ear. Her smile was beatific.

Mary Michael was there with her husband Ethan and their two children. Michael was the first to report the truth behind the Colter Canyon raid for the *Rocky Mountain News*. All the major eastern newspapers had picked up her story, and her byline was once again known nationally. She had had an advantage no other reporter had. She and Ethan were part of Ryder McKay's "cavalry." After following Jay Mac across the country to make certain he did nothing foolish, they had ended up being called upon to assist in the rescue. Michael's reporting had a slant that was the envy of all the news agencies.

Judge Halsey's eyes slid next to Michael's twin. Rennie was kneeling beside her own twins, wiping sticky red and black licorice off their hands, and asking where they had gotten the candy. Cait and Lilly were almost comically mute in their refusal to betray their father. As for Jarret, he was busy tucking strings of licorice out of sight in his inside breast pocket.

The judge's slightly crooked smile faded as he noticed one youngster had occupied the plush leather seat behind his desk and was energetically swiveling back and forth. He was about to say something when he noticed Mary Margaret's attention was drawn from the babe in her arms to her daughter. She poked Connor gently with her elbow and nodded toward Meredith. Connor put his hand out stopped the rotating chair, and that was that . . . until Meredith began rooting through the papers the judge had been foolish enough to leave out. At that point it was easier for Halsey to look away than watch the carnage.

It was then he caught Mary Schyler's eye. She was laughing

at him and making no effort to hide it. The sheer brightness of Skye's flame red hair and flashing emerald eyes made the judge feel decades younger. He found himself chuckling in return, glad for all the clan that Skye had been able to return from China for Mary Francis's wedding. Her husband Walker was the groom's best man. Now Walker tapped Skye on the shoulder lightly and passed their son into her arms.

It was then Judge Halsey realized they were all waiting on him. His complexion reddened a little, and his starched collar suddenly felt tight. He cleared his throat, more out of necessity than for dramatic effect, and nodded to Mary and Ryder. "It appears we're ready," he said solemnly.

Mary Francis looked around the room once, taking time to acknowledge everyone individually, to thank them silently for all they had done. When she turned to face Ryder a faint wash of tears glistened in her eyes. The full measure of her family's love had swelled her heart.

Ryder took her hand and drew her close as Judge Halsey began the ceremony. Later they would both admit they remembered almost nothing of what was said or done. Separately, yet together, they had been transported to a still and silent clearing in the Arizona Territory where their marriage, like all other life, had been given its nascent moment in cool, crystalline water.

It was the judge's expectant look, his nod of encouragement to each of them that brought them back to the present. Mary raised her face and Ryder bent his head. There was a collective sigh among the witnesses when the kiss finally ended.

Flushed and a little breathless, Mary smiled, radiating joy. Ryder selfishly kept the warmth of that smile for himself a moment before he turned her gently so they might greet the family together.

They were mobbed.

A warm breeze swept up from the Hudson River, crossed the field of wildflowers, and fluttered the lace curtains in the corner bedroom of the summerhouse. The scent of water; the fragrance of larkspur, zinnias, primroses, and yarrow; the gentle, almost ghostly movement of the gauzy curtains teased Ryder's senses into wakefulness. He rose from deep sleep slowly, turning on his side with a lazy stretch, and buried his face into the coolest corner of the feather pillow. His hand slid beneath the covers, searching for the familiar contour of Mary's slender arm or the shape of her rounded hip.

He opened his eyes to confirm what his blind seeking had already divined. He was alone.

Ryder smiled to himself, not alarmed by her absence. He knew where he could find her.

Mary surfaced and shook her head. The spray of water sparkled like diamonds in the moonlight before each droplet was absorbed by the larger pool. She turned in a slow circle, letting her bare arm skim the surface and creating a ripple with her at its center. Except for Mary's own light, off-key humming, the clearing around the pool was quiet.

She never heard Ryder's approach, yet she knew almost immediately that he had arrived. It was as if there had been a shift in the very air. She stopped humming and completed her lazy rotation until she faced him.

Moonshine glanced off his naked shoulders and set his features in sharp relief. He was hunkered on the lip of a rock, his predatory posture familiar to her now, more exciting than threatening. He watched her closely, his gaze gliding over her face, her neck, her bare shoulders. His quiet scrutiny infused Mary's skin with warmth, and the water suddenly felt several degrees cooler.

Ryder's voice had a deep, husky edge. "What are you doing here?"

"Waiting." She said the word simply, but could not have imbued it with more meaning. She knew about the pleasures of waiting.

He nodded and stood. "I thought you might be." He undid the button at the waist of his jeans, the only one he'd buttoned, and hooked his thumbs into the waistband and pushed the pants off, diving into the water the moment he kicked them free. His body skimmed Mary's as he surfaced. "I missed you," he said.

Treading water easily, she placed her hand on the curve of Ryder's neck and flicked away a strand of dark hair from his nape. She leaned into him and placed her mouth across his. They sank beneath the water, their lips fused in a breathless kiss. Mary wrapped her legs around Ryder's thighs and pressed her breasts against his chest. Her hair fanned out in the water, waving and undulating as they floated back toward the surface.

They headed for a shallower part of the pool. Mary's arms circled Ryder's shoulders as he lifted her. Her thighs clutched his hips. Buoyed by the water and supported by him, she felt nearly weightless. She arched her back. Sensation rippled from their joining to her fingertips. His mouth was on her breast, sucking. Cords of pleasure tugged deeply within her, as deeply as her womb. Her fingers spread widely across Ryder's damp skin, and she clung to him. His hands were on the small of her back, pressing her close. As she flung back her head, his mouth found her throat, his lips almost intolerably hot against her skin.

She felt him shudder, and the vibration of his body seemed to roll into her. Mary absorbed it as Ryder continued to stroke her. He kissed her deeply and kept his body flush to hers. Her tender breasts rubbed slickly against his chest.

She was expecting the climax, still, the power of it took her by surprise. Mary cried out, her body rocking hard against Ryder. He held her close but not tightly. His loose embrace secured her afterward when she sagged weakly against him, replete and radiant.

Ryder carried her out of the water. She pointed to the blanket she'd brought from the house and he set her on it. Her cotton shift was bunched in one corner. She raised her arms languorously as he helped her put it on. He gave her a brief parting kiss that was more promise than passion before he went around the pool to retrieve his trousers.

"You didn't have to put those on on my account," Mary said when he returned.

"I know." He dropped to his knees beside her and then stretched out, propping himself on an elbow. "I put them on because it's warmer in the water than it is out here."

"Do you want to go inside?" she asked.

He smoothed tendrils of her damp hair away from her temples. Her complexion was bathed in silver-blue moonlight. "No," he said, studying her serene, uncomplicated beauty. "No, I want to stay right here."

She smiled. Only that. It wasn't important to say anything in return.

Ryder's fingers continued to sift the slick and silky strands of her hair. "Did you ever think we should have had our wedding here?" he asked after a time.

"It occurred to me," she said. "But I didn't want to share this place that way." She imagined that he felt the same way. After all, he hadn't broached the idea *before* their wedding. "I'm quite happy with the current arrangement. My sisters and their husbands and all those children are running up and down the stairs in my parents' home while you and I honeymoon right here at the summerhouse."

Ryder's palm slid from beneath Mary's breast to the gentle swell of her abdomen. "Our child will be running up and down those same stairs someday," he said.

Mary shook her head. "I'm going to teach him how to use the banister. It's the quickest way between floors."

He chuckled. "I believe you will." He rubbed her belly idly, thinking.

"It's not a magic lamp, you know," Mary said tartly.

Frowning, Ryder stopped. "What?"

She was hard pressed to keep her stern expression, but she managed to point to his splayed hand on her abdomen and tell him, "Your son won't appear in a puff of smoke no matter how hard you rub."

Ryder couldn't have removed his hand any more quickly if he had been scorched. His grin was sheepish. "Sorry. I didn't realize . . ." His voice trailed off as Mary placed his hand back on her swollen middle.

"I don't suppose I mind so much," she said. "Just so you know these things take time."

By Ryder's reckoning it would take four more months. He had a particularly fond memory of a shared bathing tub at Doc Stanley's boarding house. Their child, like their marriage, had been conceived surrounded by water. "Do you really think it will be a boy?"

"No. I don't have a sense of it one way or the other." She studied his face. Did he want a boy because he'd already had a daughter? Was the memory still too raw, even after so many years? "Does it matter?"

He shook his head. "A daughter would be fine, Mary. I'll cherish her as much as I do her mother." He raised his hand again, but Mary brought it back to her belly quickly this time. Her expression cautioned him to be still. Beneath his palm he felt the surprisingly firm kick of his child.

"That's approval," Mary said softly.

Ryder laughed lowly. He removed his hand and lay back. Mary nestled her head in the curve of his shoulder and laid her arm across his chest. Blanketed by stars in a midnight blue sky, they enjoyed this moment in silence. Too many times over that last five months they had wondered if they would ever reach the sanctuary of this Hudson Valley clearing. The thought of being here, in just this place and in just this way, was the vision they had kept secretly in their minds' eyes as they'd faced down their critics and accusers.

Mary Michael's story in the *Rocky Mountain News* had gone a long way to helping Ryder and Mary, but it hadn't cleared every obstacle. The story was too big, the scandal at once abhorrent and compelling. Even John MacKenzie Worth couldn't stop the Army from interrogating Mary. She'd endured hours of questioning, days of defending herself for assisting Ryder in his escape and for every subsequent action that she'd taken on his behalf or at his side.

She still struggled with the irony of having to lie about helping Ryder escape the stockade in order to be in a position to be believed about everything else. Florence Gardner herself had come East with her son when the general had been summoned to Washington by the War Office. She had met with Ryder and Mary, had offered to admit the role she had played, but they had declined. General Gardner's career, already under a great deal of scrutiny because of his handling of the Colter Canyon investigation, would have suffered considerably more if it had been known he couldn't control his own mother.

From the moment Mary's family had crowded the wine-cellar stairway, it seemed there had been no end to the activity and to the lack of peace.

Ryder's memory of the commotion in the cellar was clearer than Mary's. In spite of her sister Maggie's immediate attention, Mary sported a lump the size of a plover's egg for a week. Mary was the first to admit it was an insignificant consequence of her encounter with a wine bottle. Anna Leigh Hamilton had not been so fortunate. Maggie's timely intervention only meant that the chance of infection had been reduced. The shards of glass had been painstakingly removed from Anna Leigh's face and throat, and Maggie had bathed her eyes with a steady flow of water, but no amount of skillful suturing would ever restore Anna Leigh's complexion to its former flawlessness, nor would the bathing restore sight to her eyes.

Anna Leigh Hamilton made a tragic, sympathetic figure as she testified against Wilson Stillwell. It was not difficult for her to twist the truth and paint herself as a victim of an older man's promises and power. She cleared Ryder McKay, but she leveled charges at his uncle. Anna Leigh's suffering on the stand made it almost impossible for any of the other defendants to point their fingers at her. Still, they tried . . . and failed. The efforts of Lieutenant Rivers and Senator Stillwell to portray Warren Hamilton's daughter as a temptress only succeeded in reminding the press and the public and the politicians that the woman had been a vibrant, spirited beauty, vital to dressing up the dullest Washington dinner party. The senator and the lieutenant could say nothing against her that didn't go against themselves.

Lieutenant Rivers and a handful of key conspirators were hanged in April. The full entourage of soldiers who had committed the massacre at Colter Canyon were sharing prison cells in and around Washington and were scheduled to hang in groups of three or four over the course of the summer. They were mostly forgotten now as the nation began to put the Colter Canyon tragedy out of its memory with the suicide of Wilson Stillwell. Editorials in *The Times* and *The Herald* all but came out and thanked him for his decision to end his life and let the nation move on. The publisher of the *New York Chronicle* was a lone voice in naming him a coward.

The senator died without giving up the location of his share of the gold shipment. While all the others involved in the theft had turned over their unspent bullion, Wilson Stillwell never admitted he had received any of the gold.

Mary thought long and prayed hard before she decided to confess that she knew where the senator had hidden his Judas payment. Before she shared what she knew, she struck a deal that a portion of the vast treasure would be turned over to the families of the men who had died at Colter Canyon. She also secured the War Office's agreement that Ryder McKay was done answering their questions. To her way of thinking the Colter Canyon affair was closed. The Army was in no position to argue with her.

She led her husband and Army officers back to Senator Stillwell's home and into his wine cellar. "Revelations 21:21," she said. When no one moved, she added, "The streets of the city were of pure gold, like translucent glass." Ryder began to smile at that point, but the entourage of officers continued to regard her blankly. They sincerely hoped they hadn't followed her to be quoted scripture. Sighing, Mary said, "Don't look at me, gentlemen. The answer is under your feet."

Ryder was the first to understand and the first to remove a penknife from his pocket and dig at the bricks on the wine-cellar floor. Gold was a soft metal, so he had no difficulty chipping through the paint and revealing the precious metal beneath. The edge of his knife was flecked with gold. He held it up for the officers to see. They worked hard at not being impressed. The Army had already scoured the senator's home, including the wine cellar, a half-dozen times, and had found nothing.

"How did you know?" Ryder asked her as he led her away.

So she told him how, during his interrogation of Anna Leigh, she had kept tracing the mortared edges of the bricks in the cellar floor, and that when she had looked at her hands much later she had seen flecks of gold under her nails.

Like the good poker player she was, Mary had kept the secret to herself, not showing anyone her cards until she was certain she knew when and how to play them.

Ryder McKay was not acquitted as loudly as his uncle was denounced. The Army absolved him of all wrongdoing and offered to reinstate him if he wished. He didn't, for which no one in the War Office was sorry. They felt they had lived up to their agreement with Mary and were happy to finally end this affair. His presence was an embarrassment, a reminder of the shoddiness of their organization and of the rampant prejudice in the government's Western policies against the Indians. Ryder McKay was cleared, but he wasn't a hero.

He was satisfied with that. He preferred exile to the property he and Mary had purchased at Flagstaff to a life of notoriety in Washington or New York. They had more than enough money to make a good start at ranching. His savings had bought the property, and Mary had her trust from Jay Mac to purchase cattle and hire hands. Then there was the unexpected news from Rennie just a few weeks ago: Ryder's prospecting map had led her and Jarret to a mother lode. Rennie arrived for the wedding carrying deeds and mineral rights and rights of way for Northeast Rail. She negotiated a deal with Ryder and Mary that would set them up handsomely for the rest of their lives.

And, as Jay Mac pointed out, it did no harm to Northeast Rail either.

"What is it?" asked Mary. She felt Ryder's soundless laughter as his chest vibrated softly against her arm. "What are you thinking?"

"That your father's a crafty man."

"In business they call that successful."

"Mmmm." He bent his head and kissed the crown of her head. "He was making noises about retiring. I heard him talking about it to Judge Halsey at the reception."

"I know. I overheard some of it." She shook her head. "I imagine he'll always keep his hand in some way, but he's been grooming Rennie and Jarret for a long time to take over Northeast. They're ready for it, and Mama would be happy to spend her days traveling the country and visiting her grandbabies. Jay Mac doesn't seem as averse to the idea as he once was."

Ryder agreed quietly that it was true. He felt Mary relax against him, her arm becoming a little heavier across his chest. Her breath was soft and her eyes were closed, but he knew she wasn't sleeping yet. Her lips were moving almost imperceptibly. Ryder could feel the whisper of her mouth against his skin. He smiled. This was the time of night when she protected him with prayers and gave thanks for every good fortune that was hers to share.

He had been wrong to suppose that Mary had placed her trust solely in him, that she had been certain he would protect her. He knew that now, and was able to recognize the real source of her great strength and of her love.

Mary had placed her trust solely in Him.

To My Readers

The publication of *ONLY IN MY ARMS* represents the end of the Dennehy saga. When I first began writing about Mary Michael Dennehy in *WILD SWEET ECSTASY* I had no idea that she came from such a large and interesting family or that I would be committed to writing about them for the next five years. I certainly didn't anticipate developing a story around Mary Francis. Letters from readers (and some gentle prompting from my editor) convinced me to complete the chronicle with Jay Mac and Moira's first daughter.

Readers who were kind enough to write to me and let me know how much you enjoyed the Dennehy series, I would like to thank you. I appreciate your commitment in sticking with the stories. I know you had a long wait between each sister. For those of you who read hundreds of romances each year I was especially flattered that you were able to keep track of all the Marys. Although that probably says more about your brain-power than my ability to spin a tale, I choose to be flattered. Thank you again.

ABOUT THE AUTHOR

JO GOODMAN lives with her family in Colliers, West Virginia. She is currently working on her newest Zebra historical romance, once again set in the Regency period. Look for it in August 2005! Jo loves hearing from readers, and you may write to her c /o Zebra Books. Please include a self-addressed stamped envelope if you would like a response. Or you can visit her website at www.jogoodman.com

Please turn the page for an
exciting sneak preview of
Jo Goodman's

MY STEADFAST HEART

Prologue

They came for the baby first. Colin remembered because he was eight, old enough to grasp the loss, too young to prevent it. He had expected it would happen, but expectation alone did not prepare him, nor had he been able to prepare his brothers.

Not that Greydon could have understood. He was the baby they came for. With his round face and engaging smile, it was natural that he would be chosen. Grey had no real knowledge of his circumstances or surroundings, Colin thought. At five months he did not know he already had a family, albeit a smaller one than he had had three months earlier. Young Greydon was all gurgling laughter and chubby, flailing limbs. He charmed without effort and without conscience, as naturally as breathing and eating and crying.

So when Grey sighed contentedly as he was lifted into the woman's arms, Colin tried to remember that it didn't make his baby brother a traitor.

Beside the doorway, just inside the headmaster's office, Colin stood holding his younger brother's hand. Decker was only four, but he was willing to stand at Colin's side, his small body at attention while the couple from America made their decision about the baby.

The next minutes were an agony as the headmaster indicated the two boys and asked the question of the couple with careless indifference, "Will you have one or both of the others?"

The man turned away from his wife and seemed to notice the boys for the first time. The woman did not glance in their direction.

"They're brothers," the headmaster said. "Colin. Decker. Come here and stand. You will make the acquaintance of Greydon's new parents."

The last hope that Colin had that the couple would not choose Grey vanished at the headmaster's words. Dutifully he stepped forward, Decker in tow. "How do you do, sir," he said gravely, extending his free hand to the man.

There was a surprised pause, then a low, appreciative chuckle from the man as he returned the handshake and greeting. Colin's narrow hand was swallowed in the man's larger one. In later years, try as he might, Colin could not put features to the man's face. It was the dry, firm handshake he remembered, the deep, lilting chuckle, and the momentary surge of hope he felt.

The man looked at his wife who was coaxing another smile from the baby in her arms. It was easy to see she was already in love with the child. There would be no difficulty passing the baby off as their own. No one among their family or friends would have to know it was an adoption.

"I'm afraid not," he said, letting go of Colin's hand. "My wife and I only wanted a baby." Because he was uncomfortable with the two pairs of eyes looking up at him, he added to the headmaster, "You shouldn't have brought them here. I told you from the first we were only interested in an infant."

The headmaster did not flinch under the rebuke. Instead he deflected it, turning his head sharply toward the boys and ordering them out of the room. His stiff, accusing tone made it seem that their presence in the office had never been his idea at all but theirs.

Colin released Decker's hand. "It's all right," he said quietly. "You go."

Decker's wide blue eyes darted uncertainly between Colin and the headmaster. It was at Colin's urging, rather than the headmaster's stony glare, that Decker hurried from the room.

"I would like to say farewell to my brother," Colin said. He had a youthful voice, but his dark eyes were old beyond his years and he stood his ground as though planted there.

The headmaster was prepared to come around his desk and bodily remove Colin. He looked to his guests for some indication of their wishes in the matter.

The man raised his hand briefly in a motion that kept the headmaster at bay. "Of course," he said. "Dear? This child would like to say goodbye to his brother."

With obvious reluctance, the woman pulled her attention away from the baby. Her generous smile faded as she looked down at Colin. The dreamy, captivated expression in her blue eyes slipped away. "Oh, no," she said flatly. There was a hint of gray at the outer edges of her eyes, like the beginnings of ice on a lake. "I don't want that boy touching my baby. Look at him. Anyone can see he's sickly. He may harm the child."

It was as if Colin had been struck. The impact of the words caused his thin body to vibrate. He could feel heat creeping into his cheeks as he flushed deeply with equal parts of anger and shame. In that moment he knew he was standing there because he couldn't move, not because he didn't want to.

"Is the boy ill?" the man asked the headmaster. "My wife's right. He's very thin."

"He doesn't eat," the headmaster said. The glance he leveled at Colin darkened considerably, and the warning was clear. "He's really had little appetite since he arrived. My wife believes the accident affected him more than the others. It's understandable, of course, what with him being the oldest."

As if there were no other conversation in the room, Colin said again, "I'd like to hold my brother." This time he held up his arms.

The man prompted his wife gently. "Dear? Where can be the harm?"

She did not accede immediately, but considered her options for several long seconds. Colin watched her eyes shift briefly toward the door as though she were toying with the idea of fleeing the room. In the end she gave him the baby, along with a stiff, icy admonishment not to drop him.

Colin held his infant brother to his small chest, cradling the boy as he had on so many other occasions these past three months. Turning away from the adults, ignoring the woman's sharp intake of breath, Colin adjusted the baby's blankets and smoothed his muslin gown. "I'll find you," he said, his lips barely moving around the words. "I promise, I'll find you."

Greydon cooed obligingly and beat his small fist against Colin's shoulder.

"I think that's long enough," the man said as his wife took a step forward to hover over the brothers.

The headmaster addressed Colin. "Give Greydon back now."

Colin did not so much return his brother as his brother was taken from him. He did not wait to be dismissed a second time. He could not leave the headmaster's darkly paneled office quickly enough. His gait was stiff and his spine rigid. Only his lower lip trembled uncontrollably as he crossed the floor. He barely heard the woman's words, and at the time didn't fully comprehend the impact they would have.

Tickling the baby's chin, she said softly, "I don't think I care for the name Greydon at all."

It was only three weeks later that Decker left Cunnington's Workhouse for Foundlings and Orphans. Colin had thought he would have a longer time with Decker. It was not so usual for four-year-old orphans to be placed with a family. The ones who could understand their fate at so young an age were reconciled to the prospect of servitude or apprenticeship. It seemed an infinitely more desirable alternative than remaining at Cunnington's until twelve years of age, then being put on London's unforgiving streets. A boy who didn't know how to fend for himself might be taught thievery if he was judged to be quick witted and light fingered by one of the London bands. If he caught a pimp's eye, however, he was more likely to learn the skin trade and ply his wares until his looks faded or disease wasted him.

Colin wanted none of those things for Decker, so he was resigned to the fact that Decker's departure from Cunnington's was necessary, if not welcome. He wanted to be happier for his brother, thought he *should* be happier, but in his heart of hearts he knew he was also jealous. And afraid. And now alone.

The couple who chose Decker among the score of other children were more satisfactory in Colin's eyes than the pair who had taken Grey. The wife was handsome, not pretty, but she had a serene smile and a quiet way about her that smoothed the anxious lines between Decker's brows and eased Colin's mind. Her husband was reserved but polite, a bit uncertain what to make of Decker's constant questioning until his wife said indulgently, "Why, answer him, *cher.* Just as you do me." That was when the man spoke. His voice was a deep, rich baritone, the edges of his words crisp and defined. It was a voice that inspired confidence and Colin guiltily wished that he might be chosen in place of his brother or at least that he might be permitted to accompany him.

The headmaster tried again. "Perhaps you will consider Decker's brother also?"

The woman's kind eyes alighted on Colin. Sadness and pain warred in her expression and then Colin flushed deeply, recognizing pity when it was turned in his direction. "We'd take them all if we could," she said to the headmaster. *"Ce n'est pas possible."*

Her husband nodded. "She means it," he said. "We would if we could. And the child must be healthy. There's the voyage to think of. We have a long trip ahead."

Colin slipped out of the headmaster's office quietly. In the dimly lighted hallway he sucked in a ragged breath and swallowed the hard, aching lump in his throat. If he closed his eyes he knew he would see the woman's piteous look. He didn't want her pity. If the truth were known he wanted her gratitude. Did she think her new son's sturdy little body was a happy accident of nature?

In anticipation of the evening meal, Colin's stomach actually growled. It had been a long time since he had heard that sound. In the months since coming to Cunnington's he had accustomed himself to eating less in order that his brothers might have more.

He had done what he could for them. Now he had to think of himself.

Malnourished and frail, his dark, opaque eyes like bits of hard coal in a gaunt face, Colin did not respond immediately or well to larger portions of dinner. Older boys who thought twice about tangling with him when he was championing his brothers, now found him an easy target. Soon he had little more to eat than when he was feeding Decker or Grey, and sometimes less.

Ten days after Decker was gone Colin developed a cough. At night in the chilly barracks, with one cot separated from another by mere inches, Colin kept the others awake with his deep, raspy hacking. He jammed a fist in his mouth to quell the sound, but it wasn't enough. By the third night Jamie Ferguson and John Turley had worked out a plan of their own. When Colin started coughing they rose quietly from their beds, placed a blanket over his head and took turns beating him with their fists. The following night there was no need to use physical force. They simply laid a pillow over his face and held it there until he went limp.

It was Mrs. Cunnington who first suggested that Colin's size might lend itself to a particular occupation. He was tall, it was true, but that was of little consequence. It was the width of his shoulders and narrowness of his frame that mattered. The head-master, keen to be rid of Colin, was easily persuaded.

So it came to pass that he was apprenticed as a sweep and although he displayed a remarkable aptitude for shinnying up and down chimney flues, he was too easily exhausted. His bright yellow hair, once so lovingly tousled by his mother's fingertips disappeared beneath a film of greasy soot. Colin's unnaturally flushed complexion was hidden by ash and grime, and the bruises he received from regular beatings were indistinguishable from streaks of coal dust.

He was returned to Cunnington's in a few weeks without fulfilling the terms of his apprenticeship. Mr. Cunnington cuffed him on the ears while his wife soundly scolded him. Colin's head rang without respite for twenty-four hours.

"I can't say that I like the idea of him living *here* until he's twelve," Mrs. Cunnington said. She set down her embroidery work, folded her hands on her lap, and looked at her husband expectantly. "He has the *most* accusing eyes. Had you noticed that?"

Indeed he had. The headmaster continued to clean his pipe.

"As if it were *our* fault that his wretched parents died. We have done our part. Everyone *knows* we have." Mrs. Cunnington could not speak without giving emphasis to at least one word. She believed it lent weight to her opinions. "I should say, they *could* have provided for their children. It was *obvious* they had the means to do so."

Mr. Cunnington laid his pipe cleaner aside and began to pack the pipe with tobacco. He felt the same disappointment his wife did. They had both pinned some hopes on finding relatives of Colin, Decker, and Grey. Using their own money they had placed ads in the London papers describing the three brothers and the circumstances of their parents' demise. No one had ever come forward to lay claim to the boys or suggest they might know the whereabouts of relatives.

It was the boys' clothes and Colin's polite and articulate manner that led the Cunningtons to believe there might be deep pockets in the family's coat of arms. No one at the Imp 'n Ale Inn on the post road north of London knew anything about the family who had stopped only briefly for dinner. Thirty minutes after leaving the inn their carriage had been met by highwaymen. Murder was not the usual end to these encounters, but there were always exceptions. The highwaymen made just such an exception of the boys' mother and father and the driver. Not knowing what else to do with three newly orphaned children, the local authorities sent the brothers to Cunnington's Workhouse.

The Cunningtons questioned Colin, seeking facts about his family and upbringing, but they found his stories somewhat fanciful and gradually came to believe an eight-year-old could not be counted on to know or tell the truth. The special attention given the brothers in the early days gradually waned, and soon they were treated no better or worse than any other of the workhouse's charges.

When the headmaster finished packing his pipe, he lighted it and puffed several times to begin the draw. Satisfied at last, his exhalation was more like a sigh. "You're right, of course," he said. He had learned it was always better to tell his wife she was right, even when he had every intention of disagreeing with her. Tonight, however, it was not his intention. "He can't stay here. He can't work, and I fear the consumption may infect the others."

Mrs. Cunnington's eyes widened. "Consumption?" They would have to get rid of Colin if that was the case. They couldn't wait for the boy to die. Too many other children might take ill. Why, they themselves were vulnerable. The workhouse would close, and they would lose everything. "Do you *really* think it could be?"

He shrugged and drew on his pipe again.

To Mrs. Cunnington's way of thinking her husband was too indifferent. It could only mean that he had given the situation some thought and had decided on a course of action, *"Tell* me your plan."

Jack Quincy arrived at Cunnington's Workhouse for Foundlings and Orphans the following day. Everything about him was large. His voice rumbled and reverberated as though the barrel chest and throat from which it emerged were hollow. He had thick arms, and legs as solid as tree trunks. His handshake was strong and warm, his manner a shade aggressive. Jack's eyes were widely spaced as if to suggest his peripheral vision was as good as his dead-on look. His nose had been broken on more than one occasion and had mended badly each time. It was rumored that Jack Quincy was still looking for the fight that would set it right again.

When he swept into the headmaster's office he brought the smell of fresh air and saltwater with him. And something else. Colin found himself leaning forward just to take in the scent of adventure.

Jack Quincy didn't wait to be offered the headmaster's hand. He took it in his, pumped it twice, and said without preamble, "Where's the boy you were telling me about?"

"Behind you," Mr. Cunnington said, looking past Quincy's shoulder to where Colin stood. "Won't you sit down and we'll discuss terms?"

Quincy gave Colin a cursory glance. "There's not much to him," he said in flat tones.

"He doesn't eat," the headmaster said. "At least not a lot. You won't find him terribly expensive to keep."

"And not terribly difficult to heave over the side." His eyes narrowed on Mr. Cunnington, and he jabbed a thick finger in the headmaster's direction. "More to the point, I figure the fish won't take him as bait. They're likely to throw him back. Now, what kind of bill of goods are you trying to sell me, Cunnington?" He placed particular emphasis on the first two syllables of the headmaster's name. "My ship sails in two hours and you told me you had someone I could use. What do you think I can do with this boy?"

Mr. Cunnington bristled. He disliked the Yankee's boorish manner. "He's just as I promised."

"He's sick. You didn't tell me he was sick." As if on cue Colin began to cough. Quincy glanced backward again, assessed the boy's sunken features, the shadows beneath his eyes, the hollow cheeks and pale lips, and asked bluntly, "Is he consumptive?"

"It's a cold."

Quincy walked over to Colin, raised the boy's chin, then demanded, "Is that true?"

Colin thought he would be lifted off the floor by the finger under his chin, but the large man's touch was surprisingly gentle. His lungs seemed to swell with the effort not to cough. "It's true, sir," he said. "No doctor's ever said as much."

Quincy was quick to understand Colin's game. There was no lie in his words, not when the truth was that no doctor had ever examined him. "Do you want to come with me, boy?" Quincy asked. He kept his finger on Colin's pointed chin and took measure of the grit and willfulness he saw in the boy's eyes. "Well?"

"It's Colin, sir," the lad said gravely. "My name's Colin Thorne, and yes, I want to go with you."

"Knowin' full well that I'll pitch you over the rail of the *Sea Dancer* as soon as look after you?"

In an effort to show strength where little existed, Colin held his thin body rigidly. "I'd like to take that risk, sir."

Jack Quincy released Colin's chin. "How much for him?" he asked the headmaster.

"Three pounds."

"That's a fortune," Quincy growled.

Colin grew suddenly afraid. What if Cunnington wouldn't negotiate and what if Quincy wouldn't pay? "If you wouldn't mind, sir," he said, interrupting, "I'd be honor bound to give you recompense. With interest if you'd like."

Quincy blinked. "My God, he talks like a bleedin' banker," he said, more to himself than to Colin or Cunnington. "How old are you, boy?"

"Ten," Colin said, crossing his fingers behind his back.

"Twelve," Cunnington said at the same time.

Jack Quincy grunted, believing neither. "Hell, it doesn't matter. I need the boy this trip." He opened his wool coat, reached for an inside pocket, and drew out three silver pieces. He manipulated one of the silver coins in and out between his fingers before he set them all on the headmaster's desk. "This is what I have. Suit yourself."

Mr. Cunnington picked up the silver quickly. "Get your things, Colin; then wait for Mr. Quincy at the front gate."

Colin hesitated, looking to Quincy for direction and approval, half afraid he might be set outside the gate with his bag and no one to take him away.

Jack Quincy rubbed his mouth to hide his brief smile. Damned, if there wasn't something about the cheeky little boy that he liked. "Go on with you, lad. I'm not leavin' without you."

Colin looked for the truth in Jack Quincy's eyes, then he turned and walked out of the room, wearing his dignity like armor.

Quincy watched him go. When he was certain Colin was out of earshot he turned the headmaster. "So help me, Cunnington, if that boy dies before the *Sea Dancer* makes Boston, I'll come back and take you and this workhouse apart."

"He'll arrive in Boston. After that . . ." His voice trailed off and he shrugged.

"It doesn't matter after that."

The *Sea Dancer* left London three hours behind schedule. Half expecting that one or the other of the Cunningtons would change their mind, or that Jack Quincy himself might think better of the bargain he had made, it was an agonizing wait for Colin.

The knot in his stomach didn't begin to untangle until England's coastline disappeared from view.

He was half an ocean away when Mr. Elliot Willoughby arrived in London from Somerset and began inquiring on the direction of Cunnington's Workhouse for Foundlings and Orphans. The solicitor, it seemed, was particularly interested in information on three children whose surname was reputed to be Thorne.

One

London, June 1841

It was the sound of thunder that roused him out of bed. Colin hadn't been asleep, or at least not deeply so, but he hadn't been particularly anxious to crawl out from between the sheets or to remove the length of shapely calf and thigh that had been lying across his legs.

He padded softly to the window and drew back the yellowed curtains. Lightning flashed across the sky, and for a moment his naked body was bathed in brilliant white light. He pressed the flat of his hand against the glass. When thunder rolled a few seconds later he felt the vibration all the way up his arm.

His trousers were lying over the arm of the room's only chair. He reached for them now and pulled them on. Another ragged bolt of lightning illuminated the room as Colin glanced toward the bed. He had no difficulty discerning that his companion was still sleeping soundly. That was good, he thought as he unlatched the window and threw it open. It meant he had time to remember her name.

Warm, moist air swirled into the room, and Colin put himself directly in its path. Drawing one leg up, he sat on the sill and rested his palms on his bent knee. The first fat droplets of rain touched his left shoulder on their way to the ground. He didn't move. The path of the water outlined his arm and elbow. One drop swelled strands of hair near the nape of his neck, darkening it to gold.

Colin leaned his head back against the window frame. This time when the thunder came it seemed to rumble through his entire body. He felt it in the soles of his feet, along his thigh, and across his chest. He breathed deeply and imagined the scent of the sea. He had only been ashore eight days. He'd been ready to return to his ship for six of them.

Rain began to fall faster, and the shape of the drops changed from that of fat, spattering batter to thin water lances. The sting was mild compared to what Colin endured at the helm of the *Remington Mystic*. There the spray could be needle sharp, and the pounding waves were known to scale the clipper's rails and carry an unprepared or unsuspecting sailor away.

The room Colin was shown at the Passing Fancy Inn faced the road to London. At this hour the throughway was quiet. Colin had been on the last coach from London, and that had arrived at the inn before nightfall. He and Aubrey Jones were the only two to disembark. Aubrey had immediately caught the eye of the wench who served them dinner, and had retired with her to his room shortly thereafter. Colin had expected to sleep alone, but the serving wench had produced a sister. Sibling rivalry, it seemed, had provided any number of travelers a playful romp in the upstairs rooms at the Passing Fancy.

"Here now," the voice from the bed whined sleepily. "Come away from the window. Ye'll catch yer death and toss it to me besides." When Colin didn't move or even glance in her direction, she raised herself up on one elbow and patted the space beside her. "Come to Molly, why don't ye, luv."

Molly? So that was her name. "Go back to sleep," he said. His words were not delivered kindly or as a suggestion. Colin Thorne was used to giving orders.

"No need to bark at me." Molly was quite able to hold her own. "Didn't get quite enough of the ol' slap n' tickle, is that what's keepin' ye up? I don't mind a bit more play." She yawned hugely. "If it's all the same to you."

It was so much better when she didn't talk, Colin thought. His gaze moved away from the quiet road and into the room.

It did not alight on Molly, but on the bath that had been drawn for him hours ago. He'd never had the opportunity to use it; now he felt the need. "If it's all the same to you," he said, "I'd like my bath water warmed."

That brought Molly upright, and she made no attempt to bring the sheet with her. Her heavy breasts heaved as she managed quite a show of her indignation. "Yer throwin' Molly out of yer bed?"

Apparently this was a first for Molly. "You should have gone back to sleep when I told you to," he said indifferently, turning away. Out of the corner of his eye he saw movement just below him. It had disappeared by the time he looked down. Someone just arriving at the inn? he wondered. But there had been no stage or horses. The sound of the inn's large door being slammed suggested to Colin that he'd been right about a new arrival. Probably a lone traveler surprised by the storm. Colin could have told him there was no need for panic. The rain was already letting up as thunder and lightning moved to points south and east of the inn.

Molly was of a mind to push Colin out the open window, but she remembered he hadn't paid her.

"On the nightstand," Colin said.

"So yer a bloody mind reader, too." Molly took the coins he'd put out for her and scrambled off the bed. Clutching them in her palm, she began to dress. "Me sister told me why you and yer friend are here," she said. "And here I was, feelin' like I should comfort a man about to look death in the eye. Well, I can tell ye it doesn't matter a whit to me now if his lordship puts a lead ball through yer head or yer heart."

"As long as he hits something," Colin said dryly.

"Yer too bleedin' right."

Colin came to his feet lightly. He could feel Molly's eyes on him as he walked to the door. He suspected she was glaring at him, but when he turned he glimpsed something else, something like regret perhaps, or longing. His dark eyes narrowed on

Molly's pleasant, heart-shaped face. Had she imagined herself in love with him?

"Don't flatter yerself," she said sharply.

An edge of a smile touched Colin's mouth. "Now who's the bleedin' mind reader?"

Molly's reply caught in her throat. He had no right to look at her just the way he was looking now and stop her thoughts before they were formed. It was that hint of a smile that did it. That, or the flicker of interest that was darkening eyes already as dark as polished onyx. It was just as well he was throwing her out. Given the rest of the night with him, she'd be a fool for love by morning.

"Arrogant bastard," she said under her breath. She finished fastening her skirt and shimmied into her blouse. The laces dangled and Molly made no attempt to tie them. He deserved to get an eyeful of what she was never giving him again, at least not unless he said please.

Colin was preparing to open the door for her when the knock came. It was a tentative intrusion, not a firm one. Colin knew it couldn't be Aubrey. His second in command had fists like hammers. Doors rattled under his pressure.

When Colin didn't respond to the first gentle rapping, the light staccato was tapped out again. He looked at Molly in question. When she shrugged, surprised as he, he placed a finger to his lips. She nodded her understanding.

Reaching for his boots by the door, Colin removed a knife from a leather sheath in the right one. He held it lightly in his palm, hefting it once to familiarize himself with the feel and weight of the weapon. He opened the door a crack.

The figure on the other side of the door was rain soaked. A hooded cape dripped water onto the wooden floor. The person inside the woolen garment was shivering uncontrollably.

"What do you want?" Colin asked tersely. It was too dark in the hallway to make out the features of the stranded traveler.

"The innkeeper said I would find Captain Thorne here." The

voice was husky and interspersed with the clicking of chattering teeth, but its timbre was unmistakably feminine.

Colin opened the door wider and let his visitor see the dagger in his hand. When she visibly started he was satisfied that she was unarmed. He let her cross the threshold. To Molly he said, "Perhaps you'd better see to that warm water now."

"So I'm dismissed, am I?" she snapped. "And ye already with a replacement in me bed. Heat yer own bleedin' water."

The stranger interjected, "I don't require anything."

Colin managed to grab the door before Molly slammed it on her way out. "I wasn't asking for you," he said. "I've been trying to get a hot bath since I arrived." He saw his visitor shift her head toward the bed and imagined she was able to draw all the correct conclusions. "Yes, well, you're not my first interruption this evening."

Colin thought there might be a reply, better still, the beginnings of an explanation. It seemed his visitor was mesmerized by the tangle of sheets and blankets on the unmade bed. Colin placed the flat of his knife under her chin, let her feel the cool metal, and slowly drew her attention back to him. "That's better," he said.

The tip of his weapon vibrated slightly as she continued to shake with cold. His dark eyes narrowed. Her sodden hood fell too far forward for him to make out her features. "Take off your cape."

The command shook her out of her stupor. "I'll leave it on, thank you."

"It wasn't a suggestion."

She raised her hands as far as the fastener at her throat, but there they froze again.

Colin neatly sliced the satin closure. The hood fell back and the cape opened. "Do what I say when I say it," he said, giving no quarter, "and you and your clothes will leave here in one piece."

She nodded once and then averted her gaze, uncomfortable with the way he was examining her. She didn't blush. Even if she could, it wasn't that kind of stare. His interest was more remote, almost clinical. She might well have been inanimate, a preserved specimen prepared for scientific study.

Colin lowered his knife. With a quick snap of his wrist he sent it spinning end over end until it stuck in the headboard. The sudden movement made her flinch, but she didn't cower. That in itself was intriguing. "Take off the cape."

She responded this time, slipping it off her shoulders. It was heavy now that she had to hold it, but the weight was preferable to giving it up. She clutched it in front of her.

Colin walked over to the chair and pulled his shirt off the back. He shrugged into it and tucked the tails in his trousers. He noticed her eyes were still averted.

"I take it you're not one of Molly's sisters," he said.

"Who?" Then she understood. "No. Oh, no. I've never seen her before."

Colin pitched the remainder of the clothing on the chair toward the bed. He sat down and stretched his legs in front of him. As though uncertain if she were coming or going, the woman hadn't turned yet in his direction. He studied her slender silhouette while she made up her mind. Beneath the cape which covered her forearms and hands, he could make out the spasmodic clenching and unclenching of her fists. There was tension in the line of her shoulders, and the lift to her chin suggested she was not yet resigned to whatever fate or purpose had brought her this far.

Her teeth stopped chattering and her profile became still and smooth. He couldn't be sure, but he thought she might be worrying her lower lip. The full line of it was drawn in slightly.

He gave her time. He wasn't tired. In the best circumstances sleep often eluded him, and at this moment he would wager that even if Aubrey Jones was now enjoying the pleasures of Molly's sister *and* Molly, this little diversion was bound to be more entertaining.

Colin watched his uninvited guest take a breath and let it out slowly. She hung her cape on the peg by the door, then smoothed it out, squeezing water from the hem. Apparently she was staying.

"I'll heat that water for you," she said softly.

He was going to tell her the water could wait, but she was already bending to the task, scooping water from the tub into the kettle on the hearth. She knelt on the brick apron of the fireplace and laid down kindling. After a few clumsy failures with the flint and striker she was able to start the fire.

He followed her movements with interest. She was small and rather delicate, with slender arms and shoulders and a high, narrow waist. Her hair was the color of bittersweet chocolate. Until he saw it in the firelight he thought it was merely black. Now he could see that shades of sienna and russet and coffee gave it its deep, rich shading. She wore it pulled away from her face, in a loose plait that hung down the middle of her back. The style was more for service than fashion. Colin knew women who plaited their hair at night, in preparation for bed and after giving it the requisite hundred strokes. He liked the ritual, liked lying in bed and waiting for a woman who did it, counting the strokes and watching her tresses dance and swirl as the brush was pulled through them.

Her hair shone in the firelight. Strands of dark umber whispered across her smooth cheek. Had she brushed her hair this evening? Had she done it while someone waited in bed for her?

She rose to her feet slowly, brushing her hands on her gown, and looked uncertainly at Colin. He was still watching her with that distant, narrowed glance of his. She cleared her throat.

"I imagine you're wondering who I am," she said.

"No," he replied casually. "I think I've figured that out, Miss Leyden." Her widening eyes were confirmation. Were they blue or gray? In the light it was difficult to tell. "I suppose I even know why you're here. What I don't know is what you're prepared to offer in exchange for his miserable life."

Resigned now, Mercedes Leyden let her hands fall to her sides. "How did you know?"

"Weybourne Park isn't far from here. I know because that's

where I'm going in the morning. One could manage the distance on foot; even at night it wouldn't be difficult. And you arrived on foot. I glimpsed your entrance into the inn. I'm aware the earl has two daughters and two sons. I make it a point to find out something about a man who's called me out. Since you're most definitely not one of the sons, and your clothes are too fine to belong to one of his servants, it occurs to me that you must be one of the daughters."

"Actually I'm his niece."

Colin considered that. "Aaah," he said slowly. "I remember now. The poor relation."

She winced at the description, but she didn't deny it or object to it. Mercedes had heard it before, though never so boldly pointed out. "The polite way to introduce it into conversation is to wait until my back is turned. In that manner you can console yourself with the pretense that I haven't really heard the remark. Although I understand that with Americans proper form counts for little."

One of Colin's brows raised in appreciation and approval. The corner of his mouth edged upward ever so slightly. "At least with this American," he said. "And you should be relieved. If I were an Englishman, proper form would forbid me from entertaining you in my room. Then where would you be?"

"In the hallway?" she rejoined. Mercedes noticed that her comment did not broaden the glimmer of a smile on his lips. He was not a man given to easy laughter or sudden, careless grins. She imagined the lines at the corners of his eyes were beaten into his face by sun and salt spray. His youth was captured in the sun-drenched color of his hair. It covered his head like a helmet of light and shimmered at his nape. In startling and unsettling contrast were his eyes, so deeply brown they could have been black, so polished and penetrating they reflected an image back while shuttering private thoughts.

Colin stood. "Why don't you sit here, Miss Leyden? I'll see to my own water. Unless you're comfortable by the fire."

She would not feel comfortable until she was out of his room and perhaps not even then. She shivered when he brushed past her.

"Take a blanket from the bed and wrap it around you."

Mercedes recognized it as an order. She glanced at the dagger in the headboard. It wouldn't take much effort on his part to use it on her. She picked up a blanket and did as she was told.

Colin poked at the fire. Although the rain had stopped, there was still a breeze eddying about the room. Flames flickered and danced. Shadows leaped on the bare walls. Colin dropped the poker against the fireplace and shut and latched the window. The curtains lay still again. Crossing his arms in front of him, he leaned back against the glass. "Did Weybourne send you here?" he asked.

She had to turn slightly in the chair to see him. It was natural for her to draw her feet up under her. Her leather shoes and socks were damp, and the heat of her own body felt good against them.

"Oh, for God's sake," Colin muttered. He pushed away from the window and dropped to his knees in front of her. "Give me your feet." When surprise made her too slow responding, Colin reached under her gown and pulled on her ankles himself. He removed both shoes, then the stockings, and rubbed her bare feet briskly between his hands. "Did Weybourne send you here?" he asked again.

Mortification. The word came to Mercedes's mind. But she was asking herself why she wasn't experiencing it. In all of her twenty-four years no one had ever touched her so intimately, man or woman, and yet she wasn't at all embarrassed by it. Quite the opposite. The sensations filled her with exquisite relief. It was only when he paused that Mercedes realized he was waiting for an answer to his question.

Drawing her feet away and pushing her gown back to modestly cover her legs, she found time to recover her voice. "My uncle doesn't know I'm here."

Colin wondered if he could believe her. The Earl of Weybourne was a nasty piece of work. "Really?" he asked skeptically. "Then I confess I'm curious as to what prompted your trek to the inn and why you sought me out."

Mercedes watched him rise easily to his feet and walk to the fireplace again. There was an unmistakable edge to this man, whether it was his smile or the aggressive line of his nose. He did not merely stand; he took a position. The eyes were guarded, the stare fixed. He had a well-defined, clean-shaven jaw, and he held his head at an angle that suggested he was not merely listening, but was alert, even wary.

"I know you plan to meet my uncle tomorrow morning."

Without consulting his pocket watch, Colin realized she was wrong about the time. "It's after midnight," he said. "I think you mean this morning."

Her hands folded in her lap. Her fingers ached with the effort it took to keep them still. "Yes, you're right, of course. This morning. Near the pond at Weybourne Park. I believe you chose pistols."

"That was"—he paused, searching for the phrase—*"proper form,* I believe. It was your uncle who called me out."

"He was in his cups."

"I'm sorry," Colin said, his tone indicating sarcasm, not regret. "But I don't recall seeing you in London at the club Tuesday a week past."

"You know I wasn't there. They don't allow women."

"Well, yes, I do seem to recall that. I wondered if you did." He dipped his fingers in the kettle. The water was only tepid. "What makes you think he was drunk?"

"He told me."

"And you believed him," Colin said flatly. "Why, I wonder?"

Why wouldn't I? Mercedes thought. He drank a great deal. Wallace Leyden, the sixth Earl of Weybourne, was frequently three sheets to the wind before he left his bedchamber. It was inconceivable to her that he would spend an evening at his club without a decanter of brandy at his side. "I have my reasons," she said.

"Oh, I don't doubt he's a sot most days of the week and most hours of the day, but last Tuesday he was sober. Do you require proof?"

"No." Mercedes shook her head. She believed him. It was natural that she would take the word of a stranger, even an *American* stranger, over her uncle. The point was simply that she knew the Earl of Weybourne, knew him as well as his own children, perhaps better. She would count lying as one of his smaller sins. "He may have been sober," she said. "But he wasn't thinking clearly."

"I'll concede that point. I believe a number of people, including several who call themselves his friend, tried to dissuade him from the action he took. He was set on the matter."

"He had everything to lose," she implored.

"He had material things to lose," Colin said. "Until he called me out, his life wasn't one of those things."

Mercedes's face paled. The strain of this past week showed in her clear gray eyes. The cobalt ring at the edge of her irises darkened, and she drew in her lower lip again, worrying it. After a moment she said softly, wearily, "So it's true, then. You intend to kill him." She watched him carefully, wondering if he would deny it, and if he did, if she could believe him. She needn't have bothered. There was no denial.

"If he doesn't kill me first."

She closed her eyes briefly. She tried to imagine her life away from Weybourne Manor. Where would she go? What would she do? Chloe, at least, was already engaged, and Sylvia might still make a reasonably good marriage even without a dowry, but the twins would be her responsibility and they would have no inheritance. How was she supposed to keep food in their stomachs and a roof over their heads?

Mercedes could feel her stomach lurch and roil as her thoughts began to tumble out of control. It was not like her to get ahead of herself. She was the unfailingly practical one, the responsible Leyden, heiress to virtues like honor and honesty, loyalty and trust. And where had it gotten her? She would do well, she thought, to embrace a bit more in the way of larceny and deceit. This evening's escapade was a good start. On the heels of that thought Mercedes found she could still smile.

Watching her, seeing the glimmer of a sweet, satisfied curve on her lips, Colin said, "You find the idea of your uncle killing me amusing?"

For a moment she had difficulty following him. Then she recalled his previous comment. "Oh, no," she said quickly. "I wasn't thinking about that . . . I was . . ."

"Yes?"

She shook her head. "Nothing." How could she explain that she was not quite like the person he was talking to tonight, that in other circumstances she wouldn't have left Weybourne Park after nightfall, at least not alone and never on foot. She wouldn't cross the threshold of an inn like the Passing Fancy, and she'd never even entertained the notion of joining a man in his room.

Colin tested the water in the kettle. It was finally hot. He yanked a sheet off the bed and used one corner to keep from burning his palm on the iron handle. In one easy, sweeping motion he poured the scalding water into the wooden tub. That brought the temperature up to what he called "warm enough." After setting the kettle on the floor he began to pull out his shirttails.

"You're going to bathe now?" she asked.

"I'm not waiting until the water gets cold again."

"But I'm still here."

"Are you planning on leaving anytime soon?"

"Not without discussing—"

"That's what I thought." He finished pulling off his shirt and hooked his thumbs in the waistband of his trousers.

That's when Mercedes did a surprising thing. She didn't turn in her chair or avert her head. She didn't even blink. What she did was stare.

Colin pushed at his trousers. She still didn't look away. He lowered them a fraction. The flat of his muscled belly was fully exposed, and she hadn't twitched. He swore softly and kicked the tub with his bare foot in frustration. Water sloshed on the floor and pain shot through his foot. "Very well," he said grace-lessly. "I'll wait, but state your business, then get out of here."

Taking little comfort in her victory, Mercedes said stiffly, "If you insist on showing up at Weybourne Park, then you must find some way for honor to be served without killing the earl."

Colin sat on the edge of the bed and nursed his stubbed toe. "Must I? I suppose you're going to tell me why."

She leaned forward in her chair, her expression earnest. "We'll lose everything. You can't appreciate what that means, else you wouldn't insist on this manner of addressing a fault."

He understood better than she could know about losing everything. He didn't explain because it made no difference, and was something *she* would not understand. What he said was, "You call it a fault? Is that your word or the earl's?"

"His word," she admitted apologetically.

Colin stopped rubbing his toe. "The Earl of Weybourne made a wager. A wager he hadn't the means to honor at the outset. I wouldn't have accepted the terms if I had known, but it would have been less than proper form if I had made an overt inquiry about his finances. I was prepared to cover the wager if I lost. The earl was not."

Mercedes felt a tightness in her chest. It was every bit as bad as she thought it could be.

"Do you want a drink?" asked Colin. She looked as if she might need one. Indeed, she looked as if she might faint. The only positive thing that might come of it, as far as Colin was concerned, was that he would finally have his bath. "Never mind," he said before she could answer. He could see she was preparing to reject his offer anyway. "I'll pour you one, and you'll finish it. A second, if I say so."

She nodded weakly. There was no point in arguing. She had learned living with the earl, that one must choose one's battles, and over the years she had become something of a good strate-gist.

The bottle of whisky on the nightstand had been thoughtful Molly's contribution. Colin poured two fingers of alcohol into his own unused tumbler and passed it to Mercedes. "All of it," he said.

Mercedes wrapped her slender fingers around the glass and raised it to her lips. Over the rim she caught Colin's intent stare. He looked as if he'd hold her nose and pour the stuff down her throat if she didn't drink it on her own. She tipped her head back and let the liquid slide down.

"Good girl." He took the tumbler from her and put it aside. "Let's see how you get on with that."

Her insides were on fire, that was how she was getting on. Gamely, she nodded. She hardly recognized her own voice when she was able to get a few words out. "Tell me about the wager."

Colin stuffed a pillow behind his back and leaned against the headboard. Thinking back, he raked his fingers through his hair. "You're familiar with Lloyd's?" he asked.

"The insurance house."

"That's right. They've been insuring ships and cargo for over a hundred years, and they have a good system for communicating departures and arrivals. News always seems to reach them first if a ship's foundered somewhere on the coast, or if the cargo's been spoiled, or if there've been hands lost to storms or pirates. There's an opportunity for fortunes to vanish or be made depending on the fate of ships. Lloyd's policies are really shares sold to investors, and if their ships come in they're rewarded handsomely. If they don't . . ." Colin shrugged. "Well, you can imagine."

Indeed, Mercedes was having no difficulty imagining. In her mind's eye she was seeing a man who had risked everything going quietly into a back room of the coffee house and putting a pistol to his head. Her knuckles whitened around the empty tumbler.

"Recently Lloyd's has been the site of more reckless wagering. Men are not only betting on a ship coming in, but putting down extra money if she comes in on time. There's always more to be made if a ship carrying certain valuable goods is the first of its kind to make port. Tea, for instance, from Hong Kong.

Or wool from Melbourne. If a clipper captain can be the first to reach Liverpool or London with cargoes like those, he can do well for himself, his crew, and his company."

"That's what you are?" she asked. "A clipper captain?"

"Master of the *Remington Mystic.*"

Some men would have said it as a boast, or at least with a trace of pride. Mercedes detected nothing like that in Colin Thorne's tone. He said it merely as a statement of fact. She held out her tumbler. "I think I'd like more, please."

Colin considered her request. There was a bit of color in her cheeks that hadn't been there during any part of their brief acquaintance. Her eyes—gray eyes, he could see now, with the smallest ring of cobalt blue—were clear and steady. Mercedes Leyden appeared to be holding her own. "All right," he said, leaning forward with the bottle. He gave her half as much as he had before. "Don't knock it back like a sailor this time. Sip it."

She did as she was told. The sensation was quite pleasant. "Was it a wager like that my uncle made?" she asked. "Was he betting that you'd come in on time?"

Colin set the bottle down. He drew his knees up and rested one arm across the caps. "No. That sort of wager wouldn't have had the return the earl was looking for. He challenged the *Mystic* to come in *ahead* of schedule."

"Break a record, you mean?" Ignoring Colin's earlier admonishment, Mercedes finished her drink in one gulp. "My God," she said lowly. "What was he thinking?"

"Probably that he couldn't lose," Colin said practically.

"And what prompted you to take him up on it? Was it the same for you? Did you think you couldn't lose?"

"On the contrary. I didn't think my chances of winning were very great. Your uncle only had to record his wager and wait. I had to make it happen."

Again Mercedes could detect no boast in the statement. He said it simply, accepting his role as part of the risk. "How much was the wager?"

"A quarter of a million pounds."

She blanched. It was more than everything. "The run?"

"Liverpool to Boston to London."

"And the record?"

"Twenty-six days, thirteen hours." It was becoming easier to understand why her uncle thought he had made a winning wager. She might have been tempted herself. Mercedes leaned forward and set her tumbler on the floor. When she straightened she was a little light-headed. At the moment it seemed like a very good thing.

"Twenty-six days, four hours," Colin said, answering the question she had yet to ask. "The *Remington Mystic* logged in nine hours under the record."

Mercedes stared at him. "Nine hours," she said hollowly. "My family is going to lose Weybourne Park because of nine hours."

Colin pushed off the bed and stood. "You talk as though it hasn't happened yet. Your family's already lost Weybourne Park and not because my crew had an outstanding run, but because his lordship didn't think for a moment that it was even possible."

Mercedes pressed her spine rigidly against the back of the overstuffed chair as Colin towered over her.

"Lloyd's documented the run," he told her. "It's a matter of record now. By the time I walked into their offices, people already knew your uncle had lost his wager. I found him at his club that same evening. I, too, thought he'd be drunk, but apparently his friends feared what he might do and they managed to cut his drinks with water." Colin suddenly realized he was leaning over Mercedes, and that she had pushed herself as much into the corner of the chair as was possible. She was looking up at him, her eyes watchful and wary as though she expected a blow and was preparing herself to take it on the chin. Disgusted, Colin straightened and removed his hands from the arms of the chair.

"I'm not going to hit you," he said tightly. When he noticed her position didn't change a whit he took a step backward and finally moved to the window. She had to turn in her chair to see him. It made her seem less like a cornered fawn. "In front of half a dozen witnesses the earl called into question the legitimacy of the *Mystic*'s run. He went so far as to suggest that the *Mystic* had a twin ship in the Remington line and that I had never taken the clipper the entire way back to Boston."

Mercedes's eyes widened a fraction. Her uncle had to have had some understanding of his situation to act so recklessly. Impugning a man's honor was no peccadillo, but a breech with serious consequences.

"I showed him the dated newspaper I picked up the day I arrived in Boston harbor. He claimed it was all arranged and all of it a fraud." Colin now saw on his guest's face an understanding of where this all was leading. She nodded once, slowly, bidding him to continue. "Your uncle said a number of other things. I would have been well within my rights to call him out for any one them."

"Why didn't you?"

"Because there was no point. I was already aware that he couldn't pay the debt without borrowing against the value of Weybourne Park. If he wasn't willing to do that, then the estate would be mine by default. It's all quite legal, I assure you."

Mercedes didn't doubt it. She had come to understand that Colin Thorne took calculated risks, not blind ones. What she could not comprehend was that he had a quarter of a million pounds to wager. How was it possible for a clipper captain to amass a fortune? "So when you didn't take the bait?" she prompted.

"He called me out. To his way of thinking, he had no other choice. If he kills me tomorrow he won't have to make good on his wager. If I kill him . . ." Colin shrugged. "Then he has no more worries, does he?"

The Earl of Weybourne worried very little. That was left to Mercedes. She was the one who took on the burden of managing Weybourne Park. It had been her home first.

Unfolding her legs, Mercedes moved to the edge of the cushion. She sat there a moment, perched like a skittish bird, her head darting first in one direction and then the other. She picked up her stockings, rolled them on, then slipped into her damp shoes. When she stood she felt water squishing out from between the stitching. She wriggled her toes uncomfortably.

In spite of the additional warmth supplied by the fire, her cloak was still damp. She swung it around her shoulders and drew the hood up over her head. She glanced once at Colin. He was merely watching her with the same detached curiosity she had noticed earlier. She rested her palm on the door handle, searching for something to say. In the end she left as quietly as she had come.

There were no words.

<u>BOOK YOUR PLACE ON OUR WEBSITE</u> <u>AND MAKE THE</u> <u>READING CONNECTION!</u>

We've created a customized website just for our very special readers, where you can get the inside scoop on everything that's going on with Zebra, Pinnacle and Kensington books.

When you come online, you'll have the exciting opportunity to:

- View covers of upcoming books

- Read sample chapters

- Learn about our future publishing schedule (listed by publication month *and author*)

- Find out when your favorite authors will be visiting a city near you

- Search for and order backlist books from our online catalog

- Check out author bios and background information

- Send e-mail to your favorite authors

- Meet the Kensington staff online

- Join us in weekly chats with authors, readers and other guests

- Get writing guidelines

- AND MUCH MORE!

Visit our website at
http://www.kensingtonbooks.com